RUNNING WITH THE PACK

WOLFSBANE BOOK 3

LOLA GLASS

authorlolaglass.com

Cover by Merry Book Round
https://www.merrybookround.com/

To second chances
And secret daughters

CHAPTER 1

THE SUN WARMED my fur despite the cold of the snow beneath me. A small house rested a few feet from a frozen lake to my left. The sun was setting off to my right, and the chill in the air was growing less tolerable by the minute.

A month ago, I would've been fine to sleep in the forest at night, even in the middle of winter. Now, I was already shivering.

Oh, the joys of dying slowly.

A woman with cinnamon hair stepped out onto the little house's patio and waved her arm through the air. I let out a deep sigh, the noise foreign to my wolf lungs.

If I didn't get up now, she'd start yelling. And then she'd come grab me and lecture me. I hated lectures.

And she was right; the cold was bad for me.

I stood slowly on shaky legs. Walking was easier in my furry form because if I crashed, the ground was a hell of a lot closer. Breaking my human face on the floor? Not fun.

My legs carried me to the porch slower than a damn turtle. I shifted back to skin after reaching the patio, and silently accepted the woman's help as she guided my arms into the sleeves of the fluffy robe.

"How are you feeling?" She asked, eyebrows furrowing.

I knew the exact conversation that was about to ensue, and I was way past tired of it.

"Fine." I gave her a tight smile, only because it would up my chances of not being smothered.

She pressed her fingers to my neck and lifted the watch on her wrist, checking my pulse. I stood and waited while she counted, holding myself up with my hands on the back of a patio chair.

"Too fast." She clucked, removing her fingers and slipping my arm over her shoulder so she could help me walk. "You need to mate with Ezra and let him heal you."

I said nothing. My response would've contained more cuss words than she deserved, in all her kindness.

"But you're still not going to do it, are you?" She prodded, helping lower me into the living room's giant rocking chair that could practically eat me whole. It was the only piece of furniture that smelled like me and no one else, so I pretty much lived in the thing.

"Nope." My arms wrapped around my stomach. "Thanks for the suggestions, though." I gave her another tight smile. This time, because she was my grandma… and because unlike most people, she cared about my well-being.

We'd reached a delicately balanced truce in the first few days I'd been there. After I stole her SUV in an attempt to escape… and crashed the damn thing when my legs decided to give out on me. I offered to pay for it if she retrieved my phone from the Alphas of All, but she decided I should keep my money and stay trapped.

I'd still pay her whenever I finally had access to a computer again, because she was my mom's mother. *If* I ever had access to a computer again, that is. Roman was nowhere to be found, and I had zero ways to contact anyone in New York. Although Marie and Ezra both had laptops, neither of them would give me the passcodes and I was about as far from a computer hacker as a person could get.

"Henley…" She sat on the edge of the couch, not far from me.

"Yes, Marie?"

"Grandma." She corrected.

I said nothing. We both knew I wasn't actually going to call her grandma; it was too weird.

"You have to mate with him." She said.

"I don't *have* to do anything."

Yeah, that would always be a sore subject for me. I'd always hated being told what to do.

"If you want to survive, you do." Marie countered.

"I won't give my body and soul to someone I don't love." My eyes caught on a photo above the fireplace. It was a big photo of Marie, her mate Randall, and a teenage version of my mom. It didn't belong there, but she said she brought it with her wherever she went. "You loved Randall." I reminded her.

Randall, my grandfather, died not long after my mother went off the grid because of her secret pregnancy. I was her last close relative, which was why Marie had taken work off for the entire month I'd been in Ruby City. She was determined to keep me alive, and as a trained nurse, she was more equipped than most people. If I'd been dying from a normal disease, she definitely would've dragged me through my recovery.

Unfortunately, my disease wasn't normal. Hell, it wasn't even a disease. I'd taken permanent damage from holding all those packs before I left New York, damage so bad that only a ruby wolf could heal… after I mated with him, that is. Ruby wolves had all sorts of weird shit go on after mating.

"I did." She leaned over and caught my hand. "But you could love Ezra, if you gave him a chance. He's a good man, and-"

"And I already have a mate." I cut her off. "He may have abandoned me, but he's still mine." My eyes fell to the ring on my left hand. Roman and I had never gotten around to filling out a marriage license to make things official the human way, but I still considered us permanent.

After I got over the initial shock that he'd actually dumped me in Ruby City like yesterday's poisonous trash, I talked Marie into taking me to the city's jewelry store, and I bought myself a ring like the damn independent dying woman I was.

Fine, I bought it with Roman's credit card, but only because I didn't have my own with me. I'd sure as hell be paying him back if I ever saw him again.

But the ring was a simple silver band with a single tear-drop shaped diamond, and I was completely obsessed with it.

Hell, I even bought Roman one too. Not a diamond one, obviously, but a thick ring made of metal and wood. I'd worn it on the middle finger of my right hand since it arrived, and although it was huge enough to slide off my sickly fingers, I hadn't let go of it for a second.

"The New York Alpha isn't your mate." Marie said.

I think she was under the impression that if she said it enough times, I'd start to believe it.

She was wrong.

I was as stubborn as a damn cockroach.

Which was why I'd tried to get back to New York so many times in the first week I'd been there. But I was too weak to physically fight then, and even more so now.

"In every way that counts, he is."

"He left you, Henley." Her voice raised, as it did when she got frustrated. "He wants you to be with Ezra."

I narrowed my eyes at her.

"He would never want me to be with anyone else."

Did that sound crazy?

Probably. It felt crazy.

He had left me, after all.

My body was falling apart and my spirit was going with it, sadness replacing pretty much every other feeling.

But I hadn't questioned my mind in years and wasn't starting now.

Marie's lips pressed together.

"The New York Alpha doesn't want you to die."

No, he definitely didn't want that.

If he did, he wouldn't have bothered ditching me in some other dick's house.

She stood.

"Ezra will be here soon. I'll get you some hot cocoa and then leave you two to talk."

"Yay."

Marie tutted me like she was my damn mother as she headed into the kitchen.

The front door swung open and a tall, swimmer-shaped man came strolling in. The messy, hot pink hair on his head was spiked up in its usual artsy style, and as always, he was completely naked.

"Hey, sexy." Ezra walked right over to me.

"How many times have I asked you to put pants on your tiny dick, pinky?" I drawled.

I'd have snarled and tried to look scary, but I was about two-weeks past having the energy to scare anyone. I probably just sounded tired.

"We both know this is the biggest cock you've ever seen." He gestured to his junk.

"Keep telling yourself that." I accepted the hot cocoa from Marie when she came back with two cups—always getting one for Ezra, too. Because he was the prince of the pack, and everyone absolutely adored his obnoxious ass.

Everyone other than me, obviously.

"I hear the New York Alpha has already chosen a new mate. One of his she-wolves… I believe her name is Lilac?" He lifted an eyebrow at me.

Low blow.

Yeah, that hit too close to home.

I was on my feet in an instant, too furious with Ezra to notice the way my body swayed, too damn weak to hold me up for long.

"Watch your mouth." I dared him to argue again.

"I'm too busy watching yours." He said.

That was it.

I swung my fist into his face and immediately regretted it. As my fingers collided with his face, my weak-ass bones—you read that right, even my damn bones were weak—broke on impact. A scream tore from my throat and the world went black for a minute.

Everything came back into focus and I was on my knees, Ezra's arms around me, holding me up as he licked my fingers. I could feel the bones knitting back into place quickly.

"Get the fuck away from me." I spoke through a clenched jaw. "Don't touch me."

"Let me heal you." He kept licking my fingers. I knew his statement wasn't about the hand—it was about the rest of me.

I was pretty damn weak, but not too weak to protect myself. I grabbed a hardback book off the coffee table beside me with my good hand and turned it sideways, smacking him in the face with it hard enough I hoped something broke.

He grunted at the impact but didn't release my fingers, so I smacked him again. He caught it that time before it could break his face.

"No, Henley. You like this face." He said, finally letting go of my fingers. I ducked away, stumbling over my own damn ankles.

I wanted to scream. There wasn't much I hated more than not being able to protect myself, but being told what I liked and didn't like ranked up there too.

It was time to break out the big guns.

Really, there was only one gun.

My dad.

AKA, the only dude in the pack who was stronger than Ezra.

"If you touch me again, I'll call Hansen." I warned. "He may want us to mate, but if I tell him you're attempting to force yourself on me, he's going to have problems with it."

"You wouldn't." Ezra sneered.

"Try me."

I hoped he would.

"Are you really going to let me find another woman to heal these wounds?" His cocky smirk was the opposite of attractive as he gestured to the bruise on his face. "Because the ladies are lining up. Maybe seeing me with another girl would finally push you into getting naked with me, and-"

"That's never going to happen." I interrupted him. "I have a mate, one who would never threaten to cheat on me to get what he wants."

"If he loves you so much, why did he abandon you?" Ezra stood, stepping closer. He was trying to intimidate me, to scare me into giving into him or make me sad about Roman. Some shit like that, but I wasn't a weepy girl, or one easily manipulated.

All that did was piss me off.

"He didn't abandon me. He went back to New York, taking care of his damn pack." I said.

It was a lie.

I mean, maybe it was true, but I had absolutely no idea. The last time I saw Roman was right before he dragged me into a plane with Hansen and flew me to Ruby City.

Marie told me he hadn't left my side for days while I was unconscious. He waited while Sylvie took every one of my people I'd added to my pack from me, and then he ran a background check on Marie to make sure she was trustworthy.

After he knew I was safe, he left.

The only thing I had when I woke up was one of his credit cards and a sheet of paper that said,

"Do whatever it takes to stay alive. I loved every damn minute you were mine."

He didn't even sign the thing, but my eyes burned a bit every time I read it.

Asshole.

He'd said goodbye, left me with Marie, and someone had taken my phone too, so I had no way to contact him or anyone else I loved.

Maybe I should've hated him for it. Hell, the fact that I didn't probably made me a complete fool. But I understood him too well to hate him for making the same choice I would've made in his situation.

If I could either watch him die or shove him into someone else's arms, I'd choose the latter too. And then leave like the devil himself was chasing me. The world needed Roman too much to let him go.

Just because I understood Roman's perspective didn't mean I was actually going to jump into Ezra's arms, though. I'd rather die—literally—than betray the mate I'd chosen. I'd been through worse shit than hanging around while my body shut down slowly.

Marie still assumed I'd warm up to Ruby City, that I'd fall into my role and be the happiest wolf there ever was. She didn't know what I'd been through—or what I was *going* through. But she took care of me, so I was grateful to her anyway.

When Sylvie had me dropped in Ezra's house, at least she'd given me a beautiful place to die in.

If I couldn't be with my favorite people in New York, at least I could walk out into the forest and look out at the frozen lake, marveling at the beauty of the world I'd be leaving soon.

"We're going to a party tonight." Ezra told me.

"Maybe you're going to a party tonight, but I'm sitting on my ass watching Grey's Anatomy again."

"Sylvie agreed to let you have your phone back if you'll go."

I stared at him.

Getting my phone back was a game changer. I'd searched the house for it from top to bottom before I'd tried to escape and hadn't found it. So either it was really well hidden, or Sylvie and Hansen had it.

"Swear it?"

He didn't seem like he was lying, but you could never know with a real asshole like him.

"Scout's honor."

As if he was a boy scout.

"Fine."

I was desperate to talk to Jamie and London and Arla.

And Roman, but I wasn't getting my hopes up. He hadn't ghosted me so we could do the long-distance thing.

"Great. Your dress is in our closet." He smirked, heading off to the house's one bedroom, still butt-naked.

"I'll go get the dress." Marie said quickly. I flashed her a grateful half-smile, and she returned the expression, diving into the ruby asshole's room. Both of us were living with Ezra—not by choice, in my case—so they'd gotten friendly.

In an entirely non-sexual way, despite how that last sentence sounded.

She came back with a garment bag and then helped me to the bathroom. When she unzipped it, my eyes narrowed at the white silk inside.

There was only one reason a woman wore a fancy white dress like that.

"Mating celebrations are held *after* a couple becomes mates." I said.

"Usually." Marie gave me a tight smile.

"You knew about this?"

She said nothing.

I shouldn't have let myself trust her.

"At least when I die, I'll be free of all the lying and manipulation." I muttered, tugging the tie on my robe off. I slid out of it as Marie pulled the white dress from the bag. I would've refused to wear it if it was anything else on the line, but getting my phone back so I could talk to my girls?

They were worth wearing the damn thing.

"You're not going to die." Marie said, her voice clipped. "I won't lose my husband, daughter, *and* granddaughter before I go."

I didn't argue, because that would be rude and she didn't deserve my rudeness.

But if my options were betraying my mate—the man who had saved me and protected me and loved me more than any person deserved—by giving my body to an asshole of a stranger and death, I'd choose the latter.

She zipped the back of the silky dress. It clung to every inch of my malnourished skin, the string-thin straps and open back only serving to make me look even less healthy somehow.

Funny enough, it was exactly the type of dress I would've chosen for my real mating celebration if Arla hadn't buttoned me into that hooker-bride contraption I'd worn. Simple, classy, and sexy all at once.

But now that I was dying, it just made me look like a zombie bride. The shimmering silk and ultra-bright pinkish red of my hair emphasized the lack of color in my cheeks.

"Let's put the hair up." Marie suggested gently.

I guess she got the same Walking Dead vibes I did.

"The hair stays down. Everyone needs to see that she's definitely a ruby wolf." Ezra said from outside the door. I jumped at his voice and then scowled, hating that he'd snuck up on me. My senses had gone to shit with the rest of my strength.

Dying sucked.

Ezra and Sylvie had already traipsed me around the pack the first few days I'd been in the city, so if anyone still doubted my hair color, they could go to hell.

My eyes met Marie's in the mirror and I saw the hesitance in them. She knew exactly what I was going to say. Or at least, she knew I was going to say something that contradicted what Ezra said.

"I'm thinking we do two braids and wrap them around my head like a crown. My sister-in-law wore something like that once, and it was gorgeous."

I dropped the sister-in-law thing just to bother Ezra. Marie's eyes closed for a long minute when he growled outside my door.

"You don't have a sister-in-law."

"Whatever helps you sleep at night." I called back.

His footsteps as he walked away had to be the most satisfying sound on the damn planet.

"I haven't French-braided since Hazel was young." Marie admitted.

"That's alright, let's just throw it up in a high-ponytail."

I had an ulterior motive for getting my hair up off my neck. I hoped that if Hansen could see how thin and lifeless I looked, maybe he'd take pity on me and save me from Ezra. It wasn't likely considering mating with him was my only option if I wanted to stay alive, but it was pretty much my last shot at having a peaceful death.

Marie began to coax my dry, limp hair into a ponytail. When she pulled my hair off my shoulder, she gasped.

"What?" I bent my head awkwardly, trying to see what scared her. We'd already had a conversation about my tattoo, so that couldn't be it.

"You let Ezra bite you." She whispered, her eyes glued to the crook of my neck.

Ohh… the scars from that thing Roman and I had done.

Her eyes lit up with excitement and she hit me with questions.

"When? I must've been sleeping. You could've asked me to leave, I'd be happy to—"

The door slammed in, and Marie and I both jumped back from the swinging wood slab.

"Move." The ruby snarled at my grandmother.

"Don't talk to her like that." I stepped between her and Ezra, though my legs wobbled and I had to grab the countertop to stay upright.

Ezra's eyes landed on the marks on my neck, the orbs shifting to wolf form almost immediately.

"Roman and I traded bites. It's a cute little thing regular werewolves do to mark each other as taken. And I *am* taken." I said, laying it on thick and flashing my glittering ring at Ezra.

"It's not a *cute little thing*. It's the way a ruby wolf connects their soul to one of their enforcers, allowing them a touch of power." He snarled. "Biting is the first part of the ruby mating process, too. You've sullied your soul with—"

"With my mate?" I interrupted him again.

"That's why you still smell like him; I knew it wasn't in my head."

My eyebrows lifted, and I sniffed myself. I'd know if I smelled like Roman; the man's scent was my favorite smell in the world. Though I couldn't smell anything, I chalked it up to dying.

"Cool." I shrugged, grabbing the hair-tie off the counter since Marie seemed good and spooked, just holding my hair off my neck with her hands.

"That's not *cool,* Henley. Ezra has the right to kill the New York Alpha for biting you." She pressed. Neither of them ever called him by his name; they were trying to distance me from him by calling him "the New York Alpha". As if that would work; I'd been calling him *my* Alpha for ages.

I snorted.

"Good luck with that. Roman's a lot bigger than you, and he hasn't spent his life being worshipped by everyone in the pack."

Despite my words, I really hoped Ezra wouldn't challenge Roman. Roman would probably win, but I hated the idea of him fighting for his life again because of me.

"I'll remove your connection." Ezra said, his teeth sharpening and growing as they shifted.

"You bite me right now and any chance you have to convince me to mate with you disappears." I snapped back, holding an arm out to keep him away.

"Hansen warned that he'll throw you in the basement if you do anything without her permission." Marie reminded him, stepping beside me. "Leave me to get her ready."

He stepped toward me. His nose was still busted from earlier, but I grabbed the curling iron off the counter and swung it at him. If I couldn't protect myself with my own arms and legs, I'd use what I could find.

He dodged the hot tool, barely avoiding getting his bare-chest singed. I wished he was slower, or that I was faster.

"You were meant to be mine." He snarled my way.

"I'm the only one who chooses who I give myself to." I swung the tool again. "I'm going to your damn mating party for my phone, and that's it. I'm not yours; I'll never be yours. So back the hell off."

I stabbed with the curling iron and he finally stepped out of the room far enough that I could swing the door shut. The lock was busted in, so it wouldn't do much good, but it still made me feel a little better just to have a divider between us.

"You're not really going to let yourself die." Marie said, though she didn't quite look like she believed it.

She was getting smarter.

"Arla wouldn't let me go to a party without eyeliner and mascara on." I calmly set the iron down, avoiding her question. She really didn't want to hear the answer. "I don't think we have a foundation the color of 'pale death', but a little blush could help too."

Marie slowly opened a makeup bag on the counter. I'd assumed it was hers, but she pulled out a load of brand new makeup and set it out on the counter.

"Amy had someone drop this off while you were napping." She said, her voice quieter than it had been. "Joel is worried the women in the pack won't approve of you if you don't look strong."

I lifted an eyebrow. Amy was my grandmother on Hansen's side, and I'd met her all of once, for about a minute when her mate dragged her in to meet me. Joel, my grandpa, was actually kind of hilarious. He stopped by to watch a movie with me most mornings, and the way he ignored whatever was on the screen told me it was just his excuse to try to talk to me.

Strangely enough, I didn't mind. Especially when he brought me news about the New York Pack—which was every time. He was my only connection to the people I loved.

Well, most of them. The one person he'd said he straight-up wasn't going to talk about was Roman. He'd never pushed me to mate with Ezra, but it was clear he thought I had to do it.

"Why do I care if they approve of me?"

"Because the pack's women will make your life hell if they think you aren't worthy of Ezra. A lot of them already blame you for the loss of the women who died in the trials before." She stopped.

"Before what?" I checked. "And wait, what the hell are the trials?"

"Before we knew you existed. The trials are the way a normal werewolf becomes a ruby."

My eyes widened.

"That's a thing?" I demanded. "How? Why? What does it take?"

"Slow down." Marie said, her lips tilting upward. She liked it when I had energy.

Probably because it made her think I wasn't going to let myself die.

"The trials are a month-long series of tests that turn a normal werewolf into a ruby, and anyone can go through them. But no one has ever passed the trials when there are already two ruby wolves in a generation, and if you don't pass, you die."

Damn.

"So their people died in the trials and they blame me because I didn't know I was a ruby?" I went back to the part of the conversation that had led to this, since this apparently wasn't a way I could be with Roman.

"Really, they should be blaming Hazel." Marie sighed. Her eyes filled with sadness at the mention of her daughter. "But you're the closest thing they have, so yes. They blame you."

"Cool." I sighed, grabbing the eyeliner off the counter and leaning closer to the mirror to swipe it on. My hands were shaky, so it didn't look awesome, but it was better than nothing.

I put on a little of the blush and mascara, then called it good. Ezra waited just outside the bathroom, leaned up against the wall in a tuxedo.

The outfit brought back flashes of memory.

Roman's fingers inside me in an elevator.

The way he'd held me after we survived the Alpha fight.

His tongue on my thighs as he followed the string of my thong down my ass after the mating celebration.

Hot damn.

I missed him so much it hurt.

"You like the way I look in this." Ezra purred.

My nose wrinkled.

"No."

"I can smell your desire."

Aw shit.

"What were you thinking about?" He prodded.

"Roman talked me into having sex in an elevator during our mating celebration," I shrugged.

It was mostly true.

There was sex in an elevator, but he hadn't had to do any convincing.

"Henley." Marie protested.

Ezra growled.

"Continue." He commanded.

My eyebrow lifted.

Ezra wanted more details? He was giving me the chance to piss him off?

"That's what I was thinking about. Elevator orgasms. Roman's dick. His ass. His muscles in his tuxedo." I paused for dramatic effect. *His smile* was on the tip of my tongue, but I didn't want this conversation to lead into the serious area. "That's why we'll never be mates. Roman has my heart, mind, and body. I'm his, even if I can't give him my soul."

I stepped past Ezra.

"I'm not wearing shoes to your party. My feet have to be on the ground so I have a better chance at staying balanced." I said.

He didn't respond, grabbing my arm and dragging me out to the garage too quickly for me to keep up with him. I wasn't strong enough to yank myself away, so as we went, I called a goodbye to Marie, telling her I'd see her that night.

CHAPTER 2

Ezra drove in silence. The roads were icy—especially the dirt one leading to his little house. I leaned into the door, putting as much space between us as possible.

He parked at the very front of a mansion I knew housed the current Alphas of All. Sylvie had forced me to visit a few times, and it had been insanely awkward every time. I'd only seen Hansen two or three times since I'd been there, but I knew it was his house too.

I pushed my door open without waiting for Ezra to grab it, stepping out. I had to use the door to pull myself to a standing position, but I managed. Ezra reached for my arm, and I glared at his outstretched hand.

So he just grabbed my bicep and yanked me toward the door.

I would've face-planted if his grip wasn't so damn tight.

We walked into the mansion; me struggling to remain on my feet with Asshole doing his best to knock me over. No one was inside the first room, so Ezra led me through the place into this pack's version of a ballroom. It was done up in golds and creams, fancy in a regal way some people loved. I wasn't one of those people.

The room was packed full—we were late. Every single eye turned to us as we stepped inside, and the volume of their voices rose immensely as they shamelessly gossiped about us.

My ponytail swayed, brushing the scars on my back as Ezra dragged me to Hansen and Sylvie. They stood at the back of the room, talking to different people. I knew they didn't really like each other, so it wasn't surprising that they were engaged in different conversations. They remained close to each other to uphold the idea that they were mates, but nothing in their body language gave away any type of positive feelings toward each other.

Hansen ended his conversation when he saw me and Ezra coming. He held his arms out and stepped toward me, like he was looking for a hug.

"My beautiful daughter." He announced, voice smooth and energetic.

Definitely putting on a show for his pack.

He covered the rest of the distance between us and went to wrap his arms around me. I tried to step back, not wanting to touch the surprise dad I'd never asked for, but Ezra shoved me toward him. Hansen caught me, holding me up, and shot me an apologetic grimace as he let me go.

Music began playing—I guess they'd stopped it when we arrived—and my dad bowed, holding out a hand.

"May I have a dance?" He asked.

He was a better option than Ezra, so I accepted his hand and let him drag me around the dance floor.

As we went, I caught a familiarly delicious scent.

Roman.

My eyes scanned the crowd, but I didn't see my favorite giant anywhere.

"Henley." My dad's voice was harsher than usual, and my attention snapped to him.

"Hm?" I checked.

"Your hearing is going out now? It's time to mate with Ezra."

"My hearing isn't going out. I thought I smelled…" I trailed off when Hansen spun me right into Ezra's arms. My chest smacked into his, and I grunted at the impact.

"Thought you smelled your mate?" Ezra's arms held me tightly to his chest, not letting me budge. "Here I am."

"I told you not to touch me." I growled.

"You're mine to touch." He smirked, grabbing for my boob.

I was done with this.

Stopping abruptly, I used the moment of surprise to slam my knee into his balls, my wonky-knuckled fingers meeting his cheek in a loud moment of pain and thrill.

I was finally making my stand.

The music stopped again, and gasps rang through the crowd as Ezra crumpled inward, though he didn't fall to the ground.

"This is the last time I'll say it." I raised my voice. If they were all going to watch, they may as well learn the truth. "I do not belong to you. My name is Henley Ellis and my mate is Roman, the Alpha of the New York Pack. I'm not your anything, and if you touch me again without permission, next time there will be a knife in your balls instead of a knee."

My eyes scanned the crowd. I still smelled Roman, but I didn't see him. And because my sense of smell was so crappy thanks to my sickness, I knew he had to be close.

"Now, where is my mate?" I demanded.

No one in the crowd did anything, but I noticed a woman's eyes slide to my left.

Assuming she was looking there for a reason, I tried to look confident as I crossed the room. Unfortunately, my legs were shaking like Jell-O so confidence was a pretty far reach.

I found a couple of stairs leading up to a platform I had somehow not noticed and stepped up the stairs. I teetered at the top, Jell-O-legs not doing me any favors. A small, strong hand caught mine. Her skin was wrinkled, her eyes serious as she helped me to the top step.

"Thanks." I said.

My other grandma, Amy, was the one who the hand belonged to.

She had bright red hair—the pink Ezra and I had would disappear and into a brighter red if we mated—cut to her chin, shaved in a cool pattern on one side of her head. Dark ink tattoos wrapped around her entire left arm and crawled up to her chin. Her eyes lingered on the tattoo on my collarbone; it had probably been covered last time we saw each other.

She didn't give me a 'you're welcome,' just a tiny smile as she tilted her head to the right.

I followed her, my legs weaker than they should've been. It was insanely frustrating, but there was nothing I could do about it, so complaining was pointless.

When I saw my man lying on a cot he was too big for, I rushed past her.

Mistake.

I crashed to my knees next to him, my hands finding his face and then his neck as I checked for life.

Instead of finding his pulse, my vision tunneled the moment my fingers touched his skin.

And then it was like I was somewhere entirely different, in some sort of dream or vision or something.

In front of me was a dozen werewolf bodies, some in human form and some in wolf. Though I didn't smell their death, that didn't mean anything because of my shitty senses.

Roman stood in the middle of the werewolf bodies. He carried a little girl on his back, holding her on with one hand while he fought off a werewolf in wolf form. I didn't recognize the wolf or the kid on his back, but the dead wolf bodies around me and the blood pouring from his wounds told me he'd been at this for more than a few minutes.

The little girl was sobbing into his neck, clutching him so tight it had to be painful, but he just kept fighting.

He finally got his arms around the wolf's neck in a chokehold and severed the guy's spine.

Roman dropped the wolf's body and stepped back, looking around the area for another competitor. He looked right through me, like he couldn't see me at all.

The little girl suddenly screamed. Her arms tightened around Roman's neck, and his eyes went wide as she started to strangle him. He pulled her arms from his neck and flipped her over his head, dropping her on her feet and skidding backward with his arms out.

"I'm not going to hurt you." His voice was something between a coo and a plea. "I'm here to help."

"You killed them!" She screamed, shifting forms and running at him.

Roman dove to the side, making no move to attack her. My stomach was clenched, my throat tight as the little girl lunged for him again, sharp fangs going for his throat.

A pair of arms locked around my middle, and I screamed as I was yanked from the scene.

Blinking hard, my eyes cleared and showed me the real world. Ezra's grip was iron on my waist, holding me down as I kicked and fought with everything I had.

Unfortunately, everything I had wasn't much.

"Put me down." I snarled. "He needs me. He—"

"Even you can't interfere in the trials." Amy, my grandmother, spoke coldly.

"He was fighting a little girl! Or she was fighting him, I don't know, but I have to go. I have to see, I need—"

Roman sat up suddenly, gasping for air and grabbing at his chest. His eyes were unfocused, staring at nothing. His nose twitched, and I saw him inhale deeply.

His gaze snapped to me.

"Hen." He breathed.

I couldn't help it. My damn eyes burned with tears.

He hadn't left.

Or at least, he'd come back.

And I was so in love with him I didn't even care which it was.

Amy's hand landed on Roman's shoulder and he stood, never taking his eyes off me.

Until his gaze slid down to Ezra's arms, wrapped around my waist so tight it actually hurt. Then he looked away, replacing the pain and anger I'd seen in his dark blues with determination.

Roman followed Amy to the edge of the balcony platform area we were on, looking out at the crowd. The ballroom was silent, which meant the attendees had probably heard what I said.

If anyone didn't know how I felt about Roman before, they sure as hell did now.

"The Challenger survived his third trial." Amy's voice echoed.

His third trial?

As in…

Fuck.

"He signed up for your trials?" I hissed, shooting an accusatory look at Ezra. "And you didn't even think to tell me?"

"You're mine." Ezra's teeth scraped my neck.

It felt wrong in every way, and I slammed the back of my head into his face.

Shit, that hurt.

But it did the job. He let go of me.

And then I went down.

My knees crashed to the tile, palms slapping the floor as I tried to keep my face from smashing too.

That'd hurt like hell.

Ezra's hand landed on my back and I snarled at him.

"Don't touch me."

"What the fuck did you do to my woman?" Roman's roar was followed by massive arms lifting me from the ground, cradling me to his chest.

Our eyes collided, and my heart burned at the fury in his eyes.

"She's a fucking toothpick. You're not feeding her." He glared at Ezra, tugging his eyes from mine.

"She won't eat."

"She shouldn't get a choice." My mate snarled.

I probably should've been bothered that he was talking shit about me, but my face was against his chest and I was in my personal heaven. It was really too bad he still had a shirt on.

Inhaling his scent , I rubbed my cheek against his pec. I'd gone and turned into a kitten and I didn't even freaking care.

"You're completely fucking insane if you think I'm going to send her home with you. She looks a minute away from death, you bastard."

"Marie spends all day trying to force feed her. She's not going to get better until we're mated so I can heal her." Ezra argued, stepping closer and reaching for me. "Hand me my mate."

Roman's chest vibrated with his low growl. His eyes shifted, and his arms tensed around me.

"Not while I'm still alive." He said.

...Which brought us back to what we were doing here.

"What the hell were you thinking?" I demanded.

"Fuck, Hen, even your voice sounds weak." Roman shifted my weight so held me with one arm, his fingers finding my neck and prodding like he was feeling for something. I'd had my pulse checked more than enough times for a damn lifetime and smacked his hand away.

"You're not a damn doctor."

"Please put my granddaughter down." Joel stepped up to us, tugging my eyes away from Roman. I'd pretty much forgotten there were even other people around, so it was a bit of a shock.

"No." I growled at Joel.

"He's in the process of becoming a ruby wolf, dear." Joel stepped closer, putting his hand on my arm. I didn't pull away, because he was my favorite of my newly discovered relatives. I noticed Roman's surprise that I let the guy touch me. "If you're intimate, you may permanently mate. Roman could very well die in the trials, and when a ruby dies, their mate goes with them."

"So we won't have sex—Roman was my friend before he was my mate." I leaned further into Roman's chest.

He wasn't dying in any damn trials if I had a say about it.

Which I probably didn't, in my current state. But still.

Joel looked to Roman.

Shit. He had way more of a conscience than me.

"Son, I'm sure you can understand the need to keep your distance until after the trials. If you're still together when you die, it'll hurt her that much more."

Roman stiffened.

He was going to push me away.

Roman let out a long, ragged breath and slowly tilted me, lowering me to my feet. My legs shook beneath me and he swore softly enough I couldn't hear.

"Because I understand your point, I won't drag her back to my house." He said. "But you're not taking care of her, and I didn't walk away from my perfect woman to let you kill her. I'll be living where she is, keeping her alive. That's non-negotiable."

"I'm not letting this fucker move in with me while I try to talk her into mating with me." Ezra protested, looking to Joel for support. Joel looked more than a little hesitant.

Roman let go of me, striding to Ezra and squaring up against him. Roman was taller and bulkier, but Ezra was far from afraid.

"Let's get one thing straight." Roman said, voice low. "*I* dragged her here, kicking and screaming, because *I* couldn't watch her die. *I* saved her from the asshole who held her hostage and tortured her for months. *I* protected her and her secrets from my own damn pack when they wanted to kill her for being different.

"The only reason I left her in your care is because you were supposed to heal her and keep her alive, but she's *dying* and all you're worried about is talking her into mating with you. She's the whole fucking world, not a walking vagina."

Roman paused. Ezra's face went white, and I wasn't sure why.

"And before you argue, I've heard all about your conquests. Five new women with temporary mating bonds every week. All the men who've found out their mates are still in love with the ruby bastard after he got them drunk and stole their virginity one night, years ago. If I'd thought there was a chance my girl would fall for your lies, I would've broken your damn house down weeks ago. But you were supposed to take care of her; you're the only one who was supposed to be able to take care of her."

What the hell?

New temporary mating bonds every week?

"I thought I was the only ruby." Ezra's jaw was clenched, looking between Roman and me.

"Let's not pretend there haven't been any temporary bonds this past month." Roman stepped closer to Ezra.

My knees buckled, and I went down. Joel caught me by the waist and kept me from eating the floor. He pulled one of my arms over his shoulders and held me up at his side.

Was Roman serious?

Was Ezra sleeping with other women while trying to convince me to mate with him?

"Henley and I aren't together." Ezra's words were sharp. "There's no reason for me to not to enjoy myself.

Roman snarled and Joel stared at the werewolf, stunned.

The Ezra thing was a surprise, but it's not like I was giving him a chance anyway.

"Enough." Amy stepped between them, her sleek red hair moving with her as she went. "Ezra is free to do as he wishes."

AKA, he was a grown-ass man whore and there was nothing we could do about it.

"But Roman's right. Henley's fading, and he's the most experienced at keeping her alive."

Like I'd ever needed to be kept alive before.

"The three of you will live in Ezra's house together. Marie will remain to make sure neither of you kills each other."

She glanced between the men. I resented the fact that she didn't consider me capable of killing one of them, but could admit I was too weak to catch a damn rabbit.

"There aren't enough beds." I cut in.

Namely, because I'd been sleeping in a recliner for a month—or attempting to sleep in a recliner for a month, and failing completely. Which probably contributed to my "fading".

And sleeping in a recliner was crazy uncomfortable, but also… if there wasn't a bed, I couldn't cuddle with Roman at night.

And not cuddling was insanely depressing.

"That's easily remedied." Amy brushed off my concern.

Maybe for her it was. My aching back didn't agree.

"Do you understand?" She looked between the men.

A large chunk of me wanted Roman to go all caveman and roar that he wasn't letting another man sleep in our place. I wanted him to drag me back to wherever he was living and make sweet, sweet love to me until my body shut the rest of the way down.

Unfortunately, that didn't happen.

The guys muttered their agreements, and she stepped out from between them.

"Now, Henley will dance with Ezra to make it clear to the pack that they've solved whatever problem was between them earlier, and then you can all go."

My eyebrows shot into my forehead. Roman grimaced, catching the expression.

"No." I stepped away from Joel's support, my arms folding over my chest. I wasn't steady, but I didn't fall over either. "I'm not dancing with Ezra in this wedding dress so he can save face with your pack. If he wants to look like less of an asshole, he'll stop banging everything with a face and actually listen to what I say when I tell him I'm not interested."

Amy looked to Roman.

My jaw practically fell open when I realized she was looking to him like she expected him to talk me into it.

"I can understand the need to present a united front," Roman said, looking at me.

I'd kill him.

I'd legitimately find something sharp and put it in the middle of his sexy ass and-

"But nothing binds them. They're not mates, and the pack isn't stupid enough to think they're united or in love while Ezra sleeps around. They hate Henley as it is, and if she pretends to be something she isn't, that's only going to get worse. So no, I'm not going to convince her to dance with the disrespectful bastard."

As if he could, if he wanted to.

I pitched forward again, weak legs giving out. Joel, Roman, and Ezra all lunged for me. Somehow, I ended up in all three of their arms.

So awkward.

Ezra let go first, then Roman reluctantly did the same. Joel swept my feet out from under me and started off down the stairs, headed off the platform and toward the front door. I couldn't see past him to know if anyone was following.

"I didn't know about the other women." Joel's voice was quiet.

"It doesn't change anything." I told him, though it was kind of a lie. I might not have feelings for Ezra, but it still stung a bit.

If Roman ever slept with someone else, I'd kill him.

And then whoever he'd slept with, probably.

"It does." Joel countered. "Your mother and my son weren't married. They were in love, but ultimately it was just a fling because they both knew it couldn't be permanent. Ezra could potentially impregnate one of those women, and then what? You'd be mated to a man raising a ruby child with another woman."

That situation would never occur, because I wasn't mating with Ezra. Period. End of discussion.

"I'll make sure this behavior ends." Joel said.

"How long has Roman been here?" I asked, changing the subject entirely.

His throat bobbed as he swallowed.

"He never left."

I blinked. And then blinked again.

"He's been here an entire month, and he didn't tell me? You didn't tell me?"

"We asked him not to."

Roman didn't do anything he didn't want to.

"Was it an Alpha order?" I asked.

"No. He belongs to the moon throughout the trials; our orders won't affect him. He's already become a ruby wolf in more ways than we can say."

Which meant Roman had chosen to stay away.

And now I was pissed at him too.

"He's going to die in the trials, Henley." Joel said gently, as he lowered me into the passenger seat of a truck. His truck—old and beat up, with as much of the body dented as it was smooth.

"No." I couldn't think about that; I wouldn't.

"The last person to survive them was my grandmother. The bloodline-rubies hadn't been blessed with a child in that generation, and she was the first woman to compete."

I didn't reply. Nothing I had to say would change his mind—or mine.

"They always survive the first three rounds. But there are nine challenges, and the trials grow harder as a competitor progresses through them. The next three test emotional strength, and they are rarely passed." He said.

"Roman will do it anyway." I was being bull-headed, and I knew it.

Joel pulled out of the driveway, leaving my men to do whatever they had to.

"You need to prepare yourself for the situation that—"

"No. Stop." My voice was sharp, hard. "I've been through a lot of shit, and I've survived it all. But if Roman dies…" My fists clenched. "I can't prepare myself for that situation, because I'm pretty sure it involves drinking myself to death. He was my reward, Joel. The light at the end of the hellish tunnel I walked through. I've been fine this last month because I told myself he was in New York, protecting his pack like the perfect man I know him to be. If he dies because of me, I don't think I can take it."

Joel was quiet.

"He signed up, Henley. You didn't ask him to compete."

"It doesn't matter." I grabbed my hair, tugging the tie out of my bun so it fell around my shoulders and down to my waist. It was longer again, growing out past the length it had been before my hairdresser cut it during that girls' day so long ago. "He did it for me. He does everything for me."

"We won't let you die after we've just gotten you back." Joel said.

"Haven't you lived long enough to understand that there are worse things than death?"

He didn't respond to that.

"If you haven't, you've led a damn easy life."

We drove a few more minutes in silence before he pulled up into the dirt in front of the little house.

"I'll stay with you until the sleeping situation is worked out." He said, gently.

I opened my door, but he came around and helped me out before I could climb down myself. It was probably for the better.

He pretty much carried me to my recliner, lowering me to my bed-slash-chair.

"I heard your stomach growling. What can I get you to eat?" He asked.

"Nothing. I'm not hungry." I grabbed my blanket—the crazy-soft one Marie brought for me when she first dragged my half-dead ass here—and dragged it up to my chin. She was a good grandma, even if she was still trying to shove my ass into Ezra's arms.

"Henley." He protested.

"Don't worry about me." I told him. "I just want to sit in the quiet. To think."

"Would Roman let you do that?"

"I don't know." I admitted. "He left me in this hellhole alone. Knowing Ezra was sleeping with other women. With no contact with the only people who love me, and not a single word or note or anything. I love him, but he ditched me. The Roman I know wouldn't have done that."

"In his defense, the woman he loved was dying. Is dying. A man who really loves a woman will do whatever it takes to keep her alive, even if that means walking away."

We heard tires on gravel outside, and though neither of us said it, we knew this conversation was over.

Joel turned on the TV and went to Netflix.

"I think a comedy would best suit this night." He said.

I closed my eyes, pulling the blanket tighter around me and leaning my recliner back. I didn't care what he turned on; I wouldn't be watching anything. Not while my mind was so troubled and my body so sore.

Then again, I wouldn't be sleeping either. That hadn't been in the cards for me in a month.

CHAPTER 3

THE FRONT DOOR opened and footsteps thudded the ground. When the door closed, it slammed harder than expected. I tried not to flinch, but failed. My eyes opened, and I saw Ezra stomping behind Roman. His usual flirty mask was nowhere to be seen, his eyes cold and angry and dead.

"When was the last time you ate?" Roman growled at me. He didn't look nearly as shitty as Ezra, though I was probably biased.

Did hot chocolate count?

"A few hours ago." I lied, having no idea.

It had probably been longer.

Roman stared at me long and hard before shaking his head roughly and storming to the kitchen. He muttered something under his breath, but my dying senses gave no hint as to what he said.

"So where are we going to put another bed?" Joel scratched his chin. "The spare room is full with you and Marie, but we can probably fit another mattress in Ezra's space."

I frowned.

Cabinets were opening and closing, water running and shutting off as Roman threw together whatever he was going to attempt to force down my throat.

"There isn't a spare room."

Joel frowned.

"Of course there is. It's in the basement."

The basement?

"There isn't a basement." I said, suddenly unsure of myself. I had explored the first day or two I was there, but I was mostly just searching for my phone. Since then, I'd been choosing to spend what little energy I had on shifting forms and hanging out outside in my fur.

"Yes, there is." Joel said, confused.

"No, there's not." My arms tightened around my stomach. "Ezra told me I could sleep with him in his bed or on the couch. I've been sleeping in this recliner for weeks."

Anger flashed in Joel's eyes, but both of us turned to the kitchen at the massive thud of a fist entering a wall.

Roman.

"He let you sleep on a fucking *couch*?" My mate snarled, stalking out of the kitchen with plaster on one of his hands and a plate of scrambled eggs in the other.

"It's as much your fault as his." I glared at him, my anger rising. "You're the dick who left me with some asshole you'd never met. He could've killed me and you wouldn't even know because I don't have a fucking *phone.*"

"You don't have your phone?" The plate of eggs shattered in Roman's hand and the food fell with the broken glass to the floor.

"If I did, I wouldn't be so damn *lonely.*" I tried to say it with fury, but I'm pretty sure it just came out sounding sad.

Roman spun on his heels, reentering the kitchen. There were more cabinets slamming and water continued to run, and I shut my eyes.

Fucking Ezra.

"I'll prepare the basement." Joel's voice had growl to it too.

I'd been sleeping in the recliner, but Marie had been sleeping on the couch. She was going to be pissed when she found out about the basement, too. She was too old for this shit, and I'd already tried to argue that to Ezra. No one's grandma should be forced to sleep on a *couch.*

I cuddled into the most comfortable spot on the recliner, my eyes closing as I tried to doze. It wasn't successful; my stomach churned, and my mind brought back images of Roman surrounded by dead bodies, that little girl trying to choke the life from him.

Roman came out a few minutes later and dropped onto the edge of the couch, just a foot or so from my recliner.

"You're shaking." He growled at me. "You're starving, Hen."

"Not starving." I forced the words out, keeping my eyes shut.

"Open your mouth." He ignored what I'd said.

"If I try to eat, I'll puke."

"If you don't eat, I'll strap you to this damn chair and force it down your throat."

"Wow, you always say the sweetest things." I drawled, finally opening my eyes. My hazels collided with his blues, and it was like every damn thing in the world was right again.

"This isn't a fucking rom-com, Hen. You don't eat, you die. I'll call a doctor to insert a damn feeding tube if I have to, but I'm not losing you." He dared me to argue, and I'd never had a problem standing my ground with him.

"Says the guy who signed up for a competition no one ever survives." I scoffed. "Without even telling me. Do you care at all how much it'll hurt me if you die, Roman? How do you think I'll feel when I lose you to a competition you signed up for because of *me*?"

Roman barked out a laugh.

"You think I signed up for the trials for you? If I was that good a guy, I would've left you to fall in love with the bastard in the back room." He gestured to the direction of Ezra's space. "I'm doing the trials for me, Hen. I'm a selfish asshole who can't stomach walking away from you forever. I'd rather lose my life in the damn challenges than let you go."

"Your pack." I protested.

"They're fine—and they don't want me to lead anymore, anyway. They blame me for keeping your secrets about the deaths."

"I'm so sorry. The pack means a lot to you, and-"

"And you mean a hell of a lot more." He reached for my hand, but stopped a few inches from me and pulled away. "So eat the damn eggs."

"I'll seriously puke."

"And I'll *seriously* pay a doctor whatever it takes to put a tube in your stomach if you don't."

"Roman." I complained.

"Henley." He mocked me in the same tone of voice.

With a drawn-out sigh, I finally opened my mouth like a damn toddler.

He put the eggs in, and I took a bite. As expected, my stomach churned even as I chewed. And he was already stabbing more eggs.

"No, I can't." I said, though my mouth was still full. I tried to swallow and gagged. Roman's eyebrows lifted, and he dropped the plate on the couch, striding back to the kitchen and coming back with a glass of milk. I accepted the glass and took the tiniest sip, managing to get down just a little of the liquid.

When I'd finally cleared my throat, my stomach was churning again, worse.

"Get a bowl." I managed to say.

Roman ran to the kitchen and came back with a bowl lightning-fast. Just in time for me to barf my guts up.

He held my hair back, his other hand on my back.

"This wasn't supposed to happen." He said, frustrated.

"A lot of people died because of me." I croaked. "This is karma at its finest."

"It's not karma, it's fate." Ezra said from his bedroom's entrance. "Get your hand out of her hair." He snarled at Roman.

Roman glared back but let go.

Just long enough to grab the hair tie off my wrist and tug my hair into a quick ponytail at the back of my head. I'm sure it looked like shit, but if Roman was touching my hair again, I couldn't have cared less how it looked.

He stepped away, fists tight as his sides.

"Liquids are all she can keep down." Ezra strolled toward the front door just as someone knocked on it. He'd heard the person coming; lucky sucker with his good hearing. I was so damn jealous.

He tugged the door open and Marie stepped inside. She wore a fancy dress, her eyes going straight to Roman and then sliding to me.

As she slowly made her way to me, I caught the guilt in her eyes.

"You knew he was here." I said.

Not a question; a statement.

Her head bobbed once.

"It was better for you not to know."

I shook my head slowly.

"I bet my mom would say those exact words if you could ask her why she kept me a secret." My fingers caught my soft blanket and tugged it back to my chin. I could see how much the words hurt her.

It was cruel of me to hurt her the way she'd hurt me, but I said it all the same.

"It would've been better for you not to know if he lost his life in the trials." Marie said.

"Better for you." I tossed the offensive words like a softball.

"Enough." Roman growled at me, stalking back into the kitchen. "What have you been feeding her?" He asked Marie.

She followed him into the kitchen and Ezra's gaze met mine.

"We're not that different, you know."

Maybe the words were supposed to hurt me, but I knew he was wrong. Ezra and I were different on fundamental levels that couldn't be explained to him. He'd been given everything he could've ever wanted throughout his life, and I had less than nothing for most of mine.

"I went to your party. Give me my phone." I said, ignoring his dig.

He pulled it out of his pocket and tossed it my way. My hands lifted, but I was too slow and it crashed to the ground. If it was broken, I'd rip the balls he loved to parade in front of me off his damn body.

"If you smell like him tomorrow, I'll challenge him for you." Ezra said. "He might win, but he'll at least take a few injuries. ."

I glared.

"Do whatever the hell you want. I'm done playing your games—all of your games." I shot Roman with the same glare, followed by Marie.

Ezra's expression hardened, and he walked out of the house. The door slammed behind him.

Roman came back with a cup of broth and a pack of crackers. His face was nearly as tense as Ezra's had been, though Roman was better at feigning neutrality. I could tell he was pissed.

Marie followed my man, her eyebrows knitted together in concern.

"Apparently there's a spare room." I told her.

Her lack of surprise shocked me.

"You've been sleeping on the couch—I've been in this damn recliner! Because you wanted me to climb into Ezra's bed? I struggled to my feet, and Roman pushed me back into the squishy chair with a gentle hand on my stomach. "Stop." I snarled at him before my attention went back to her. "You've manipulated me—tried to control me. I'm not your daughter, or some doll you get to control. Find someone else to take care of."

I struggled back out of the chair, my muscles crying and my body throbbing with the effort.

"Where will you go?" She demanded.

"I'm a ruby wolf. I'm sure someone will rent me a house. And if they won't, I'll sleep in the damn forest."

Stalking out of the house, my knees knocked together. Joel stepped up out of the basement.

"Wait, Henley." He protested.

I liked him more than the others, but ultimately, he'd kept as many secrets as Marie had.

"No. This is my life, Joel. If I want to wither away, I'll wither. And I'm not going to do it while you guys tug me around on a string like I'm some puppet. I'll love who I love and I'll do what I want, and if you want to stop me, you'll have to chain me to a wall like the other assholes did."

I headed into the trees, my legs just a minute from giving out. Walking took less effort and balance in my wolf form, so I pushed the straps of the white silk dress from my shoulders and slipped it off, shifting through the underwear beneath it and sliding into the trees.

My steps were slow, paws soft on the icy snow beneath me. I'd only been walking half a minute when I started shaking, the cold seeping into my bones quickly. It took more effort for my body to keep me warm than I had to give.

Snow crunched behind me. I couldn't smell whoever it was on the breeze, but my gut said it was Roman.

That asshole.

I growled at him when he caught up to me, hands in the pockets of his dress pants. He had on a button-down shirt for the party—which I now assumed was to celebrate or mark the trial he'd been taking part in.

"You're shivering, Hen." His voice was gentler, now. Softer.

I growled again, telling him to fuck off in fewer words.

"I shouldn't have left." He said.

This time, my growl was one of agreement.

"In my defense, Marie looks just like you. And I've got a weakness for nice old ladies, though she isn't as old as Mimi was. They told me being near Ezra would heal you, but they didn't mention they'd force you to live in his house. If I knew they'd make you choose between sleeping in his bed or on the couch, I'd never have left. Fuckers." He growled, now.

My legs gave out, and I flopped on my belly. A whine slipped out of me as I crashed to the snow.

Roman dropped to his knees beside me and caught my furry head in his hands.

"I'm sorry, Hen. I am. I'm so fucking sorry."

He rubbed my head, but I pulled away from him as much as I could. He let me move away, his hands landing on his knees as he sat in the snow, probably freezing his ass off and soaking his pants at the same time. He didn't seem to care, though.

"I saw the ring on your finger. Thought it was his, at first." Roman said, his voice softer. "When you head-butted him, I saw you were wearing the other one too."

I didn't respond. Didn't need to. He'd obviously put two and two together.

"You bought us wedding rings after I left you there, alone?" He asked.

I growled at him, and his lips twitched.

"Yeah, it didn't change how I feel about you either. Just made me miss you." He reached for me.

With another whine, I nuzzled my head into the crook of his neck and took in his scent deeply while his arms wrapped around me.

I'd missed him even more than I realized.

He scented my neck too, and his chest rumbled.

"You stink of that bastard."

I coughed out a chuckle.

It wasn't like I'd had a choice. I lived in that bastard's house.

"Can I carry you home?" He asked.

Home?

I tilted my head to the side. His cheeks—already a bit red from the cold—reddened further.

"To my home, I mean." He stumbled over the words.

The fact that he still considered his home mine made me so damn happy I could've smiled.

Hell, it had been a long time since I smiled.

"I bought a house here. Had to pay double what it was worth, but to be near you I'd have paid a hell of a lot more. I—shit, I'm a babbling teenager again." He rubbed a hand over his shaved head, his baseball cap nowhere to be found since he'd gotten dressed up.

I laughed another cough-sounding wolf-chuckle and bopped his cheek with my nose. His fingers slid into the fur around my head, and I don't even think he realized he'd done it.

"I think that's a yes." He said.

I bobbed my head and a ghost of a smile crossed his face before it faded. He pulled me into his arms, belly up, just in case I shifted.

"I've missed you." His voice was soft as he carried me further into the forest. "I've wandered these woods so many times, trying to catch any hint of your smell. Feel like I'm going a bit crazy without you." He admitted, his fingers digging further into my fur. "I'd never met Ezra before tonight, but just thinking about you in another guy's bed…" He swallowed, hard.

"I didn't realize how much it would hurt." He said, then changed the subject. "The girls call me every night to ask if I've seen you. You'd laugh if you heard how many times Arla has cussed me out for refusing to storm your dad's house and demand to see you. But he said you'd be safe and healthy, and I couldn't hang around to watch you fall in love with that bastard. That would kill me."

I snapped my teeth toward his neck and he didn't fight me off.

"I knew he was a player, but I didn't think he'd disrespect you. Making you sleep on the couch is fucking low, especially knowing how sick you've been. Manipulators can turn into abusers in the blink of an-" His eyes darkened as he stopped walking to meet my gaze. "Did he hurt you?"

I shook my head and Roman let out a breath of relief.

"I don't care what color his fur is, I'd kill him for that." He mumbled, resuming his walk. "We probably should've taken someone's car, but I couldn't stand taking you back into that house. The way your scents were layered together..." His shoulders tensed. "Damn, I'm a mess."

I rolled my eyes at him and shook my furry head.

"I know your scents weren't merged. You weren't together, at all." He said. "But just having him so near to you has me wanting to tear into him. Our mating bond might've faded, but it's hard for me not to think of you as mine. Even harder to think of you as his."

I growled at him and his lips tilted upward.

"I know. You belong to yourself."

Satisfied, I leaned my head against his shoulder. The comfort of being in his arms, of having his smell around me, of knowing I was completely safe... It put me right to sleep.

I woke up when Roman stopped moving. He tugged a door open, carrying me into a house. The smells inside were purely Roman, and it was like my own personal heaven.

Nudging Roman's shoulder with my nose to warn him, I shifted back to my human form. His eyes locked with mine instead of traveling up and down my naked body the way I'd expected them to.

"Perfect." He muttered. "So damn perfect."

I wrapped my arms around his neck and pulled myself against him, gentle so I didn't spook him—or hurt myself.

"I missed you too." I murmured, then let go. "And I hate you." I said.

His lips curved upward.

"It'll pass."

I stepped back, folding my arms over my bare chest just to see if I could still get a rise out of him. His eyes flicked down to my boobs and lingered for a moment before he dragged them back to my face.

"You need pants." He said.

I snorted.

"That's a terrible rule. You can't last a day without touching my legs."

His laughter boomed.

"Throwing my words back in my face, huh?"

"Well, one of us has to." I shrugged. His eyes dropped back to my chest, and he groaned, turning away and shoving a hand over his head.

"You're too damn sexy."

"You say that like it's a bad thing." I taunted him with more of his own words.

"We can't have sex. If I die…"

"You're not going to die." I interrupted. "And if you do, I'm fine to go with you."

"No." He spun back to me, covering the distance between us and catching my shoulders in gentle but firm hands. "You aren't going to die, Hen. You've earned a long, amazing life, and I'm going to give it to you. Either by surviving the trials and mating with you, or dying so that fucker is your only choice."

Anger flooded through me.

"He'll never be my only choice. Even before I knew you were in the trials, I didn't consider him a choice. I chose *you*. A werewolf only has one mate, and you're mine. End of story."

"If that's the theory you're going with, Ezra's your only choice." He gestured toward the door. "He's the only one you're physically compatible with."

"Physically compatible?" My eyebrows shot into my forehead. "You're joking, right?" When he didn't confirm that, I stepped closer to him.

He eyed me with suspicion, releasing my shoulders and taking a single, small step backward.

When I was close enough my boobs nearly brushed his chest, he took his first real back.

I moved forward.

He backed away.

"What are you doing?" He warned.

"Reminding you how *physically compatible* we are."

Though I couldn't see evidence of his erection through his pants, I rubbed my hip against him and found what I was looking for.

"Obviously, I remember." His hands found my hips and eased me away from his dick.

I grabbed his pants, undoing the button and tugging the zipper down. He tried to grab my hands to stop me, but I rubbed my hip against his dick. He swore and grabbed my hips again, shoving me away gently.

"I've only got so much control, woman."

"I know." I gave him my most wicked smile, pushing his pants down a few inches. His cock strained against his boxer-briefs, and I swear I almost purred.

Hell yes, I'd missed him.

"We can't, Hen." He snagged my wrist with one of his hands, holding my hips from his with the other.

"You told me I can use force whenever I want." I said.

His throat bobbed as he swallowed.

My fingers found the waistband of his underwear, and I pushed them down with his pants.

He hissed when my fingers wrapped around the heavy silk of his erection.

"Fuck." His jaw was clenched so damn tight.

"That's what I'm aiming for." I grinned. My legs were shaking like mad, so I lowered to my knees and wrapped my lips around his dick. He let me suck him for all of half a second before throwing me over his shoulder and stalking into a room that didn't smell much like him. He tossed me to the bed, and I let out a shout of protest.

"We're not doing it until I win the trials, Henley. End of discussion. If I die, I'm not taking you with me."

"It's not your choice." I sat up, cheeks red with anger. "Whether I live or die—it's not your choice."

"It's not." He agreed. "But I get to choose whether I take you with me when I go. And if I die in the trials, I sure as hell won't be dragging you down too."

He left the room, slamming the door behind himself when he went.

I dropped my head back to the bed, letting out a frustrated groan.

Did he have to care so damn much?

CHAPTER 4

ROMAN CAME BACK with one of his t-shirts, a bowl of chicken broth, and some ritz crackers twenty minutes later. I slipped the shirt on, had a sip of the soup and half of a cracker, and then had to quit. He left me in his spare room—alone—to sleep, then.

Staring up at the ceiling, my mind brought back everything I wanted to say to Roman. Some of them were things I wanted to yell. Others, things I wanted to whisper while our bodies melded and our souls merged. The rest were just stories; funny things I'd noticed or thought that I'd wanted to tell him when I heard them.

Roman had left me with his phone after 'dinner' and told me to call his sister.

His sister.

Like we weren't mates.

I hadn't called her—or answered when the phone vibrated. I'd let it go to voicemail and then sent a text pretending to be Roman, telling her that he was fine and that he was just dealing with stuff. Though I didn't read her response, she called six more times, so I didn't think she appreciated the avoidance.

Though I wanted to talk to the girls, I was too uncertain of myself and my future to do it now.

After a few hours of thinking, nature got the best of me and I slid out of bed to go to the bathroom. I used the facilities and washed my hands, my eyes catching on my reflection. I'd tried not to look at myself lately, too disturbed by what I saw.

Skin and bones.

Dark circles beneath my eyes.

Bruises I couldn't remember getting in splotches over my arms and legs and stomach.

Toothpick limbs.

Dark hazel eyes, lacking any sort of light.

I'd been in bad shape before, but this was new territory.

This was the verge of death.

"I'm dying." I whispered the words, trying them out in my mouth. "I have a few days left. Maybe a few weeks, if I stop getting out of bed."

But what kind of life was that?

What kind of life would I have even if I did get out of bed?

I let air out of my lungs slowly. Even that was uncomfortable.

Was I really ready to die?

"You enjoy living too much to tie yourself to me right now, Hen." I hadn't heard or smelled Roman approaching, but his voice was soft enough not to scare me. "You've got a lot to live for."

"And you don't?" I eyed him pointedly.

His lips quirked upward.

"I do too. It's why I'm going to beat the trials."

"If you're so confident, why don't you want to mate with me?"

His expression faded to a serious one.

"I can't see the future, Hen. Confidence isn't a guarantee. And I won't risk your life just because I'm too cocky."

I smiled softly.

"Too cocky, or too *cocky*?" I wiggled my brows. His lips lifted again.

"Both."

"Well, you wouldn't be risking much. My life's pretty darn close to over as it is." I looked back to the mirror. "I really do look like death. It's no wonder Ezra's still sleeping with other people."

Roman stepped closer, his fingers landing on my shoulders and curving over my weak bones and muscles.

"You're beautiful for more than just the way you look. If he can't see that, he can go fuck himself while I win the right to be yours forever." His lips met my head, then my neck, then my shoulder. I stepped back and leaned into him.

"Do I smell like death?" I asked. He shook his head.

"You still smell like you, but there's a thick layer of the scent of pain over you. When I came out of the trial and caught your scent, I thought someone was hurting you. I was ready to destroy the whole damn ruby pack. But when you hugged me, I realized you were just hurting."

I made a face.

"So I smell like a serial-killer's wet dream. Great."

Roman's lips lifted. He played with a strand of my hair, then stopped and slowly let it slip through his fingers.

We both watched the hair fall back to my shoulder.

My eyes closed.

"Did you text me?" I asked. "When I didn't have my phone, did you call me or text me?"

He hesitated, so I opened my eyes.

"Once." He admitted. "I was drunk."

Drunk?

I spun around, grabbing his shirt in my hands.

"What the hell?"

"Easy. It only happened once." He ran his hands down my arms. "After the first trial. Well, I drank once before that. Not a huge fan of it. But after the first trial, I was shaken. It felt too real. I either needed you or the alcohol, and since I couldn't have you…" He trailed his fingers from my ear down my neck, shoulder, and arm. I shivered, leaning into his chest.

"I drank. I didn't turn into an abusive asshole, somehow. It did make me weepy, though. Not fun. I missed you, so I called you. When you didn't answer, I texted you a dozen times. Don't read the messages. I thought you hadn't texted me back because of what they said."

"I didn't grab my phone from Ezra's place, so I have no way to. But you should tell me what they said."

He shook his head.

"Not happening." His fingers trailed back up my arm and shoulder to my neck.

"Please?" I turned so our chests met, lifting my arms to wrap around his neck. All I had on was his shirt, and we both knew it.

"Nope." He brushed hair from my eyes. "I should let you sleep."

"I haven't slept in a month, Roman."

"That's not helping you heal." He frowned.

"There's no healing from this." I gestured to my chest. "Those packs I held damaged me permanently. The only person who can heal me is a ruby—my mate. Which you could possibly become. Right here, right now." I shot him a stare, quietly challenging him.

"We can't mate, Hen." He growled at me. "Wrap your gorgeous head around it and get the hell over it. Three weeks from now you'll either be in my bed, moaning my name, or burying me in a casket."

"Don't say that." I smacked him on the chest with all my might—which wasn't much. "You're not going to die. I won't let you."

He laughed darkly.

"There's nothing you can do to stop it. It is what it is."

"I saw your trial, today. When I touched you, it was like I was there. You couldn't see me, but I saw you. With the little girl, the dead bodies. It was horrible."

His eyebrows lifted.

"How?" He asked.

"I don't know." I admitted. "But Ezra and Marie said that biting each other is the first step in the mating process. I thought it was just sex, but I guess maybe that's different for me too. They said it links our souls—that a ruby can bite a regular werewolf to give them some of our power so the werewolf can be an enforcer."

"Shit." Roman ran a hand over his head. "We need a rulebook or something."

I snorted.

"Like I'd follow a rulebook."

He flashed me a grin, ruffling my hair.

"We'll have to find a way to break the connection before my next trial, just to be safe. They're every three to four days, so we have time to figure it out."

I didn't think there was anything to figure out. Ezra threatened to bite me to remove it, so that was probably all there was to it. Not that I would let him bite me; I wanted my connection to Roman.

"Hen?" He tapped my cheek with his finger. "Hello?"

"Hmm?" I looked up at him, feigning innocence.

"You know how to break the connection."

"Nope." I lied through my teeth.

He studied me.

"Does it have something to do with the pain I felt months ago when one of my wolves broke through the bite scar on your neck?"

Shit.

"Not that I know of."

Lie.

I was a good liar, but Roman could read me like a damn book.

"So to break the connection, I'd have to let another guy bite you." Roman's grimace was deep.

"It's not your choice." I folded my arms.

"It's not yours, either." Roman grabbed my upper arms, fingers gentle but strong on my skin. "It's up to both of us, Hen. We're a team. If we're going to do this, these trials and all the shit that comes with them, we've got to make our choices together. And if we're going to be the next Alphas of All… then we've got to come up with a way to do it better than Hansen and fucking Sylvie."

"We haven't agreed on anything since I found you at that party. How are we going to make decisions together?" I eyed him, fairly confident this wouldn't work out.

"We agreed that Ezra's an ass. And that you shouldn't have to sleep on the couch." He paused, eyes softening. "And that we missed each other. We've done the decision-making thing together, and we're good at it. We can figure it out."

I sighed, pushing my hair from my eyes.

"Fine. Okay. You're going to have to compromise on some things though, because I hate most of your decisions right now."

He chuckled, swiping his thumb over my cheek.

"Another thing we have in common."

I rolled my eyes, but my lips twitched.

"Alright. You're eating more crackers while we talk it over." He said, scooping me off the ground and hauling me to the couch. He lowered me to the corner, propping me up on the pillows and then dropping a kiss on my head before he went into the kitchen. A minute later, he was back with a glass of chicken broth—blah—and the crackers.

He lifted my feet to his lap and leaned back into the couch cushions. I wiggled my foot toward his junk, prodding his dick with my toes. He swore and grabbed my toes as they met his erection.

"I said no." He growled at me. "Damn seductress."

"I wasn't going to give you a rub-down. Just wanted to see if you're still affected by my presence." I said, innocently.

Roman shook his head at me.

"Definitely still affected." He brought my toes to his cock and rubbed them up the hard length of it, making me laugh. "Alright. What will it take to get you to make that sound for the next three weeks until we can get naked together again?" He pulled my feet from his junk but kept ahold of them.

"I don't know." My shoulders lifted. "I feel better when I can sleep, and I sleep better with you."

It was ridiculously cheesy, but he kept my nightmares away.

"Okay, we'll share a bed. You've got to wear pants, though, or my dick might find its way into you during the night."

I lifted an eyebrow.

"Bullshit."

"I'm serious, Hen. We were having sex three or four times a day, and it's been nothing for the past month. Now that we've done it…" He shrugged. "There's no way to forget what it feels like to be inside you. It's like I'm going through puberty all over again with all these damn wet dreams."

I blinked at him. A lot.

Something about imagining Roman orgasming in his sleep was incredibly sexy.

"Hello?" He waved his hand at me.

I cleared my throat, and he groaned.

"You're turned on by my wet dreams?"

"Am I the star of them?" I checked.

"Every damn one." He growled.

"Then yes, I'm definitely turned on by them. You should describe one right now. In detail. And touch me."

He smacked my feet gently.

"You're going to kill me."

"I'm still not wearing pants." I wasn't even slightly apologetic. "If your dick finds my vagina and you don't want to mate with me, you can just pull it out. It's not like I'm really in great shape to be having a lot of sex, or tempting you."

"You've got great shape. Always." He squeezed my foot. "But food will make you feel better." He paused. "And if that was a question of whether I want to mate with you, the answer is and will always be 'fuck, yes'. You're it for me."

He lifted my toes and sucked one of them into his mouth. I squealed at the weird sensation and yanked it away, regretting the girly noise immediately. The jerky movement knocked me off balance, and I rolled off the couch.

Roman caught me just before I hit the ground, my hands pressed to the floor in an effort to save my face.

Lifting me onto his lap, he checked my hands to make sure I was okay.

And then he roared with laughter.

"Asshole." I complained, smacking him on the chest.

"Like that's news." He grinned, grabbing my face and kissing me hard.

I slipped my tongue in his mouth and he let go of my face, grabbing my hips instead. He lifted me onto his lap and I wrapped my legs around his waist, pushing my core into his hardness. He groaned, meeting my kiss stroke for stroke. I tugged at his shirt and he pulled away, grabbing my hands.

"We can't." He growled.

"I know. I just want to feel your skin while you kiss me."

He shucked the shirt, grabbing the hem of mine, and tugging it over my head. I was naked underneath, and he grabbed one of my boobs in his hand, squeezing and feeling and prodding. My fingers brushed over his abs, tracing the lines and dips and pressing into the muscles I loved so much.

My eyes landed on his collarbone, and I froze.

"Roman." I said, the mood gone. "What the fucking *hell* did you do?"

He glanced down at his collarbone, then back up at me.

"Tell me it's fake."

He said nothing.

My body began to shake. Not with the effort of holding back from shifting—but from pure, undiluted fury.

"You put my tattoo—the one I've hated since I was held down and branded at eight years old—on your own fucking collarbone." My voice shook.

"It means something different to me than it does to you." He said, voice growing gentler again.

"What could it possibly mean to you to justify putting it on the collarbone I'm going to wake up on top of for the rest of my damn life?" My voice rose.

"To me, it means survive." He trailed his finger over my tattoo—the one that matched his damn collarbone, now. "Push through pain. Brighter days follow the dark ones."

The responses surprised me, killing my anger.

His voice dropped lower.

"And most of all, it means that I'm yours. That every day, for the rest of my life, when I look at my body, I'll see you. Or at least a part of you." He ran his tongue over my tattoo. "You're Wolfsbane, and I'm yours." He pressed a kiss to my neck. "How can you be angry at me for wanting to belong to you, even in this small way?"

I scoffed, but couldn't think of anything.

His reasoning was actually sound. At least, to me it was.

He kissed me again, slow enough to wipe the rest of my thoughts from my mind while his fingers stroked my skin and slowly moved me closer, pressing me further into him.

"Also, Amy may have told me I had to get a tattoo if I wanted her to let me go through the trials."

"I knew it wasn't your idea." I grabbed a pillow and smacked him in the face with it. He laughed—my favorite damn noise. "I just can't believe she actually let you into the trials."

"Oh, she didn't have a choice. She has to let anyone who wants to do it attempt them. I just didn't know that before I went into her tattoo shop. But I still like it, for the reasons I told you." His fingers trailed over my tattoo, though we were talking about his. "You're tired, Hen. You're hurting. How can I fix it?"

He saw it in my eyes, what I was going to say to that, and interrupted me before I could.

"Other than mating with you."

I sighed.

"Don't know."

And I didn't.

As far as I knew, there was only way to fix me and it involved the naked bits of two ruby wolves.

"We need you to heal, Henley. I don't know if you can wait twenty-seven days." His eyes met mine again, his concern heavy.

I guess that was how much longer he had until he finished the trials.

And yeah, there was no way I'd make it that long.

"I'm fine." I said.

It was far from the truth.

"You can't even stand for more than a minute without collapsing, and you think you're fine?" He called bullshit.

I shrugged.

"I'm tough."

He growled at me, grabbing my face that way he always did, sandwiching me between his hands.

"Stop, Hen. Stop lying to me. I need the details, the shitty truth."

"Fine." I pushed his hands off me and leaned my back further into the couch. "The shitty truth is that I'm dying and there's nothing I can do about it. And don't say I can mate with Ezra, because I can't." I paused, knowing he'd argue with that. "Maybe I can, but I *won't*. I've lived enough shit not to resign myself to an existence like that."

Roman snarled.

"Are you pissed that he's my only option, or that you're not one?" I asked.

"Both." His voice was rough with frustration. "I thought he was going to keep you alive while I went through the trials. I'd come back, you'd kiss the hell out of me and mate with me in the bathroom during whatever celebration party this pack throws, and everything would fall into place. But the trials are timed with the moon, so we can't do them more quickly. And if you don't have that long…" He shoved a hand over his head.

"Maybe I'll last another month." I suggested. It felt like a lie, but was one of those kind lies you tell people so they don't feel crappy.

"How long have you not been able to keep solid food down?"

"Technically, crackers are solid food." I pointed out.

Mostly to avoid his question.

"The shitty truth, Henley." His chest rumbled.

"Two weeks."

He grabbed a book off the table and chucked it at the window. It broke through the glass, and a gush of icy air blew in. I shivered, grabbing Roman's shirt off the ground.

"Fuck." He snarled. Picking up one of the decorative pillows his sister had probably shipped to his place, he stalked to the window and shoved it into the hole.

The window cracked further, and then the rest of the glass fell from the frame completely.

We were both quiet for a minute.

And then we burst out laughing.

"Shit, I'm a mess." He said when we'd stopped laughing.

"Everyone's a mess sometimes."

He moved to the couch, grabbing a blanket off the far end and wrapping it around me a bunch of times.

"Let me tape this up. Didn't mean to lose my temper on you." He dropped a kiss on my forehead. I grabbed his arm, pulling him back for a longer, deeper kiss.

After he taped a garbage bag over the window, he dropped to the couch beside me.

"I'm thinking there's not any good—or safe—option here." He said, face twisting in a grimace.

"Pretty much." I agreed.

"Our choices…" He drummed his fingers on his thigh. "You mate with Ezra, he heals you. I probably die in the trials because I'll have no reason to fight if you're already mated."

I gave him a big thumbs-down.

"I'm not mating with Ezra. You're not dying. Neither half of that situation is actually an option."

"Alright. I want you to stay alive no matter the cost, but—"

"Roman." I interrupted, sitting up straight. "I'm not a puppet. You don't get to make decisions for me."

He shot me a disapproving stare.

"I was going to say, 'but if you're not willing to mate with him, it's off the drawing board'."

Oh.

Good.

I nodded and leaned back into the couch cushions.

"So really, we have to choose between mating now and risking me losing the trials, or waiting as long as we can in case I die early. If I do die early, you could still decide to jump in the sack with Ezra… Shit, I can't believe I just said that." He shook his head in frustration. "I'm not going to die."

"You're not." I agreed. "So let's just get naked, then you can heal me and everything will be perfect."

"Henley." He growled. "We're having a conversation here."

"You're having a conversation here. I already know what I want." I shot back.

He growled.

I growled back.

"Hen," He grabbed my hand and lifted it to his lips. "There's more to this than just what we want."

I knew that. I did. But I was selfish, and although I'd give most things to help someone else, I wouldn't give my freedom or my body. And those things were exactly what it would take to do what Roman was asking.

"If you don't mate with Ezra, women in the pack will keep sacrificing themselves in the trials." He said.

That was true. But mating with Ezra fell in the "sacrificing my body" column, which meant I wasn't responsible for it.

"But more than that, there has to be someone to take over as Alpha of All in place of Sylvie. You've known more of the Alphas than anyone, and if you were in charge of the male Alphas… Hen, you could change a lot of lives. A lot of *women's* lives. I can't take that from you if I die in the next trial, or the one after that."

He had a point.

Mostly.

"You're not taking anything from me. I wasn't going to mate with Ezra, even before I knew you were a possibility. By mating with me now, you'd be giving me the chance to live, Roman. Even if just for a few weeks. I'd be alive again. Not just waiting to die; *alive*." I lifted our intertwined hands to my lips and kissed the back of his hand the way he'd kissed mine

"We're never going to agree on this." He sighed, leaning into the chair with our fingers still intertwined.

"We're not." My head bobbed.

"So I guess we meet in the middle, then. If it becomes clear that you won't survive to the end of the trials, we'll mate."

"Romantic." I drawled.

"We had our romantic mating." He kissed my fingers. "This is the realistic one. If you're clearly going to die, I'll heal you. And then it's on me to survive."

"Good thing you're tough." I squeezed his bicep with my free hand.

He laughed dryly.

"Good thing."

A massive yawn stretched his cheeks.

"Can we go to bed?" He asked.

"Dude, I'm sleeping more than I'm awake these days. You don't even have to ask."

He scooped me up and carried me to his bed. It smelled so damn good. And even though I hadn't showered off whatever was left of Ezra's smell on my skin, Roman held me and we fell asleep the same way we had so many times before.

But this time, everything was different.

CHAPTER 5

ROMAN WAS GONE when I woke up, and there was a sticky note on top of his phone—right beside my pillow—that said he'd gone to the store. At the bottom, it said 'CALL ARLA'.

I slipped out of bed, my body crying out in protest. My damn limbs would've been happiest if I just sat in bed and stared at the ceiling while I waited for death to come for me.

But now, I had a renewed hope.

I wasn't going to die because Roman was going to keep me alive. If I got too sick, we would mate. He would heal me.

I would survive.

It was a beautiful thought. Maybe the most beautiful I'd had in an entire month.

Even though things had changed when Roman got me out of Ezra's house, I decided I'd keep going with the routine I'd started when I was living with Marie and the asshat. I threw on one of Roman's sweatshirts—yes, I dug it out of the dirty clothes basket like a crazy stalker—then rifled through his pile of hats until I found a beanie.

After tugging my leggings on, me and my bare feet walked out onto the porch of Roman's house. It wasn't a mansion, and it wasn't fancy.

And I loved that. So freaking much.

The steady wood of the patio was smooth beneath my feet. Grabbing a snow shovel leaned up against the wall beside the back door, I dragged it down the steps that led into the forest.

I'd taken to spending most of my awake time in the woods. The forest was alive in a way I just wasn't, and I craved that.

The snow beneath my feet canceled out any of the warming effects from my beanie and sweatshirt—not really warm enough for a winter so close to the Canadian border, anyway.

But I scraped off the snow in a yoga-mat sized area, jumping into the gap I'd created. The dirt was still icy beneath my feet, but not nearly as bad as the snow had been.

After I dropped the shovel in a bed of snow beside my homemade yoga mat, I shut my eyes and focused on my breathing. My senses were shit, but I could feel the forest in my soul.

That had nothing to do with my hair. It was just part of being a wolf.

My fingers stretched toward the sky, my back arching gently. I couldn't bend the way I had during those yoga classes I'd taken at Roman's gym for fear I'd break something in the process, but even just a little stretching felt good. It gave me time to reflect, too. Time to consider my future, however bleak. And time to let my mind linger on the good memories I'd created in New York.

I'd come to cherish my yoga time, if only because it reminded me how happy I'd been.

And how happy I'd felt only hours ago, cradled against Roman.

And now, how happy I could be again.

My fingers trailed toward the sky as I bent over. I'd trained my body to bend well before I got sick, and at least that still showed. My stomach met my thighs without strain as I held the next pose in the routine sun salutation I'd decided was all I could really handle as I grew weaker. My palms were flat on the icy ground, and it made me shiver.

"Damn, you're bendy." A female voice commented.

I had heard her coming only seconds before she spoke, but it was long enough that her words didn't scare me.

"Who are you?" I continued with my sun salutation. If this chick wanted to talk, she could talk to me while I did my yoga.

"Roman's friend."

My eyes narrowed at my feet.

He hadn't mentioned a female friend. Definitely not one who was a normal werewolf, someone he could actually mate with.

Although if he was transitioning to a ruby wolf, maybe that was off the table now for him too…

"I work at the bar across from the ruby mansion." She said, when I didn't respond, just continued through my poses.

"What do you want?" I asked, tired. Of everything, really.

And the one thing, the main thing I knew, was that no one in this pack had ever done something for me out of pure selflessness. They weren't taking care of me to take care of me; they were taking care of me because they wanted something from me.

Even Marie, though she just wanted me to be a stand-in for the loved ones she'd lost. Maybe that was why she didn't follow me and Roman to our place.

My sun salutation led me to stand, fingers stretching to the sky again. My eyes made contact with hers.

She was my opposite. Soft and curvy, wavy hair in a pretty, neutral brownish-blonde color, and warm blue eyes. She even had smile lines on her face, despite only being somewhere around my age.

"Just to talk." She said, innocently. But her cheeks reddened, a dead giveaway.

Lie.

"The last time someone said that to me wearing an expression like yours, he acted like I mattered for all of three minutes before he said I could either strip and let him fuck me or die slowly and painfully." *Cough, cough, Ezra.* "The time before that, a different fucker chained me to a wall and made my life hell when our little 'talk' didn't go the way he wanted." I paused, watching her eyes widen fractionally.

"That's not—"

"Roman is one of the most private people on the planet, which is saying something coming from *me*. He doesn't just make friends. So either you're lying, or a good portion of his personality up and changed, but he didn't feel the need to tell me."

Truthfully, I'd been so unsure for the past month that I could admit the second option actually sounded like a possibility.

My muscles screamed as I lowered myself to pushup position and lifted my ass in downward dog position.

"We only talked a few times." She admitted. "So calling us friends is a stretch. But I need to talk to you."

And there it was.

"What do you want?"

As I expected, she needed something. They all did. They couldn't get off their high-and-mighty Ruby Pack privileged asses to worry about the real world. Which was why Roman thought I'd make a good Alpha of All.

Not that it'd be hard to be better than Sylvie. Killing people without reason and setting assholes up to run packs was about as crappy as it could get.

My knees knocked together as I rose into the next position in my sun salutation.

Shit, I was getting weaker.

"Ezra will die if you don't mate with him." The girl finally said.

To be honest, I'd sort of forgotten she was there already.

I skipped a few positions, making the transition back to my feet look smoother than it felt as I rose to a standing position. Setting myself into warrior pose, which I could hopefully hold for a minute while we talked, I met her gaze again and ignored my damn quivering muscles.

"Have you had sex with him?" I skipped the polite conversation, going right to the point.

Her face went red. Her mouth opened, but I cut her off with my own words.

"Look, even if I liked Ezra—which I don't—I believe in choosing a mate and being loyal to him. I was a virgin before I was with Roman, and I'll never sleep with anyone else. He's mine and I'm his, and it's a connection I won't betray. I'm loyal to my mate, even if there's not an official bond tying our souls together."

"You're selfish enough to condemn him to death by choosing someone else." She said, as if that was the most shocking thing she'd ever heard.

"You were selfish enough to sleep with a ruby wolf you knew was fated to be with someone else. Selfish enough to give your body to someone you knew could never be your mate, though you knew whoever you'd eventually choose was saving himself for you. If keeping promises I've made to someone I love—someone who rescued me from a life that felt like hell—makes me selfish, then sure. I'm a selfish bitch. I'll die and take Ezra with me if I have to, because unlike you, I'm *selfish*."

The crunch of tires on snow and gravel was loud enough even I heard it.

Roman was back from the store, finally.

"You're going to kill him." She said, even knowing her argument was weak. "His death will be on your shoulders, even if Roman survives the trials and you live long enough to mate with him."

My gaze darkened. She might not realize it, but I'd been fairly friendly to her. Giving her the benefit of the doubt, explaining myself politely.

I leaned toward her.

"I've got deaths on my shoulders, far too many of them. But Ezra's won't be one. I'm not responsible for that asshole, and if you suggest I am again, you're going to find out how I survived growing up in hell. If anyone's to blame for that, it's this fucking pack that scared my mother so thoroughly she hid me from her own parents. I can't say I blame her, after spending a month here."

I straightened. My legs wobbled fiercely, and I was glad I'd bent into warrior position because it was the only reason I was still upright.

"Go." I said, simply.

She didn't budge.

"Henley?" Roman's voice was edged with panic, though I knew he could easily follow my scent trail here.

"If you really want to help Ezra, sign up for the trials yourself." I told her. When she glared at me, I spoke again.

"Here's something a real friend would understand about Roman." I said casually, though I felt thirty seconds from passing out. "He's a pretty nice guy until you disrespect one of the women in his pack. Offend one of us, and you lose an eye. Or an arm. Maybe even your head." I threatened her in a calm, rational voice. "I won't be pushed, or used, or manipulated. And if I were you, I'd get out of here before my mate finds out you spent the last ten minutes trying to guilt-trip me into giving my body to Ezra. He's not very forgiving when it comes to things like that."

She glanced at the house.

The back door slid open and closed, my man stepping out onto the porch.

"Hen." Roman's voice was halfway between pissed and relieved. "What the hell are you doing out here?" He crossed the yard. I hadn't gone far from the porch, knowing it'd take a lot of energy to get back inside.

His arm swept under my knees, and he cradled me to his chest. I leaned into him, enjoying his warmth and his muscles.

Thank the damn heavens.

I'd been so close to collapsing.

He shot the woman beside me a suspicious glance and asked,

"What are you doing here?"

As expected, they weren't actually friends. He'd have used her name if he knew it.

She somehow grew even paler.

"I—" She stopped, not sure how to continue.

"She just stopped by to remind me that if I don't get naked with Ezra, his death will be my fault."

Roman snarled and set me down. I pitched toward the ground with a yelp and he caught me around the waist, dragging me back into his arms and holding tight.

"I gave that fucker a month to convince Henley he wasn't a complete asshole. He made her sleep on a couch—and didn't give a shit that she was dying right in front of him. If I was his Alpha, he'd be in the hospital with every damn bone in his body broken, not a drop of painkillers in his system. You think he deserves to be saved, join the fucking trials yourself." He stepped toward her, and she stepped back.

I'd never really seen him intimidate a woman on purpose, but he needed to make a point with this one or there would be more after her.

"If you step foot on my property to threaten Henley again, you won't leave alive. You've got a minute to disappear."

He grabbed my snow shovel off the ground, hauling it and me into the house. The door slammed behind us, rattling the walls.

"What the hell was that?" He demanded, setting me on the kitchen counter.

I grimaced.

"I guess Ezra won most of the women over when he was sleeping around. I didn't think they'd actually be brave enough to hunt me down, but he must be damn good in bed, because—"

"Not that." Roman brushed the conversation with that woman aside. "What the hell were you doing with a snow shovel and bare feet on icy dirt?"

Oh.

"Yoga." I said.

His eyebrows lifted.

"Yoga?"

"Yeah. I used to do two classes a day, remember? I'm getting decent at it, and it makes me happy."

"You can do yoga inside, Hen."

"Well, yeah, but it's not the same. When I do it outside, I feel alive. Like I'm in-tune with nature or something. I like it."

"You're fading to nothing, doing yoga outside without anything in your stomach because you *like it*?" His voice was dangerously low.

"Yup." I wasn't afraid to argue with him. "Are you going to break another window because of that?"

He growled, yanking the lid off the blender on his counter and grabbing some crap from the grocery bags he'd left on the table.

"There's always a chance." He muttered.

"Do what you've got to do to cope." I patted him on the arm.

He dumped a couple types of liquid and a couple types of powder into the blender and hit the mix button. When it finished mixing, he dumped the liquid into a cup—the thermos kind, so I wouldn't feel the cold of the drink on my hands—and passed it to me.

Surprisingly enough, it wasn't too much for me to drink it all.

"Thanks." I said.

"Outside yoga ends today." His fingers found the edges of the counter, gripping so hard I wondered if he'd crack it.

"No." I wouldn't give him that.

I'd give him a lot, but not my favorite part of the day. Yoga was keeping my spirit alive, even if it was hurting my shitty body.

He swore.

I sipped my drink and made a face.

Protein powder. Mixed with who knows what other vitamin-shit Roman thought might keep me alive.

"Drink it." His voice was heavy with a threat.

I knew he would legitimately call the doctor for that feeding tube. So I drank.

After I'd slurped down three-quarters of the special sauce, my body was so heavy and exhausted I started to fall asleep. Roman carried me to our bed.

"You weren't kidding about how much sleep you need." He murmured.

"Mmhm." I agreed, only half awake. "Can you stay close? My nightmares are bad lately."

"Of course." His lips met my forehead. "I missed seeing you in my clothes."

"Me too."

I fell asleep against him again.

CHAPTER 6

I WOKE up to pounding on the front door. Roman's eyes met mine, pulled from whatever he was working on from his laptop.

"Did you invite someone?" He asked.

"No."

There was a cracking noise as the door broke open.

Shit.

Roman sniffed the air and grimaced. His lack of fur and fury told me we weren't in danger even though my nose couldn't.

Maybe it was Joel, or Hansen.

"You didn't call Arla." He said.

Nope.

"Where the hell is my sister?" Her demand floated in from the front room.

"In here." Roman called back, shooting me an exasperated look. I shrugged at him.

I would've kept in contact if I had my phone, but *someone* ditched me with a bunch of manipulative assholes. And since I'd been back, I was too busy trying to figure things out with Roman.

Arla came stomping in, but she wasn't alone.

Jamie, London, Kyler, and Oliver were behind her.

Double shit.

"Who's watching the pack?" Roman scanned their faces. His expression hardened when his eyes landed on Kyler, but he moved past him. Mostly because we weren't sure to what extent my crazy-ass ruby power had affected him, I thought. Maybe he hadn't been thinking clearly even when he turned me in to Ledger all those months ago.

Though, I *had* been thinking clearly and was sure he wouldn't take back the decision to save his sister.

"The new Alpha of New York." Arla's face went dark. "Jett Larsen."

The name was familiar. Jett had been one of Roman's enforcers—an MMA fighter, probably the only one who was a real competitor for Roman.

"He challenged you?" Roman scanned his sister for injuries, then looked to Kyler.

Wait, had he left Kyler as the Alpha?

"No. He staged a coup. The pack's still pissed about the murders. We thought we'd managed a tentative peace, but they cornered us and gave us the option to fight or hand the power over. Kallie," Arla glanced at me, probably wondering if I knew who Kallie was. I couldn't recall her face, but I knew she was Jett's sister. "She's been training for months and I wasn't sure I could win.

"The pack didn't want us there, so rather than risk our lives, we left. There wasn't time to grab our stuff, so this is all we've got." She gestured to the group. She and Jamie carried purses, but other than that, they had nothing.

"Shit." Roman stood to pace. I grabbed his hand and pulled him back.

"At least we don't look as bad as Henley." London offered.

Roman snarled, but I threw my head back and cackled. My damn frail body shook with the effort of the laughter, but I didn't care one bit.

"I'm so glad you guys are here." I said, my eyes scanning each of them.

"Will she survive a hug?" Arla checked.

"She's fine." Roman's voice was gruff, and Arla tackled me to the bed. I hugged her back, tightly, but Jamie and London were on top of us both a second later.

I sniffed Arla's hair and gasped.

Kyler.

Her hair smelled like Kyler.

Not just him, but both of them. Their scents were intertwined.

"You bitch!" I smacked her on the head. This time, she was the one cackling. "You wouldn't even tell me about your secret love affair, and you went and mated yourself to him? You nosy, secretive bitch!" I looked to Kyler's sheepish grin. "Get in here." I barked at him.

He looked to Roman, and I rolled my eyes at Roma's reluctant nod.

"If you kiss him again, I'll kill you." Arla whispered conspiratorially. I snorted.

"If I kiss him again, Roman will kill him too and then you'll both be alone."

"Let's not discuss this." Kyler winked, before sliding onto the bed where Arla was and joining our dog pile, pretty much only touching his mate. The glances he sent Roman's way told me that was for my man's sake, not mine.

Arla was mated.

So crazy.

But so freaking exciting.

I guess I knew why he'd given me all his properties in New York. And I felt less bad about keeping them knowing he'd only signed them over to me to save face with the girl he wanted to bang.

I glanced at Oliver on the outside of our dog pile. Plus Roman, but he wouldn't join unless I invited his ass in.

"Come on, everyone in my bed." I glanced at Roman. "Our bed." I clarified, catching Roman's little grin at me for stealing his furniture.

Though he'd probably change the sheets before we went to sleep that night.

Scratch that—he'd probably clean the whole damn mattress before we went to sleep that night.

The rest of them joined the pile a bit hesitantly, but we scooted over to make room. Roman was the only one sitting out, so I reached out expectantly for his hand. He took it, and I yanked him toward me. Though I wasn't strong at the moment, he let me tug him, and maneuvered his way to the very bottom of the pile so my body draped over his.

When everyone made their way out of the pile and went back to talking about what had happened in New York, I looked around and realized that the people in the room had become my family.

There I was, in a pack full of relatives I'd never met or hadn't known long, and the people I still felt the most connected to were the ones I'd chosen.

Roman ordered sandwiches and then blended me another glass of nasty protein-stuff. I reluctantly drank it, envious of everyone's future food and regretting that my stomach was such a wreck. Everyone spread out in the kitchen and living room. There were only two spare bedrooms, but we hadn't really talked about what we'd do… about anything, really.

"So this bastard tells you, on the first day you meet him, that you can strip and get in his bed or sleep on the couch?" Arla leaned toward me, like she couldn't believe what I was saying.

"Yep." I confirmed, sipping at the nasty stuff in my glass. My stomach wasn't churning, just a little upset.

"And your Grandma didn't argue? Not at all?"

"Nope." I shook my head. "But in her defense, everyone's pretty much brainwashed to do whatever ruby wolves want. If I walked into a clothing store and loaded my cart, the employees would just let me walk out with it. In her mind, because he's a redhead and I'm a redhead, jumping into bed together is all there is to it."

"Damn." Arla whistled, leaning back into Kyler's arms. He nuzzled her neck, and she protested, but the way she laughed while she pushed him away told me she didn't really want him to stop.

Roman was talking to Oliver in the kitchen. I glanced over at him, and he met my gaze with the tiniest smile that made me irrationally happy.

Jamie walked into the room with a glass of water, and I gasped.

"Jame. You're pregnant."

I struggled off the couch, smacking Arla's hand when she reached out to help me.

"I'm fine." I scoffed, hurrying over to my friend. She laughed when I lifted her shirt to poke her little baby bump—even though she was holding the both of us up. The three of us, if you counted her baby.. "Oh my gosh. Your squish is already freakin cute."

"You can't even see him." She smiled.

"Didn't anyone tell you that x-ray vision comes with the red hair?" I tutted her, though that was a joke.

"What?" Jamie looked to Roman, who shook his head no.

"Spoilsport." I shot him a saucy glare.

"Go ahead, flip me off." He smirked, shooting me a knowing look as he said it. My body flushed in memory of his mouth around my middle finger.

"Oooh, what's the story behind that?" London sat in a big, decorative chair off to the side of the couch.

"Nope." Arla lifted a hand, palm out in a stop sign. "Sister here. Don't want to know."

"Now who's the spoilsport?" London teased her.

"I guess it runs in the family." Arla glanced at Roman. "You okay with that?"

"Perfectly fine with it." He agreed.

"Yeah, right." I collapsed next to Arla on the couch again. Kyler was playing with her hair, and it was so freaking adorable. "I recall your name on a paper taped to that hideous leather lingerie you trapped me into wearing. You're an instigator, which is about as far as you can get from spoilsport."

"When it comes to Roman's sex life, I'll go with spoilsport." Arla shook her head at me.

"Lingerie, Arla. Bedroom clothes. Want me to tell you what happened when we got to our apartment while I was wearing that? It started with—"

Roman's hand covered my mouth. He lifted me off the couch as I protested into his palm, sitting back down with me on his lap.

Jamie was laughing in her chair, and Oliver's eyes were glued to her from his place in the kitchen. On second thought, every time I had looked at him since they'd been there, he was looking at her.

It was so freaking adorable.

"So what's our plan?" Arla wondered, leaning further into Kyler. His fingers trailed up her arm.

"We need to buy a house. I'm not living here with Roman and Henley while they go at it like rabbits." London said. "Actually, I'm not living with Arla and Kyler, either. Jamie?" London swiveled her head to find our round-bellied friend.

"We're on the same page." Jamie nodded quickly.

I snorted.

"We're more like bears than rabbits."

Roman coughed behind me, choking back a laugh.

"Plus, we can't have sex or I'll die. So the only ones you have to avoid are these hot fools." I gestured to Arla and Kyler. His fingers paused on her arm.

"Alright, we need to buy two houses." London waved her hand like that didn't matter.

"I hardly convinced the Alphas to let me buy this one. They claim all their apartments are occupied, too." Roman brushed my hair from my neck so it wouldn't yank when he tugged me closer. "I'd be surprised if—"

He stopped talking when someone rang the doorbell.

Considering Arla had broken the door when she kicked it in, that was pretty polite of whoever was there.

Roman sniffed and swore under his breath, slipping out from under me.

"Want me to grab it?" Arla checked, standing.

"Not this time." He stalked to the door. From where I sat, I'd be able to see whoever was there, and they'd see me too.

The door opened to Joel and Hansen. Hansen looked uncertain about being there, but I imagined Joel hadn't given him much of a choice. Joel was a decently cool grandpa other than the lying, but Hansen pretty much avoided me.

His eyes landed on me and he swallowed.

Was he disgusted that he'd had a child without realizing it?

Or did he just see her, every time he looked at me?

"We heard you had guests." Joel scanned the group for threats. His eyes met mine, and I saw the question in them. Since I'd told him in nicer words to fuck off the last time I saw him, I wasn't surprised by the caution in his gaze.

"This is my family." I told him, watching carefully for his reaction. Whatever he felt, it didn't show in his eyes. "You tried to alienate me from them by taking away my communication, but you failed."

He frowned.

"I was unaware that you'd had your phone taken and didn't have access to the internet for anything but television." Joel said.

I mostly believed him.

"It's nice to meet the people who kept my granddaughter alive when I couldn't." He nodded at the group.

"It's time to come home, Henley." Hansen interrupted his dad before Joel said anything else he didn't like. "We've spoken with Ezra, and he's agreed to stop the inappropriate behavior. He'll apologize if you'd like—take you to a nice dinner, buy you jewelry. You can stay in my home, if that makes you more comfortable."

I scoffed, holding up my left hand and pointing to the diamond I'd bought myself. Roman's eyes flashed with humor, enough that I could see it from my seat on the couch.

"I'm perfectly capable of taking myself to a nice dinner and buying myself jewelry, dad." I snarled the last word, using it as an insult rather than a term of endearment.

Hansen's face strained.

"Sylvie is very attached to Ezra. She thinks of him as her child and has had a lot to do with raising him. She already hates you because of what

I did with your mother, and if you take away his chance at living, she will kill you."

Roman stepped up to my father. Daddy dearest was only a few inches shorter, but Roman managed to dwarf him all the same.

"You'll want to be careful about threatening my mate."

Hansen's eyes narrowed.

In the past, he'd seemed fairly reasonable. I guess me messing with Sylvie and the ruby wolf way had pissed him off.

"I assume you'll need some place to hold all of these people." Joel changed the subject, gesturing to our group.

"We'll find someone to bribe." I said.

"Yes, but that will take time neither of you have." He said. "We'll have the houses on either side of this one vacated for you." Joel said.

"As a sign of good will?" Arla strolled up beside her brother to join the conversation. I looked at Kyler, and he looked at me. We both shrugged.

Sometimes, it was better to sit back and let the Ellis twins do their thing.

"No. They're only offering because they want something from us." I said, easing off the couch. "From me."

The men didn't deny it.

That was just how this damn city worked.

They did wait for me to make my way to Roman's side and lean into him so he could wrap his arm around my waist and keep me on my feet.

I didn't ask another question, instead waiting for them to just come out with it.

"Let Ezra break the connection between you." Hansen's eyes jerked to my neck. The bite marks there. And then he looked back to my face.

"And then go to dinner with him. Just the two of you. Give him a chance."

"You mean like he gave me a chance, when he told me to sleep on the couch until I was ready to have sex with him? Or maybe the way he gave me a chance by sleeping with other women while trying to force me into giving myself to him?" I folded my arms.

One of my girls growled behind me, and I knew they'd all have my back if I needed them to.

"It wouldn't cost you anything."

"It hurt like hell the last time someone tore through the bite on my neck." I gestured to the scar.

"Ezra will be careful." Hansen assured me, though the way his jaw was clenched said he either didn't believe it or was just plain old pissed. I wouldn't be surprised by either answer.

A soft hand landed on my shoulder and London stepped around me, sizing the men up.

"Look, bastards." London's voice was honey-sweet as she smiled humorlessly at them.

Oh, great way to start a conversation with the male Alpha of All and his dad.

"Hazel left your pack and hid her daughter from you. A woman doesn't just jump into single-motherhood at eighteen for fun. She must've been afraid for her life and Henley's. If you want Hazel's daughter to trust you, you've got to do something trustworthy for at least one damn minute."

The men just sort of stared at her.

My dad shook his head and looked back to me.

"Think it over. A date and a bite; That's all it'll take to get the space you need. Don't bother trying to find a way around it; property doesn't move hands in this city without my approval."

Hansen strode back to his truck, but Joel lingered.

"Can I bring you all dinner tonight?" He asked, scanning the faces in the room. "There's a new movie I thought we could watch."

Joel and his movie nights.

Roman and Arla looked to me.

"Are you going to try to talk me into sleeping with Ezra?" I checked.

He chuckled.

"I'm about done trying."

Finally.

"That wasn't really an answer." I said.

"I'll say nothing about your love life." He glanced at Roman, and I understood. If we agreed to the movie night, he'd keep his mouth shut about both Ezra and Roman.

"Then we'll see you tonight." I gave him a quick smile, only somewhat genuine. He looked a bit sad, and I felt crappy for that, so I stepped toward the door as he turned to go. I lowered my voice to a dramatic whisper, catching his arm.

"I'll trade a hug for a milkshake." I said.

His big grandpa-grin stretched his cheeks.

"Am I allowed to share that trick with my son?" He checked. I laughed.

"As long as you don't let Roman get his hands on the milkshake; he'll add protein and vitamins and shit." I shot Roman a teasing glance and his lips lifted.

"Yes, ma'am." Joel tipped an invisible hat my way, and I feigned a curtsy. Of course, bending my legs wasn't really a great plan those days. My legs gave out, and Roman barely caught me before I face-planted.

"Dammit." I muttered, a little unsteady.

Joel roared with laughter, shaking his head as he turned and headed to the truck my dad waited in. I hoped that someday, we could have a conversation about my mother without anyone else around. I wanted to hear his side of their story.

"I'll see you at five." Joel called over his shoulder.

The door shut, and Roman carried me back to the couch.

"Well, they're pieces of work." Arla grumbled, following me back.

"You have no idea." I drawled.

Roman's lips pressed to my temple, and he deposited me on the couch… disappearing into the kitchen to make me *another* glass of protein juice as someone arrived with the food they'd ordered.

And damn, I couldn't wait for the moment Roman finally agreed to heal me.

CHAPTER 7

JOEL BROUGHT steaks and potatoes from a local steakhouse for my friends, a smoothie and milkshake for me. I think he felt bad for everything and was trying to make it up to me by feeding the people I cared about.

I fell asleep on Roman only a few minutes into the movie and didn't wake up until well into the next day. Roman was pacing the room with a glass of protein-crap in his hand when I finally opened my eyes.

He relaxed when he saw that I was up.

"Every time you go to sleep, I'm terrified you won't wake up." He said, dropping beside me and handing me the drink. I made a face at it, but accepted it.

"I'm fine, Romeo." I caught his arm and gave it a gentle squeeze. He tugged it from my grasp and wrapped it around my side, dragging me closer.

"What do you think about Joel's offer last night?" Roman asked. We hadn't talked about it since—I think everyone realized it was my business. I'd punch any of my friends who told me I needed to let another guy bite me.

I looked him up and down.

Fingers in a loose fist.

Shoulders tight.

Lips pressed together, not on my skin.

"You think I need to do it." I said.

"If it's part of the mating process and I don't make it through the trials, we don't know how my death will affect you." He didn't confirm my assumption; he didn't have to.

"I'm not going to let him bite me." I countered.

"Hen." He shut his eyes and kept his breathing level. Fighting the frustration and fear I could scent on him.

"It's my choice."

"I hate it when you get to make decisions." He muttered, opening his blues and wrapping his arms around me, hugging me to his chest. The movement dragged me onto his lap, and I buried my head against his neck.

"I'm not apologizing for being free." I said into his collarbone.

"I know." His hands lifted to my back, rubbing circles over the big long-sleeve I'd stolen from his dirty clothes basket again. "I wouldn't want you to."

"Would you even be able to stay calm if I permanently smelled like Ezra?" I asked him.

Roman paused.

And then chuckled, his chest rumbling against me.

"I didn't consider that." He admitted. "There's a good chance you'd need a fly-swatter if you agreed to it."

I snorted.

"Yeah, like that would stop you. A spray bottle would be the smarter choice."

"Good point. A taser, maybe?"

"Nah. I think I'd need a full-on gun."

"I'll buy you one." He teased, his fingers lifting to comb through my tangled hair. "Ezra's hair is pink too. Does the color change when you mate?"

I nodded.

"To make it obvious which ruby wolves aren't mated. A new pink ruby is always born within nine months of the Alpha of All mating. It's actually kind of interesting. There are only ever two pink wolves. One genetically connected to the Alphas of All, and one born to a random couple in the Ruby Pack. They call the random one the 'blessed' ruby.

"The blessed ruby is always the pack's favorite, and a lot of couples will try to get pregnant in the months before the pink ruby mating so they have a chance at bearing the 'blessed'." I made air-quotes around the word.

"That's messed up." Roman grimaced.

"Yup." I popped my lips with the "p". "Did anyone try to talk you into convincing me to do it after I went to bed?"

He lifted an eyebrow.

"You think someone here would try to talk me into getting you to let Ezra bite you?"

Good point.

"They didn't. They value their lives too much." He pressed a kiss to my forehead.

"Knock, knock." Arla said as she pounded her fist twice against the door. "Hennie, we heard you do yoga when you get up and we're dying for some girl time." She called out.

"Coming." I called back, lifting my lips to Roman's. The kiss was meant to be quick, but his fingers tangled in my hair and my tongue slipped into his mouth. We lost ourselves to the kiss, Roman's erection jabbing my ass when Arla banged on the door again.

"If I don't get to have sex, you don't either." She yelled.

Roman's face twisted with disgust at the mention of his sister and sex in the same sentence.

"Love you." I patted him on the cheek and slid out of bed, wincing at the aches and pains I'd forgotten.

"Hen." He warned, grabbing the protein drink I'd left on the bedside table. I'd put it there, hoping he'd forget about it, but no luck.

"Fine, fine." I took a swig and made a face.

Not good.

But I didn't puke, so it was alright.

I pulled my coat from the closet. Roman came over to help me slide my arms in, the concern evident in every line of his tight expression.

"Really, Romeo." I forced a smile, sipping at the drink while he zipped my jacket up. "I'm okay."

"You're far from okay." He murmured.

I kissed him quickly and headed outside. Arla was leaned up against the wall, waiting.

"Damn." She said.

I lifted an eyebrow, silently asking her what the 'damn' was about.

"You look worse every time I see you." She said.

I rolled my eyes.

"I'm fine."

Maybe if I said it enough times, it'd end up true.

Unlikely, but a girl could dream.

"Sure." She grabbed my arm, pulling it over her shoulder as we started toward the back door.

My toes met a shoveled path through the snow, still ice cold. Roman must not have noticed my bare feet, or I'd definitely be wearing boots.

We slowly made our way to the other girls, and I joined them in their stretching, enjoying the feel of the dirt on my toes—even if it was cold.

We went through my sun-salutations together, though I only made it through two that day.

I'd been able to do fifteen without a break a month earlier. Before I tried to hold the New York Pack, I could go on indefinitely.

Arla looked worried after I called it quits and sat on the icy dirt, but I pasted on my calm mask and acted like it was normal.

The next day and a half passed quickly, and then we all accompanied Roman to his next trial. He didn't seem nervous, but let me lace my fingers through his as I leaned into him so he could keep me upright. The pack threw some sort of party to honor every trial—it would turn into a celebration of the victory, or a memorial of the loss.

This time, it was an indoor barbecue. Not all of the pack members went—there were multiple parties thrown, and there was a rotation of who got to attend with the ruby wolves each time.

The barbecue was inside a school gym, so the pack members dressed casually.

We left our friends to the party, slipping into the room where the trial would take place. It was a small classroom, and the small mattress for those competing was on the ground. Sylvie and Hansen stood off to the side, Joel watching the door while Amy went through the medical cart she'd wheeled in. Ezra wasn't there—probably off in a room with some chick, hoping Roman died tonight.

Roman kissed my head and sat on the mattress, rolling one of the long-sleeves of his shirt upward and holding out his arm while Amy went over to him with what looked like a shot.

Sylvie left the room and announced the start of the trial to the pack somewhere outside the room, while Amy injected the inside of Roman's elbow. She slipped the syringe in a hazardous material bin and stepped back, taking a place right beside me.

"What is that stuff?" I asked her, gesturing to the needle.

"Wolfsbane." A bit of sly humor brightened her eyes. "It's not actually poisonous, you know—at least, not entirely. It connects us to the moon. To our beastly sides. Only when used on certain phases of the moon will it begin changing someone to a ruby wolf."

"Huh." I said, watching Roman lie back on the mattress. "How did you learn about this way to turn someone into a ruby?"

"It's existed as long as we have." She said.

"Does it hurt?" My arms wrapped around my middle, my eyes glued to the man I loved.

"No. But it lingers in the system, changing cells and tissue and who knows what else. If the werewolf doesn't continue with the trials, it will kill them slowly." She glanced at me. "And more painfully than what you're experiencing."

I grimaced.

We were quiet. The party went on behind us—we were in a room off to the side. Amy and Joel—the Ruby Elders—made it clear that only ruby wolves were allowed in this room, so our friends and family were out in the party somewhere.

As far as I could tell, Ruby Elders were just ruby wolves who no longer had Alpha power—so basically, just werewolves with red hair.

Roman's body was still, but he was breathing. At least there was that.

"Do you love him?" Amy asked. Her words were soft, though there was curiosity in them.

"More than I thought I could." My eyes didn't move from him.

She was quiet.

I couldn't stand any longer and sat down in the chair Joel had placed behind me for this reason.

"Are all the trials about physical fighting?" I asked. "When I touched him last time, I saw what he was facing. It was… disturbing."

"It depends on the person. The first three trials typically are, as they test the wolf's physical strength. The second three focus on emotional strength and are often much harder. Few wolves survive the second set of trials. There are nine in total, and each set of three is more difficult than those before."

"How many?" My voice dropped. "How many of the girls who fought in the last few years survived the second set?"

Amy's lips pressed together, her eyes going back to Roman and lingering.

"Amy." My voice was quiet but sharp.

"Three."

My eyes widened.

"Of how many?"

"Seventy-three."

My stomach turned.

"None of those three made it past the seventh trial." She didn't look away from Roman.

I slipped off the chair, moving toward him, but she caught my arm.

"You can't intervene."

"I just want to see." I tugged my wrist, but she held tightly.

"You can't." Her voice was firm, unmoving.

I tried but couldn't get free of her, so with a heavy sigh I let her tug me back to my chair.

"How long have you been together?" She asked. I think she was just trying to distract me.

"Depends how you define together. I think he considered us 'together' the moment he saw me." My arms wrapped back around my nervous stomach.

"Will you tell me about it?" Amy prodded.

None of my newfound family had ever asked about him before—they hated it when I mentioned him. And some part of me was desperate to have a connection with them—the people who knew my mom, who were my family by blood.

"It was September or October. I can't remember which; the days all blurred together, then. I was so afraid of Ledger—" I glanced over at her. "He was the Colorado Alpha. He had me chained in his basement for months, torturing me. Trying to talk me into mating with him." Her expression went tight. "If I'd know sex wouldn't mate us, I probably would've given in."

I was damn glad I hadn't known.

"I'd escaped him and had been free, hiding in New York City for a few months. But still scared. I only left my apartment at night, thinking every other werewolf was stuck in their wolf form then. The first time my boss talked me into working a day shift, I met Kyler. The owner, and one of Roman's enforcers. I ran from him, but Roman caught me. I followed him to his skyscraper, and he told me his pack would pay me to stay, so they didn't have to shift. Offered me so much money I couldn't turn it down."

My lips lifted, just the tiniest bit.

"He pretty much just inserted himself into my life. Wormed his way into my trust and my heart. I was so stubborn, I'm surprised he didn't just walk away, but he loves a challenge. He protected me, and took care of me, and let me set the pace… And damn, did I make it difficult for him."

Amy's eyes were bright with interest.

I brushed hair from my eyes and noticed off to my side, Hansen was watching me intently.

Listening.

"Back before I joined the New York Pack, I never told anyone anything. I never let people in."

"I guess that's a good excuse as to why you won't give Ezra a chance." Amy said.

It was time to change the subject before someone decided to try to talk me into choosing Ezra again.

"Did you know my mom?" I asked.

Amy's posture changed, her eyes flicking to her son.

"I did." She said.

"What was she like?"

"Sweet. Friendly. She made it difficult for people to dislike her." Amy tilted her head toward Hansen. "Your father would be the better person to ask. They were best friends through most of his life, even after I tried to convince him to break her heart and walk away."

My eyebrows lifted, and I looked at Hansen. His face reddened.

Sylvie hadn't returned after announcing the beginning of the trial. If she had, I didn't think Hansen would say anything.

"She knew me better than anyone." He admitted. "Made me laugh all the time, made life seem easier, simpler too."

I studied him. His whole body language had changed when I brought her up.

"You loved her." I said.

He bobbed his head.

"I spoke with my mom's best friend from the Georgia Pack. That's where she raised me, until another pack wiped us out. My mom never spoke about your pack. The only time her friend even heard anything about you, they were drunk. Mom told her friend that she still loved you. That she missed you so much it hurt."

Hansen's fingers lifted to his chest briefly.

"Thank you." He turned, walking to the doorway and turning so we couldn't see him, looking out at the party.

Amy grimaced, looking back to Roman.

"If he dies, will you mate with Ezra?" She asked.

I swallowed.

The idea of Roman dying was too much to take.

"No. I won't betray him, or myself." My arms folded over my queasy stomach. "If he goes, I'll follow. I've only got a few days left anyway; the doctor gave me about a week to live when I saw him on Wednesday." It was Monday, so I'd already breezed past most of my week. And while that was just his guess, he knew more than I did.

She nodded.

"You'll condemn Ezra to death."

"He wouldn't be the first." I said, guilt tugging at my conscience. "But if I die, another girl should be able to win the trials."

That thought triggered a realization.

If I killed Ezra, Roman would probably survive the trials.

I brushed the thought away, because it was more than shitty. I'd killed people, but I wasn't a murderer. And I knew with certainty that Roman wasn't either. He'd rather lose fairly than take a life without reason.

The only person who might act on the knowledge was Arla, but even that, I doubted.

Amy said nothing.

"What are the emotional strength trials usually about?" I changed the subject again.

Roman was supposedly going through the first emotional strength trial, and if I couldn't touch him to see it, I'd try to figure it out from where I was.

"Watching people you love suffer without losing your mind." She watched Roman too. "Sometimes, making difficult decisions that will hurt at least some people."

"He won't break." I maintained my confidence in Roman. He needed me on his side, and I sure as hell needed him to keep fighting.

"We'll see." Amy said.

It was thirty minutes before Roman emerged from the trial. He was barreling across the room to wrap me in his giant arms before I knew what was happening.

I hugged him fiercely, squeezing his body to mine. His arms were iron around me, holding me like an anchor. When he leaned away to meet my eyes, they were dark as midnight.

"You're safe." He murmured, like *he* was the one comforting *me*.

"Of course I am." I whispered.

"They were—you-." He shook his head, burying his nose against my neck once again.

"You don't have to talk about it. I'm fine, and you'll keep me safe."

He grunted his agreement, holding me tighter and just breathing in my scent.

If he was this shaken up after the fourth challenge, I wasn't sure I wanted to know how bad the next ones would be.

CHAPTER 8

Arla walked me outside for yoga the next morning. We'd all been quiet the night before, leaving Roman to his thoughts. His face was still pale, and he hadn't let me out of his sight after the trial. Even as I headed outside with Arla, I could feel his eyes on me.

"So you might have already answered this question before, but why aren't you getting any better?"

I wasn't sure if I had answered it or not either. There was a lot going on in my mind, and I'd sort of avoided the question so it didn't lead to Roman learning answers that would freak him out.

"The damage from holding all those packs is permanent until I can be healed by another ruby wolf—my mate." I explained quickly. "My organs have gone to shit. Most of them are in some stage of failure. The doctor I saw last week was surprised I'm still breathing. A regular wolf or my grandparents could try to heal me, but they wouldn't be able to undo the deep damage that needs fixing."

Arla's eyes widened.

"How long did he say you have?"

I shrugged it off. I hadn't told Roman yet, because I knew it would freak him out and wasn't about to force him to mate with me. Especially when the horror of whatever he'd lived in that trial was still obviously with him.

"Doesn't matter." I lied.

"Henley." She protested.

I glanced over my shoulder. Didn't see Roma, so I assumed he'd gone to the bathroom or something and lowered my voice.

"He didn't think I'd last through the week."

Roman snarled somewhere behind me.

Shit.

Arla let go of my arm just before her brother swooped in front of me and grabbed my face.

"How long ago was that?" He demanded.

I met his eyes.

"Not long."

"Tell me."

I said nothing.

All it would do was hurt him.

I'll call fucking Ezra for the answer if I have to." I could barely make out the words through his growl.

"Wednesday." I finally said.

He let go of my face and a string of curses spewed from him as he stepped away. According to the doctor, I had only a day left.

"We can talk after yoga." I told him, voice small and soft.

Arla's arm wrapped around me again, and she eased me toward the door. I left Roman in the kitchen, knowing he'd let me know when he wrapped his head around what I'd said—and when he'd come up with a resolution for it.

The other girls were all outside, standing and stretching around something that looked like a giant lamp. There was no snow around it for a few feet in each direction.

"What's that?" I glanced at my sister-in-law.

"Outdoor heater." She said. "It was here when we came outside."

Roman.

He didn't want me doing yoga in the cold, so he took care of it.

Took care of me.

My throat caught, and my eyes stung.

No tears. Fuck the tears. I hadn't cried since I woke up alone in that damn bedroom, and I wasn't crying now.

"Oh no, Hennie," Arla stopped walking and wrapped her arms around me. "What's wrong?"

"I'm just really glad you're here. All of you. I spent the last month thinking I'd have to die alone, and I—" The rest of the words didn't make it out, but I brushed at my eyes with the back of my hand.

The girls had me wrapped in a giant bear hug so fast it was almost funny.

"You're not going to die." Roman's breath was on my ear, his arms wrapping gently around my middle before he extracted me from the group of women and lifted me off the ground like I was some kind of delicate flower.

"I'm not going to break." I mumbled.

"Nope. I won't let you." His lips tickled my ear as he lifted me in his arms.

He grabbed his keys off the counter.

"Where are you taking me?" I asked at the same time Arla followed us out the front door.

"Where are you going?" She called out, mirroring my question.

"On a date with Ezra." Roman shouted back, opening the truck's door and sticking me inside. It was a different truck than the one he had in New York, so it didn't smell like us yet.

"What the hell?" I shot him an irritated glance. "I tell you I could die today and you want me to go out with Ezra?"

"I didn't say *you're* going on a date with Ezra. I said *we're* going on a date with Ezra." He said, twisting the keys in the ignition.

"Roman."

"Henley." He met my stare with his own. "Your dad and Joel didn't say you had to go alone with him. And any good negotiator starts with a higher price than they expect to leave with."

"I'm not letting him bite me."

"I think you should, but it's your decision." Roman wasn't intimidated by me, and I loved that. "They're probably expecting you to shoot that part down anyway. If not, you'll talk them out of it. There isn't much your stubborn ass can't convince someone to do."

I scoffed.

"My stubborn ass?"

"Sorry, your *sexy* stubborn ass."

He smirked when I smacked him on the leg.

"You didn't really think I'd leave you to die alone." He said, growing serious as we drove. My eyes trailed the forest, and I didn't respond. "Hen." He repeated.

"You left me. Walked away. What was I supposed to think?"

"That you were better off without me. That he was the only one who could heal you." Roman's voice was low, lower than usual.

"I knew you *thought* that. You didn't purposefully hurt me. But waking up alone in a stranger's house, in bed next to some other naked guy, still sucked."

"Wait, what?" He sat up straighter.

"Ezra thinks he can convince me to mate with him by walking around naked all the time. I mean, maybe it would've worked for you. But him? Blah."

"Marie told me she'd protect you." I smelled his frustration, but it was nothing compared to mine. "I thought she'd keep you safe."

"Not all grandmothers are Mimi, Romeo." I shook my head and looked back out the window. "Her definition of protection is different than yours and mine. And to her, boning Ezra is the only way to ensure my safety."

He swore under his breath.

"I wish she was wrong." He shoved a hand over his face. His stubble was longer than usual, I noticed.

"What have you been doing for the last month?" I changed the subject.

He laughed humorlessly.

"Fighting."

I shot him a questioning look.

"Bought a gym here and turned it into an MMA place. I started teaching, since none of the ninnies here have had a reason to learn to fight. The classes are mostly full of women." He shot me a sheepish glance. "But you know I don't encourage them, and there are a few guys happy to take a couple hits for the sake of learning. We're kind of…friends."

"Friends?" I lifted my eyebrows.

"The first I've had in a long time." He admitted. "Some of my enforcers were cool, but I was always their boss. These guys are my equals—except when I stomp them, but that's for fun."

"Damn, Romeo. Look at you, making friends. Next thing I know, you'll be yelling at a football game on the TV like a real human."

He laughed.

"I doubt I'd ever pass for a real human."

My eyes swept his muscles and mischievous grin.

"Probably not. But this is one step closer."

We pulled up in front of the Alphas house.

"How many of them tried to make a move on you?" I asked, trying to keep my voice casual so I didn't come off as a jealous bitch.

Roman shut the truck off without answering.

I growled, and he captured my face between his hands.

"None of them were you, so it really doesn't matter." He said, and I could smell his sincerity.

"Yeah, because having healthy women you can actually mate with hit on you in workout clothes is nothing. I'm sure you'd feel that way about shirtless ruby men hitting on me." I muttered, pushing his hands off my cheeks. "Probably didn't help that you're the only available guy with experience in bed…and there are dozens of women who want someone who knows his way around a woman thanks to Ezra." I grumbled.

Roman tugged a strand of hair, lifting it to my nose.

"At least none of them were naked in my bed." He said.

Bringing that up again? Low.

"That was your own damn fault, and I still blame you for it." I shot back.

Roman chuckled, pressing his lips to my cheek.

"I only ever dreamed of you." He murmured.

And damn him, it made me feel better.

We stopped in front of the door and Roman knocked. A middle-aged woman with long, ruby hair answered.

"What do you want?" Sylvie's gaze locked on me, her eyes angry.

"Nice to see you too." I said, voice heavy with sarcasm.

Roman squeezed my hand, telling me to stay calm without saying the words.

"Hi." Roman bowed his head slightly, a move of respect. "Hansen and Joel are waiting for us."

Sylvie scowled but stepped back, opening the door for one of us to fit through at a time.

Roman went first, releasing my hand so we'd fit. He cleared the doorway and I followed him, but as soon as the door was closed, Sylvie had me pinned against it. Her voice dropped low.

"Ezra is the closest thing I'll ever have to a child." She snarled in my face. I tried not to wince. "If he dies because of you, I don't care what color your hair is. I'll remove the skin from your body inch by inch, strip by strip, until you've suffered enough to make up for the years I spent begging the moon for a—"

She staggered backward, my mate having shoved her a bit when he stepped between the two of us. One of his arms wrapped around his back to find me, fingers catching my hip gently.

Sylvie tried to slam her power into him. Though she was strong, her power couldn't touch him while he went through with the trials.

"I may not be a ruby wolf yet, but if you touch my mate one more time, I'll break your fucking neck." Roman's voice was low and deadly.

"What's going on?" Amy demanded, strolling out of another room. Her gaze trailed from Sylvie's pissed-off glower to Roman's heaving chest, and then to the protective arm around me. "Sylvie." She said sharply.

"I'll discipline Hansen's bastard any way I wish." The ruby woman spun on her heels and stalked back to whatever hellhole she'd crawled out of.

Amy's eyes met Roman's.

"I wouldn't recommend threatening an Alpha of All." She tilted her head in the direction I knew Hansen's office was. "Come on."

We followed her. Or at least, Roman followed her. He scooped me up and carried me like a damn infant.

Joel was relaxed in a rocking recliner off to the side of the room, a highlighter and a newspaper in his hand. I didn't even know printed newspapers were still a thing. He looked up with an amused smile as we entered, though his son's expression was neutral.

"What was the yelling about?" Hansen looking at Roman.

"Your lovely mate." I said, and the blood drained from his face. "It's not like you don't know she's a bitch. You told me before you knew I was your daughter that you hated her."

"I don't hate her." His voice was gruff. "She's my mate; I could never hate her. We just don't see eye-to-eye on much."

...Or like each other.

He didn't say it, but I knew it was true.

"We're here to negotiate." Roman tugged a strand of my hair to distract me from my anger again. It didn't really work, but the change of subject did. "Henley will go on a date with Ezra in exchange for the houses on either side of ours, along with some information."

Joel and Hansen looked at me. I nodded my agreement, though Roman hadn't told me what information we were looking for.

"What information?" Hansen asked.

"What are the steps to the ruby mating process?" Roman spoke again. Good thing he was there; it legitimately hadn't occurred to me to ask.

"You're going to try to mate before you know if you'll survive the trials." Hansen's voice dripped with disapproval.

"I won't make it to the end of the trials." I cut in before my man changed his mind. "I'm falling apart. I can hardly walk, can't keep down solid foods… Hell, I wouldn't be surprised if tomorrow, I can't even keep down liquids."

Hansen's grimace was deep.

"Ezra is still an option." He said.

"For you, maybe. Because you chose Sylvie over the woman you loved." I leaned toward him. "Tell me, how much happiness has that choice brought you?"

"It kept me alive to meet my daughter." He countered.

"The daughter you would've had a chance to raise if you'd stayed with my mom instead of letting her run away. Maybe letting her go was easier for you, but in the long run, your life—and my life—would've been better if you'd held on."

My dad's face remained calm, though I could feel his frustration.

"I would've died years ago."

"Maybe." I nodded. "But you'd have died happy. In love. Honest with yourself and the people around you. And that means more to me." I leaned into Roman's side when he tugged me closer.

"Dammit, Henley. You're twenty-one years old; you need to *live*." Hansen slammed his fist on the desk.

"Then you'd better hope mating with Roman works now that he's turning into a ruby." I gave him a tight smile. "And that he survives the trials."

"I accept your deal." Joel said, from behind my dad. "I'll sell you the homes if you go on a date with Ezra—just you and him, Henley." He glanced pointedly at Roman, and I swore mentally. "And I'll tell you the mating process, when I've seen photographic proof that you went on a date and really gave him a chance."

Damn.

Roman grimaced, looking to me. I knew what he wasn't saying; that it was my choice, and he'd support me whatever I decided.

Without knowing the mating process, we couldn't exactly become mates.

Which meant I had a grand total of one option here.

"Alright. One date, with proof that it's legit." I agreed. "Ezra has to wear clothes."

"That's reasonable." Joel nodded.

"When doesn't he wear clothes?" Hansen wondered.

I barked out a laugh and Roman grimaced.

"It doesn't matter—plan on five this evening." My dad said.

It was so weird to think of him as my dad.

"She'll be ready." Roman's voice was low and growly. I felt shitty for him; I'd sooner rip my own nails off than send him on a date with another chick. He had more protective and possessive instincts than I did, so I couldn't imagine how much he hated the idea.

We left a few tense minutes later, Roman's hand gripping mine so tightly I thought my fingers might break.

Considering what I was doing that night, the tight grip was a bit of pain I'd happily take for him.

CHAPTER 9

I SPENT an hour in Roman's bedroom with him, Arla, Jamie, and London. Kyler was in the process of making dinner, and Oliver was helping. Roman was "working" on his laptop. Translation: watching me and the girls.

"This would make you look even closer to death." Arla suggested, holding one of Roman's puffy coats up to me. Since I didn't have any clothes there other than what the girls picked up on a trip into town, we didn't have a lot of options.

"Plus, you'd smell like Roman so he wouldn't touch you." London's grin was devilish.

They were there for moral support more than anything else.

"Or smelling like Roman would make him want to touch me even more." I countered, from where I sat in a chair we'd dragged in.

"Enough, guys." Roman growled from across the room, tossing his baseball cap to the bed beside him and scrubbing his hand over his face. "She's going to wear clothes that fit and give him the benefit of the doubt."

I turned in the chair to face my man as the girls exchanged concerned looks.

"I don't have to do this, Romeo."

His eyes closed, and he took a measured breath in and out before he opened them back up.

"There's not another option." He said, voice forcedly calm.

We could walk the streets, asking people for information, but that likely wouldn't get us anywhere in a city that hated us. I'd tried calling Marie to ask her—but she hadn't answered. And really, she was the entirety of my contacts in Ruby City.

"There is, though. We could camp out in Hansen's office until he tells us what he knows." I said, knowing that really wasn't an option.

"Or we could drive around and ask people. Someone else in the pack probably knows something, if not everything." Jamie offered.

"Or we could abduct someone to demand they tell us what they know." London threw in.

We all turned to look at her, and she shrugged.

"What? It's true."

"We want these people to like us." Roman growled. "They're Henley's family. Maybe if she goes on this date, they'll give up on trying to talk her into giving him a chance and accept that she's going to be mine."

"Or maybe they'll think I'm interested in him and pull more of this shit." I threw back.

Roman shook his head.

"They care about you, in their own messed-up way. So you're going on this date you promised them, and you can politely tell them to go to hell if they try to force another." Roman said.

I scowled, but agreed with him.

At least, enough not to keep the fight going.

"Fine. Just grab the least-sexy clothes I've got and we'll go with that." I told them.

They helped me into a pair of warm black leggings and a big, comfortable, black long-sleeved tee. Somehow, it made me look even more frail.

London braided my hair out of my face. I shot down makeup so Ezra didn't get the wrong impression, and then it was about time to go. Roman walked me to the door, his hand on my arm instead of my waist to keep me upright.

"It's okay if you like him, Hen." Roman said, his voice soft but unsteady. "I know you've been pushing him away because of me over the past month, but if you like him… Well, you're supposed to be together. It wouldn't be bad or wrong. And you should be with the guy you're fated to if you like him. I know that. So forget about the other women he's slept with and think about giving him a chance."

He actually looked… vulnerable.

I loved it, but hated it.

"Roman." I grabbed his face, going up on my tiptoes and leaning against his chest for balance. "It's been a month, and he hasn't tried to get to know me, or make me laugh. He's never even tried to *talk* to me about anything other than mating. Even if you weren't in the picture, I wouldn't choose him."

Roman nodded, though he still didn't look convinced.

"I'm worried that ten years from now, you'll look back and wish you'd at least tried to be with him—that you'll regret choosing me so quickly." He admitted.

"That's bullshit. Not even possible. But to make you feel better, I'll start a conversation with him tonight—a real one, about my mom or something. Then you won't have to worry about this down the road when you and I have an argument, okay?"

"Alright." He pressed a kiss to my forehead. Ezra knocked on the door, only inches from us, and Roman stepped away to answer it. He pulled it open and sized Ezra up. The ruby wolf was as cocky as ever, wearing a smirk I'd only seen on him when he was attempting to manipulate me into sharing his bed with him—or talking about his dick.

"Ready to do this?" He held his elbow out to me.

A soft, warning growl rumbled from Roman. I squeezed his ass to reassure him as I stepped past him, ignoring Ezra's elbow to walk by his side

My damn legs shook, and he grabbed my arm to hold me up.

"I'm only doing this because I have to." I warned him.

"You'll be mine by the end of the night." He promised, shooting me a smug grin. I had a shitty feeling about it, but just rolled my eyes and slipped into the passenger seat while he walked around to the driver's side. He turned the car on, and I looked out the window to see Roman.

One of his hands was tight on the door, the other fisted at his side.

Hopefully he could meet up with his friends to punch some of that frustration out before we met with my dad and grandpa.

I texted Kyler, asking if he'd drag Roman to the gym so my mate wouldn't feel quite as shitty. Kyler sent back a thumbs-up, and I felt slightly better.

Ezra made no effort to talk to me on the drive. I considered making the effort myself, as I'd told Roman I would, but just really didn't want to talk to the asshole.

When we pulled up in front of a fancy restaurant, he turned to me and draped his hand over my thigh. My very, very upper thigh. Like, he almost grabbed my damn vagina.

I shoved his hand away, but was too damn weak to do anything.

"Get your hand off me." I growled, shoving at him again. London had slipped a knife in my bag—she was crazy—but I wasn't fast enough to get away with stabbing him.

"You're mine to touch." He smirked.

Since my knife wasn't an option, I grabbed a plastic water bottle out of the door and shoved it at his face. He smacked it with his free hand, squeezing my upper thigh as he did.

"Last warning. Let go of me, *now*." I gritted my teeth against the feeling of being violated. I wasn't new to it, but it was just as bad now as it had been the first time.

"Henley, babe." He finally let released my leg, shutting off the car and stepping outside. "It's time you accept who you belong to and get over the idea that you get to choose. You're mine. End of story." He said, wrapping his arm around my waist and dragging me inside.

"Let go of me." I hissed as eyes and bodies turned to watch us.

"I don't think so." He pressed his lips to mine, and I jerked backward, nearly falling on my ass.

"Whoa, easy there." The waiter caught me with hands on my shoulders. Gentle hands, unlike Ezra's.

"Sorry." I mumbled, sliding away from him and barely dodging Ezra's grabby arm.

"Hey, you're Roman's... friend." The guy said. "Henley, right?" His eyes caught on my hair.

He must've been one of Roman's friends from the gym.

"Yep." I gave a tight smile, the expression vanishing when Ezra grabbed my wrist.

"Don't speak to my future mate." Ezra's voice was sharp and cruel.

"Don't talk to people like that." I snarled back, ripping my hand from his grip. "And stop touching me."

"I'll touch you however the fuck I want."

He shoved me into a corner and I almost fell on my face. Stunned by the physical mistreatment, I reached for my phone but came up empty.

My bag.

He held it in his hand.

"Looking for this?" He taunted.

"Give it to me." I warned.

"I don't think so." He sneered. "I've had enough of you refusing me and calling for help. Sit down and shut the hell up." He waved for a waitress. Ours was a woman, who came running the second he lifted his hand.

"She'll have a glass of water. Get me my regular."

He sent her away as fast as he'd demanded her there.

"Yeah, I'm done." I tried to slip out of the booth. His fancy shoes smashed into my kneecap when I did, and I barely bit back a pained cry.

"You'll leave when I say you can leave."

He still had my phone and bag. Everyone in the pack loved him and thought he was perfect. They'd never believe that he'd hurt me, and they definitely wouldn't intervene.

Even as they witnessed the mistreatment.

"You've embarrassed me, Henley. Do you think I want to mate with a weak shell of a woman who argues with everything I say? I assure you, I don't. Because it's our only option, I'm going to eat, and then we're going back to my place together. Understand?"

"Fuck you."

"Oh, you will." His face practically begged to be punched, but with his leg stopping me from moving and my own damn weakness, I was trapped.

Anxiety rose within me, and my body quivered with the need to shift.

Go.

Run.

Escape.

I should never have left Roman. Bad shit happened when I was alone.

I caught the waiter's eye—he was watching me. And I mouthed, "Call Roman."

His head jerked in a nod, and he vanished.

Ezra's food arrived quickly, and he lifted the gigantic burger to his mouth. He ate messily, and I scowled at him.

"Is everything alright over here?" Roman's friend, the guy waiter, came back to our table with a calm smile.

"Fine." Ezra barked.

The waiter set a plate down in front of me, and I glanced down at the food I hadn't ordered. It was a burger; definitely wouldn't be able to keep that down.

My eyes caught on a napkin beneath the plate. It said:

HE DIDN'T ANSWER.

My heart sank. I'd gotten too used to having someone to rescue me in shitty situations like this.

"She's sick, and feeling the effects of fighting fate." Ezra's voice was sugar-sweet. "She doesn't want the burger. Take it and go."

The guy looked toward me, and I nodded.

"Go." Ezra repeated, louder.

The guy left, glancing over his shoulder at me.

My water had arrived with Ezra's food but I had yet to touch it, so I grabbed it and chugged some. It probably wouldn't help, I knew, but it was something to distract me from my dire situation.

Alone with an asshole who was determined to make me his.

Someone who wasn't afraid to hurt me and had less than no respect.

"Here's the deal, Henley." Ezra said, after swallowing a mouthful of meat. "After I eat, you're going to climb back into my car, and we're going back to my place. You'll mate with me, and I'll heal you."

Yeah, I'd rather die.

"You've been sick. I'm tired of having this up in the air. We're fixing both things tonight." He added.

"You just proved you're not afraid to physically hurt me, and you think I'm going to agree to mate with you?"

"No. I think you're going to mate with me because I'll kill you if you don't." His voice was easy and calm. I noticed a few people near us shoot him shocked glances. "I won't die alone so that you can be with someone else; I don't give a shit about what you want. Better accept it now."

I lifted my hand, calling the waiter over. Our waitress showed up, depositing our drinks beside me and looking at me.

"I've decided to have some food after all. I'd like to try one of everything on the menu—drinks included. No rush, I'd rather you just bring one thing out at a time." I pasted a smile on my face, though it probably looked more scary than nice.

I hoped ordering a lot of food would buy time for the waiter to get Roman to answer his phone.

"Put it off as long as you want." Ezra said casually, popping another bite of steak in his mouth. "You'll be mine tonight."

Yeah fucking right. I just had to put it off long enough for Roman to chase me down.

I grabbed my water and took a big swig.

Talking to Ezra was pointless, so I just sat there staring at the ceiling, drinking my water. None of my food came out, but Ezra finished his.

"Ready to go?" He asked me.

"I'm waiting still." I shook my head, and the movement felt sort of slow. Disconnected, almost.

"Weird." I said. My word slurred, and I frowned. I felt almost… drunk. But not like my usual pissed-drunk, but a tired, dizzy drunk. "What the hell?"

"Don't worry." He tugged me out of the booth and wrapped his arm around my waist. I stumbled, but his iron grip kept me upright. I opened my mouth to argue but forgot what I was going to say as he led me out of the restaurant. No one stopped us.

He lowered me into his car and sleep threatened to overwhelm me.

"No, no, stay awake." He snapped his fingers in front of my eyes. I shook my head again, trying to stay up. "It's just a few drugs, Henley. A ruby shouldn't be so easily affected.

Drugs?

"You roofied me." I slurred.

The water…

He hadn't touched it.

"Technically, the waitress did." He offered. "Elizabeth, her name is. She's delicious."

I slouched into the seat.

He was going to try to force me into mating with him.

It wasn't possible, right?

For normal wolves, it wasn't.

The world spun, and I couldn't see much of anything through the spinning.

But Roman hadn't answered his phone, and everyone else thought Ezra was a great guy. If I was going to get out of this, I'd have to get myself out.

The only way I could think of was to knock Ezra out, or kill him, when he came close enough for me to make out his features.

Was I willing to take his life?

In self-defense, yes. I'd killed to protect myself before, and I wasn't proud of it. But I'd do whatever I had to do to defend myself.

"I hear biting is crazy erotic. Can't wait to sink my teeth into you." He flashed me his fangs as he pulled up to the glass house. Sylvie opened my door as soon as Ezra had his car parked.

She knew?

What kind of woman could ever support a plan like this?

"Hurry up." She snapped at him, grabbing me and yanking me out of the vehicle. I'd have landed on my face if she didn't catch me. "Hansen and Joel are going to hear about your disappearance from the restaurant."

Roman would too, if Ezra actually bit through the scar on my neck.

Sylvie shoved me onto the couch and I landed half-on, half-off.

Ezra rolled me over, positioning his body over mine. I was too sedated to feel much terror or dread, but I was still ready to protect myself.

"I hope this hurts." Ezra sneered, lowering his teeth to my neck. He bit down on my skin, and the white-hot pain of the disconnection from me to Roman broke through even the drug-induced haze.

Ezra wasn't expecting my fingers to shift..

He didn't see my hands to lift to his neck.

But he definitely noticed my claws gouging into his throat as I fought him away.

Sylvie screamed, diving toward us as I pierced veins and arteries, blood pouring down on me as Ezra threw me off the couch. He was gasping, grabbing at his throat, as I flew through the air. I was so dizzy I couldn't decide if life was going in slow motion or faster than it should.

I slammed to the ground, head colliding with wood so hard I lost consciousness for an undetermined amount of time. I don't think it was more than a minute or two.

A familiar roar ripped me back to the real world, though everything was fuzzy.

I blinked and saw Ezra's bloody body hit the ground.

Another blink, and a man—Hansen, I thought—threw himself in front of a half-shifted giant with blood on his claws.

A third blink and Amy was on the floor, her fingers on Ezra's neck, while a female ruby wolf licked at the wounds on his throat—Sylvie.

Even as I lost consciousness, I could smell death in the air. She was too late.

The fourth blink had Roman at my side. His hands were on my face, but I couldn't feel them. He was speaking, but his words were distant. Far away. Someone else was talking too—yelling, maybe?

When I blinked the fifth time, Roman's eyes were watery as his teeth lowered to my neck. I felt more pain—more burning, white-hot pain, as some part of my soul latched back on to Roman's.

My eyes closed and didn't reopen.

CHAPTER 10

I WOKE UP IN A HOSPITAL.

At least, it smelled like a hospital. I still couldn't get my eyes to open, but there was the beep of a heart-rate machine off to my side so I figured I'd somehow managed to stay alive.

I really was a damn cockroach.

How many people had to stomp on me to finally end my life?

"There's no other choice." A deep, male voice said. I couldn't tell who it belonged to—I was too disoriented for that.

"I knew that before you asshats decided to risk her life." Another voice snarled.

That one, I would recognize anywhere.

Roman.

I tried to move, but my body felt like it was made of sludge.

"It shouldn't have been a risk." A third voice said. "We had no idea he and Sylvie were planning something so horrible or we would've stopped it long ago. We wanted Henley to mate with Ezra, but we would never try to force her."

The words brought back memories.

Flashes.

Ezra on top of me.

Pinning me.

His teeth in my neck.

My claws in his throat.

Our broken bodies on the floor.

A massive shudder went through me.

"Hen." Roman's hands were soft on my arms, my neck, my shoulders, my face. "Henley." The bed shifted, and the side of his body pressed into mine as his fingers felt my throat for a pulse despite the machine clearly declaring it was still beating.

I wrestled my eyes until they opened…

And met the concerned blues I loved so much.

A relieved breath left his throat.

"How do you feel?" He asked.

I glanced at as much of my body as I could see without moving my neck.

"Like Ezra roofied me." I said, clearing my throat as Roman's body shook like a damn leaf in the wind. *He was furious.*

How long had he been shaking like this? Fighting not to shift forms?

My gaze brushed over Hansen and Joel. They looked like shit—long stubble on their faces, dark circles beneath their eyes. I looked back to Roman and realized he too was growing an accidental beard, his circles as dark as theirs and his eyes even a little red.

"How do *you* feel?" I asked, lifting my hand to his face.

Holy shit, my fingers were heavy.

"Fucking terrified." He growled, his hands cupping my face and his forehead leaning down to rest against mine. "You scared the hell out of me. I don't think I'll ever sleep again."

"I'm fine." I murmured, my eyes closing as I blinked. They stayed shut a minute as I tried not to relive everything at the forefront of my mind.

"Stay awake." He barked. My eyes opened again, sleepily. "You've got to stay awake, Hen. We have to talk." He looked nervous, almost.

I glanced at Hansen and Joel.

"About what?" I asked.

My dad and grandpa made their way over to me. They both looked hesitant, and apologetic.

"Do you remember what happened two nights ago?" Joel asked.

Two nights ago?

Shit, had I been out that long?

"Went on a date. Got roofied." I rubbed at my aching head, a memory of my claws in Ezra's neck hitting me again. "He… bit me." My fingers reached up to my neck, feeling for an injury. It had been healed, and I glanced at Roman inquisitively. He rubbed the back of his own neck.

"I bit you after him." There was so much regret in his voice I had to lift my eyebrows.

"Why do you feel bad about it?"

"You were unconscious." He said.

I guess it was sort of a violation, but sure as hell didn't feel like one compared to what else had happened.

"You were dying with Ezra. His bite alone was enough to take you with him when he died. Roman bit you to keep you alive." Joel said gently.

"I would never have done it without your permission if there was another option." He said, voice dripping with apology. "I'm so damn-"

"Roman." My fingers curled around the neckline of his shirt, and I tugged him closer. Though I was too weak to really pull him, he moved for me. "I let you bite me ages ago. I wanted it. Don't apologize for that—especially if it saved my life."

He jerked his head in a nod, and I looked back to Hansen and Joel.

"So Ezra's dead." I said.

The men both nodded.

"Sylvie tried to heal him, but you'd cut too many major arteries."

"I killed him." I said, my voice monotone.

"Yes."

I wasn't sure how to feel about that. On one hand, anyone who would try to rape someone should burn in hellfire. Death was too small for them, too simple. That wasn't the issue—he'd deserved to die for that.

The part where I was the one who killed him, using my own damn claws, was the part I didn't know how I felt about.

With a heavy sigh, I leaned back into the thin pillow behind me and closed my eyes again.

"Open." Roman growled.

I obliged, just to glare at him.

"I'm fine."

"You're still dying." He argued. "We don't know if we can mate at all, and now I'm your only chance."

"You were always my only chance. I knew he was a dick the whole time. Didn't expect him to try to force me—how would that even work?"

"Sylvie wasn't sure it would, but she was desperate. She loves Ezra." Hansen said.

"Love isn't an excuse to drug someone and attempt to rape them." Roman snarled, shooting my dad a threatening look that had me putting my hand on his shoulder. Not to stop him; I completely agreed. "It definitely isn't an excuse to *help* someone else drug and rape."

"How many of the abusive assholes who hurt me did Sylvie choose to be the Alphas?" I poked the bear. "How many terrible men has she put in a position of power, knowing they'll use violence and cruelty to control their packs?"

Hansen said nothing. I think he had nothing to say… or at least, nothing he felt like he *could* say.

"We can't sit back and let this happen." I told Roman. He met my eyes. "We've got to fix it. To change things."

"You want us to be the Alphas of All after I pass the trials." He said.

"No. But we can protect people when no one else will, so I don't think we have much of an option." I said, looking back to Hansen. "Will we have to fight you for it?"

He grimaced.

"No, but my pack won't follow you." He said. "And Sylvie will try to kill you if you take her power."

"They'll learn to accept us over time." Roman wrapped an arm around me, turning to size my dad up. The pack adored him and Sylvie the same way they'd loved Ezra; Hansen never would've needed to learn to fight. "And we can deal with your mate."

"We'll consider it." Hansen said, his eyes softened as he studied me. "I'm sorry I didn't know what they were planning early enough to stop it, and I'm glad you protected yourself." He slipped from the room, leaving us with Joel.

"He's being weird." I muttered into Roman's shoulder.

"I almost killed Sylvie and he would've died with her." Roman said, his lips meeting my forehead.

"Hansen and Sylvie have always had a rocky relationship, but I think seeing her help Ezra try to force you frightened him." Joel said, crossing the room to sit on the edge of the bed. His palm landed on the top of my calf, near my foot. Since there was a pile of blankets over my leg, it wasn't strange. "It frightened me and Amy as well. She and Sylvie were close, once. When our son was around your age, before they became Alphas of All."

"Power corrupts people." I said.

I'd seen it happen to too many Alphas not to believe that.

"It corrupts *weak* people." Roman agreed.

I snorted, and his lips tilted upward.

"Still cocky." I commented.

His lips brushed my ear, and he murmured,

"Only for you."

Goosebumps climbed my skin until Joel cleared his throat. Then I looked back at him.

"The mating process is relatively simple. You exchange bites, then bodily fluids—" AKA have sex, "and then blood."

Blood?

My nose wrinkled.

"We drink each other's blood?"

"I'm sure it sounds odd, but for ruby wolves to bind together, you must be connected in every way. Usually, a pairing will spread out the exchanges as they meet and grow closer—the way the two of you exchanged bites before you were intimate."

I looked to Roman and found him studying Joel.

"If it takes more for ruby wolves to be mated, are there more benefits to the mating as well?" He asked.

"Yes." Joel's head bobbed. "You'll be able to heal each other from any physical injury—even so much as healing scars from old wounds."

My eyes widened.

My scars could be healed?

Did I even want them gone?

"You probably know that some Alphas can speak into the minds of their co-leader and pack members in wolf form. Ruby wolves are able to speak into their mate's mind without effort, regardless of the distance between you or which form you're in."

Damn.

"Your very souls and lives will become connected when you mate. Your existence depends on each other, and your happiness lies in the hands of another. You live or die together, which is a bit intense."

No kidding.

"At this point, we just have to hope you're able to mate. Without Ezra as an option, I'm afraid Roman may be the only ruby wolf alive come this time next week."

Wow, dark.

Roman growled at my grandpa.

"We're thinking positive thoughts." He warned.

Joel chuckled.

"I suppose that's a good way to prepare yourselves for what's to come if the mating works." He stood. "I'd recommend waiting until you're back at your own home to complete the process. The connection to each other can be overwhelming at first."

Joel stepped around Roman to kiss the top of my hair.

"I'm glad you're alright. Amy has Sylvie locked in a room in our house until we can be sure she's not a danger to you any more, and I swear we won't allow her to hurt you again."

"Thanks." I said, awkwardly.

Inwardly, I was thinking she needed a hell of a lot more than to be locked in a room. There should've been consequences for what she'd done.

Joel left the room then, leaving us together.

Roman's eyes met mine.

"How are you feeling?" He checked, his hands on my face again as he gently turned my head to one side and then the other, looking for injuries or something.

"You already asked me that." I reminded him.

"I'm worried about you." He admitted, His fingers found the hem of the hospital gown I had on, and he undid a snap on the side so his fingers could touch my hip. I thought he just wanted to touch me, but winced as he gently pushed on what felt like a bruise.

Ducking his head, he studied it.

"Bad?"

"Not good." He said, redoing the snap after he slid his fingers back out. "I wish you wouldn't have killed Ezra. I wanted to feel his heart stop as I crushed the life out of him."

I snorted.

"Dark, babe. Really dark."

His lips twitched.

"It was self-defense. Would've saved him for you if I could." I rubbed at my neck, shivering at the memory.

Roman's fingers went to the scar of my bite mark on his own skin.

"I know. I was looking for you, after Carson called me. I'm so fucking glad Ezra was stupid enough to take you to his house." Roman's hand trailed down my hair. "I don't know if I could've been there in time to keep you alive if he wasn't."

"Don't think about that." I said. "Are you okay with the blood exchange thing? It sounds kind of weird, but..." I shrugged. The movement reminded me how much my body hurt.

"I think it sounds hot." He said. "Your blood smells delicious."

I wrinkled my nose at him and he grinned, leaning in to kiss the damn thing.

"You're fucking adorable." He nuzzled his nose into my neck and I swatted him away. He just caught my hand and lifted it to his chest.

The nurse came in and Roman chatted her up like they were friends. She got the paperwork together for us, and we were driving back to our place an hour later.

I expected it to be empty, but all our people were gathered in the living room, waiting for us.

"Hennie!" Jamie shrieked, throwing herself at me. Roman grabbed me, keeping us both upright.

"Oh my gosh, your baby is poking me." I breathed, excitement in my eyes.

"I'm not apologizing."

"Don't. It's cute."

Arla and London were close behind Jamie, their arms wrapping around both me and Roman. He'd told me in the hospital that he kept them updated on how I was doing, but the ruby wolves hadn't allowed anyone else in the hospital with me.

We talked to them and luckily Roman had already explained what happened so I didn't have to. Though they seemed reluctant, they all left without complaining when Roman told them I needed to rest.

The wink London shot me with over her shoulder told me they knew exactly what kind of "rest" I'd be getting.

CHAPTER 11

THERE WAS a bit of quiet tension between us when they left for the houses Hansen and Joel had cleared for them. Not an angry kind of tension, or an awkward kind. Just the tension that accompanied two people, knowing they were about to make a decision as big as this one.

I sat on the couch while Roman made a protein drink for me. He sat beside me, watching to make sure I drained every drop from the glass. When it was empty, I sat it on the floor near my foot and turned to face him, my legs folded up on the couch with us.

"So." I said, watching him.

"We don't have to do anything tonight, Hen." He said, suddenly. Like he was worried I didn't think we had a choice.

"You know I still want you, right?" I checked.

I'd gotten lucky with Ezra. Lucky that nothing really, truly horrible and scarring had happened. If he'd been expecting me to fight, or if I hadn't had claws, things could've gone much worse.

But another round of my life's shitshow wasn't going to change how I felt about Roman.

He rubbed the back of his neck.

"Yeah, but—"

I scooted closer to him, my knees bumping the side of his thigh before I swung one of my legs over him so I could straddle him.

"I'm dying, Roman. You left me with my shitty family, but I understand why you did it. I would've done the same in your situation. You've been nothing but loving and protective and so damn perfect I sort of want to strangle you for it—even if that's an awful joke considering what just happened. So why the hell wouldn't I want to do anything tonight? I chose you ages ago."

He shut me up with a kiss, his tongue plunging straight into my mouth as he pulled me closer with a gentle hand sprawled over my lower back.

"I get it." He murmured, pulling away and then kissing me again, lazily this time. It was beyond perfect.

"I missed your mouth." I said, pulling him back to me when he ended it again.

He chuckled, his chest vibrating against mine.

"I missed your ass." His lips met my neck. "Your hair, too." He dragged the hem of my shirt up over my belly, lifting it and my bra up to free my boobs. "And your damn nipples." He groaned after capturing one in his mouth. I arched into him as he sucked, a soft moan escaping me when I felt his dick hard against my core.

"What about my vagina?" I breathed.

He growled into my boob.

"I could climax just thinking about it."

I laughed, my breath catching when he released that nipple and caught the other one.

"Shit, Roman."

"Call me Romeo." The command was so low and sex-laden I wanted nothing more than to obey.

"Shit, Romeo." I corrected myself, cracking a smile when he met my gaze over my chest, eyes narrowed at me.

"Again." He said, sucking hard.

"Dammit," I moaned, grinding against his erection. "Romeo."

He grabbed my thighs, lifting me from the couch and stalking into his bedroom with me in his arms, my shirt and bra still bunched up above my boobs. He didn't take his mouth off my nipple the whole time we went.

"We'll have to be careful." He murmured, setting me on the bed and crouching over the top of me. "Take it slow."

"I hate it when you say that." I grabbed the button on his pants and struggling with it. "Dammit, why do they always make these things so hard?"

"You're the only one who makes this thing hard." He rubbed himself against my hand and wrist, and I laughed.

"Then unbutton your damn pants."

With a grin, he rolled his weight to one hand and deftly undid his pants, sliding them down far enough that I could see his erection straining through his boxer-briefs.

"Yum." I licked my lips.

He threw his head back and roared his laughter.

"I fucking love you."

"Good, because I fucking love you too."

He kicked his jeans off, and I wasted no time dragging his boxers down so I could grab his dick.

I loved the feel of his heavy silk in my fingers.

"I missed you." I told it.

"You can't talk to my dick, Hen." Roman caught my face in his hand, tilting my head up so my eyes met his instead of his boner.

"Sure I can. It likes me." I tossed the words at him, looking back at his cock. "Bring it up here so I can show it how much I like it."

He shook his head at me, grinning broadly again.

"You can blow me after you're healed. It's been so long, I'd probably lose it the second your tongue touched me."

"Let's try." I said.

"You're in bad shape, Hen. We're not trying anything except slow, vanilla sex and some vampire role-playing."

"Damn, you're a spoilsport." I sighed, letting go of his dick. "Alright, stick it in me already."

"The romance in that comment was overwhelming." Roman said dryly, his fingers kneading my nipples.

"You called sex with me 'vanilla'." I countered. "Not exactly romantic."

"Hen." His fingers slid down my bare stomach and found the waist of my leggings. His mouth met mine, the kiss a slow dance of tongue and lips as his fingers teased my lower belly before finally sliding inside my leggings. I sighed against his mouth when his fingers stroked my center, arching into him when they slid inside me.

"Already wet." He growled his approval into my mouth.

"For you, always." I stole his words, scraping my teeth over his bottom lip just to hear him growl again. "Tell me how much you missed me." I breathed, moving slightly against his hand.

"I couldn't sleep without dreaming of your body." His lips were on my ear, licking and teasing as he whispered. "Woke up wet, like a fucking teenager."

"What did I do in your dreams?"

"Moaned and groaned and writhed while I worshipped you." His teeth scraped the bite scar on my neck. "Orgasmed around my dick." He bit harder. "Sucked me while my tongue was inside you."

I grabbed his dick again, pushing his boxers down further.

"I don't want to go slow." I tugged him closer to me and he did what I wanted, tugging my pants down so my underwear was the only thing between us.

"Take them off." I commanded.

He shot me a dark grin.

"Yes, ma'am."

His tongue trailed up my inner thigh, and I gasped, arching more. The motion hurt, but was so freaking worth it.

"Easy." He growled, one of his hands on my hip, pushing my ass back to the bed. "Be careful."

I opened my mouth to tell him to shut up when his tongue stroked up my core, over my panties. Even with them on, I bucked against him.

He growled again, holding me down harder before licking me again.

Since I couldn't move, I grabbed fistfuls of the sheets and moaned.

"Better." He rumbled his approval, his teeth catching the crotch of my panties and tugging them downward. I hissed at the feel of the fabric moving down, painfully slowly. He abandoned them just above my knees and his tongue found my center.

Gasping, I wrapped my thighs around his face and held him to me while he feasted on my body. Tension grew inside me, and his emotions hit me hard.

Heat.

Desire.

Love.

Excitement.

Hope.

Lust.

They had me arching harder into him. This time, he didn't push me back down.

I went right to the edge, and he stopped entirely, his mouth still on my core, fingers inside me.

"Keep going." I moaned, trying to move against him.

"Not yet. You can't finish until I'm inside you." He growled against me.

I panted against the effort not to rub myself against his face.

"Please." I breathed.

He was back on top of me in an instant, ripping my shirt and bra the rest of the way off me. His dick slid inside me, and I lost it.

"Romeo." I groaned as he slammed into me, following me over the edge. Our emotions mingled, and then our souls.

Tears stung my eyes as we connected—it was like I could see straight into Roman's soul, the fabric of our beings knitting together. Roman groaned against me, rolling so I was over the top of him and holding me to him tightly.

"Tell me you feel it now." He whispered, his hand trailing up my inner thigh, feeling the place we were connected.

"I feel it." I breathed. "Everything."

His hands found my waist, holding me in place, and I opened my eyes to see him staring at me like I was more than a person.

Like I was the whole fucking world.

"Bite me." I whispered.

He wasted no time. His fangs sank into my scarred neck, and he swallowed a mouthful of my blood. He rumbled and shook beneath me, groaning and growing hard inside me again.

"Henley." He snarled softly into my ear.

I knew what he wanted and gave it to him, my own teeth shifting to slide inside his skin.

"Take it. Take *me*." He murmured, hands kneading into my ass.

I sucked on his neck, and the tang of his blood entered my mouth. It didn't taste like blood—it tasted the way Roman smelled. Like my own personal dessert.

"Fuck, yes." I moaned, pulling away and licking his wound.

My eyes widened when I watched the skin knit together, scar disappearing entirely to leave his neck smooth and perfect.

Mated.

We were mated.

Roman was moving inside me again, lifting my hips to slam into me. He rolled me back beneath him, sucking my nipple into his mouth and biting. I gasped at the feel, and Roman rumbled.

"Moan for me."

I moaned, lifting my head to his chest and letting him have his way with me as he slid himself in and out, working my body.

"Fucking yes." He groaned and slid out of me, lifting my legs up to his shoulders.

"Does she like this?" He said, sliding in and out.

I opened my eyes, frowning at the weird comment.

"Nope." He said, lowering my legs to his hips. Sliding out, he stopped when he noticed me watching him and opened his mouth to speak.

"You okay?" His eyes furrowed, and he spoke again. This time, his lips didn't move. "Is she hurting? Shit, I haven't been careful enough."

My eyes widened.

"What?" He looked around. "What's wrong? You're panicking, I can feel it."

"Roman. You were talking, but your mouth was closed."

He stilled.

"You can hear my thoughts?"

"Yes?"

"Fuck, she's going to know every time I think about her ass."

I laughed, and he grimaced.

Now that his dick wasn't inside me and my thoughts were slightly clearer, I could tell when he was speaking or thinking. When he spoke, I could hear it. But when he thought, I could *feel* it.

"I wasn't getting any words from you. Just feelings." He said, and I shrugged.

"I don't think in words when we're doing it. Mostly I'm just watching you enjoying my body and loving the way it feels."

"That's so fucking hot."

His fingers slipped back inside me, and the conversation was over. He parted my legs again, his lips meeting my core in my favorite kind of kiss.

"You like that?" He thought.

I groaned a yes, wrapping my thighs back around his face.

"I hope you come on my tongue."

I lost it.

Roman talking dirty? Definitely did it for me.

Definitely.

My body quivered as I shattered, Roman holding my hips down so I didn't hurt myself.

"I'm going to heal you now." He spoke the words into my core and I shivered, trying to reach toward him mentally.

"Afterward, you're finishing inside me." I thought.

"Hell yes I am."

Then his tongue met my lower belly, and my thoughts dissipated into feelings.

He made his way up and down my body, rolling me over when he was done with my front and I was practically a puddle of orgasmic goo. He had his fingers inside me, working me while he healed, and I lost count after the third orgasm.

He hesitated before licking my back, and I turned to look at him.

"Your scars." He murmured.

My damn body was so broken, he'd need to heal every part of me to make sure I was better. Including my back.

While I'd always worn the scars without fear of judgement, I didn't *like* them. Hell, I didn't like the memories they connected to, either. They were just a way for me to remember that I was a survivor.

"They're just marks." I said, lowering my face back to the bed. "I'll be the same person without them."

He lifted my arm then, showing me the front of my wrist. Where I'd had the word "free" inked into the scar he'd given me when I joined the New York Pack. He hadn't healed me there yet, either, I guess.

"Even this one?"

My lips tilted.

"That's yours. You decide."

He chuckled, licking my wrist in one long stroke before moving to my back

When he'd licked every inch of me, his fingers slid out and he wasted no time.

We were shattering together in seconds.

Both of us spent, he collapsed beside me and wrapped his arms around me, rolling to the side and pulling my back flush against his chest. His fingers stroked up and down my arm, tugging and twirling my hair as he held me close.

"She's mine." He thought. *"You're mine."*

"We're permanent now." I thought back. *"Forever."*

"Finally." He murmured against my neck.

He'd doubted it would happen, and I had too.

But after everything, we were finally one.

"I hope you never get tired of my body." I thought at him, lips curving up when his hand slid to my boob, squeezing and playing.

"Not possible." He blew against my neck. If I wasn't so thoroughly worn out, I'd have shivered.

My stomach growled, and Roman chuckled into my skin.

"How are you feeling?"

I stretched my arms out, tentatively feeling for soreness.

There was no pain.

Easing away from Roman, I sat up.

It didn't hurt.

Hurrying out of bed, I stretched and spun and jumped a bit. Roman laughed, and I noticed his eyes watching my body bounce.

"I feel good." I said, half-shocked as a grin stretched my cheeks. "Alive. I feel alive. Let's go do something." I said, feeling so much lighter and happier than I'd been. "We could shift. Or go for a run. Or —" my stomach growled again.

"How about we go to dinner and do something afterward?" His grin matched mine.

"Deal." I bounced to the closet, excitement thrumming in my veins. "I need clothes. I need…" I grabbed a bra from the drawer I knew they were in, but hadn't touched.

Sheer lace.

A sticky note on it marked it as another bit of the payment the girls owed me from that little bet we made about Roman's reaction to my hair.

I dug through the pile of underwear.

Everything was either sheer lace or made up of some sort of netting.

And it was mostly all thongs and unlined bras.

Roman walked up behind me, bare-assed and practically glowing with happiness as he wrapped his arms around my waist and kissed my shoulder, then my neck, then my cheek.

"What are we looking at?" He murmured.

"The evil sex-geniuses are at it again." I held up a hot pink lace thong and a sheer black bra.

"Mmm." His lips lifted in a grin against my neck. "I should write them a thank-you letter."

"Don't encourage them." I grumbled, leaning over to dig through the built-in drawer. I still needed to get my revenge on them, but I had no idea what to do. "Help me find the least-sexy ones."

"I don't think any of these wouldn't look sexy on you." He said, feeling my ass. "Damn, I've missed this."

"Pretty sure my ass was always available to you." I shot back, still slightly miffed about being ditched. I was one boob squeeze away from getting over it, though—too well-pleasured to hold a grudge any longer.

"Not your ass—though I've missed that, too. I missed hanging out with you, hearing your voice and joking with you. I love your body, but I'm in love with your personality." He said.

Then squeezed my ass again, just for good measure.

And I was officially over the thing where he ditched me.

I tossed him a pair of crotchless underwear that was going right in the trash—seriously, what was the point?!—and kept digging through the pile. There was a ridiculous amount of shit in the drawer.

I decided on a pair and tugged them on, pulling my mass of tangled hair over my shoulder to get it out of the way of my straps. When I saw the color of my hair against my pale skin, I gaped.

"Holy shit." I hurried to the bathroom, flipping the light on to gawk at myself in the mirror. "It's red."

"I thought it was always red." Roman leaned up against the bathroom door, a smirk on his sexy face. I smacked him in the chest, lifting the strands up to the light.

"Hot damn, I look scary with red hair." I said.

He coughed on a laugh and I shot him a glare.

"Very. Very scary." He cleared his throat, still trying not to laugh.

"Asshole. Yours is red now too." I turned back to the mirror, studying the change to my appearance. His wasn't a big change, because he had hardly any hair. The only place you could really tell it had changed was on his chin, because he seriously needed to shave.

Roman stepped up behind me, lowering his head so he could check out the teeny stubbly hair on his head.

"Shit." He muttered, straightening to look at his eyebrows. They were red too. "I'm a ginger."

"You're a ruby." I corrected him, lifting my fingers to run over his eyebrows.

"You should wear see-through bras all the time." He said, his attention on my boobs again. He flicked one of my nipples so he could watch it go pointy, and I rolled my eyes.

"You should go commando all the time." I countered.

"Done." He didn't bat an eye at the request.

My eyes caught on my back in the mirror, and the breath whooshed out of me. Turning slightly, I tilted my head over my shoulder to look at myself from behind

My back was clear and unblemished. Like my scars had never been there at all.

"Damn." My voice was lower, my hand slipping over my shoulder to feel for a scar nearest my shoulder blade that I'd always been able to run my fingers over. Where the skin had been rough and bumpy, it was now smooth and soft.

Roman said nothing, letting me take in my new appearance.

I tugged my hair over my other shoulder, still studying my skin.

I'd gained Roman when he healed me. Plus the ability to control my ruby power without dying—a necessity, obviously.

But I'd lost the marks I'd collected over my years of pain. The proof that I'd survived.

Truthfully, I wasn't sure if I should be glad the scars were gone or miss them.

My eyes landed on my crooked fingers, resting on my shoulder, and widened when I saw that they were straight.

The evidence of punching Ledger in the face—gone.

"You look beautiful." Roman's fingers trailed over the smooth skin on my back, his expression neutral as he tried to figure out what I was thinking. I could feel it now—the way our minds weren't touching. Like it was a physical choice we had to make, to communicate mentally. And right then we weren't, so he didn't know what I was thinking.

"I know." I said, softly.

He waited.

And I just looked.

My feelings were so mixed, there was no use in trying to interpret them.

"My new hair makes me scarier, but my new back makes me look wimpier." I finally said.

Roman chuckled, lifting my wrist to his lips and kissing my ink. Somehow, it looked even better without the scar beneath it.

"Between the two, no one will suspect a threat when they see you. That's even better than coming off as intimidating." He said.

"Let's get dressed." I led him back into the closet, pulling on a long sweater dress the girls had bought me. I didn't usually wear dresses, but it had been so long since I felt this good that I wanted to celebrate.

"I want to get out of here for a while." I said, spinning to face him. "I want steak. And ice cream. And pizza."

"Deal." Roman grabbed my face and kissed me hard.

"Let's bring the girls. And their guys." I went back into the bathroom and swiped on mascara and eyeliner.

Damn, I looked weird in makeup after so long without it.

"I'll call them." He disappeared into the room for a minute, coming back with his phone to his ear.

"Hey. How is she?" I heard Arla's voice on the other side of the phone.

He glanced at me, eyes sweeping up and down as I brushed my teeth.

"Perfect. Better than perfect." He was quiet for a minute, then chuckled. "Yes, we're mated. It's incredible."

The smile on his face was so real, so genuine, I could've melted into a damn puddle of happiness.

I'd put that smile on his face. I was the reason he was happy.

"Yes, you are. You're my everything." His voice stroked my mind.

"Ditto."

I pushed a mental image of his head between my legs at him and watched his pants tent.

"Gorgeous devil." He murmured, tucking the evidence of his desire out of sight and leaning his head up against the door. "Everything's great, but Hen's hungry for pizza, ice cream, and steak. And you."

Even I heard Arla's taunting laugh.

"You get her back in bed and the first thing she asks for is me? That's rich." She hooted. I laughed, and Roman lifted an eyebrow at me, but the grin he wore told me he wasn't bothered.

"Having to keep our hands to ourselves for a few hours will make the sex hotter when we're back home." Roman said, his voice casual. And his grin remained when she scolded him for talking about our sex life.

I put the makeup back in my bag and crossed the room to Roman.

"We'll be ready in twenty minutes." Arla said. "I don't want to come smell the nastiness in your house, so walk over here."

Roman agreed, hanging up.

"What are we going to do for twenty minutes?" He murmured, tugging me up against his chest.

"No clue." I tapped my finger to my chin. "We could probably scrounge up a chess board or something.

"I've got a different game in mind." He lowered his lips to my ear and whispered. "I bought a replacement for that vibrator you mentioned."

I bit my lip, heart thrumming with excitement.

"Let's go." I dragged him back to the bed.

He chuckled as we went, both of us shedding the clothes we'd just put on.

CHAPTER 12

THE NEXT NIGHT was the fifth trial.

Amy eyed us solemnly as we arrived. Everyone else did too. The entire pack was dressed in black, and there was no party going on this time. It looked like a funeral.

The giant room in the Alphas' house was silent as hundreds of eyes tracked us across the floor. I hoped we didn't reek of sex, so they didn't hate us for celebrating after the loss of their douchebag Blessed Ruby.

"Nice party." I muttered.

"They loved Ezra." Roman murmured the reminder, though he tugged me a bit closer.

There was no music playing, so with all the stares it was a bit eerie.

Arla and the rest of our people had gone back to New York to grab their stuff, planning to move wherever we decided to go. We'd never force ourselves upon the New York Pack, so we figured we'd have to make a pack of our own.

Arla hadn't wanted to leave while Roman was still going through the trials, but he and Kyler worked together to convince her he'd be fine. Seeing them work together was a bit of a shocker, but in a good way.

Roman and I stepped together through the doorway to the small room used for trials. Hansen and Sylvie sat at the back of the room, studying us, while Amy withdrew some wolfsbane liquid from a jar into a syringe attached to a needle. Joel sat near the room's entrance, grimacing deeply.

"Creepy." I whispered.

Roman squeezed my fingers before releasing them. He tilted my chin up and pressed his lips to mine. Though he'd never admit to being afraid, I could see the edge in his eyes. If anything went wrong, he'd blame himself.

Not that either of us would be alive to place that blame.

He sat on the small cot set up for this purpose. Up until a few weeks ago, it had only ever held women—which explained why my giant male's feet would hang off the edge.

"The fifth trial is another test of your honor." Amy's solemn voice and eyes had me grimacing the same way Joel was.

She'd told me the second set of trials was testing emotional worthiness… *how the hell did a person prove their emotional honor?*

The way Roman's expression tightened told me the previous honor test sucked.

He silently held out his arm, and Amy wiped it with alcohol to clean it before injecting him.

I looked away. Something about seeing a needle go into Roman's skin would make my stomach churn, even now that I was healed.

Roman lowered himself to the cot, his eyes closing and his breathing leveling out, like he was falling asleep.

Amy threw out the needle and alcohol wipe, stepping over to stand at my side. Hansen's and Sylvie's eyes were focused on me, so I said nothing to her.

"Congratulations are in order." She murmured. "You look much stronger."

"Thank you." I stared forward, watching Roman carefully.

"Act like I'm telling you a story." She said, voice even lower.

My eyebrows lifted.

"Really?"

"Sylvie's plotting your death. Hansen's trying to stop her, but she loved Ezra like a son. The pack will move against you tonight."

"Oh, wow." I maintained a neutral expression.

"They'll likely attack before the trial ends so they don't have to deal with Roman. She's fed them lies that you're not worthy to lead, that you killed Ezra so Roman would survive the trials. They won't follow you."

"That's funny." I forced a smile.

"To take over as Alphas of All, you just need to pull the power from Hansen and Sylvie. The new generation takes over whenever they feel it's time—and you need to decide it's your time."

"Did they make it?" I didn't let my eyes flick back to my unconscious mate, hoping my grandmother would understand that I was asking if Roman could hold the ruby power despite still being in the transition process.

"I don't know." She admitted. "But he's over halfway through after this one, so I think he'll survive, if it works at all when he tries to take the power from Hansen."

I nodded.

"I'm glad." I continued to feign listening.

"Make sure you grab the jar of wolfsbane—you'll have to continue with the trials, regardless of where you go."

I nodded again.

"Good luck." Amy ended the conversation.

We both looked at Roman, watching the steady rise and fall of his chest.

I reached out to him mentally, the way I did when I tried to talk into his mind. The response was almost instant. His mind tugged on mine, and I was ripped into another trial.

I fell hard on my hands and knees, looking around the space I now occupied. Though it felt real, I knew it was part of Roman's test. Part of his mind.

The smell of gunpowder caught my nose as I rose to my feet. Everything was dark around me, but I put my hands out in front of me. Feeling for anything that might be in my way.

"You don't want to do this." Roman's voice echoed around me. It wasn't his usual calm growl. The words were edged with panic.

"Of course I do." My own voice sneered back.

I followed the gunpowder scent, the light increasing as I moved closer to the smell.

"They don't deserve this, Hen. The Alphas did, but these are just people. They didn't know what was going on, and if they did, they were just afraid." Roman's voice was grew louder, the echo greater as I continued to move.

When I finally stepped into the area, I could see what we were arguing about.

Bodies surrounded the trial's version of me—my hair still pink, my hands on some sort of automatic gun. Rows of werewolves were on their knees in front of me, their chins to their chests as they looked to the ground, their hands raised beside their heads. There were at least fifty of them lined up, and more than that dead on the ground.

Roman stood in front of them, his arms out as if he could protect all of them .

"They hurt me." The trial's version of me didn't shake or quiver. She radiated hatred and anger, Ruby Alpha power pouring off her as she glared her male down. Roman's hair wasn't ginger yet, and he took the hit of my power. His body quivered with the effort of remaining on his feet.

"It wasn't them. Their Alphas didn't give them a choice." He pressed, fighting me still.

"They could've challenged the leaders. They didn't have to sit back and watch me suffer. They chose not to help—and now they'll deal with the consequences. Karma's a bitch."

The other version of me lifted the gun to the person on the far right. Roman lunged to the side, blocking my view with his body again.

"Don't do this." He pleaded with me.

Roman wasn't one to beg, so seeing him plead with this angry version of me was a blow to my chest.

"There's no other option." The trial version of me swung my gun to the left, firing before Roman had time to dodge.

Time slowed as he lunged.

Not between the bullets and the person I was shooting at.

He lunged for the pink-haired version of me.

Someone shook my shoulders, and my consciousness was ripped backward, careening back into my own mind and eyes. I gasped, clutching my chest as I took in the situation.

I was on my knees, on the floor of the room.

Amy stood in front of me, shaking my shoulders.

Joel stood in the doorway. Werewolves pushed him, trying to get in, but his fingers were shifted and his shoulders thrown back, blocking those of us in the room. Sylvie fought Hansen's arms around her middle, a knife in her hand as she stood mere feet from the love of my life.

"They don't deserve to be ruby wolves!" One werewolf shouted from beyond the doorway.

"Kill them for what they did to Ezra." Another snarled.

"Let Sylvie slit her throat!" A third crowed.

One of the wolves rammed Joel, and I saw red.

My grandpa.

My father.

My mate.

All the men I cared about—some more than others—in one room, being threatened.

I reached for Sylvie's power the same way I'd learned to reach for Roman's mind. She gasped, the knife clattering to the floor as I ripped her ruby power from her body. It hit me like a damn tidal wave, but I didn't have time to think about that.

She elbowed Hansen in the face and leaped toward me. I threw my body to the side, smashing my power into Sylvie as I shouted,

"Back off!"

She crashed to the floor beside Amy, who barely moved out of the way in time.

Sylvie's chest heaved as she shakily stood, her fingers shifting to claws while her fangs lengthened and she faced me.

Hansen's power crashed into the werewolves trying to get past Joel, forcing them back. The women in the group staggered backward, but the men snarled and fought harder.

I threw my power in with his, the force of it hitting the men hard enough that they flew backward.

Shit.

Stronger than I'd expected.

I hurried to Roman's side, leaning over him to watch his chest rise and fall. I'd have felt for a pulse, but I was afraid touching him would pull me back into the trial with him.

"You can't intervene, Henley." Amy's expression was one of fear. "There last time someone intervened in the trials, both wolves died. You can't intervene."

"You should both be dead for what you did." Sylvie snarled. "Ezra deserved to live."

"For what I did?" I demanded, stalking away from Roman. Though I was pissed, I kept a leash on my power just in case it could hurt Sylvie. She was a bitch, and probably deserved to die, but I wasn't about to make that call—or be the reason my dad died, since his life was connected to hers through mating. "I killed him in self-defense. You helped him pin me to the couch, you told him to bite me without my approval, and you would've helped him *rape* me. You're the one who should die for your actions."

"He was the closest I'll ever have to a child, because of *you*." Hatred dripped from her every pore. "And you were going to let him die out of your own selfishness."

"That doesn't give you the right to force me into anything—especially mating." Rage was pouring off me. "You're lucky I killed him before anything happened, because I would've torn you both to shreds regardless of the consequences if he'd touched me."

Roman gasped behind me, and I fought the urge to spin to look at him as he scanned the room for threats. His arms locked around me, and he smashed my body to his chest.

"You can't hold them back forever." Amy's voice was soft, worried. "You have to go."

Sylvie snarled at her, but Roman didn't release me.

"Try to take Hansen's power." I mentally urged, pushing the memories of me taking Sylvie's toward him, hoping it would help him figure out how. Though I wanted to give him time to recover, we were in a shitty position.

Roman was silent for just the tiniest blip of a moment before shaking his head against me.

I pulled his arm off my waist.

"We've got to leave." I warned. Roman's head bobbed. I grabbed the jar of wolfsbane off the medical cart, took his hand, and pulled him toward the doorway.

"I'll keep the women back." Hansen said quietly. "And do what I can to diffuse the tension here. Return after the trials to take my power."

I nodded.

"Thank you." I hoped he could see that I meant the words.

"You shouldn't have to thank your father for keeping you safe." He tilted his head toward me. "Go."

With another nod, I led Roman from the room.

Some guy's mind slammed against the control I was using to hold him back, and I winced.

Amy was right. I couldn't do this forever.

Another hit, and I snarled.

"Everyone back up." I commanded.

The men skidded backward, their bodies controlled by my words.

"Don't follow us." I added, hurrying from the building.

Roman's truck was still outside, but he was subdued. His eyes were wild, haunted.

I dug my hand into his pocket, grabbing the keys. When he didn't move to get in, I opened the passenger door and climbed inside, dragging Roman into the passenger seat as I scooted over to the driver's. The truck roared to life, and I slammed my foot into the gas.

Our tires squealed, and we flew away from the Alpha House.

I didn't know where I was going; just *away*. The jar of wolfsbane was pinned between my thighs, trapped upright. That shit was going to keep my mate alive, so I'd sleep with the damn thing if I had to.

"You okay?" I glanced at Roman. Flying down the highway, I couldn't give him the attention needed to really talk to him, to prod for answers —or determine If I shouldn't prod.

It would have to wait.

"Sure." His voice was quiet, unsteady.

"Don't lie to me."

"I'm not ready to talk about it, Hen. Please don't push." He was almost hoarse.

I understood what he was asking for—and why.

I'd been through enough of my own shit to respect his request. Dropping my hand to his thigh, I squeezed gently to let him know I got it.

He put his hand on mine, and we drove like that in silence for a long while.

When signs came up, warning me that I'd have to pick which direction to head on the highway soon, I thought about it.

We could go back to New York. We'd grab our stuff and meet up with our family and friends to decide where to move. That had to happen at some point.

But there were a lot of Alphas all over the U.S. who didn't deserve to lead. Alphas who'd hurt and abused and mistreated their people. Hansen wasn't with me and wouldn't be able to change the female leadership, but there were less shitty female Alphas than males, mostly because of how the Alpha Males tended to treat their mates.

I could help people—heal packs, replace shitty leaders with those who would protect their wolves.

It's what I was born to do.

And well, I wasn't going to be the reason assholes remained in power. The people being used and abused had become my responsibility when I took the ruby power from Sylvie, and they'd been mistreated for long enough.

So when the sign asked me which direction I wanted to go, I turned down the highway toward a pack I knew needed me.

Oregon.

I would do what I'd spent my life wishing someone would do for me.

I'd free them.

CHAPTER 13

We stopped halfway between the town the Oregon Pack occupied and Ruby City. Roman still hadn't said anything yet, and I needed to sleep before I crashed at the wheel and accidentally drove us off a damn mountain. We needed to hold each other, shower and change, and maybe talk things out a bit.

He stayed in the truck while I ran into Walmart to grab us a few changes of clothes. I'd left my purse in the vehicle when we went in for the trials, so luckily money wasn't an issue.

I grabbed what looked comfy and stretchy so it had a better chance of fitting us, throwing a couple pairs of shoes and a shit-ton of underwear and socks too. After adding shampoo, conditioner, and body wash along with some other toiletries—Arla has spoiled me with that shit, and I was too prissy to use the hotel stuff now—I bought a few snacks too.

After I checked out, I grabbed a few sandwiches from the Subway inside Walmart, and then hauled our bags back to the truck and loaded everything into the backseat.

Roman had his chair leaned back and was staring up at the ceiling, his face pale and his eyes dark.

I drove us to a hotel nearby, deciding I'd wait until we were clean and full to figure out why he was acting so unlike himself. What I'd seen of the trial was freaky, but whatever had come after must've been even worse.

It was a fancy hotel—the kind Roman usually picked when we went places. I didn't really care about fanciness, but I wanted him comfortable so I'd pay the outrageous fee.

Roman shuffled into the lobby of the hotel beside me. He let me take his hand, but made no move to get closer to me or lace our fingers together.

I did it for him, pasting on a friendly smile when we approached the desk. I wasn't feeling all that smiley, but people usually responded better to pleasant interactions. And in a fancy place like this, we needed them to want to help us.

"Hi. My husband and I would like a room." I draped my hand over the desk so she could see the diamond on my finger and know that we were serious customers despite how laid-back we looked. Her eyes dropped to the ring, as I'd expected.

"Wow, that's a gorgeous diamond." She smiled back, her eyes sweeping up and down Roman's figure. Checking him out right in front of me.

My fingers tightened on his, and my smile went brittle.

"Thanks. A room?" I prodded, trying not to let my ridiculous jealousy show.

"Right." She clicked a few times, eyes scanning the screen. "One bed, or two?" She asked.

"One. Biggest bed you have."

She glanced at Roman again, and I wanted to punch her for the intensity in her stare.

I'd introduced him as my husband. What kind of woman checked out someone else's husband?

"Alright..." She rattled off a price, and I handed her my card.

She glanced at him again.

"Do you have a question?" Roman's voice was tight and low.

"Hmm, what?" her cheeks reddened as she'd been caught.

"You keep looking at me." He said flatly. "It's rude to check someone out so obviously in front of their wife. I can't imagine the owner of a hotel with prices like these would be happy to know their employees are eye-fucking their customers."

I could smell her embarrassment and wanted to kiss Roman for standing up for me. Well, for himself, I guess. But it felt like he was standing up for me, considering how much she was pissing me off.

"I'm sorry. You just look more like siblings than a couple, with the matching hair." She looked back at the computer, and I choked back a laugh. "Here's your room key."

I took the card, and Roman's fingers tightened on mine as he led me to the front doors. We still needed to grab our bags from the truck—just in front of the building.

"If she's staring at my ass, I'm calling her boss." He muttered.

I bit back a grin, glancing over my shoulder to find her staring studiously at the computer screen.

"You're fine." I said.

He went silent again, grabbing the bags and taking my hand again as we made our way back inside and to the elevator.

"Siblings." He grumbled. "I need a hat."

"Maybe some eyebrow dye too." I teased him. He flicked me on the nose, and I bit his finger.

We found our room and slipped inside. Roman dropped our bags on the desk off to the side of the large space, and I kicked my jeans off, tired of wearing pants.

He eyed my bare legs, but pulled his gaze back to the sandwiches when his stomach growled.

"I should've stopped for food earlier." I grimaced, feeling shitty for not realizing I'd been starving him.

"I should've said something." He kissed my head, grabbing the sandwiches and carrying them to the bed. After he dropped the food on the mattress, he tugged his shirt off and tossed his sweatpants on the floor so I wasn't the only one not wearing pants. Climbing into bed in his boxer-briefs, he pulled all six sandwiches I'd bought out of the bag.

Yeah, six sandwiches. I was hungry and still trying to regain the weight I'd lost when I was sick. And Roman ate a shit-ton, always.

He sniffed one of them, tossing it to the other side of the bed when he smelled the vinegar on it. He didn't like vinegar on sandwiches, but I did. It made it easy to tell our food apart.

He opened the first one he found without vinegar, taking a giant bite. I slid into bed, giving him space so he didn't feel like I was pushing him, and opened my own sandwich.

We ate in silence, but I finished before him because he had twice as much food.

"I'm going to shower." I said, sliding back off the mattress. Roman caught my hand, lifting the back of it to his lips before releasing me.

Hopefully, he'd appreciate the time to himself and figure out how he was feeling about everything he'd seen in the trial.

I turned on the water to let it heat, stripping and tossing my clothes into the laundry basket beside the toilet. Usually it was meant for towels, but Roman liked to keep his space clean so I'd pull the clothes out later.

Stepping under the falling water, I sighed at the comfortable warmth. It was still freezing outside, being the middle of March and all. I tried to keep my hair out of the water since I'd forgotten to grab my shampoo from the grocery bags, but it got wet anyway. It was longer than it had been in a while, falling nearly to my ass.

I tried to consider what Roman might be feeling. The trial was gruesome; me, killing who knew how many people. The fake me had shot someone just as I disappeared. I wasn't sure what had happened after, though.

Had I killed Roman in the trial? Was he afraid I'd go crazy and hurt him or something?

It probably felt real; maybe he was seeing the crazy version of me every time he looked at me now.

I thought through the possibilities as the water ran down my skin.

"You're thinking pretty loud there, Hen." Roman's soft voice had me spinning.

"You scared me." I scowled, turning back to the water.

The fact that he was naked—and hard—hadn't escaped my notice, but he wasn't acting like himself, so I wouldn't assume anything.

"Sorry." His lips brushed my ear as he whispered the apology, his arm wrapping around my middle and drawing my back to his front. His erection pressed into my lower back; he was too tall for it to hit my ass unless I went up on my tiptoes.

"I didn't realize I was broadcasting my thoughts. I'm sorry, I was trying to give you time alone." I said, tilting my head back so I could kiss the side of his neck.

"I like hearing your thoughts." He said, tugging my hair out from between us. A few of the strands had wrapped around his dick, and his lips twitched with humor as he detangled it. After my hair was draped over my shoulder, falling down the front of me, his lips met the top of my head.

"I shouldn't have left you to wonder." His fingers latched gently on my hips. "I've been fighting to keep you from seeing my memories. I'm sure I'd broadcast the images right into your head if I stopped trying."

"So stop." I wanted to turn so I could meet his eyes, but didn't want to stop him from telling me.

"I'd rather tell you first." He said. "It was a test of honor—you saw part of it. To protect hundreds of people, I had to kill you."

Oh.

Oh.

No wonder he was being quiet.

"You killed the fake version of me." I said.

He nodded, and I felt the movement against my head.

"Didn't feel fake." He admitted. "Seeing you die at my hands…" He let out a slow breath. "It reminded me of my dad. I don't think I'll ever forget that."

There was nothing to say that would fix that—or change it.

So I finally turned, wrapping my arms around his neck and pressing my body to his. We were naked and warm and wet, and the moment felt really vulnerable.

"I love you." I squeezed him to me.

"I love you too." He pressed his lips to my neck, lifting me so I wasn't squashing his erection so uncomfortably. I wrapped my legs around his back, my lips twitching when he throbbed against me.

"Would it offend you if I asked you to help me forget?" The low growl of his voice tilted my lips upward.

"Nope." I captured his lips in a kiss.

His chest rumbled against mine, and he turned to press me into the shower's wall. The damn thing was slippery on my back, and I latched onto him more tightly just to stay upright as our tongues battled.

Roman's fingers gripped my thighs. Usually, he'd warm me up before plunging his dick in me. This time, though, he wanted an immediate distraction. He lifted me, adjusting my position above him and thrusting in with one movement.

I gasped, arching into him and loving the growl the movement earned me.

Roman moved, then stumbled and grabbed the wall with another growl.

"Did you almost just fall?" I breathed, moving my hips to rub him against me.

"No."

Lie.

I laughed into his neck.

His breathing was unsteady, his nose against my throat. He growled a complaint. "I can't smell you. Fuck the shower." He cranked the handle to shut the water off, grabbing a towel and carrying me to the bed. Throwing the towel on the mattress, he draped me over the edge without sliding out of me. My hair sprawled over the bed, probably soaking the damn sheets, but I was too occupied to care.

He lifted my legs to his shoulders, pounding in and out. My fingers twisted in the sheets, gripping the blankets as he slammed into me again and again.

Tension grew in me, and when his hands found my boobs, I arched into him and shattered. He went with me, body shaking as he lost it.

He collapsed beside me, his arms cradling me into his chest.

"I'm sorry I didn't tell you earlier." He murmured.

"I get it. You don't have to apologize." I nestled against him, embracing the afterglow as he held me tightly. "We're going to Oregon. I'm going to free the pack." I whispered, hoping he'd tell me it was a great idea.

"By giving them a better Alpha?"

"Yeah." I snuggled further against him.

"You're amazing." His hand dropped to cup my ass, tugging me even closer so all of me pressed into all of him.

"I know." I smiled against him, loving the chuckle that shook his chest against me.

"I think your hair soaked our bed." He grumbled, lifting a few strands and tugging them toward the towel we were only half on.

"I think your dick soaked my vagina." I shot back.

He grinned, pulling away just enough that his blues met my hazels.

"Is that a challenge?"

"If it is, you already won."

His grin grew wider. I slid away from him, grabbing my dripping hair off the bed and shivering when the icy strands hit my back.

"I've got to wash all this." I gestured to all of me.

"I hope that's an invitation." He sat up, eyes lazily sweeping my figure.

Crossing the room, I dug through the bags and grabbed my bathroom stuff, cramming it in my arms. It was freezing against my boobs, and I shivered again.

"Only if you bring your tongue and fingers this time." I taunted, crossing the room.

Roman was right behind me. I leaned down to put the stuff on the floor of the bathroom, and his fingers slid inside me. I stopped abruptly, eyes slamming shut.

"How's this?" He murmured, his thumb stroking my center while his fingers moved inside me.

"You're invited."

We didn't turn the shower back on for at least an hour.

THE NEXT MORNING, we drove away from the hotel as the sun rose in the sky. We hadn't gotten a lot of sleep—Roman's nightmares kept us both up—but there was plenty to distract ourselves with.

The Oregon Pack was a few hours from us, so we arrived there right around lunch time. It was one of the bigger packs I'd lived in, so I wasn't surprised to see the bustle around the Alpha's house.

"How are we playing this?" Roman studied the craziness. This pack lived on the outskirts of a fairly large city, so their Alpha's house was a mansion with a gigantic yard. The yard bustled with kids and their mothers—most of the men would be working, since it was the middle of the day. Women with children weren't allowed to work in this pack. If that was what they wanted, I totally respected it. But it should've been their choice, and I knew it wasn't.

"We're not playing it." I met his eyes, ignoring the many gazes on our vehicle. "We're going to be ourselves. Christopher, the Alpha here, was green on your map; he's not a threat. But he's an asshole sexist who thinks he gets to control what women do. We're taking him off the throne."

Roman nodded, reaching for the handle to his door.

I dropped a hand on his leg.

"I have to be independent here. The women need to see that I'm strong and that we're equals. So don't be overly nice to me." I said.

He lifted an eyebrow.

"You're telling me not to treat you like I love you."

I nodded.

He shook his head.

"If we're being ourselves, I'm going to treat you exactly the way I would in my own pack, Hen."

Valid point.

"Alright. But no holding my door."

He shook his head at me, but we opened our doors at the same time.

Stepping out of the truck, I walked around to the front just as Christopher strolled out of his house.

"Wolfsbane." He held his hands out. "You've come to enlighten my pack again."

"You could say that."

Roman took my hand, and I laced my fingers through his.

Christopher studied Roman.

"I heard you took a mate, but I didn't realize it was the New York Alpha."

"I'm not the Alpha of New York anymore. We're the Alphas of All." My mate said. His mind touched mine, and he told me, *"Let them feel your power."*

I released my power gently, pushing the ruby power out so it touched all of the pack members but focusing it on Christopher. His smile wavered, his eyes on the red of my hair.

"Why don't you join us for lunch?" He gestured to the picnic tables set up outside around us.

"We'd love to." I didn't smile.

Not in a pack of women who'd been told constantly that their worth was defined by their damn smile.

"Gina, show the Alphas of All to a table." He ordered. Gina was his mate, and she hurried over to us with a giant smile pasted on her face.

"That won't be necessary, Gina." I said. She stopped in her tracks. "We'd like to walk around the pack's land while we're here."

Gina glanced back at her mate, still smiling.

"You don't need his permission." Roman's words were smooth, though I could hear the bite in them. "Your mate is meant to be your friend and lover, not your boss."

Hell yeah, that was my man.

She said nothing, but her smile did falter.

"Would one of you be willing to show us around?" He looked at the women, who all looked at their Alpha. "I'm sure the pack has changed a bit since Henley was here."

"I'll do it." One of the women stepped forward, a chunky baby girl on her hip. She didn't smile, which led me to like her immediately. That, along with the fact that I didn't recognize her from when I'd been in the pack years earlier.

"Thanks." I nodded.

"This way." She led us inside the Alpha's mansion. Christopher stepped out of our way, though he looked pissed to be doing it.

She showed us around the mansion—exactly the same as it had been last time I saw it.

"Lunch is about ready, so I can finish the tour afterward." She said, leading us back outside.

"What was your name?" I prodded.

"Leah." She gestured to her baby. "This is Annie."

I was terrible with kids, but Roman cooed and waved one of his giant fingers at the little girl. She grinned back at him, and he let go of my hand.

"May I?" He checked, holding his arms out.

The little girl leaned toward him, reaching for my mate, and Leah's eyes lit up as she handed her baby to my man.

For once, I was okay with sharing him with another chick.

"I don't think Christopher has ever even looked at her." She admitted, meeting my gaze.

"He's an asshole." I agreed.

Her lips twitched, and I glanced at her kid.

"Sorry, uh, jerk."

I'd have to work on the cussing when Jamie had her baby.

"What's your mate like?" I asked.

Her lips lifted further.

"Not like that asshole." She nodded toward the table the Alpha occupied, and I grinned.

Roman sat down at a table, Annie's chubby little fists wrapped around his fingers as he held her up on wobbly legs.

"I heard your mate is a good Alpha. We've been thinking about moving to New York for a year or two, but don't have a way to afford a place to live." She admitted.

"We're going to turn this pack into a place you want to stay." I said, watching Roman with the baby. "And he *is* a good Alpha. The best."

The little girl cooed, and Roman talked to her in a cutesy little voice.

It had to be the most adorable thing on the planet.

CHAPTER 14

WE WALKED around the pack's land most of the day, staying until the working men were home from work. The pack wasn't nearly as bad as I remembered—they were just struggling.

Much to Christopher's displeasure, the pack gathered around the Alpha's house as the men arrived. Leah's husband Andrew arrived with a group of construction guys, laughing and talking with them. The laughter died as the group noticed Roman and I mingling, of course.

Andrew saw us with Leah and headed over, abandoning his conversation with one of the other men.

"You're thinking they should lead the pack." Roman murmured mentally.

"Yes." I agreed. *"You?"*

"Yup."

"But we need to talk to him first, to see if he's as cool as she is."

Roman murmured his agreement as the guy walked up, his arm wrapping around his mate's waist at the same time he captured his daughter, who had leaned toward him, waving her chubby arms around and babbling.

"Hey." Andrew seemed cautious.

"Hi. I'm Roman Ellis, this is my mate Henley." Roman's arm draped over my shoulders, marking me as his territory the same way Andrew had done with Leah and their daughter. "We're the new Alphas of All."

Andrew's eyes widened, just fractionally. I liked that he was real, that he hadn't perfected the neutral mask most Alphas and assholes in general had.

"Wow." He said, glancing around the pack and pulling his mate a bit closer. "Is something wrong? We've never had Alphas of All here before."

"No." Roman let his gaze land on Christopher, the Alpha who was eyeing us like a damn hawk. "We're just planning on running things differently than the last Alphas." He said. "Part of that is checking in with the packs now and then, making sure the leadership is up to par with our standards."

Really, I didn't think our standards were that much of a stretch. "Not an asshole" pretty much covered it.

I studied the way Andrew held his mate. Gently, like she was important to him. But also close and careful, ready to protect her.

Their eyes met, and I saw the question in his. He respected her enough to look to her for her opinion, and that said a lot about his personality.

"Do you know how to fight?" I asked him.

Roman shot me a look that said, "SHUT UP", and I shrugged at him.

"Um," Andrew glanced at his mate again. "I haven't trained extensively, but I know enough to protect my family. Why do you ask?"

"I want you to be the new Alpha." I said.

I heard Roman's inward groan.

"We don't know anything about him, Hen. We were going to get to know him."

"Just go with it."

"You want me to..." Andrew lifted his eyebrows, then fidgeted. "Wow." He said. "Can I get a few days to think about it?"

I mentally went through the days. Roman's next trial would be the next night, so we needed an answer before then so we could be far enough from this pack that he'd be safe.

"All we can give you is twenty-four hours." Roman spoke for me.

Andrew grimaced.

"Would Leah take the Alpha Female position?"

"Definitely. Couples who respect each other can lead a lot more effectively than two random people." I said.

"We'll have an answer by tomorrow morning." Leah said, glancing sideways at her husband before looking to Christopher. "Can we keep this from the current Alpha until we've made a decision?"

"Of course." Roman said smoothly.

"Thank you." Leah cracked a smile as someone on the other side of the yard announced the start of dinner.

We went to eat with and chat with another couple who could be promising if Leah and Andrew turned the position down.

The dinner was long and slightly uncomfortable, but we talked to a bunch of couples and got a nice feel for the pack. All in all, they could have a good thing going with a little nudge.

Roman and I went out for ice cream out in the city before heading back to our hotel. Sitting in a booth in an old-fashioned diner, we ordered our milkshakes before talking about the pack.

"What do you think?" I asked Roman.

He lifted an eyebrow.

"I think you jumped into that a little quickly."

Well, he wasn't wrong.

"I had a gut feeling they'd be good." I admitted.

"I'd like my opinions to be considered too, if we're going to do something as important as choosing new Alphas."

Good point.

"You're right, I should've asked you."

"I don't think you're wrong about them, though. They could be great." He slurped his chocolate milkshake, and I sipped the strawberry one in front of me.

"It's so good to eat again." I sighed, leaning into his shoulder. We'd sat in the booth together, side-by-side instead of across from each other.

"I bet." He draped an arm over my shoulder, snagging my milkshake. I grabbed his, sucking down the chocolate deliciousness.

Mmm. Maybe I'd keep his.

"Gross." He wrinkled his nose at me, handing the drink back. I held his shake tight. "Hey."

"You'll have to fight me for it if you want it back."

I slurped down some more.

"Damn stubborn woman." He shook his head, drinking more of my shake and making another face. "Trade back." He shook it toward me.

"What will you give me?" I countered.

"What do you want?"

"My own chocolate milkshake." I grinned, and he chuckled a chest-rumbly laugh.

"Deal." He captured his shake back, drinking it as he swaggered back to the cash register to order me another one. He was back a minute later, and I was reluctantly trying to finish the strawberry one.

"Life's too short to drink nasty milkshakes, Hen." He grabbed it, tossing it in the trash bin behind our booth. I didn't even protest, just laughing at his ridiculousness.

My milkshake was ready a minute later, and I drummed my fingers on the table while I sipped it.

"So, what's a good method for deciding who will be the best leader?" I wondered.

"I don't think your gut is a *bad* method." Roman offered. "But it's not a reliable one. You can have a wrong gut feeling, so we need a way to prove whether we're right. I think talking to them can help, but asking others in the pack about would be better."

"Hmm." I nodded. He had good points. "But the only way we would really know is through trial and error. Maybe we go with our gut after doing some research, and plan a few secret visits over a few months afterward."

Roman nodded slowly.

"That could work, but we've got the fifty U.S. Alphas to check in on, as well as however many European packs there are—which we know little to nothing about, and need to ask Amy for more info on."

"Valid point. Do you have a better idea?" I checked.

"We could set up some kind of survey or website where pack members anonymously vote on whether they like their Alphas and can tell us about any shit they pull."

"Sounds good to me." I agreed.

We stayed a bit longer, talking about the pack before heading back to the hotel for some sleep.

• • •

THE NEXT MORNING, we headed over to the pack lands bright and early. It wasn't even 7 AM when we arrived, but there was already chaos.

We got out of the car and heard the fighting—then smelled the blood. I broke into a run, and Roman ripped his clothes off to shift forms, passing me on our way to whatever fight had broken out.

Christopher was in human form, naked-assed and almost entirely covered in blood. From the smell of him, most of it wasn't his.

Male werewolves bled all over the gigantic yard, and I hoped most of them were still alive.

The women were huddled together on the edge of the yard, a ring of bleeding male wolves around them, protecting them. The women formed a circle around their children as well, protecting the kids with their own bodies.

Roman wasted no time. He tackled Christopher to the ground, snarling at the man's face. I felt Christopher throw his Alpha power at Roman—and felt through the bond as it did nothing to my mate. Like a breeze against a boulder.

I ran to the women, jewel-toned hair flying around me as I went.

"What happened?" I looked to Leah in the front of the group. One of the male wolves in the outer protective circle snarled at me, and I snarled back. He stood between me and the women, but I wouldn't move.

"He found out you wanted to make us Alphas." She said, her voice wavering. Her arms were scratched and bleeding, and although she was at the front of the group, I noticed her palm pressed to her side and smelled more blood than just what I could see on her arms.

Shit.

Apparently 12 hours was too much time to let them decide when the threat of another Alpha loomed over them.

"Where's your mate?" I scanned the wolves on the ground, not sure what Andrew looked like in wolf form. The scent of blood was too strong to narrow down what each wolf smelled like.

She looked to Christopher—and to Roman, Both were in wolf form now, across the yard, but I'd seen Roman fight enough times to know that he wasn't really even trying. Christopher was crazy, but untrained and unpracticed. His Alpha power would've made it difficult for the rest of the pack to fight him, but we didn't have that problem.

"Here." She moved from the protective circle, and the male wolves released her with another growl in my direction. That growl was much less threatening, probably because Roman had contained their threat.

Leah led me around the Alpha Male fight, and Roman's mind touched mine for just a moment.

"Be careful." He warned, easily sidestepping Christopher's teeth.

"Don't kill him yet." I whispered back.

Though I didn't hear his agreement, I felt it.

He had the Alpha pinned the moment I felt his agreement, but I left him to it, still following Leah.

We made our way into the living room in the Alpha's mansion.

A dozen men were in a pile of blood and fur. One wolf bled freely, but he was licking the others as quickly as he could, keeping them alive.

Leah shifted immediately, healing the wolf who was still on his feet even as he growled at her and jerked his head toward the pile of men.

There wasn't time to waste.

I ducked outside, and Roman's voice was already booming,

"I have the threat controlled. Heal your people as fast as you can." He commanded.

There was no ruby power in his order, but the protective circle scattered as the pack's women shifted together, dividing as they all found someone to heal.

I reached for the hem of my top, planning to heal someone myself.

"No." Roman's voice touched my mind. *"They need to do this together so they know that they're strong enough without us. They can't rely on us."* He paused. *"And I'm messed-up so badly right now that if I smell another man on you, I'll probably rip his throat out."*

"But this is our fault."

The words I'd heard months ago echoed in my ears.

Death follows blood wolves.

In Ruby City, they considered us treasure.

Everywhere else, we were death.

And really, I'd been the one who jumped into choosing an Alpha too fast. Roman wasn't at fault here. I was.

"We're still figuring this out." Roman said, though even in my mind his voice was grim. *"There's a learning curve. At least now, they'll be free."*

I slipped outside the door of the Alpha mansion. Each of the men on the ground had a female poised over him, healing him.

"Are we any better than Sylvie?" I wondered.

"She left packs broken and breaking. We'll leave this one healing." He said firmly.

I wasn't completely confident, but I'd fake it. Because if Roman believed it, I would too.

Eventually.

Most of the wolves recovered. Christopher had gone crazy but he wasn't trained, so all he really had on his side was fury and Alpha Power. Which was a good thing for the rest of the pack.

I made my way to Roman's side. He'd knocked Christopher out, but remained by the Alpha so he was prepared to fight again if he had to. Probably for the pack's peace of mind, more than anything.

Everyone made their way to the middle of the field as time passed, and Leah and Andrew slowly made their way to our sides. Christopher's mate followed them up.

"We'll do it." Andrew said.

I nodded.

The couple looked out to the pack.

"This will never happen again." Andrew's voice was hard, but confident and warm as well. "This show of cruelty will never be allowed to happen again. We won't allow it."

Murmurs of agreement came from the pack, as mothers cradled their babies and husbands cradled their wives.

"We've walked on eggshells around each other too long. It's time we become more than just a pack—it's time we become a family." Leah said.

The murmurs grew louder.

"The New York Pack will send support and money to ease your transition." Roman said, raising his voice.

I smelled the shock coming off the group.

"We all need to help each other—no matter which states we live in, who we are, or what we do for a living. Henley and I won't be like the previous Alphas of All. We won't sit back and let packs fall apart. We're in the process of creating a system to keep packs balanced and fair, and it will be implemented here as soon as it's ready."

That was a bit of a stretch considering we'd only talked about it for a bit the day before, but I could see the worth in a little stretch of the truth to give the pack hope.

The people murmured their surprise, and Christopher's mate stepped up to Leah. She took the woman's hand, meeting her eyes.

"Take my power." She said, and I felt the Alpha power move from her to Leah.

"Thank you." Leah bowed her head at the previous Alpha Female, a sign of respect. I could smell the shock Leah was feeling, and the fear too.

She was worried she wouldn't be good enough.

And that was a sign she'd be a damn good Alpha.

I transferred the power from Christopher to Andrew without any sort of ceremony, and that pulled the old Alpha male from unconsciousness. He came to snarling and swearing, and as a whole the pack seemed to take a sharp breath in.

"Stop." I barked at him, putting my ruby power into the command for the first time that day.

He froze, blinking at me in shock and then fury.

"You've been removed from the seat of leadership. Andrew and Leah will lead this pack now. You can choose to support them, or you can choose to leave. And if you do neither, we'll kill you." I said it simply. It seemed pretty simple. He could stay and shut up, leave in a hissy fit, or throw his life away for some stupid revenge plan.

It was his choice.

Because regardless of the power I held, I would never take someone's freedom unless they were using that freedom to hurt people.

I saw his decision in his eyes.

He wasn't going to surrender or leave.

"You'll have to kill me." He snarled.

I looked at Roman, and he looked at Andrew.

"What will you do, Alpha?" Roman tilted his chin toward the man who held the power now.

Andrew looked unsteady, but I couldn't scent any indecision.

When he looked to his mate to get her input, my approval skyrocketed.

He'd be a good leader.

Leah looked at the pack.

"Does anyone want to challenge Christopher for what he's done?" She lifted her voice.

Silence echoed at first, but one of the men finally stepped forward.

"You trapped my mate." His voice was a low growl, his eyes locked on Christopher. Christopher's confidence faltered—he'd probably reached for his power, planning to use it to protect himself.

"You hurt my daughter." Another stepped forward.

Roman caught my elbow, his fingers gentle on my skin.

"This is their business, not ours." His words brushed my mind.

"Here's our number." He handed a business card to Leah. She accepted it, tucking it in her pocket. "Someone will be in contact soon about the financial assistance."

I had a feeling the financial assistance would be coming out of Roman's bank account. Or one of Roman's bank accounts, since I still didn't know just how rich the man was.

She nodded, and I could smell her gratitude.

"We'll leave you to it."

I didn't look at the old Alpha.

He was an asshole, but I didn't want to watch anyone else die. I'd seen enough—and would continue to see enough death.

Roman and I walked back to his truck together while the pack continued with their decision.

"Will they be alright?" I wondered.

"They'll be fine." His fingers slipped down my arm, sliding between mine and giving a quick squeeze. "You did a good thing, Hen."

"*We* did a good thing." I corrected, tilting my head to his shoulder. "Where to next?"

"We need to go to New York." He admitted, turning the truck on and pulling away from the Oregon pack. "But not until I've survived the trials. So for now, I'm thinking we head to Washington. Check in on the bastard Alpha there."

Marcus.

He'd forced me to take his pack by becoming his Alpha of All before I'd been ready. It had hurt like hell, but I understood why he'd done it. Even if it had contributed heavily to me nearly dying.

"We're not killing him for being a bastard." I warned.

"I know." Roman's hand slid up my thigh. "But he deserves another broken nose, at least."

"I'm not disagreeing there."

We didn't mention the trial Roman would have to survive that night, though we stopped at a medical supply store to pick up a few needles and syringes before we went back to check out of our hotel.

CHAPTER 15

We drove until the sun began going down. Roman checked us into another hotel, then, and hauled our stuff up without letting me lift a damn finger. He dropped the bags on the desk and kissed me before heading into the bathroom for a shower. I thought he needed time to think, so I left him to shower alone.

I checked the jar of wolfsbane a few times, anxiety churning my stomach while I fiddled with the hotel bed's pillows and blankets way too many times.

The shower shut off and Roman came out in a towel, wrapping his arms around me.

"Stop fidgeting." He murmured, licking up the side of my neck. I pushed him away, too worried to laugh.

Only three people out of—how many had Amy said?—had survived the second set of trials. And even though Ezra was dead, even though there were supposed to be two ruby wolves in every generation at all times, I was still freaking out. This was the last of the three trials in that second set, so statistically, our chances weren't great.

"It'll work out, Hen. Just breathe." He pressed his lips to my neck then, rather than licking me again.

"I'm supposed to be comforting you." I said. "You're the one going into the trial."

"We can take turns." He shot me a little grin, but the expression faded quickly as his eyes went serious. "I won't lose. I can't. I refuse to be the reason you die. The world needs you." His lips met my hair, then my forehead, then my cheek. His fingers dug into my hair, twisting the long strands around his palm in a mass amount rather than taking a few strands of it the way he usually did.

"Well, the world needs you too, Romeo. So you'd better not die." I warned. His lips lifted.

"That's the spirit." He squeezed me close. "Love you, Hen. Don't panic. I'm a giant, remember?" He teased me, using my own thoughts about his size against me. I snorted, pushing him to the bed.

"Shut up." I grabbed the needle.

"I can do it." He held his hand out.

"You wouldn't be any better than me." I moved it out of his reach.

Neither of us liked medical stuff, but he was the one who needed to suffer through the damn trial, so I'd take the injection job. At least I could run to the toilet and puke afterward if I was that affected by it.

"Alright."

My fingers shook when I opened the plastic on the needle, slipping it into the jar of wolfsbane and drawing liquid into the needle. When it was full, I stepped back to Roman's side and opened up an alcohol wipe.

Cleaning the inside of his elbow, I ignored the way his eyes traced every inch of me, like he wanted to remember every single piece of me.

"Don't let me go dark again. If it's bad, push me to forget. Help me remember that it wasn't real."

I jerked my head in a nod.

"You'll be fine." I said, more to convince myself.

"Of course I will." He pressed a kiss to my hand as I tossed the alcohol wipe to the nightstand beside me. He lowered himself to a laying position and I leaned over his elbow, trying to find a vein like the internet had shown me. His veins stood out thanks to those sexy-ass muscles of his, so it wasn't all that difficult.

Pushing the needle into his skin, my stomach turned harder, and I clenched my jaw, hands still shaking as I injected the wolfsbane into the man I loved.

"Good." He murmured, his fingers stroking my arm. "I love you, Hen."

His eyes shut, and the trial took him quickly.

His breathing was even, as always, giving away nothing about what he was experiencing. I tossed the syringe and moved to the bathroom, scrubbing my hands while my stomach kept rolling. I washed them twice, then a third time.

Striding back out to the main part of the hotel room, I watched Roman breathe.

And then paced across the room.

He was right; pacing helped.

So I paced back and forth for a few minutes until it made me more stressed than just sitting down. Then, I collapsed into the fancy chair in front of the desk. As soon as I was sitting, I saw a flash of an image.

Me, strapped to the wall in Ledger's basement, screaming and bleeding.

I breathed in sharply, unprepared for the shitty memory.

My eyes landed on Roman, his steady breathing only making me less certain of what he might be seeing or living.

Another flash, and I saw Arla chained to the wall beside me.

A third flash, and Roman was chained across the room.

I blinked away the images, head swiveling around the room. Then it occurred to me, what was happening.

It wasn't a memory.

I was seeing Roman's trial, though I hadn't reached out to him. He was broadcasting to me.

But I needed to try to stay out of his mind, to stay away from the trials. Amy had been serious when she warned me I couldn't intervene, and as crappy as most of the Ruby Pack was, I believed her.

Another flash hit me, this one longer. I saw Roman's dad touching me, a knife to my throat while he groped me.

I gagged, the images vanishing as my stomach flopped. Lunging for the bathroom, I barely reached the toilet in time for everything I'd eaten to come back up when the images returned and Roman's dad became Ezra, sneering and stripping me while I fought to be free.

I pushed Roman's mind away from mine, one arm draped over the toilet while the other wrapped around my stomach as if that would make me feel better.

Another image tried to reach me, and I pushed Roman further, harder.

When I heard the bed move, Roman's body shifting, I froze.

He'd never moved during the trials before, had never even budged.

The movement stopped, and I was hit with another image.

Roman yelling, fighting the chains, while Ezra's fist met my face.

He didn't move in the bed when I didn't fight his mind.

My throat swelled.

I couldn't push him away, couldn't touch his mind when he was in the trials. That would be intervening, which could kill us both.

I'd just have to survive, like Roman.

Rinsing my mouth with shaky hands, I tried to ignore the images.

Tried not to scream when Arla became the focus of the torturers.

Tried not to let the images join my own shitty memories.

Tried not to let my body quiver when the trial version of Roman collapsed to the ground, chained wrists beside his head while he wept over our broken bodies.

Tried not to *cry* as Roman's face went neutral and slack while he tried to survive watching another round of the physical abuse we took.

My eyes scanned the screen when my phone vibrated, and the images abated for the tiniest minute.

AMY: Tonight's trial tests the wolf's emotional endurance. We've lost more to this round than any other.

I shut my eyes, breath staggering as I tried not to let the newest round of images hurt.

But it was useless; the horror would always remain.

Roman had been through a lot, but this was a trial meant to push him over the edge and see if he'd survive the fall.

And the images… they made me want to scream. But for Roman's sake, I couldn't. I had to stay calm, had to do whatever I could to help him through. The same way he would've if it was me.

When the images finally stopped, I curled into bed beside Roman. His breathing changed, staggered, as his body began to shake. I draped myself over his chest, my head against his neck as I focused on calming thoughts.

The ocean brushing the shore in calming waves.

Wind rustling the trees.

Walking through the forest in wolf form, dirt beneath my paws and branches brushing my fur.

Yoga in the snow, feeling life in the nature all around.

Roman didn't hold me.

He quivered, and I felt wetness on my hair but said nothing. He wouldn't want me to acknowledge it.

Tears were for the weak, and neither of us was weak.

I don't know how much time passed before he eased his body from mine. His hands barely brushed me, like he was afraid I might break.

"I need to shift." His voice was rough, hard.

"I'll come." I whispered, sliding out of bed on the other side.

"No." The word was sharp, and stunned me a bit. "I'm sorry." He shoved a hand over his head. "I just need to be alone."

He grabbed his keys.

I followed him out, and he turned when the door closed behind me. My back pressed to the door, only inches between us. Nothing about the moment was sexy, or even intimate, as anger rolled off his skin.

"I want to be alone." He repeated. I tried not to wince at the volume, the fury in his words.

I was trying to be there for him, to stop him from going dark like he'd asked, but he was pushing me away. Usually, that was my job. But I was ready for it; I'd deal with his anger the way he'd always dealt with mine.

"I just want to drive you there."

His eyes closed for a long moment. When he finally opened them, he jerked his head in a nod and spun around. I followed behind him, keeping my distance. Though I didn't think he would hurt me, I'd seen his trial. It wasn't just flashes for him—he'd lived it. Every minute, and every pain.

I knew first-hand how trauma could change you, so I gave him space.

I said nothing all the way to the truck and remained silent when he turned the music up so loud it nearly deafened me as soon as I turned the truck on.

Pulling away from the hotel, his fingers were white on the handle beside the top of his door and his seat belt.

We were quiet through the drive. I'd pulled up a hiking trail on my phone on our way down to the truck, so google took me to the woods. It wasn't far.

The moment I parked, Roman had his pants on the snowy dirt and was in his fur, sprinting into the forest. My eyes dropped to the gas gauge; nearly empty.

Shit.

Neither of our wallets were with us, because that's just how crap worked in my life.

With a long breath out, I shut the vehicle off. The sudden silence in the truck added to the chill that returned immediately, and I pulled my knees to my chest. I would've shifted, but Roman made it clear he didn't want me in wolf form with him. Whether that was because he was working off what he'd lived through or because he just didn't want to be near me, I wasn't sure.

When my fingers began to tingle and my breath didn't feel hot on them anymore, I let out a frustrated sigh and slipped out of my clothes, swapping skin for fur but staying in the truck.

Roman would just have to deal with that compromise, because I wasn't about to freeze to death in his damn truck.

It was amazing how much warmer I was in my fur, now that I was healed.

A pained howl miles away caught my ears, and I tuned into Roman's thoughts to make sure he was okay. His mind slammed mine away so hard my ears rang, and I whined as I changed positions, trying to get comfortable in the truck's seat.

An hour went by, and then another and another. The sun began to rise, and I wasn't sure how much time had passed. My stomach growled, but I ignored it. Roman needed this—this time—and I'd give it to him if that was what would get him through the trials.

It was the middle of the day when he finally emerged from the trees. My eyes lifted, wary of my male.

He bared his neck toward me, a sign of submission as his mind touched mine.

"Run with me." He said.

I said nothing back, just watching him. Waiting for another explosion, or a sign that he was alright.

"I need you." His words were more vulnerable this time. He'd beg if I made him, or apologize if I demanded it, but I didn't need him to. Hell, I didn't even *want* him to.

I shifted to open the door, shifting back to wolf form as I slipped out, and walking to my mate. His neck was still bared, open for me to bite or punish him if I wanted to.

Nuzzling against his neck, I licked him and cuddled him.

"I love you." I murmured, after pushing gently into his mind and then withdrawing so he'd have that privacy he wanted.

He made a choking sound, dropping to his belly and burying his nose in my furry chest. I shifted, clutching his gigantic wolf body close to my skin and stroking his fur. It was darker than I'd thought, halfway between his usual dark brown and my ruby red, and the color was beautiful.

He whined into me, and I wrapped my arms around his entire body. He licked my belly, like he wanted to reassure himself that I was really there—that I was okay. He whined again, and I whispered,

"Shh," while running my hands up and down him.

He'd had his time to accept what he'd seen and cope with it as well as he could on his own. And now, he just wanted me to hold him.

I understood so well it nearly brought tears to my eyes.

No one was really too tough to cry. Not even me or Roman.

At some point he shifted, and I was rubbing skin instead of fur. I didn't stop, moving my hand in circles on his back and holding him close to me. His head was against my chest, his body shaking as he wrapped his arms around me to pull me even closer.

My fingers lifted to his head and neck before moving back to his shoulder blades.

"I'm sorry." He finally said.

I didn't know how much more time had passed, but it was easily the middle of the day.

"I lashed out at you, and I shouldn't have. I'm sorry."

"It happens." I murmured. "I understand, and you know you didn't hurt me."

We heard the crunch of tires on snow and dirt and turned our heads. It was still a minute away, but a minute wasn't long considering we were naked in the damn dirt and snow.

We were up in an instant, Roman grabbing me by the waist and practically throwing me in the truck before jogging around to yank his sweats—wet now, the rest of his clothes shredded—off the ground and up to his hips.

I tugged my sweatshirt over my head, shimmying into my panties so I was at least somewhat covered.

Roman waved a hand at the guy in the Jeep that pulled up a few parking spaces away from us, then slid into the driver's seat and closed the door behind him.

"Damn, that was close." He muttered, glancing at me. "You're okay?" His eyes scanned me for injuries even as he asked.

"I'm fine." I dropped a hand on his thigh and made a face at the cold wetness that was his pants, lifting my fingers away and shaking the water off.

"Should've stripped in the car." He said, grimacing.

"Then I wouldn't get to see your ass in dripping wet sweats." I countered.

He shot me a half-smile.

"I really am sorry, Hen." He copied my move, dropping his hand on my thigh. Where his was covered in soaking sweats, mine was bare. I shivered away from his cold fingers.

"Stop apologizing. I don't want to have to say sorry next time I act bitchy, so I don't want you apologizing for being a jerk."

He chuckled, his eyes softening.

"You're never a bitch, Hen. Stubborn and defensive, sure, but not bitchy."

"You're the only one who thinks that." I said, tugging my semi-wet hair over my shoulder and shivering. "Can you take us back to the hotel? It's freezing."

He let go of my leg long enough to back out and get us on the road, then grabbed my thigh again.

"Do you want to talk about it?" I checked.

"Nope." He didn't hesitate. I turned the radio on, fine with that. I'd tell him I saw parts of the trial later—after he had more time to wrap his head around it.

Though he'd said he didn't want to talk, he opened his mouth a few minutes later.

"It was bad. I'm going to remember it a long, long time."

He ran a hand over his head.

"They were hurting you, and there was nothing I could do. I know it wasn't real, but it felt like it was and that's probably the shittiest part of the whole thing."

"Sounds shitty." I agreed. "Amy said it was a test of emotional endurance. Apparently most people fail the trials on that round." I told him, focusing outside so he didn't think I was too worried about him, although I was.

"I don't blame them." He said frankly. "If I wasn't fighting for you, I'd have given up too."

We were both quiet. The sounds of the music, the heater, and the tires on the road were loud enough to fill the silence.

"If we have kids, they're going to have to marry other ruby wolves." I told Roman.

"I know." His grimace told me he'd considered it.

"What if the others are like Ezra?"

"Then I'll kill them." Roman didn't even hesitate.

It probably made me a terrible person, but that warmed my damn heart.

"Do you want kids?" I wondered.

He'd asked me before, but it occurred to me that I'd never reflected the question back.

"I do." He didn't hesitate. "Two or three, if you're up for it. There's nothing I want more than to see a little boy or girl with your smile."

I bit my lip.

"You said you'd like to try it, last time I asked." He reminded me.

"Yeah, but that was before. Now, I don't know. The world's a shitty place."

"A beautiful shitty place." He said, soft but sure.

It was probably the most soulful thing I'd ever heard Roman say.

I guess something about suffering reminds you to look for what's still good.

"I want him to have your eyes." I said, focusing on the trees. "Also, your height. Tall guys are the best."

"What if it's a girl?" Roman countered.

I shrugged.

"I'd do much better with a boy. I'm not empathetic enough to have a daughter."

"You underestimate yourself." He said, as we parked in the space the hotel had designated to us.

I reached for my door, and he grabbed my leg.

"I'll get it." He said.

I could've said no, but this was one of his ways of showing me he cared. So I sat back while he walked around the truck, tugging my door open. Roman's arm wrapped around my waist as we headed for the elevator.

"Let's sleep the rest of the day." I said.

"That's the best idea I've heard all damn year."

We crashed without even exchanging kisses.

CHAPTER 16

WE DIDN'T LEAVE for Washington until the next morning, and then we reached the pack a few hours after lunch.

Marcus came out of the Alpha House only moments after we arrived. I couldn't read his expression, but his stance told me he was ready for a fight. Roman and I had spent a few hours in the hotel's gym before leaving that morning, so we weren't itching to punch anyone.

Or at least, I thought we weren't.

We walked up to Marcus's porch, Roman's left arm around my waist. The Alpha opened his mouth to greet us when we made it up the stairs, but before he said anything, Roman's fist was flying at Marcus's face.

Marcus didn't move to stop the punch, but I jumped away.

Roman had mentioned punching him in the face, but I didn't think he'd actually do it. I underestimated my mate, I guess.

"What the hell, Roman?" I demanded.

"He hurt you. It's my right to break his nose."

"I already did that last time we saw him."

"Well, you aren't me. He would've been waiting for me to retaliate through our entire conversation if I didn't do it now."

I didn't exactly agree with it, but there was no point in arguing. Roman would protect me however he thought he had to, and I was alright with that for the most part.

"You gave my people back to the Alphas of All." Marcus glared at me, even while he cradled his bleeding nose. Someone I faintly recognized brought him a wad of tissues, and he held it to his face.

"I was dying. An unmated ruby wolf can't hold packs like I was doing." I stated.

"And now?" He looked to Roman, his eyes focusing on the nearly invisible glint of red shadow Roman's cheeks. He'd shaved before we left the hotel—I think because he didn't want anyone to think we were siblings again. But his stubble grew so fast you could already see it.

"She's mine." Roman's arm tugged me closer. "Permanently."

"And we're the Alphas of All." I added, since that was the real question he was trying to ask.

"Here to take my pack back?" Marcus asked, looking a bit suspicious. "Or replace me altogether?"

"Neither. We're here to make sure you're still worthy of being Alpha. We're replacing anyone who doesn't qualify."

His eyebrows lifted.

"You're fixing the system that hurt you." He said, obviously speaking to me.

"We're fixing a broken system so no one else has to suffer." Roman cut in, protecting me from the conversation he thought might hurt me. I was fine to talk about it, but appreciated the gesture anyway. "So, show us your pack."

Marcus led us inside, giving us a tour of the Alpha House—the size of a normal house.

I knew his pack was scattered through the outskirts of a decently large city, and that the wolves would travel to Marcus's place on the edge of the forest when they wanted to shift and run. So visiting all the pack members wouldn't be realistic, as I'd warned Roman, but Marcus could call them all to his house like Christopher had.

After we'd seen the house and turned down the guest room Marcus offered us for the night, we spent a few hours in wolf form in the forest together before meeting the rest of the pack.

When we headed back to the Alpha's house, we heard the noise of the pack's chatter and laughter before we saw them.

"Good sign." Roman murmured.

"Definitely."

We made our way to the back door, ignoring the surprised murmurs of everyone who saw us and our red fur. Roman's was darker and less red, but I figured they'd just assume there was variation in the color of ruby wolves.

After getting dressed quickly inside the house, we stepped out to greet the pack. They were waiting for us, and for the most part quieted down when we stepped beside Marcus on the porch. The pack waited, but I looked to Marcus for an introduction.

This was still his pack, and I sure as hell didn't want to lead it for him. That was his job.

"Everyone, this is Roman and Henley Ellis. The new Alphas of All." He said.

A stunned silence killed whatever had been left of the chatter.

"When I left to find us protection, they were who I went to. I trusted them with our lives then, and I do the same now. So please, give them the warmest Washington Welcome you can muster."

Deafening claps, whoops, and whistles sounded instantly from the crowd. Though there were only fifty-some wolves, they were louder than you'd expect.

I knew the "trusting us with their lives" bit was an exaggeration, but would say nothing of it. He trusted us because he had no other option, and *only* because he had no other option.

We walked through the pack, greeting the members. There were a few I knew by name and I wasn't surprised when they treated me vastly different than they had when they'd seen me last.

Back then, I was an object to them. A useful one that prevented them from shifting at night, but an object. Now, I was their superior. Someone they needed and had to respect for the sake of their own lives and wellbeing.

I didn't think that should affect how well they treated me, but it did.

It didn't take long to see that Marcus was a good Alpha—something I'd assumed even after I was taken from the pack there. He'd been young, then. Only eighteen.

The people talked freely, seeming unworried and friendly enough.

Roman and I agreed that we didn't need to stay any longer, and we headed back to our truck to find another hotel.

On our way to the hotel, Roman's phone rang.

I glanced at the caller ID as I handed it to him.

"Thomas Caine?" I checked. The name was familiar, but I couldn't remember why.

"One of my unmated enforcers, before." He explained, hitting the green button and lifting it to his ear. "What's up?"

"Things are bad." Thomas said, not bothering with greetings. "The pack was pissed at you, but Jett's worse. He's got Lilac and Sky locked in the jail cell. I think Charlie's dead, and Matt and Jordan are in bad shape. Do you have any ideas how to stop him? He hired some outside assholes to come help regain control, but they're only making things worse.."

Roman glanced at me, fingers tightening on the wheel.

His pack, broken.

Once again, it was my fault.

"Let's go." I said, answering the question he hadn't dared ask.

Would I go with him to New York?

Hell yes, I would.

"I'll be there as soon as I can. Probably around twelve hours." He glanced at me again as I pulled up google maps, taking us to the airport. He plucked my phone from my fingers, holding his cell against his ear with his shoulder as his focus split between the road, the directions, and the conversation. "If Jett has the Alpha power, all you can really do is challenge him or obey. No one in the pack can beat him, so just play along until I get there and do what you can to heal the others."

"What should I do about Lilac and Sky?" Thomas checked.

"If they're not dying, leave them. Focus on keeping everyone alive and preventing Jett from doing any real damage."

"Alright. Thanks."

"Any time. I've got to book a flight, but call me if you need anything else. Call Henley if I don't answer."

Roman was about to hang up, but Thomas cleared his throat.

"I don't know how the pack will do if you bring her back." He admitted.

"We're a packaged deal. They can suck it up or I can leave you to Jett." Roman growled. He didn't mention we were the Alphas of All yet;

probably for the better. We didn't want Thomas spreading that news, putting Jett on the defensive.

"Alright. We'll figure it out."

Thomas hung up, and Roman handed me his phone.

"Can you call the airline for me?" He asked.

I knew which ones he had connections to and found the number in his phone. A few minutes later, I had us booked on a flight that left in an hour. Twenty minutes later, we were moving through the airport's security.

We had to make a connection and then our second plane was delayed, so we had a bunch of time to grab food on our way. That was nice.

I slept against Roman's chest. The roomy chairs in first class were barely big enough for my gigantic mate, but massive enough for me to snuggle against him. His fingers brushed through my hair when he woke me up with a kiss and an ass-squeeze as the plane landed.

His truck was still at the airport, so we didn't have to call an Uber.

Walking up to the skyscraper after a month in Ruby City was surreal. Roman's fingers held mine tightly, and we strolled inside together.

The front desk chick, the kick-ass one who always had at least a couple guns on her, was gone. Replaced by a huge-ass male with actual frown lines despite looking around my age.

"Conrad." Roman nodded, easing me to the other side of him so he stood between me and the other man. I knew that regardless of my power, Roman would always do what he could to block me from perceived danger.

"Turn around and I won't have to kill you." Conrad's snarl would've scared most people, but not my male.

"This is above your paygrade." Roman said, leading me past the desk.

Conrad stepped between us, throwing Alpha power at us. It was enforcer-level strong, and probably would've stopped us if we weren't who we were. But it didn't even touch us.

Roman dropped my hand, stepping up nose-to-nose with Conrad. My male had plenty of practice when it came to intimidating people. Being taller and stronger than pretty much everyone helped too.

"You don't want to threaten an Alpha of All." Roman warned.

Conrad tensed.

"You're not an Alpha of All." Conrad said, though he didn't sound entirely convinced.

"What do you want to bet?"

I hit him with a bit of ruby power, then. Just to emphasize Roman's point.

Conrad staggered backward, and Roman stepped toward him.

"Now, are you going to let us past or do you want to challenge me?" Roman's voice was normal, neutral and calm.

Conrad didn't answer, but he did step to the side.

I caught up to Roman quickly, staying on his left so he didn't have to maneuver himself to separate me and Conrad again for his peace of mind.

We strode to the elevator, Roman's hand on my lower back as he directed me in front of him, maintaining his position between me and the front desk.

"Was he one of yours?" I asked as the elevators shut. I didn't remember him, but Roman did have a bunch of enforcers and I wasn't his Alpha Female for long.

"No, he was too bloodthirsty to qualify. I always made my enforcers take the same psychological exam police officers take. Conrad failed four times." Roman's hand was still on my lower-back, and he used it to tug me closer.

"Did Jett pass the psych test?" I checked.

"Narrowly." Roman grimaced.

Too narrowly, we were both thinking.

"Maybe we should have all the Alphas take that test." I said.

"Probably should."

The elevator went to the top floor without a single pause. Traveling had ended up taking somewhere around fourteen hours, so it was early evening. The skyscraper should've been a mad house of people. The silence of the building was a bad sign.

We said nothing when the elevator dinged and the doors opened. And then said nothing again, as we sniffed the air.

I gestured in the direction of our old apartment, and we headed down the hall.

"You don't think he…" I trailed off, but Roman understood I was wondering if he'd claimed our old place.

"He'd need more than just power tools to get in. I have it locked up tight."

I nodded. We found our door—chunks of wood surrounding it, fallen off the actual door. Which was apparently made out of metal, since I could see the dented door standing strong. There were holes in the walls randomly on either side of the door, revealing more metal.

"Damn."

"I had it fixed up after I met you. Couldn't risk my mate getting taken from my own damn apartment. Your old one is similarly impenetrable, though it was more difficult to install with you constantly there." He said.

I shot him a look of disbelief.

"You had your apartment fixed up under the assumption you'd be able to convince me to mate with you right after we met?"

His crooked grin and shrug were too damn adorable when I was trying to be annoyed with him.

"I'm persuasive."

I shook my head as I walked beside him to the room across the hall. I'd never seen its owner. But by the smell of it, it now belonged to Jett.

Roman didn't bother knocking. He twisted the doorknob, finding the room left unlocked by the cocky asshole messing with our pack. We stepped inside and stopped abruptly when we saw Jett on the couch.

All he had on was jeans. The girl on top of him, who he was making out with, wore absolutely nothing.

Jett dropped the naked chick on the floor on her ass, ignoring her shriek as she scrambled for his shirt. Roman's eyes didn't dip to her, landing on the asshole who stood in front of us, throwing his Alpha power at us without a shred of control.

"Well, can't say I expected this." Roman drawled, draping his arm over my shoulder. "Who leaves the door open when they're going at it?"

He looked at me, and I shrugged.

"People who don't give a shit, I guess."

"Back down, Ellis." Jett stood, feigning casualness. The smell of lust around him was too strong to smell whatever he was really feeling. He was threatening Roman, but I liked that I was included just because we shared a last name.

"How many of my people have you killed?" Roman demanded, dropping the guise of calmness he'd adopted.

"They're mine now." Jett sneered.

"Are they?" I lifted an eyebrow. "Did you ever meet the Alphas of All?"

His forehead wrinkled.

I was pretty sure he'd been with us when they visited one of the times, but he didn't seem to remember.

"What does that have to do with anything?"

I grabbed Roman's baseball cap off his head, pulling it over mine. Jett's eyes landed on Roman's head, and he scoffed.

"Dyed your hair to match your mate's?"

"Nope." Roman didn't hesitate.

I pushed Jett back with my power and he stepped back, confidence faltering.

"Did you see the color of their hair, Jett?" I pushed again, and he stepped back again. This time, his eyes widened just fractionally. I assumed he'd put two and two together. "That's right; we're the new Alphas of All. And we're not letting assholes like you control anything —or anyone."

My power pushed him back again, and he stumbled.

"Easy." Roman murmured into my mind. *"Just take his power."*

It was nice to have Roman balance out my bitchiness, sometimes.

So I did as he said, pulling Jett's Alpha Power into myself. It settled with the other power I had, but I didn't want to get used to it.

"We need to find another Alpha." I said.

It couldn't be Roman; he was becoming like me, still.

"Kyler." Roman said.

He and Arla were the best bet. She had experience, and everyone liked Kyler. He'd been an enforcer long enough to know how everything worked, too.

Jett staggered to the couch, holding himself up with the back of it and glowering at us.

"Kyler's not here." His voice was uneven as he adjusted to the loss of power.

"What do you mean, he's not here?" I frowned.

Kyler and the girls were headed back here before we left Ruby City—they should've been back in New York days ago.

"He never showed up." Jett said. I guess he'd heard our people were coming back, too.

"Did Arla?" Roman demanded. "Jamie, Oliver, and London?"

"No. We haven't heard from them since they called to warn me they were coming." Jett grumbled, collapsing on the couch.

"Shit." Roman grabbed his phone, hitting Arla's number.

"Maybe they decided to drive." I said, though I was pretty sure that wasn't the case.

That would be a long-ass drive.

The phone rang and rang, then went to voicemail.

He dialed Kyler, leading me from Jett's apartment with a string of curses when Kyler didn't answer either.

We headed down the hall, passing a few of Jett's enforcers. I sent them on their way, stripped of their power, while Roman continued dialing our family. He grew more desperate with each person he called, since none of them answered.

We reached the jail cell, and Roman stayed outside to keep trying their phones when I went in. Lilac and Sky were locked in the room, sitting on the edge of the one bed together. I tried the old passcode—Roman's birthday—and grimaced when it didn't work. Hitting the speaker button, I leaned toward it.

"Hey, ladies. Any idea what the code is?"

The girls both jumped up, their eyes on the window I was looking out through.

"Henley!" Sky exclaimed.

"We have no idea." Lilac groaned. "Jett's the only one who knows. You'll have to go get it from him.

"Alright. I'll be back in a bit." I said, releasing the button and stepping back into the hall just as Roman slammed his fist into the wall beside the door. Jumping away, I swore and snarled at him.

"What the hell?"

"My sister's probably still in Ruby City." He snarled back, shoving his phone at me and stalking down the hall. "We need to go back. Now."

"Call Joel." I said, handing him his phone back as calmly as I could. "Go to our apartment and get it figured out. I'll deal with the pack."

He jerked his head in a nod, stalking down the hall with his phone back to his ear. I'd never really seen him lose it like that… but I'd never seen him when his twin was in danger, either.

Then again, he also still hadn't forgotten the torture he'd seen and lived through in the trial. I was sure that was where his mind went when she didn't answer. And I seriously hoped that wasn't what was going on.

I made my way back to Jett's apartment. I stepped in, and we made eye contact. He shoved me up against the wall the moment he realized I was alone, his fingers wrapping around my throat.

"Let go." I said, remaining calm.

"Give me back my pack."

So he knew I was the one who took his power. He must've noticed me and Roman communicating.

"Last warning. Let go." I forced my voice to remain neutral, even as my damn scarred memory brought back flashes of other hands on my throat throughout the years.

He squeezed my neck.

I dropped my calmness and slammed my knees toward his balls while I threw my power at him. He dodged the kick to the balls but couldn't avoid my power, skidding backward a couple feet and crashing into the wall. The noise was a loud thud, and Roman came barreling in.

He stopped at my side, looking to Jett.

"What's the passcode for the jail cell?" I tossed the question out.

The guy on the floor said nothing.

"Don't make me throw my power at you again." I snapped.

He grumbled but said,

"8325."

"Thanks." I called out, as Roman and I headed back down the hall. "How's Arla?"

"I don't know. Joel and Amy didn't answer either." Roman admitted, seeming much calmer than before.

"Shit." I grimaced

"They can all defend themselves." Roman said, a slow breath leaving his lungs. He was definitely trying to convince both of us, not just me. "We're needed here. We'll head back to Idaho to make sure they're alright when we know this pack is safe."

I nodded.

It was true; they were all adults who could protect themselves. This pack was littered with kids and teenagers who needed protection, and from what we'd seen of the skyscraper, they were in deeper shit than our friends could likely be."

We reached the cell and Roman typed the code in on the keypad. It flashed red.

He tried again.

More red.

"Son of a bitch." I swore. "He didn't."

Roman shot me a dry grin.

"Should've thrown your power at him."

"Should've had you kick his damn ass." I shot back, standing and hitting the buttons myself.

8…3…2…5…

Red lights.

"Asshole!"

Roman leaned over to the intercom and hit the button.

"Where's Thomas?" He asked, not bothering with an introduction. The girls jumped to their feet, eyes on the glass once again, though they couldn't see anything through it.

"Thomas called me. Where is he?" Roman repeated the question.

"How are we supposed to know?" Lilac folded her arms. "We've been locked in here for an entire day."

Roman let go of the button and strolled out of the room.

I hit the button again.

"We'll be back for you soon. Sorry!"

Catching Roman was easy, since he was walking slowly so we could walk together.

"We need to check the offices on the north side and the west side." He said. I had no idea which way was north and which was west, so I nodded like I understood. His lips tilted upward, and he pointed in the direction of one hallway we hadn't been down, and then the other.

"Are we staying together, or splitting up?" I checked.

The question was for the sake of Roman's sanity.

He was the one dealing with shit right then; if he wanted to stay together, we'd stay together.

"We'll split up. Tell me if you find them, and I'll do the same." He said, tapping my temple. "Use your power first, ask questions afterward so you don't get that sexy little ass of yours kicked again." He said with a grin.

I scoffed, smacking him on the arm before heading down one of the halls he'd pointed to.

CHAPTER 17

I CHECKED EVERY DOOR, knocking and then stepping inside. I didn't find a single person in any of the apartments, offices, or meeting rooms. The place was a ghost town, reminding me of the empty elevator when we'd arrived.

There weren't even any recent scents.

I reached the final door at the end of the hall and didn't bother knocking, just opening it up since I expected it to be empty.

A battle-cry roared out of a tiny female. Her weight came hurtling toward me, her body jerking to a halt as she reached the ends of her chains.

Chains.

She was chained to the wall, like I'd been in Ledger's basement.

In my own fucking pack.

I saw red, barreling toward her. She backed up a bit, her eyes shocked as I grabbed the chains and tugged.

"Henley?" She asked.

I recognized her now. The receptionist I'd always admired, the chick who'd pointed a gun at Ledger all those months ago.

"I thought you and Roman left." She eyed me suspiciously as I followed the chains to the wall, testing the weight of the thick screws in the metal plate.

"We did." I bit the word out. "We're the new Alphas of All. It's why people were dying here—my damn hair." I gave up on the metal plate, hurrying to the kitchen. "Who did this?" I demanded over my shoulder.

"Jett brought some new guys in from another pack. They do what they want." Her words were bitter, her voice hard.

I found a flathead screwdriver in the kitchen's junk drawer, but it was too big for the screws in the thing—and would do nothing for the nails. I snarled in frustration, grabbing a butter knife and a butcher's knife from the other drawers and going back to the receptionist. Now, she looked a bit worried.

"What are you doing?"

"Freeing you." I growled. "The way I wish someone had freed me."

Her eyes widened, and I realized I'd just dropped a massive chunk of my past in her hands—and I didn't even know her.

When the hell did I become the kind of person who spilled intimate details of their life with strangers?

"You were… chained?" She asked.

The damage was already done, so I didn't bother hiding the truth.

"For far too much of my life."

I wiggled the screwdriver, wedging it between the metal plate and the wall. Moving it back and forth, I got to work prying the thing out. It was slow-going and incredibly frustrating, because the damn thing barely budged at all.

"I thought all the packs wanted you." The receptionist said.

"They did. I was an object to them; a *thing* that would get them what they wanted."

"And they wanted not to shift at night." She lifted her eyes to the ceiling, and I wondered what she was looking at for all of half a second before I focused back on the plate.

I pried.

I wiggled.

I yanked and tugged.

The damn thing wasn't moving.

With a groan, I gave up on prying it from the wall. I stepped back to study it, looking for a weakness.

The receptionist shuddered.

"It's almost time." Her voice was half-growl, half-whisper.

"Time for what?" I looked to her face and saw wolf eyes staring back at me.

What the hell?

"You didn't ask why I was chained." Her whole body shivered this time, and I saw the war in her eyes as she fought back the shift. "You just came to help me."

She shook her head hard, her eyes going back to human.

"We split the pack. City and Countryside. Most of our people are upstate, refusing to follow Jett. I'm the Alpha Female."

A massive shudder quaked her and the chains. I'd never seen someone forced by the moon to shift, and I stepped back to watch in a dark fascination as she physically fought to stay in human form.

Another shiver, another shudder, and she snarled as she shifted to a furry blonde wolf.

"Shit." I murmured.

And then my eyes went back to the chains.

I'd kill the bastards who did this to her. No one should be chained—no one should lose their freedom like that without doing something truly and disgustingly horrible.

"I'll get you out." I told her, my eyes steeling as I focused on the chains.

And dammit, I had no idea how to break them.

"I found them." Roman's mind touched mine. *"Thomas saved the others—they're all in bad shape and chained up, though. I'm getting the key from Jett."*

"He chained the receptionist too." I said. *"I've been trying to get her out."*

"With your bare hands?" I could hear his humor and scoffed.

"With a screwdriver. And a butcher's knife."

His amusement ramped up, and I bit back a grin.

"Wish I could've watched that."

"Yeah, yeah. I'll meet you in Jett's apartment." I looked back at the receptionist. "I'm going to come back with a key. I don't know how long it will take, but I'll be back for you. I won't leave you here." I told her.

She bobbed her wolf head and showed me her neck in submission for the briefest moment.

I made it back to Jett's apartment in record time, barely glancing at the door to the place Roman and I had called home. Nothing would ever be the same for us again. Not New York, not our friendships, and definitely not our pack.

But we'd find a way to deal with it. We had each other, and that was what mattered.

I found Roman's hands around Jett's neck. My male was bleeding—I couldn't see the wound, but I could smell the blood. A lot of blood. And there was a knife on the ground, which I assumed Jett had stabbed my mate with. Or at least poked him with.

"I killed your enforcers and I'll kill you too if I have to." Roman snarled into Jett's ear. "Last chance."

"Do it." Jett snarled back. "I won't surrender."

I saw the conflict in Roman's eyes.

And though I didn't know what had happened between them, Roman didn't look confident he should end Jett's life and I didn't want him carrying any guilt.

I hit Jett with my power.

"Where are the keys for the people you had chained?" I demanded, crossing the room and forcing him to answer.

Roman released Jett's neck but pinned him to the wall.

The ex-enforcer and Alpha gritted his teeth together, fighting against my control.

I hit him with the full force of my strength.

"Tell me where the keys are."

"With the Georgia men I hired. Twenty-sixth floor." The words poured from Jett's mouth like water.

"And the code?"

"0809." He said.

He'd only switched one of the numbers in Roman's birthday, which had been the old code. Bastard.

"If you're not convinced he deserves to die, let him go." I murmured to Roman, spinning on my heels and stalking from the room. The apartment's door slammed when I was partway down the hall, and

Roman caught up to me almost instantly thanks to those damn long legs of his.

We were headed to the jail cell—though we hadn't talked about it, I think we both agreed Sky and Lilac would be more useful to us free.

"He let half the pack go." Roman bit out. "They didn't want to follow him, so he let them go. Feels wrong to kill him knowing that, regardless of the other shit."

"He's got that pack's Alpha Female chained in my hall."

"If the Georgia assholes have hurt anyone else, I'll kill them—and Jett for bringing them here." Roman said as we approached the cell.

Freeing the other girls took all of one minute. They were fine—only their egos were bruised—and split up to go watch the chained people to make sure no one touched them.

Roman and I went back to the elevator, riding down to the twenty-fifth floor.

When the doors shut, the scent of Roman's blood intensified and I spun to him.

I'd forgotten about his injury.

What kind of shitty mate was I?

He leaned up against the side wall, watching me. Like he was waiting for me to explode.

I grabbed the hem of his shirt—black, hiding the red of the blood—and tugged it upward. He winced when it stuck to his skin, and I had to ease it from the wound.

When I saw the injury, I nearly puked. I lifted his hand, using it to hold his shirt up, and hit the button to freeze the elevators.

He only watched me.

"Shirt off." I told him, dead serious.

"They need us." He said, not moving.

"They can wait three minutes. That's awful." I pointed to his stomach with my thumb. The wound was jagged and rough, like the blade he'd been stabbed with was dull.

"Henley…" He sighed. "Fine."

"This is where you say, 'I love you for caring so much about my health, my perfect, sexy mate." I drawled.

He snorted, and I kneeled in front of him. His body leaned toward me, arching just a little when he saw my face in front of his dick.

"Easy, big guy."

"We don't have time for sex, Hen." He growled. "That's why I didn't tell you about the injury. If you heal me, I'll be fucking horny."

"Then I guess it's a good thing we're adult enough for self-restraint." I said. "Because you're not going anywhere with your damn organs nearly hanging out."

Roman grumbled again but leaned back against the elevator as I moved toward him. The licking would go faster in wolf form, but I didn't want to add the extra time that would come with stripping, shifting, and getting dressed again.

I tried to stay clinical about it, making quick work of licking his injury. One of his hands gripped my head halfway through, his fingers in my hair as he pulled me closer. His erection pressed into my boobs, and like the good Alpha I was attempting to become, I didn't acknowledge the way he moved against me—just slightly—to ease the discomfort.

When I was done healing him, I took a breath I hadn't realized I was holding. His fingers slid from my hair, and he adjusted his pants while I hit the button to start the elevator again.

His breathing was unsteady, his eyes squeezed shut, his hands on the metal walls like he was trying to use them as an anchor.

I reached for Roman's hand and he jerked it away from me.

"Don't touch me, woman. Even your hands are sexy." He said.

"Dude. Dude. Dude." I repeated the word he considered unsexy. "Birds. Arla. Arla and Kyler, doing it."

He grimaced, but there was still a massive bulge in his pants.

"Jamie's pregnant belly. Jett's ugly face. Me, bleeding and—"

His hand clapped over my mouth.

I spoke into his hand when the elevator doors opened.

"Ready?" I asked.

"Are you ready?" He countered.

I knew what he was asking.

The Georgia guys had hurt our people. When we'd seen them last time, they were wild and cruel. We were the Alphas of All—we had to keep the peace and protect our wolves, no matter the cost.

I'd killed people before, but I'd never looked them in the eyes and decided they didn't get to live. That didn't feel like a choice me—or anyone else—should make.

Yet someone had to choose, and it looked like we were the ones in that position.

I wished there was a guidebook, and a thought occurred to me.

"I think we need laws." I told Roman as we walked through the halls. I could smell the Georgia males and assumed Roman could too. "There should be rules with consequences if you break them.

It was a basic idea; one that should've occurred to the Alphas of All long before us.

But the Ruby Wolves were usually preoccupied by leading Ruby City and only interacted with the packs when they had to step in to "right" a wrong.

Their definition of wrongdoing and their way of righting it was shit.

"Seems like an obvious answer to the problem." Roman said. "I don't know why no one's thought of it."

"Because it's not natural to us. We're not human; we don't like rules. But I think it could protect people."

The conversation ended—tabled for later—when we approached the apartment the Georgia men were living in. Loud music played from the room, and I could smell beer and sex.

Roman opened the door, stepping in first.

Human strippers—women, wearing nearly nothing—danced at the front of the room. The three Georgia men—all mated—sat on the couch, their hands underneath the clothes of their mates, who sat on their laps while they all watched the strippers dance.

Empty beer bottles were scattered at random on the floor, glass bottles of cheap whiskey and vodka on the coffee table and countertop with various levels and amounts of liquid.

A memory from Roman hit me hard enough to nearly knock me over.

A young Roman and Arla, walking into the kitchen for a snack and finding his mom on his dad's lap, a bottle of whiskey in one hand and the other in his mom's shirt. The kids were too young to realize what was happening, but old enough to know they shouldn't see it, so they ran from the room.

His dad had shouted profanities at them, dropping Maisy on her ass and following the kids into Roman's room. Arla had ducked into the closet while Roman tried to hold the door shut, but his dad shoved it open hard enough to throw little Roman across the room.

Roman stood on shaky little legs, glowering at the large man he resembled, and his dad stalked across the room with his fists clenched.

He slammed the door to that memory, knocking me right the hell out of that nightmare.

"Get out." Roman snarled at the strippers. He grabbed a wallet off the counter, shoving it at the first of the women while turning to the men on the couch. Their mates hurried off while Roman grabbed the first guy by the throat. "Who sent you here?" He demanded.

Another guy lunged toward Roman, and my mate leaned down to dodge so the guy flew past him.

"Hit them." Roman growled into my mind.

I knew what he meant and threw my power at the asshole Roman had pinned, forcing him to tell the truth when Roman demanded an answer again.

"Who sent you to destroy the New York Pack?"

"The Alpha Female of All." The guy struggled beneath Roman, fighting to get free. Both the other guys launched toward my mate. Roman dropped the first guy and stepped back in time for the two men to slam into each other, collapsing to the ground.

"Sylvie." I grimaced, asking my own question next. "When did she send you?"

"After you killed our Alpha and she replaced him." The guy who'd been pinned glared at me for forcing the answer from him. I didn't feel bad for invading his privacy, since he was one of the ones who chained the receptionist-turned-Alpha to the wall after coming to New York to tear my pack apart.

"You've got two options." Roman said, stepping back to me and scanning the men. "Attack me or my mate and die at my hands, or stay and bear the consequences for your actions, as decided when we learn the extent of them."

Personally, I'd rather they all die. But as much as we wanted to kill them, Roman and I weren't gods. That wasn't only up to us.

Roman was getting damn good at acting like we'd figured out Alpha shit we'd barely put in the works, and I definitely admired it.

One of the men lunged for Roman again. My mate sidestepped, catching the man by the throat and twisting.

A sickening snap echoed in the air before his body dropped to the floor.

"I've trained with professional fighters for nearly ten years." Roman said, his feigned calmness hiding the fury I felt coming off him. "Surrender or die."

One of the men glanced toward the room the women had run off to.

His mate.

He lifted his hands in the air, lowering to his knees.

I felt the slightest, tiniest bit of compassion for him. Only because he gave up for her.

"I surrender." He said.

The third man looked torn. His eyes moved from the body on the floor to the man kneeling with his arms up.

He gritted his teeth and lifted his hands, surrendering without lowering to his knees.

Roman grabbed the guys by their shirts, lifting the one to his feet.

"Where are the keys for the people you chained?" I asked, using my power again to get a true answer.

They directed me to a drawer in the kitchen. I went to dig through it, pulling out a ring of keys.

My eyes widened and met Roman's.

"How many people are locked up?" I asked them.

The reluctant guy met my gaze in a fiery glare.

"As many as wouldn't obey."

Roman shoved the guys through the door.

"Wait for the next elevator, please." His mind touched mine. *"I don't want these assholes near you any longer."*

I didn't think it was a big deal to be near them, but after seeing Roman's memory, I sure as hell wasn't going to argue. It had me a bit spooked. Not because of what I'd seen—as horrible as it was—but because of what it could mean.

More nightmares for the both of us. Roman living my hell, me living his.

"Sure. I'll talk to the women." I headed into the backroom, mind reeling until I saw the women.

They held knives, standing ready for a fight.

I raised my hands beside my head.

"I would never hurt you." I told them. "I know your friends. They came to me to free them from your Alpha after your change in leadership."

They lowered their weapons slightly.

I scanned them, head to toe. They were on guard and defensive; not as weak as they'd looked in the other room.

"My mate and I replaced the old Alphas of All. We're creating a justice system to punish people like them. One of your mates was killed already, and the others will probably die after their trials." I turned, leaving the room with the assumption they'd follow me.

They did.

"I can tell you've joined this pack seeing as you're in human form right now, but you may not be allowed to stay when the new Alphas take over." I warned.

They didn't seem to care.

"My mate isn't as bad as theirs." One of the women said, hurrying beside me. "I don't want him to die."

I sniffed the air, finding she was mated to the one who'd surrendered quickly.

"Then you can say that in his trial." I said.

But one woman's opinion of her own male wasn't enough to keep him alive if he was the kind of bastard willing to chain people to the damn walls.

We caught the elevator, heading up in silence.

CHAPTER 18

THE WOMEN and I made our way down the hall together. I didn't really trust them enough to let them go on their own, so I'd have to stick with them for a bit.

And though I wanted to free the receptionist, it was more important to get the men Roman had said were in bad shape, first.

I asked the women to stay outside while I stepped inside the room with the injured people. I could hear the women where I left them, so they wouldn't get away if they sympathized with their men more than they seemed too. Plus, from outside, they wouldn't be able to hurt the injured men for the same reason.

Though they seemed like they were glad to be rescued, I'd seen enough Alpha Females support their mates silently to know they might not be what they seemed. A woman had to use what she was given, after all. And sometimes that meant playing into how fragile people could think we were.

There were five men chained up—more than I expected, and all in wolf form. The only one I recognized was Thomas, so I tried keys in the lock until one worked. When he was unchained, I let him lead me to the one he trusted next.

Roman came in while we were unlocking that guy. He made quick work of unchaining the rest of the wolves while me and Thomas went over everything that had happened—in our minds. I could speak with my wolves mentally, almost the same way I spoke with Roman. It was much more difficult though, and sort of tired me out.

According to Thomas, Jett hadn't known anything about the Georgians until they showed up. When they appeared and threatened his life, he gave them free range in the skyscraper.

Jett did let most of the pack slowly disappear upstate while he acted as a puppet for the other men, though. The Georgians had only found out about the pack splitting the day before, which was when they'd nearly killed Thomas—who was apparently the upstate Alpha Male—and had chained the ex-receptionist, Molly.

The moment we all stepped back into the hallway where the women were still waiting, Thomas let out angry snarl. One of the women screamed, throwing herself at the Upstate Alpha. Her nails shifted to claws, her fangs aimed at his furry face.

"Easy." Roman caught the woman around the waist, dropping her back by her friends. I stepped between her and Thomas, looking to him first since we knew and trusted him.

"She spoke for the women and their mates." Thomas growled, stepping toward the woman. *"She's the ringleader."*

He looked straight at the one who had asked me to spare her mate.

I repeated his words out loud, and snarls and protests rang through the air from all sides.

"Enough." Roman boomed, ending the arguments. "We'll put the women in the cell with their mates, since they get along so well, and we'll figure out what to do with everyone in the morning. After we've all had time to calm down."

It was a smart move, and Roman shot me a tired half-smile when he felt my approval.

We escorted the three women to the jail cell, and Roman closed them in with their mates. He changed the passcode—to my birthday, I realized, when he told me mentally. We didn't trust even Thomas enough to let him have the code during the night.

After we unchained Molly, the receptionist/Alpha, she and Thomas took the keys to check out the rest of the building, to find the others who'd been locked up. Because there weren't labels on the keys, they'd have to go floor to floor together, no splitting up. But they were adamant that they'd take care of it, sending a few enforcers to check out the floors before they did to make it faster.

They assured us we'd "done enough" and told us to go to bed.

In the process, they made it clear that because of the deaths before I learned I was a ruby, they still didn't trust us.

And that was their right, so we went home.

Roman's fingerprint unlocked the fortress of safety that was our space. He twisted the knob on the door, swinging it open and leading me inside. Everything was exactly the way we'd left it, down to the blankets on the floor and the hospital-smell in the air.

Damn, it felt like ages ago that we'd last been there.

"I need a shower." Roman murmured, kissing my forehead and heading toward the bathroom. He was still a bit bloody from the wound on his abdomen and the fight with Jett.

I went into the bedroom, trailing my fingers over the comforter.

I'd been in a lot of places, moved too many times to count, and it had been years since I missed a place or my things there. But feeling the comforter that had warmed us as I laid in Roman's arms for so many nights, I missed this place.

Our apartment.

Our home.

It seemed silly, but I missed our things too. Our bed, our couch, our kitchen.

Our life.

I'd been born a ruby wolf, but I was reborn in New York. I became myself. I found people who loved me—and found people to love.

And I missed it when I had to leave.

"I don't want to stay in Ruby City." I spoke to the walls, sitting on the edge of our bed. "I want to live in New York."

Ruby City was just a place full of regular werewolves, run by Alphas who happened to be ruby wolves.

So why couldn't me and Roman make our own version of that, here? Why couldn't we turn the New York Pack into a new Ruby Pack?

There was the issue with the pack hating me, of course. And honestly, I deserved that. But the people were already in two groups; maybe we could change the way it was split. Haters and non-haters.

Yeah, it sounded ridiculous, but I still had a little hope. I always had a little hope. If I didn't, I would've lost the will to live a long time ago.

Standing up, I walked inside the closet. My fingers slid over the clothes, brushing the rows of fabric. Roman had more stuff than me when we left, but now there was a whole chunk of new clothing on my side of the space. It looked like my girls had spent a little more of the bet money they owed me. Hell, they'd probably already blown through it all.

A mental image hit me and I stopped in my tracks.

Roman had glanced down at his body—his dick standing ready for me—showing me abs and biceps.

Yum.

"Come join me." Roman murmured into my mind, showing me an image of his fingers sliding up and down his cock.

I wasted no time, stripping as I walked to the shower. When I stepped into Roman's arms, naked, he held me tight.

Skin on skin, our hearts thrumming together, some invisible part of me finally healed.

I wasn't alone.

I wasn't trapped.

I wasn't helpless, and I wasn't in pain.

I was free.

Free to love Roman, free to help women who'd been through the same hell I had. Free to live whatever life I wanted.

In that moment, in Roman's arms, safe and happy and loved, I knew exactly what I wanted to do with my freedom.

I wanted to make other people free.

And fate, in all her wisdom, gave me the one tool I needed to do that.

My damn red hair.

I laughed—a full-belly laugh, the kind that shakes your whole body.

Roman's lips tilted upward, though he looked a bit confused. Our minds weren't connected at that moment, so he couldn't read my thoughts.

"I really hope you're not laughing at how horny I am." He rumbled.

I grinned, going up on my tiptoes and kissing him, hard.

"I'm *always* laughing at how horny you are."

He growled at me, his nose finding my neck as he tilted my head to the side for better access. His teeth slid into my skin, and I gasped at the sudden shock of pleasure that had me arching into him, my body melting for him the way it always did. He claimed me with his teeth, his erection pushing against my core as he walked me into the shower's wall.

"It's not my fault you're so damn sexy." He released my neck, licking the wound as one of his hands found my boobs, the other on my ass.

"What part of me in particular has you so horny right now?" I teased, still catching my breath from his bite.

"You kneeling in front of me in that elevator, my dick against your boobs and your tongue on my skin."

"Should we replicate it?" I lifted an eyebrow.

"Hell yes." He growled, his hands finding my hips and moving up the curves of my side as I sank to my knees. His fingers tangled in my wet hair as I leaned toward him, his erection wedging against my chest while my tongue found his lower belly, my fingers wrapping around to the inside of his thighs as I slid down, lower.

Roman turned us, his back finding the wall as his hand tangled in my hair with the rest of his fingers.

My tongue went lower and lower, his hardness sliding against my chest, collarbone, and neck until I closed my lips around his erection.

Roman groaned, tugging on my hair, pulling me closer. My tongue slid up and down the bottom of him, and Roman's mind met mine.

"Fuck yeah. Harder, baby. Faster. Make me forget."

I took his thoughts as a challenge, ending the teasing to give him a real suck. His body quaked against me, every shred of his being at my mercy. No one else ever had or ever would see him like this—so completely vulnerable. And so completely mine.

"Always." The words were more intense, more real, when our beings were so connected. It would only get better when his dick was in me, but for now, I wanted to give him the escape he wanted. *"Only yours."*

He pushed himself further into my mouth and shuddered as I did what he wanted, faster and harder.

My fingers found his balls, and that was all it took. He lost it, his body shuddering as his orgasm shattered him.

I felt what he felt, the numbing bliss of the escape, though I didn't physically experience it myself.

Releasing my mouth from him, I swallowed and lifted my face to the water streaming from the showerhead above. Roman lifted me back to my feet and his hands found my body, stroking and feeling and petting in slow motions while I rinsed my hair.

"Thank you." He murmured out loud. "I think I needed that."

"I hope you need another." I said, grabbing the shampoo off the shelf that held it off to the side. It was my fancy hairdresser stuff—and I'd missed it when I was in Ruby City. It made my hair so damn soft.

"I think I need three more."

"Maybe four." I said.

"I'll give you six." He snagged the shampoo from my hand. "Suck me again and we'll make it twelve."

I rolled my eyes, biting back a grin.

He had the best sense of humor.

He squeezed the shampoo into his hand and lathered it against my scalp. I leaned into the feeling of his fingers on my skin.

"You should wash my hair for me every day." I told him.

"You should suck my dick for me every day." He countered.

"A scalp massage for a blowjob? Sounds fair."

He chuckled.

"Am I allowed to massage any other parts of you?" He grinned.

"I don't know. You'll have to test it out, to see if I like it before I agree to anything. Maybe you're not any good." I said, poker face on strong.

"That sounds fair, too." He agreed, rinsing the shampoo from my hair for me. "We already know I can do this." His fingers rubbed my scalp, the way he pushed eliciting a moan. He grabbed the conditioner for me, putting it all over my blood-colored strands before resuming his exploration of the rest of me.

"How's this?" He rubbed down my neck, thumbs pressing into my shoulders and rubbing over the muscles there.

I sighed, my ass pushing against his junk as I stepped back into him, lifting up so he could feel me against him. He was already hard again, ready for what was to come.

But the tension we liked to build was delicious, and neither of us would sacrifice that. It was just too damn much fun.

"Alright, you can rub me there." I moaned.

He murmured his agreement, his fingers sliding over my collarbone and finding my nipples. He pinched them, chuckling when I wriggled against him.

"Easy." I shot.

"You like it." His teeth scraped my neck as he palmed me. His dick throbbed against my ass as he felt me, squeezing and prodding and pinching and flicking.

Damn, that was good.

"Do I get the pass for this one?" He murmured.

"I guess." I mumbled, eyes closing as the back of my head rolled side to side on his collarbone.

His hands slid down my curves to my backside, gripping and squeezing and kneading.

"Damn, I love your ass." He growled, lifting me just a bit to rub me against his hardness.

"It's a nice ass." I agreed, lips curving as his hands slid back to my front without asking if he had my approval. We both knew he did.

My excitement rose as his fingers dipped toward my center, my stomach tightening as they brushed my core—before finding my thighs.

I groaned, and his chest rumbled against my back.

"Can't forget these beauties." He said, sliding down so he could massage my thigh with both hands. He focused on one, moving down to massage my calf as well before moving to the next one.

My body was crazy tense, but he moved down to my feet. I had to plant my palms against the wall, leaning over him to stay upright, when he lifted it off the ground, his thumbs gliding over the pads on my feet.

"How do you even have sexy feet?" He mused, thumbs stroking my arches in a way that had me imagining those same fingers on my center.

He lowered his lips to my feet, sucking one of my toes into his mouth.

Holy hell, I drove straight past horny and shattered. My body quivered, one of his hands catching my backside to keep me upright while the release shook me. And hot damn, it had to be one of the best I'd ever had.

Roman's chest rumbled his approval—probably having felt my orgasm the way I'd felt his—and his lips found my toes again.

I don't know why, but it was even hotter than when he sucked my fingers.

He massaged and sucked, paying more attention to my feet than he had most of my other parts. And after that one damn lick shattered me, I couldn't complain.

His hands trailed back up my thighs, stroking and rubbing and pushing. His tongue followed the trail his fingers made, leading up to my center. His thumb brushed over me, and I arched with a cry.

Roman kept rubbing and licking me, and the image of him on his knees while he devoured me body and soul was one I hoped to never forget. One of his fingers slid inside me, pumping into me while he stroked and licked. I climaxed again before my damn legs were too jelly-like to hold me up.

Roman lowered me over his pelvis, aligning his erection to my center. I moaned when he entered me, and held myself against him until we shattered together.

He dried us both and carried my floppy self to our bed. When he peeled back the comforter, the smells on it were stale and sickly.

"Blech."

He grinned, setting me down and dropping a kiss on my forehead while he swaggered to the hall closet to grab a clean set of sheets. I rolled off the bed, plopping to the floor while he switched the sheets.

"You did me too well." I groaned at him, the man still grinning like mad as he switched the sheets.

"Damn straight." He kept grinning.

"What's got you so perky?" I complained.

He laughed—the man actually *laughed* at my question.

"I felt you orgasm." He said, wearing a sexy-ass smug grin. "I orgasmed *with* you—four damn times. I'm the luckiest fucker alive. That's why I'm *perky*."

He finished changing the sheets. I started climbing to my feet—and stopped when he walked around the mattress to lift me to his chest.

"You're perky because of a few orgasms?" I lifted my eyebrows. "That's a good reason to feel like a gazillion bucks, but perky?"

He laughed again.

"It's not the orgasms, Hen. It's you. I'm perky because I just had the time of my life in the shower with you, and I feel better than I ever have. I'm perky because I've got you here, in my arms and in my bed, and our souls are so damn connected that I literally *felt* your orgasm. And I'm perky because I know that whatever comes next, I have the privilege of facing it at your side." He kissed my head and then my mouth, lowering me to the mattress and sliding in behind me to wrap his body around mine.

We were naked, but both too spent for it to be sexual.

"You've got to be the most perfect male specimen there ever was." I mumbled, my eyes starting to close. He chuckled, rumbling us both.

CHAPTER 19

We dozed until Roman's growling stomach woke us both up—sometime in the middle of the night. Then we ordered food, and I slipped into my favorite long-sleeved pizza shirt and some underwear while Roman went down to pick it up.

Before everything went down, his assistant would've grabbed the food for us. Now, he was likely upstate and we were on our own.

I kind of liked being on our own.

There was a knock at the door, and like a love-drunk idiot, I assumed it was Roman and opened it without peeking through the peephole. Maisy stood in the doorway, clutching her side. Her left eye was swollen, the start of a black eye forming. Her hands were covered in blood, spots of the stuff on the rest of her like it had been spraying toward her.

She fell toward the floor, and I lunged to catch her. Her arm went over my shoulder and I dragged her inside, closing the front door with my foot. Lowering her to the couch was a real struggle, but we landed on our asses without taking any real damage so that was a win. The blood on her didn't smell like her own, and I was fairly certain I could guess who it belonged to even though the smell wasn't familiar.

"What happened?" I forced my voice to come out gentle, not knowing exactly what had happened, though I had a sinking suspicion.

"I love him." She said, shock in her voice. "I love him. My mate. My husband. Jude. I love him."

"Of course you do." I kept my voice calm.

"I love him." She said, leaning into the couch. Her heart beat rapidly—so loudly my enhanced hearing could pick it up. And though she would soak the material in blood, I didn't give a rat's ass about our furniture when Roman's mom was sitting there, covered in his dad's blood.

"He's your mate." I said softly. "Of course you love him. Nothing changes that."

"He wouldn't stop hitting me, and I just—I just couldn't—and I lost my temper, and-" She stopped talking, breaking into sobs. She leaned into me, and I wrapped an arm around her to hold her, to comfort her. "I love him. I didn't mean to. I love him." Her tears soaked my shirt, and I tightened my arms around her.

The door to our apartment swung open. Roman said,

"The delivery guy couldn't find the damn skyscraper. You should've seen the way he gawked at me when—" He stopped, eyes landing on me and his mother. His fingers tightened around the bag of food.

He took a deep breath in, letting it out slowly before he walked to the kitchen and put our food on the counter.

"What happened?" His voice was neutral.

Maisy looked up at him, pleading with her eyes.

"I love him. I didn't mean to. He just—and I-" she bawled again, burying her face in my soaked pizza shirt.

"In your house?" Roman's voice stayed neutral.

She nodded against my boob. Roman's eyes met mine, and he shoved a hand over the ball cap on his head.

"I can't leave you here alone." He met my gaze. Whether it was for safety reasons, or because of the trials that were still haunting him, I didn't know. Either way, it didn't matter.

"We'll come and stay in the car while you fix things. It'll be nice." I forced my voice to sound cheerful. Only for Maisy; Roman and I didn't need cheery shit.

Roman nodded. He grabbed me some pants and then had to help me into them when Maisy wouldn't let go of me long enough for me to get dressed. We wrapped her in a blanket and dragged her out to Roman's truck, me scooting into the middle so I was between her and Roman.

His finger were tight on the steering wheel.

"You surviving?" I murmured mentally.

"I'm fine. This has happened before. My dad's always okay. Not that I'd care if she killed him; the fucker deserves it." His voice was dark, but still mostly neutral. He was forcing himself to stay calm, like I knew he would.

Because some feelings were too big to feel. And Roman was always the tough guy. When we were alone again, he would let himself feel it.

He parked in front of a giant house in the fanciest part of the city, catching my face and kissing me gently before he slid out of the driver's seat.

Maisy was huddled against the car's door, weeping. Her fingers were still wrapped around my bicep, her grip on me iron.

"I love him." She whispered. "I love him, I love him, I love him. It was an accident, I didn't mean—I'd never…"

"Of course." I patted the woman on the back.

The first time we'd met, she tried to strangle me—so I knew she was capable of serious violence. But she didn't need me to argue, she needed me to keep her from flipping her shit while Roman dealt with the damage.

Like the damn saint he was.

"Jude wasn't always horrible." Maisy wept. "He was so, so good. Determined not to become like his father. But we lost the baby, after my twins…" Her tears were thick, her whole body drooping with sadness. "He was so sad. And I was too, but it felt like my fault. It *was* my fault. So his drinking, the anger, the violence… it's my fault too."

I would've liked to argue the hell out of that statement. A miscarriage wasn't anyone's *fault*. And Jude turning into an abusive asshole meant he needed to learn to cope with his shit like the rest of us did. That was on no one but him.

But Maisy didn't need arguing. She needed therapy. And that wasn't my job, or Roman's job, or Arla's job, but the twins had more than done their part.

So I held Maisy, ignoring the memories of her hands on my neck. I'd never trust her—not completely—after what she'd done to me, but I could support her for a couple hours.

Roman came back to the truck ten minutes later. The scent of death was on his skin, and I met his grimace with my own.

Maisy had killed her mate.

And while the man deserved it, and Roman had considered doing the same dozens of times, Jude was still dead and Maisy would have to carry that.

Maisy reached toward Roman, weeping and wanting a hug. He leaned over me, his hand landing on my thigh while he gave her a half-hug.

"Where do you want to go?" I asked Maisy.

"Just let me stay with you." She bawled at Roman. His whole body seemed to deflate. His mom was a damn handful, and Roman was going through other shit with the trials too. "I can sleep in your apartment—do the cooking and cleaning. We can be a family."

I didn't have to see Roman's memories or read his mind to know that this was far from her first plea that they be a family. And that despite his father's death, Roman didn't want to build a relationship with his mom.

That was his right, and I'd do what I could to protect his freedom the same way he'd protected mine.

"You can stay in my guest room, but Henley and I are leaving after we get things sorted with this pack." Roman said, firmly.

His mother was far from stable enough to help us find our friends—and rule as Alphas of All. There was so much more me and Roman still needed to learn about what we had to do—and so many plans we still had to talk about and make.

"I'll come with you. I can take care of you, and-"

"You need help, mom." Roman said, his voice tired. "You've been abused for twenty years, and you just killed your mate. As much as he deserved it, a person doesn't take the life of the person their soul is bound to and walk away fine. You're going to stay in my apartment and go to therapy, or I'm going to check you in to a mental health facility where they'll force you to heal."

Maisy bawled harder. I was dripping in her salty tears, but her fingers still twisted into the fabric of my pizza shirt and clutched me tightly, turning me so my eyes met hers. There was a ferocious sort of desperation in her that I'd rarely seen in anyone.

"You'll let me come with you." She snarled at me.

I wasn't about to challenge her in her instability, but Roman didn't seem to have the same reservations.

"Take your hands off my mate or I'll throw you from this fucking truck." He said, voice calm but sharp.

"You wouldn't-"

"I would." There wasn't an ounce of hesitation in his voice. I believed him. *"Now."* This was more of a growl than what he'd said before.

"Roman-" She protested, fingers tightening and shifting so her claws scratched my skin.

The lock on the doors clicked when he hit the unlock button and she screamed, releasing me and jumping away from Roman's hand as he reached toward her.

Truthfully, I wasn't sure if he'd actually follow through with the threat. But nothing in his words or expression told me he wouldn't.

Maisy went from angry to scared to fucking *possessed*.

"You're nothing more than a spoiled child, always ungrateful for everything your father and I gave you. Even without the alcohol, you have become the worst parts of your father and—"

Roman had stood up for me, but he wouldn't stand up for himself. And I wasn't about to let him be threatened or mistreated any more than he'd let me.

"That's enough." I snarled. Though I didn't use my power on her—and wouldn't unless it was necessary—she shut her mouth. "Roman isn't Jude, and he's far too good to become like him. If you ever want to be around your children again, you'll check yourself into a facility, because without a really fancy letter from a damn good therapist, I'm not letting you near my mate. He is *nothing* like you and Jude."

"I can't believe you have the audacity to—"

"Think carefully about your next words, mother. Henley isn't just my mate; she's the Alpha Female of All."

He didn't mention what that made him.

She looked at me, lips parting and eyebrows furrowing as she opened her mouth to say something else—probably something that would piss me and Roman off, all things considered.

Before she could speak, Roman hit the button to turn the radio on. The heavy pounding of his typical rock music shook the car, cutting Maisy off. I smelled her fury on the air.

"Turn this noise off. This isn't music." She shouted, loudly enough that I could hear her over the "noise".

Roman turned it down a little, but not enough to really have a conversation over the noise.

It occurred to me then, that maybe he listened to rock music because it wasn't country or pop, the genres his parents were famous for singing.

...Or maybe he just liked the way the heavy bass could drown out your thoughts.

We pulled up in front of a building without a sign overhead, and I knew instantly it was the facility Roman had mentioned.

He shut the music off and stared forward.

"You have two options." He told his mom, without looking at her. He was so protective, it had to be killing him to do this. "You check yourself in and stay until the doctor gives you a clean bill of health, and I'll let you live near me and Arla.

"Or I can check you in as a concerned son, and you'll be forced to stay until they decide you're not a risk. Choose that option and you won't be welcome in our pack any longer—or near any future children we may or may not have. And if you take this moment to insult me, I'll understand you're choosing option two."

Maisy stared out the front windshield, her lips tight and her body tensing. Whatever remorse she'd been feeling after taking her mate's life seemed to have found a back seat to her anger at being forced to make a choice.

Finally, she undid the seatbelt I'd buckled over her hip. Her fingers latched on the doorknob, and she looked to me and Roman.

I waited for some final, inspiring words or a grand apology to the son who'd stood by her for so long. If this were a movie, there would've been one. But it was real life, and in real life, things were messier. The hero didn't always get an apology—and his family didn't always regret mistreating him.

Sometimes, you just had to accept life for the shitshow it was and move on. Get over it.

Even if I was horrible at doing that.

We stayed together in silence, watching through the glass doors as Maisy stepped up to the reception counter. She signed a few papers, and someone in scrubs came out of the back room to lead her further inside the building.

She never glanced back.

I wanted to know where Roman's head was at, but this was his shit we were dealing with. It was his turn to set the pace, his turn to decide how much to share. And truthfully, that was sort of unexplored territory for us. He knew much of the details of my past, but I'd never pushed to know his.

But I hoped he trusted me enough to share his pain at some point.

We sat there for a long few minutes, both of us silent and staring ahead.

Roman finally pulled out of the parking lot.

A few minutes later, he opened his mouth.

"I should feel worse." He said.

"Why?" I wasn't mincing words. Roman and I didn't really do that.

"My mom just fucking *murdered* my dad. I should feel bad, but when I saw his body, all I felt was *relief.* I was glad he was gone, Hen. He was my dad. Shouldn't I have felt bad?"

"Should I have felt bad when Ledger died?" I asked. Roman growled at me.

"He hurt you, but he wasn't family. It's different."

I nodded. It was different, definitely. To me, it seemed worse to be betrayed by the people who were supposed to love you.

He groaned and grabbed his hat off his head, throwing it at the windshield.

"I need a break for six damn minutes." He pulled off the road, into the parking lot of some place I hadn't been before.

"If we're asking for breaks, I'm going to ask for a hell of a lot more than six minutes." I tilted my head back, my hair sliding down the back of the center console turned seat that I still occupied.

"Good point. Let's make it six days. We'll go on a vacation again. The beach was nice."

"Six days? Where's your sense of adventure?" I teased. "We could take at least six *weeks*. Maybe six *months*."

"How about six years?" Roman's eyes softened, though his lips didn't tilt upward. "Where should we go?"

"Europe." I tilted my head to his shoulder. "I've never been to Europe. Heard they have great food."

"We can try pizza in Italy." Roman offered.

"And eat pastries in Paris." I sighed dramatically. "You could kiss me at the top of the Eiffel Tower, and I could finally give you your ring." I wiggled my fingers toward him, flashing my diamond and his wood band.

"We're not married, woman." He caught my fingers, tugging at the diamond.

"Says the bastard who'd happily introduce me as his wife."

"I've never introduced you as my wife." He countered. "You haven't said 'I do'."

"That can't be true."

"It is."

I thought about it, and couldn't think of a single time he'd actually called me his wife.

"So what, you want to do a real wedding? Trade vows and shit?" I lifted an eyebrow. "Seems a little too human to me."

"You're wearing a ring you bought yourself, Hen. We're mates, and we're permanent, but I won't call us married until you've said the words and signed the damn paper."

"Seriously?" I lifted an eyebrow. "Our souls are bound together. That's about as intense as it gets."

"Mating isn't marriage." Roman shrugged. "Sex and biting aren't the same as a verbal promises."

"Fine." I grabbed my phone out of the cupholder, googling "simple vows", clicking on the first result and scrolling past the ones that looked religious. I wasn't confident about what I did or didn't believe in, so I wasn't going to swear myself to Roman with something religious.

"Alright," I scooted across the bench, sliding onto Roman's lap so I straddled him, but not in a sexy way. Clearing my throat, I read the first line and looked into Roman's eyes. His hands found my hips, his grip soft.

"I Henley, take you, Roman, to be my wedded husband, and to live together in marriage." I looked to the phone for the next line, then looked back to Roman. His eyes were serious, his expression solemn. "I promise to love you, comfort you, honor and keep you."

Roman's lips lifted, just barely. His eyes were lighter, brighter. I read the last line, then met his gaze again.

"For better or worse, for richer or poorer, in sickness and health, and forsaking all others, I'll be faithful only to you."

The website added a "so long as we both shall live," but for me, my promise wouldn't end when one of us died. I'd honor my vows, even if our mating didn't bind our lives.

Roman took the phone from my hand, glancing down at the screen. He lifted his eyes a moment later, looking at me.

"I Roman promise to you, Henley, to stand by your side, to share and support your hopes and dreams." He lifted the tops of my fingers to his lips, pressing a soft kiss as his eyes didn't leave mine. "I vow to always be there for you. When you fall, I will catch you. When you cry, I will comfort you. When you laugh, I will share your joy."

My heart caught in my throat. Roman's vows were prettier than mine, and I didn't even care. Somehow, this moment in his truck after his father died and we'd dropped his mom at a facility, had become something cherished.

"No matter what lies ahead of us, I will see it as a journey that can only be completed together. I promise this now and forever."

We were quiet for a moment. I broke the silence by saying,

"I think this is where the minister would tell you to kiss me."

Roman chuckled, low and deep.

"I fucking love you, woman."

And kissed the hell out of my lips.

"You have to wear your ring now." I told him, sliding the comfortable weight off my middle finger.

"I'm buying you a diamond." He warned, letting me slide the giant ring on his huge-ass finger.

"I'm not giving up my ring." I fluttered it at Roman. He snagged my hand, tugging the jewel off despite my protests.

"I'll put it in a necklace." He pressed his lips for mine. Protesting, I tried to grab the ring, but he wrestled me until I gave up. "You'll like mine more." He promised.

I believed him.

We drove back, knowing our world wasn't done changing and there was no way to guess what the future would hold. But those things didn't matter, because we had each other. And we were permanent.

CHAPTER 20

When we got back to the apartment, we were both ready for bed. Unfortunately, there was too much shit to do. Sometimes being an adult really sucked.

The laws we had to throw together were at the top of our priority list. Neither of us was into politics or particularly liked rules, but maybe that made us better for the roles because we'd keep things simple and fair.

We showered off the blood. Roman hadn't had time to accept losing his parents, but we didn't have the time—something he knew as well as I did. Arla and the rest of the people we loved were likely trapped in Ruby City with my bitch of a stepmother, the New York Pack was falling apart, and there were still dozens of Alpha assholes we needed to replace.

But none of those things could be dealt with until the morning, so we needed to focus.

I pulled on some sleep shorts and one of Roman's long-sleeved tees while he stepped into sweats. He grabbed his computer, I grabbed a notebook from inside his nightstand, and we headed out to the living room so the bed wasn't a temptation.

We started by making a list of which packs we needed to visit—the worst-off first, the best last. Thanks to both our notes on his U.S. Alpha map in his computer, it wasn't difficult to figure that out.

We then decided we needed to come up with a basic draft of the werewolf rules; we weren't gods, and it shouldn't be up to us alone. We'd have a vote or something afterward, but for now, we'd focus on coming up with an outline.

"We've got to keep it simple." Roman said, opening up his laptop and connecting it to the giant TV on the wall so I could see his map of states.

Most were green or yellow—which had meant they weren't a threat to me, when Roman created the map. Those who were red had been a threat to me, and for the most part, they were the assholes we needed to focus on. Only a few were red, but they were our first priority after we got things sorted in Ruby City and with our friends.

"The basic rules should probably be to keep our existence a secret from humans and to respect both werewolf and human lives. Most people follow the first, but not so much the second." I said.

When Roman nodded, I scribbled it into the notebook.

"Laws would have to be more specific, though. If a man hurts his mate, he should be executed." Roman said.

I lifted an eyebrow.

"You'd have yourself executed if you ever hurt me, even if it was an accident?" I asked.

Roman leaned toward me.

"If I ever hurt you, I want you to rip my heart from my fucking chest yourself and then hang it from your ceiling like a chandelier."

Dark.

Really, really dark.

"Should we talk about the memory you flashed me earlier?" I asked, voice softening.

Roman's expression hardened.

"Not tonight, Hen." His hand found my thigh. "Not because I don't trust you, it's just… raw."

I could tell it was hard for him to admit so.

"Whenever you're ready." I kissed his cheek, scribbling 'execution' on my paper even though I was damn sure I didn't want to have anything to do with that part of our justice system. "We don't want to be the Alphas of All who murder everyone. There should be consequences less drastic for those whose crimes are less horrible. But everyone should have some consequence when they break a rule or law."

My mind went back to that night in the club, when Gunner had nearly killed a human man and he hadn't received so much as a slap on the wrist.

"A few nights in a jail cell should be for small things. But anyone who hurts someone—human or werewolf—should have a bigger punishment, a way to repay the person for what they did. I'm just not sure how we'd make that happen." I drummed my fingers on the table.

"Maybe they repay the packs as a whole, by doing some boring shit no one else volunteers for. We could have them on cleaning duty, or acting as assistants, or something like that." Roman suggested.

I thought the idea was moving toward where we wanted to be, so I wrote it down.

WE WERE up all night brainstorming, and when Thomas and Molly knocked to ask us to come deal with the pack, we had a tentative plan that would probably get ripped to shreds by our friends. But we were proud of it.

A conversation with the men and women from the Georgia pack determined that they'd broken too many laws—and ultimately, purposefully hurt too many people. Sylvie's command hadn't required the deaths of the people those couples had chosen to kill. We let Thomas and Molly take their lives, despite the foul taste in my mouth that caused, and headed upstate with the Alphas.

Thomas and Molly sat in the back of the truck. We'd needed a chance to talk to them, and this was the easiest way to get privacy while also getting where we needed to go.

"So, about you being Alphas." I said, opening what would undoubtedly be an awkward conversation.

"The pack won't follow you." Molly said without hesitation—and without emotion, too. She was remarkably good at keeping her feelings out of her judgement, and I liked her immensely for it. "Some of the people, maybe. But most won't."

I nodded. We'd expected that.

"We've got a proposition for you." I said. "We want to keep the New York Pack split. Most wolves will remain yours. Those who want to join our pack will become part of a new pack; our Ruby Pack. The Alpha of All Pack, I guess." We hadn't thought of a name for the pack Roman and I would run—we had bigger fish to fry.

"The Wolfsbane Pack." Roman corrected me.

Something in me turned.

Not my stomach, for once. Maybe my damn softening heart.

Up until recently, the name had been nothing but negative for me. But now it was engraved on my favorite collarbone—AKA, Roman's—and it was the name of the herb that gave me the chance to mate with the man I loved.

I couldn't hate it when I considered that.

"Would you want the upstate neighborhood or the skyscraper?" Thomas asked.

"Whichever pack is bigger at the time of the split should take the skyscraper permanently. If your pack is bigger, Roman will sign the building over in exchange for the properties in the neighborhood that belong to those who stay with you. If ours is bigger, we'll keep the skyscraper and do the same with the neighborhood for you."

The Alphas looked intrigued by the offer.

"That sounds fair." Molly said. "Some of the members might not be willing to part with their properties, but if it's that or having you lead, we can probably convince them by selling apartments rather than renting them the way you've been doing.."

"Your pack will have to shift with the moon, as you've realized." Roman reminded them.

They nodded.

Seemed like they were willing to sacrifice that.

"A lot of people from both packs need open access to the city for work, so we'd have to agree that everyone can enter and leave each other's land at all times without penalty." Roman added. "We'd be splitting peacefully, so we'd consider you our allies and you could rely on us to have your backs as long as you don't break the laws—which are still a work in progress, but you'll have a chance to vote on them.

"That sounds better than anything we've come up with." Molly admitted.

"I think it's the best way to keep the most people alive." Roman agreed. "And the most fair way to split."

We discussed logistics for the rest of the drive, calling it quits when we arrived upstate—where our pack's refugees were hiding out.

Or our old pack's refugees were hiding out, I guess.

After a long, drawn-out meeting, we gave everyone a few days to consider and spread the word while Roman and I went back to Ruby City.

• • •

We flew halfway to Idaho, landing in Minneapolis and grabbing a hotel room. The last time we flew, I'd had to store our wolfsbane in a little perfume container after dumping and cleaning it out, so that wasn't an issue.

I showered while Roman went for food—his choice, since he was the one who'd be fighting for us.

He was on his seventh trial—the one no one had made it past since the last woman who became a ruby wolf. Joel's grandmother, I believed.

And if everything went to shit, we were in the last hours of our lives.

I stepped out of the shower, wringing my hair out and drying myself. After I got dressed, putting on comfortable clothes that would be easy to get out of if this trial was as horrible as the earlier one and I needed to shift.

He still wasn't back, so I sat on my bed and dialed Roman's number.

"Hey." His voice was muffled, like his hand was over the speaker. I dropped to the bed.

"It doesn't take this long to get food." I told him.

"Nope." He didn't argue. I loved that we didn't lie to each other, even if it pissed me off sometimes too.

"What are you doing?" I pressed.

"Don't worry about it, Mrs. Ellis." He said.

I pushed hair off my face and reached my mind toward him. He blocked me out like a freaking brick wall.

"You'll find out soon." He said, humor in his voice. "Love you, Hen."

He hung up without giving me a chance to mirror his goodbye. I scrolled through my contacts, hitting Joel's number when I found it.

The phone rang, but went to voicemail. I tried Amy next, with the same results.

With a sigh, I dropped my phone on the nightstand.

We'd have four days after this to get everything sorted with the Ruby Pack. Then there would be another trial.

If the seventh—this one—was as rough as the sixth had been, realistically, we only had three full days to get that shit sorted. If it was worse, our time would be cut even slimmer.

But we would figure it out. We had to. There was no other option, because we wouldn't leave our people in Sylvie's hands.

Roman finally came back ten minutes before his trial needed to start. I was reading a kindle book on my phone, trying not to panic as the minutes ticked by and he was later and later.

"Where were you?" I demanded, dragging him to our bed and pushing him to the mattress. He lowered to the bed, lips quirking upward in a grin.

"Close your eyes." He said.

I scoffed.

"You're about to fight for your life. I'm not—"

"Close your eyes and shut that sexy, smart mouth of yours." He growled playfully.

How he was so happy before a trial was beyond me, but I finally obliged.

His fingers met my left hand, and I opened them as he slid a ring on my finger. Lifting my hand to check the jewelry out, I sat beside him and admired the damn gorgeous thing.

A tear-shaped diamond like my old one was haloed by small, glittering stones. Rose gold wrapped around all of them, the band delicate and sparkling. I'd never been into glittering jewelry before, but damn.

"Good job." I said, still admiring it.

"You approve?" He checked. "They didn't have time to use the diamond from your other ring, but-"

I shut him up with a kiss.

"It's perfect."

And then I stood.

"Now, roll up your sleeves. You've got to fight for our lives." I smacked him on the shoulder and he grabbed my hand, pressing his lips to the top of it.

"I love you, Hen. Whatever happens. You know that, right?" He looked up at me, his dark blues piercing.

"Duh." I forced a smile as he lowered himself to his back on the mattress, rolling his sleeve up to his bicep for me.

I filled the needle with wolfsbane, injecting it inside his elbow and ignoring my suddenly-queasy stomach.

Roman's eyes closed and his breathing evened as the drug worked on his system, drawing him into his seventh trial.

The first in the third category… Testing mental strength, according to Amy. I didn't remember which aspect of mental strength it was testing, but I was sure I'd see glimpses of it as Roman went through the trial.

I was right, to an extent. It was a long while later—maybe twenty minutes of pacing and trying not to panic—when I got something from Roman.

He wore armor like a damn knight and stood on a giant chessboard that sprawled out in front of him. Instead of chess pieces, there were groups of people. Some dead, some dying, and some shouting obscenities. Roman argued with a few other men in armor that matched his—I assumed they were all the leaders or something.

The mental images from Roman's vision spiraled away as fast as they had come on.

I itched to touch him, to step inside the trial and live it with him. But Amy said not to intervene, and I didn't have a death wish.

So I waited.

I saw two more flashes—both even shorter than the first—in four entire hours.

My eyes were getting tired, my body growing more tense, but Roman had never seemed worried when I saw him. He wore the knight armor like a damn hero, commanding his armies the way an ancient Alpha may have done.

Nine hours passed, the sun began to rise, and I tried not to panic. When I reached for Roman's mind, I found a wall blocking me out.

I watched his chest rise and fall obsessively, waiting for the breathing to stop. Waiting for both of us to die.

After over eleven hours, Roman's breathing finally changed.

There are no words to describe the level of relief that flooded me.

I threw myself at him, hugging him tightly as he left the trial. His arms wrapped around me, and he squeezed me too.

"How was it?" I breathed.

"Kind of fun." Roman admitted.

I lifted my head to meet his gaze and saw the ghost of a smile on his face.

"It was just a game of strategy. I won."

"Of course you did." I kissed him, hard.

He grabbed the comforter, pulling it over us.

"You're cold." He frowned at me.

"I was too nervous to care." I said, dropping my head to his chest and burying my nose against his neck. From there, all I could smell was his scent. And damn, he smelled good.

His fingers twisted in my hair.

"I'm so fucking glad it wasn't more torture." He murmured. "Not sure I'd survive that round again."

"You and me both." I agreed, wiggling my nose against his neck. He chuckled, the movement rumbling both of us. "Damn, I love it when you do that." I sighed happily. Like a damn fairytale princess.

"Do what?"

"Laugh." I squeezed him.

He laughed again, rumbling against me.

My fingers trailed up his face, feeling his neck and his stubble. It was longer than usual, so I reached for his hair. That was growing out too, longer than I'd ever seen it.

He'd buzz it when he shaved, I knew.

"Why do you wear your hair so short?" I asked. I'd looked at his head enough to know he wasn't balding early, so there had to be a story behind it.

"Why? You'd like me better if it was long?" A soft grin teased the edges of his lips.

"Definitely."

He caught my sarcasm, but his smile faded a little into seriousness.

"When I was sixteen, someone told me I looked like my dad. Said that between my hair and my eyes, I was a dead-ringer for him. I went home and shaved it off that night." He was still smiling, but the smile was more sad than anything else. "I've thought about letting it grow back, Arla said it makes me look more intimidating like this, so I've left it short in hopes that it'll keep my pack a little safer."

I nodded, lowering my nose back to his neck.

"I love it buzzed." I said. "And since my scars are gone, we need your scary-factor high."

His fingers twisted into my hair, and I moved my head to free a chunk that was trapped between us.

Some light coming in from a crack between the curtains hit my bright, ruby red strands as I moved.

"Do you miss the pink?" I asked Roman.

His obsession with my hair had gone far from unnoticed. I freaking loved it.

"I did at first." He said, wrapping the ruby strands tightly around his fingers and tugging softly enough not to hurt—but hard enough to make me horny. He knew exactly what he was doing, the sexy bastard. "But then I remembered that it's red because it's mine. Forever. Fuck pink; I'll kill to keep the red."

I laughed, and Roman's other hand ran down the curve of my back, running over my ass and squeezing. He grabbed my thigh, sliding it higher so I could feel his boner against my leg.

"You want to have sex now? You just finished the damn trial." I raised my eyebrows.

"Victory sex." He rubbed my thigh against his hardness—more for his benefit than mine, I thought. But his grin made me smile.

"I don't think that's a thing."

"It definitely is." He tugged my hair again before letting go, his hand sliding down my back and into my pants so he could squeeze my ass again—this time, from inside my pants. "Damn, that's a nice ass."

"That's a nice dick." I countered, rubbing my leg against him again.

He chuckled, rumbling his chest—just because I'd said I loved it.

Letting go of my ass, his fingers slid up to my bra and undid the clasps, sliding my shirt up and tugging it over my head when I lifted for him. Our chests pressed together, bare skin on bare skin, and I decided that had to be one of the best feelings in the world.

We made love and fell asleep together in the hotel bed.

And despite all the shit going down around us, life was so beautiful it almost hurt.

CHAPTER 21

After a few more hours on a plane the next morning, we landed in Spokane and rented a car, driving toward Ruby City.

We made it to the city around noon, driving straight to Roman's house. The scents there and in the houses on either side were stale, so we headed to the ruby mansion.

The people on the streets didn't pay us a shred of attention, which was probably for the better considering what had happened last time we saw them.

We slipped out of the car together. After we stepped up on the porch, Roman blocked my view of the doorway.

The door opened, and I went up on my tiptoes to see who it was. Her lips curled upward in something between disgust and pleasure.

She stepped back and held the door open, letting us inside. Roman's fingers caught mine, and we followed her in.

"We've been waiting for you." She said, leading us through the house and stopping in a living room I'd never been inside before. The lights were off, and the scents of sweat and anger made my nose twitch.

When my eyes landed on Hansen at the same time I smelled that he was the source of the anger and sweat, I halted.

My father was chained to the wall with the same chains we'd seen in New York.

The same chains that had been in Ledger's basement.

And suddenly, everything made sense.

Alphas finding me every time I moved to another pack.

The pain I'd experienced at the hand of almost all of them.

The uncontested cruelty time after time, pack after pack.

The insanity I'd seen in so many of their eyes, the crazed determination.

Sylvie was connected to all of it.

"You knew I existed." I said.

Sylvie sneered at me.

"Of course I did. He came home to *me*, smelling like *her*. I forced her to leave the pack, but I smelled the bastard child on her skin."

The shock of that revelation had me reeling.

Not every Alpha was violent and dangerous, but most of mine had been.

She must've forced them or broken them to the point of obedience so that when she told them where to find me, they would hurt me.

I'd thought Alphas in general were bad. I'd blamed the male population as a whole. I'd thought people with power were just shitty.

But I was completely wrong.

"You broke the Alpha's mind before he visited Georgia. Made him burn my family to the ground." I stared at her, revelation after revelation tumbling through my mind like a damn hurricane.

"If I couldn't have a child, Hazel couldn't either." She bared her teeth at me.

Her anger couldn't affect me anywhere near as badly as the rest of the shit she had done to me, even if that had been indirect.

"You left me and my mom alone for eight years." I said. "Why?"

"I was young and desperate and stupid. I assumed you'd be born a werewolf, not a ruby. And it took eight miserable years of tears and despair for me to realize what had happened. She stole my ruby child."

Damn, that was some messed-up logic.

"Why didn't you kill me, then?" I demanded. Roman took a step back, protecting me with most of his own body. His stance told me there was a threat nearby, but my mind was spinning too rapidly to notice. "There are always two pink ruby wolves, so why not kill me and have your own?"

Sylvie laughed darkly. She lifted her hand, and the wolves attacked. Six were on me in an instant, biting into my skin and ripping me from my mate.

I kicked one away, pushing power at them in attempt to force them to back down. It worked for a moment, but they were back on top of me even faster the second time.

Something closed around my wrists, and they burned as I fought, shooting power and kicking with everything I had. There were too many of them, though, and I was dragged toward the wall. Power spiraled from me, but slid off them like oil.

Like after the trial, my power alone wasn't enough to take complete control.

My back and head slammed into the plaster on the wall, chains locking around my wrists and ankles. Despite the new revelations Sylvie had given me, bad memories were still assaulting me with the feel of my wrists trapped like that. I shivered horribly, and fought to keep myself in the present so my mind would stay out of the horrors in my past.

"I kept you alive so Ezra would have a back-up if the trials failed to find someone more suitable. The Alphas I forced to abuse you should have broken you and made you compliant, so you'd mate with him to save your life."

What she didn't say coursed through my veins.

I wasn't broken—even after everything I'd lived through. I wasn't compliant or weak at all. I was strong—so damn strong I hadn't mated with the asshole willing to force me to give myself to him, even to save my own life.

"I never considered you might run from the Colorado Alpha—or meet one of the Alphas I hadn't gotten to yet."

She hadn't planned on me falling in love with him, either. Or him protecting me.

"Hansen didn't know." I said, tugging on the chains that held me. Roman was chained now too, locked to the wall with me and Hansen. Though we spoke about him, he didn't join the conversation.

Sylvie laughed humorlessly.

"Of course not. He's never gotten over the whore who gave birth to you. I knew that the moment he saw how much you looked like her, he'd never stand for me killing you. Now, he's not going to get a choice." She focused on Roman, bleeding and pissed, glaring at her like he was imagining his hands around her damn throat.

I was in his mind—and knew he was doing exactly that.

With nothing left to say, Sylvie started to walk away.

"Your life has been hard." I called, growing desperate as my freedom was taken from me again. "You think revenge will make you feel better, but it won't. The only thing that will make you feel better is getting away from the past, sipping margaritas on a beach somewhere in Europe, as far away from all the hell you've lived as you can get.

"My bank account is massive." I continued, since she'd turned to face me. "I'll put it in your name if you let us go. You'll have all the money you could ever want or need, and you'll be free from all of this."

It was a long shot, but I had to try.

Sylvie strode toward me, reaching for my face. Her fingers trailed over my forehead to my chin, and I remained still.

"I'm going to make you hate your mother for sleeping with my male. And then I'm going to remove your heart from your chest and watch the life that should've been my child's drain from your weak, repulsive body."

She tapped my nose, turning and striding out of the room.

The moment she was gone, Roman and I looked to each other.

"Are you hurt?" He demanded, at the same time I said,

"My family is fucking crazy."

"I'm fine." I gave him a tight smile. "The chains are bringing back some shitty memories, but that's to be expected."

Roman nodded, grimacing and tugging at them.

After that trial, he was probably fighting the same kind of memories I was.

"We've got two days and a few hours to get out of here." I looked back at the chains, studying the way they were connected to the walls. The damn things were as solid as any I'd ever seen, which didn't help anything. "After that, the wolfsbane in you will start killing you and Sylvie will probably watch with popcorn as we die together."

Then again, she wouldn't be able to see our hearts if she just watched on with popcorn while nature ran its course.

"I'm sure she doesn't want us to die that quickly." Roman growled, yanking the chains connected to his wrists.

They didn't even seem to budge at all.

He snarled, rearing back and throwing himself as hard as he could to see if he could use his weight to break the metal restraints. When he crashed against the end of the chains, jerking his body painfully enough it brought tears to *my* eyes, a string of curses left his mouth.

"I've been trying to escape for days." My father said, his eyes full of pain and expression dark. He looked like he was on the verge of death —it was no wonder he hadn't thrown his power into the fight to help me. "I didn't know she was this twisted. I'm so, so sorry."

"It's not your fault." I told him, frustration building as I pushed back another damn round of shitty memories.

"Fuck this." Roman snarled as he ripped at the chains again and again.

The torture was more raw for him, even though I had some of his trial-memories in my own head too.

I stepped as far toward him as my bindings would allow me to. He stopped fighting when he saw what I was doing, and did the same Our fingertips barely brushed before the chains pulled us to a stop.

"Are Amy and Joel okay?" I asked Hansen.

"I don't know." He admitted. "I believe so, but I have no way to be sure. The last time I saw them, I found them locked in her office. My parents were about to take them somewhere safe, when Sylvie realized what I knew. She made her move, then, and I've heard nothing about your friends or my parents since."

I nodded, eyes closing tightly as I ran through our options and came up with nothing.

At least our family and friends were probably okay. That was something.

"We'll figure a way out of this." Roman's mind touched mine, though I could feel the worry behind his words.

"I love you." I told him.

"I love you too." He murmured out loud. "And if that's your way of saying goodbye, then when we get back to New York, I'm going to force an entire damn pineapple pizza down your sexy little throat."

I flashed him a smirk, loving the glint in his eyes.

"That sounded like a challenge, Romeo."

"Oh, it was."

We chatted—out loud, bringing Hansen into the conversation—until we were tired of talking, and then we sat on the floor, as close to each other as our chains allowed us to be. Acting like we weren't chained up and sitting on the floor in his living room, trading stories and experiences, made me feel closer to my father than I ever had.

And closer to my mother, as she was the star in most of his favorite memories.

There was no amount of pain Sylvie could inflict that would make me dislike the woman who loved me for the first eight years of my life. That, I was sure of.

WHEN SYLVIE RETURNED, hours upon hours had passed.

My mouth was dry, my stomach rumbling alongside Roman's.

But when I saw the knife in her fingers and the darkness in her eyes, my survival instincts kicked into gear, my heart rate picking up.

I knew the feel of steel parting my skin. Knew the pain of my blood on someone else's hands. And I'd protect myself and my mate from it in any way I could.

I gathered my power as she approached Roman.

Her knife met his cheek, and I exploded.

"Step back." I commanded, throwing everything I had at her.

It was more than I'd pushed at the Alphas we faced, and more than I'd used on Jett and the men from Georgia. Hell, it was more than I'd used to spare my own damn life when her people were chaining me.

But for Roman, I threw everything I had.

It hit Sylvie and she laughed, turning to me instead. Roman roared, ripping against the chains, struggling against the iron holding him back as she moved toward me instead.

"Don't touch her." He snarled, ripping and yanking. The iron scent of his blood touched the air, and my chest tightened.

His mind clutched mine, and I felt it when something inside him snapped into place.

His power.

It rushed out of Hansen and into Roman in a tsunami, crashing into him and somehow managing to make my mountain of a man seem even taller and stronger.

Sylvie didn't notice, her knife moving toward my neck. As she nicked the base of my throat, Roman attacked.

Where my power was a brick wall, his moved like a freight train. It slammed into Sylvie, and she dropped her knife and reached for her heart as she skidded backward, her movements uncontrolled.

"You shouldn't have access to your power." Her gaze snapped to Hansen, slouching further now. "And you shouldn't be able to control me. Amy said-" Her words stopped abruptly, and I could smell her horror—which was rapidly replaced with fear, and then anger. "She lied."

Like she couldn't believe Amy would lie to her.

"Release us." Roman slammed his power into her again. This time, she was ready for it and fought against the power, her own anger and hatred fighting off Roman's ability to control her.

There was a new fear in her, and I could still smell it alongside her fury. She wasn't as sure as she had before, when she threatened to watch the life drain from my heart. Strolling from the room like we couldn't smell how terrified she was, she left.

No one replaced her.

"I didn't know you were far enough in the trials to use Alpha power yet." Hansen's voice was quieter than before.

"I didn't either." Roman admitted.

His eyes swept my body until he was satisfied that I was uninjured besides the small cut on my throat. Then he gestured to the floor, where Sylvie had dropped the knife she'd threatened us with.

"Kick that knife over to me?" He asked. I did as he'd asked, and he caught it with the side of his shoe, bending down to pick it up.

Straightening, he stuck the knife in the keyhole over my wrist, wiggling it around. The weapon would be useless against the bolts holding it to the wall, so picking the lock was our only real chance. And doing it with a knife? Really unlikely.

"She'll be ready next time, so we've got to get out before then." Roman said, voice as hard as the chains holding us. "Why hasn't she just killed you for the power?"

Hansen answered for us both.

"Because if she kills you two, the power goes back into the Ruby Elders. She's always respected my mother, and wouldn't be willing to kill her to get the power back."

Roman focused back on the lock, jiggling the knife in the keyhole. I winced at his lack of precision.

"Do you know how to pick locks?" I asked him.

"Not a clue." He growled, jamming it to the side.

"Easy." I stepped toward him, as far as my chains would let me. "You'll break the tip off, and then you really won't have a chance.

He looked to me. I felt Hansen's eyes on me too.

"You know how to pick locks." Roman said.

I thought it was obvious.

"Of course I do. If you get trapped in a room, you just use your giant-ass self to kick the door in or ram it down or something. When I get trapped in a room, I've got to find another way out. And I've been trapped in more than my fair share of rooms." I said. "I haven't picked a lock in a few years, though. No idea if I can still do it. Even if I can, I doubt it's possible with a knife."

Roman set the knife down and gently kicked it my way.

"You're our best bet." He said.

Hansen muttered his agreement.

I grabbed the weapon, sitting on my ass and lifting the tip to the keyhole. Getting the damn thing unlocked with regular lock-picking tools would've been difficult. With a knife? The odds were pretty much zero.

But I didn't want to die chained to *another* wall, so I tried anyway.

"You really didn't know that I existed?" I glanced at Hansen. In my month in Ruby City, I'd only seen him a few times. Never for long enough to have a conversation, just the two of us, and never to ask about that. "Because I swear if you're working with her to mess with me, I'll kill you."

"You'd have to get in line." Roman growled mentally.

"If I'd known you existed, you would've been raised here. We would've been a family. Hazel would've gotten over me and mated with a better wolf, and Sylvie would've been a real stepmother. A good one, too. She was always good with Ezra." He said, his voice hollow.

I studied him, pausing with my knife in the keyhole.

There was a slouch of his shoulders, a lack of fight I'd never noticed before he knew about me. A haunted look in his eyes, too.

I didn't blame him for feeling hollow and disturbed. If I found out I had a secret daughter who'd been abused by my mate for more than a decade, I'd be shattered in so many pieces there would be no recovering.

"It would've been a good life." I finally said, looking back to the knife.

Maybe it would've been, but it hadn't happened. Now, it was too late. I wasn't the kind of person to dwell on the past, but I said it to make him feel less shitty if I could.

"I would give up my very soul to have had that." My dad said, his words quiet but rough. "And I'll do whatever it takes to make sure your children get to have that life."

Yeah, if Roman and I had kids, Hansen would have nothing to do with how and where they were raised. But I wasn't going to crush his dreams; there was no harm in letting him hope and wish.

"Protecting them isn't going to be up to you." Roman warned.

"I would never try to take that privilege from you." My dad's words were quiet. "Sylvie is my mate, so she's my responsibility. I'll do what's required to keep her from hurting you again."

I glanced at him, eyes narrowing.

"You'd be killing yourself if you took her life."

"Death would be a gift after what I've learned this past month." The words were angry, but he just sounded tired. "I've been so stupid."

"We'll find a way to deal with her without killing her. There are prisons that hold people for life; we can build something like that." Roman said. Werewolves were always careful to keep our people out of human prisons. The chance of keeping our existence a secret in a place that was slim to none.

When neither of us said anything about the jail thing, Roman changed the subject. "Getting close?" He asked me, trying to step closer and swearing when the chains tugged him back.

I laughed humorlessly.

"Yeah, right. This is like trying to cut hair with a wooden stick." I pushed my own strands from my face.

"You'll get it." Roman said.

I snorted.

"You will." Hansen insisted.

I don't know how long we sat there, mouths drying and stomachs rumbling while my hands began to shake, but I still kept trying to pick the damn lock.

CHAPTER 22

I WAS PRETTY sure I was on the verge of having dehydration hallucinations when someone finally brought us water. I'd given up on lock-picking with the knife earlier when I trembled so badly I nearly cut my finger off.

The guy who came in with water was a man I didn't recognize, and he kept his eyes down as he set water glasses down in front of each of us.

"Did Sylvie send you in as some kind of sacrifice?" I asked, not bothering with my power when I was nearly positive she had.

"It's my honor to serve the ruby wolves." He murmured, bowing his head.

No doubt she'd decided to send a male inside with the hope that Roman wouldn't have a chance to learn to control his power on a woman. But after all his years as Alpha of New York, I was fairly confident he wouldn't have a problem with control. Ruby power worked pretty much the same as regular Alpha power.

"What did she put in this?" Hansen asked the guy who'd brought it in. His voice wasn't unkind, just tired and scratchy.

"It's my honor to serve the ruby wolves." The guy repeated, before leaving the room.

Picking the glass up, I sniffed the liquid inside. It smelled like water, but that didn't necessarily mean anything.

"Should we take the risk?" Hansen wondered, looking to me and Roman.

"Probably not." Roman sniffed his glass too. I knew his expressions well enough to know he hadn't smelled anything out of the ordinary.

"We don't have much of a choice. I don't know the exact timeframe, but if we don't drink soon, our bodies will start to shut down. I've been there, and it sucks." I swirled my cup around, looking for anything floating. "If there's anything in the water, it's probably the same shit she and Ezra drugged me with."

Roman's expression darkened.

"We could just sip at it." Hansen said. "We'd be affected by the drug less if we only drink small quantities."

He might have been right, but I didn't understand medicine or drugs well enough to say if that was true.

"Both of you should drink." Roman said. "I'll wait to see how it affects you two. I'm the only one who might be able to stop her if she comes back in, anyway."

Hansen and I agreed.

"Bottoms up." I lifted my glass in the air toward my dad.

"To second chances." He said, lifting his glass toward mine.

"And secret daughters." I sipped the water.

Damn, it tasted good.

Hansen sipped, his lips curving slightly upward as he looked at me.

"Hazel would be so proud to have a daughter as strong as you." He said.

Since they'd been in love and he'd known her better than anyone, it was probably true. And that warmed my damn heart.

I would always admire my mother, regardless of what Sylvie or anyone else said about her. She was the woman who'd loved me, who'd carried me to Georgia to protect me, and who had died still trying to keep me safe. She was a damned saint.

I took another sip, and another.

My body loosened by the minute.

"Definitely drugged." I mumbled, my mouth feeling dry again while my head spun a bit.

"I've got you." Roman said, reaching his hand to the edge of the chains as we'd taken to doing. I met his with mine, the tips of our fingers barely connecting.

Since it was going to knock me out anyway, I swallowed the rest of the water and shut my eyes.

When I opened them again, we were in the same places. Roman snored away, having drunk his own glass, and Hansen was awake, watching us both.

"How long was I out?" I asked, groggy still.

"Hard to say." He said softly. "Roman was getting dizzy from the dehydration, had to drink."

I nodded.

He couldn't always be the hero, after all. I just hoped Sylvie didn't come back while he was out.

Of course, we couldn't be that lucky.

She came waltzing in, sealed water bottles in her hands. And hot damn, I'd do just about anything for a bottle of untainted water.

The fancy cocktail dress she had on was my first warning that this wasn't going to go my way.

"What do you want, Sylvie?" Hansen eyed her warily. I couldn't imagine what he was feeling. They hadn't really liked each other, but finding out you'd shared a bed with someone so terrible had to hurt.

She flashed him a smirk, eyes traveling over Roman to land on me. Her smile widened.

Shit.

This wasn't going to be good.

Crossing the room, she grabbed my chains and unlocked them.

"Just like that?" I lifted an eyebrow.

I could've attacked her, but I wanted to see what she had planned first.

"Just like that." Her smile widened as she spun on tall stilettos. "Tonight's going to be the night of your mate's eighth trial—or it's going to be the night you both die. If you want the wolfsbane that will trigger his trial, you'll have to do what I tell you to do." She said.

"What do you want?" I followed her out of the room, into the hall.

"Give your power back to me, permanently." She said as we went. "In front of everyone who attends the gala."

"Should I know what gala you're talking about?" I asked, even as I thought back to Christmas, all those months ago.

"The Annual Gala for Influential Werewolves." Sylvie waved me into what I knew was a large bathroom. "It was postponed until now, at his mother's insistence. She funds the whole thing." Sylvie scoffed. "Put the dress and makeup on. You have to make it believable if you want to keep yourself and your mate alive." She said, slamming the door shut and locking me in the bathroom.

I stared at myself in the mirror.

There were lines beneath my eyes. My hazels were dull, my hair greasy and tangled. I didn't look great, but I looked a hell of a lot better than I had when I was dying.

Funny how that had become my way to measure my appearance.

I grimaced at the frilly dress hanging off the door. Light pink, made entirely of lace and tulle, the damn thing was strapless and fluffy. I'd look like a cake in it.

There wasn't another choice that I could see though, so I quickly washed what I could of my body in the sink to remove any stink, and stepped into the cake dress. I had to contort my arms to zip myself into the thing, but I made it work.

After it was on, I turned to study myself again.

Damn, I looked ridiculous.

I dry-shampooed the hell out of my roots, leaving my hair big and messy and dramatic. Grabbing makeup off the counter, I put the eyeliner on thick and layered my mascara on like a fiend.

There wasn't much I could do to the dress, but I shifted my fingers to claws, slicing a few of the layers of tulle from the inside to shrink the dress and make it sheer enough that you could see my legs through the skirt.

That change didn't do much for the dress's overall girlishness, but it helped with the volume and the frills.

Sliding my feet into the flats Sylvie provided, I stepped out of the bathroom just as she came to get me.

Her expression was flat when she saw me. Whatever she was feeling, it didn't show on her face.

This didn't seem like the ultimate *make-you-regret-living* torture she'd promised, but I guess her plan had to change when she realized Roman could control her.

But then again, she'd gotten me away from him, so it seemed like she could pretty much do whatever the hell she wanted to me now.

"What will people think when Hansen's not at the party with you?" I asked. Not mentioning that they'd have even more questions when Roman wasn't there with me.

"Everyone who's met us knows I'm more powerful than him. Female ruby wolves are stronger than males because we control men." She said, like it was obvious.

I didn't reply.

If I had, I'd have called bullshit on that. Male wolves were physically stronger, sure, but females were more manipulative and often more vicious.

"Most people didn't know why my hair was so red." I said. "Have you always gone to galas like this?"

Sylvie scoffed.

"I don't make a habit of spending time with regular wolves, no. They're holding the gala here to honor the first time the Alphas of All will deign to attend their little party."

I knew why she'd decided to make this her first appearance. I'd forced her into it when I started replacing Alphas, declaring me and Roman the Alphas of All.

We slid into a limo together, just the two of us. Angering her wouldn't get my dad or mate anywhere, so I kept my mouth shut through the drive, only opening it to eat the food she had in a basket by the door—all the bags and packages sealed until I got them. So, safe.

I guess having me pass out from hunger and thirst while giving back her power wouldn't do her any good.

We pulled up to a massive building I hadn't seen before. The kind of building you would expect the pack to use when announcing that they'd found a ruby wolf who had been in hiding, or when there was someone new attempting the trials in an attempt to become a ruby.

But I guess that's where Sylvie came in, cock-blocking us in ways we hadn't even realized.

Every time I thought about her setting up the shit in my past, I had to force my fists not to clench. Had to resist shifting and ripping her to shreds. If she wasn't connected to Hansen, I would've done it. Because I'd suffered so damn much, and it was all because of her.

I hadn't just been hurt; *she* had hurt me.

Repeatedly.

In so many ways, I wanted to scream just thinking about it.

But I kept my damn mouth shut and my claws to myself, because I wasn't sure I could live with being the chick who killed her own father. And when we parked, I followed Sylvie inside that damn massive building.

We stepped inside the grand entrance, and walked down a short hall before reaching a staircase that led down into what I imagined was a gigantic ballroom. There was music playing, and the sounds and scents of many werewolves.

Sylvie left me in the hall, and I heard the music change. Someone with a microphone announced her name. I didn't have to imagine the overly sweet smile plastered on her face or the self-assured way she held herself.

When I stepped down the fancy staircase, the music shouldn't have changed like it did for Sylvie. But it did, and I felt the stares on me even as I focused my gaze straight ahead. Trying to look stronger than my frilly dress, trying not to show what I was thinking.

I was thinking that I shouldn't have been walking into that party alone. I should've been walking in on the arm of the yummiest man on the damn planet, and I should've been grinning at whatever he was saying to me mentally. And I should've danced the damn night away like a freaking princess in his arms, wondering how the hell I'd gotten so lucky.

Instead, my flats were silent against the stairs. My fingers curled around the railing.

My hair fell around my shoulders, ruby red without a hint of the pink some of the attendees might have expected.

And the room went silent, every eye and every ear on me.

I didn't look at a single one of them. The only person I let my gaze land on was Sylvie.

And she was *pissed.*

The feeling was mutual.

Her fingers wrapped around my bicep as I stepped off the final stair, and she tugged. Since I was in flats, I didn't stumble. She dragged me to the side of the room, and I hit her with my most neutral stare.

"Take your hands off me *now*." My face didn't give away my emotions, but I hoped she could smell my fury the way I could smell hers.

"I'm in charge here." Sylvie hissed, her face going red somehow despite the thick layer of makeup she wore.

And in that moment, I actually felt a little bad for her.

Her life had sucked in a lot of ways—and parts of that were probably my mom's fault.

But that wasn't an excuse for her to abuse an eight-year-old girl. There was no excuse for forcing a child to watch her mother die, or to have her branded like a fucking farm animal and then hurt by powerful men time and time again.

Maybe I'd accepted the tattoo on my collarbone and the nickname that came with it, but I sure as hell would never accept the way and reason it had been forced upon me.

"You may be running the show as far as I'm concerned, but don't think for a second that anyone in this room would obey you over me." I said softly, putting as much venom into the words as I could. "You're a ruby wolf, but *I* am the Alpha."

She snarled, but I didn't flinch.

Not in front of the woman who'd been the source of so damn much pain.

"Careful, Sylvie. Your insecurity is showing." I spun away from her, somehow landing in the arms of one of my favorite people.

"Joel." A smile curved my lips.

I'd stopped worrying about him when Hansen told us he'd helped his parents and my friends escape, but it was still good to see in person that he was fine.

"Henley." He ducked his head, leading me across the dance floor. "One must be careful when they poke a bear." He said, a grin teasing his lips.

"All it takes is a couple of wolves to bring down a grizzly." My eyes lit. "Tell me you have a way to free Roman and Hansen."

I didn't care who was listening, or what they heard. If news spread that Sylvie was holding her mate and mine hostage, I hoped attitudes would change toward her and people would actually want to help us.

"We're working on it." He said, his grin holding as he spun me away from him and then back into his arms. "Sorry we couldn't answer your calls. Sylvie's taken to tracing phones."

Ah.

I nodded.

"She's going to make me give her the power back." I warned.

"Don't." He said, spinning me into the arms of another man.

I inhaled sharply as my hazel eyes met my favorite dark blues.

"How?" I demanded.

"My sister's almost as resourceful as I am." Roman's eyes were soft, staring into mine as he spun us around the dance floor. He still looked tired—those drugs were serious shit.

"Nearly? We both know Arla makes a better rich person than you." I said, teasing a smile from him. He dipped me low, curving me in an arch before lifting me back to him so our chests met.

"When did you learn to dance?" I asked, a bit out of breath.

"My parents are famous. Dance class was one of my chores." He said, twirling me.

I felt eyes on us; Roman in his sexy-ass tux and me in this awful frilly dress.

"So what's the plan?" I asked, our bodies practically glued together as Roman did all the work in leading us across the floor.

"This was the extent of it." His lips twitched. "None of our people understand what's going on. I doubt Joel and Amy know the full extent of what's been going on, or for how long. They went off the grid to protect themselves and our friends from Sylvie, but that didn't clue them in to her plans."

"So they didn't know Sylvie was the one making demented Alphas and torturing me throughout my life?" I lifted an eyebrow. He nodded.

"Wasn't sure you'd want to tell anyone." He glanced left and right. People were gawking at us, whispering loudly, but I didn't pay them any attention.

"Secrets and lies fester in the dark, Romeo. It's time to bring everything into the light."

Roman studied me for a long few minutes before bobbing his head and leading me toward the staircase.

Sylvie followed us up, reaching for my arm about halfway up. Roman spun me away from her, snarling at the woman.

"You'll never touch my mate again."

The music halted.

Whoever controlled the damn stereo must've had a real taste for drama.

Sylvie looked to the crowd, her face red and borderline purple as she stared out at the people. Somewhere in the massive crowd was Arla, Jamie, and London. And damn, I missed them. We needed a seriously long girl's day after this shit was over.

"Roman Ellis and Henley Clark have been planning to take the Alpha of All positions since they met." Sylvie announced, her face still flushed and her hair wild as she called to the crowd, attempting damage control before any damage was done. "They've been killing Alphas, trying to set up worse leadership while I struggled to keep the peace."

People below us exchanged confused looks.

Probably because Sylvie had never kept the peace a damn day in her life. Or, more likely, because they had no idea what was going on.

None of the werewolves below knew what it meant to be a ruby wolf —or even that there was such a thing. I hadn't known, and I *was* one.

"It's time for the truth to come out." I shouted to the crowd.

To hell with being tactful or winning people's trust.

They could take the truth and think what they wanted, because the lies and secrets weren't getting us anywhere worth going.

"I am a ruby wolf. It's why this word," I tugged the top of my dress down to expose my collarbone, and the ink there. "Was tattooed on my skin at eight years old. People in my pack don't shift when the moon comes up, and it's because of the color of my hair. Ruby wolves are—"

Sylvie cut me off with a shout as she slammed her stiletto into the back of Roman's knee and dove toward me. Roman ripped her away from me before we collided, and the two of them rolled down the stairs together in flashes of skin, fabric, and ruby hair.

The crowd gasped, moving backward as one, and a sound like thunder clapped through the room. I realized it wasn't thunder, but the sound of many doors being opened at once.

And then the occupants of Ruby City were flooding the room.

Wolves and humans charged the Influential Werewolves who'd come for the gala, and suddenly, my hair wasn't the reddest thing in the room.

Blood spurted and flowed, fur and fangs and skin clashing.

What had started as a party had turned into a battle.

And I had no clue how to stop it.

CHAPTER 23

The building shook with snarls, howls, and roars.

My options were to let the fight continue, or do something about it.

The latter was the obvious choice, but I couldn't exactly battle my way to peace like Roman could.

So I shifted forms, tearing through the girlish lace and tulle that hadn't accomplished a shred of whatever Sylvie hoped when she bought it, and howled.

Power coursed through me and into my cry, halting every man and some of the women in the crowd for half a second. Without the pressure of more ruby power from Roman, those who'd been stopped ripped themselves free of me.

"Help." I snarled to my mate, wherever he was in the crowd.

I saw a flash of red and a flying fist off to my right, and then Roman was howling. His cry pierced what mine couldn't, crashing through the walls of the wolves who refused to follow my command and slamming his will upon them.

I howled again, this time with my mate, and a massive shudder shook the crowd.

And then every person in the damn place joined in. Some responded to our cry instantly, howling with us. Others fought the pull of our voices and power for as long as they could, giving out and joining in when they couldn't fight any longer.

Our voices merged, everyone there howling as one. Even the building seemed to shudder beneath the combined strength of every werewolf in the room.

And when the howl faded, leaving silence and calming peace in its wake, I traded my fur for skin once again. Roman would hate me standing in front of all these people in the nude, but it felt necessary to speak to them in my barest, most vulnerable form.

I'd been reluctant to lead since the first time Roman asked me to be Alpha Female of the New York Pack, but the time for reluctance was over. It was time to accept the future I'd been born into.

"We have been fighting for too long." I lifted my voice, the way I'd lifted my howl. "My name is Henley Ellis, but most of you know me as Wolfsbane. I am a ruby wolf, born to be an Alpha of All. I've bled and suffered for this role, and I will fight tooth and nail to keep it. My mate, Roman Ellis, has nearly completed the trials that have taken the lives of dozens who've considered themselves worthy to lead as a ruby. He will lead the packs with me."

Silence echoed, and my black wolf leaped up the stairs to stand in front of me, glowering out at the crowd. Daring them to disagree.

And covering me up with his damn body.

No one spoke, and I hoped they weren't getting ready to try to kill us.

My father stepped up the stairs, and everyone watched him move. Everyone but me; I didn't want a glimpse of his junk.

"Many of you prefer the old ways of the Alpha challenges to determine who leads." He spoke loudly, with more confidence than I'd seen him before. "You prefer to see someone fight for the right to lead; to prove their worthiness by proving their strength. So I challenge Roman Ellis for the role of Alpha of All."

It took a moment for what he was saying to set in. Both for me, and everyone else in the room.

A challenge for Alpha always ended in death.

And then the crowd was cheering, their voices raised to the heavens. Because they all knew or knew *of* Roman Ellis, and he had never lost a challenge.

I spun to my father.

"What are you doing?" I demanded.

His lips lifted sadly.

"Making up for the damage I've done."

Roman's mind didn't touch mine, his wolf eyes meeting my father's instead. I imagined that if Roman mentally reached for Hansen, the men could communicate mentally, similar to the way I'd been able to speak to Thomas in New York.

"Hennie." Jamie's voice was barely a brush. She and London maneuvered some piece of clothing over my head—probably at my mate's request. If anyone else had tried to touch me, I'd have fought them off. But my girls, I trusted.

"Don't do this." I said to my dad.

I knew what he'd planned.

Roman wouldn't submit in the Alpha fight. And he wouldn't lose; he never lost. If Roman was fighting for both of our lives, he'd fight like a damn monster.

All of which Hansen knew.

Which meant he was sacrificing himself to rid the world of his mate.

Roman licked my arm before he descended the stairs with Hansen, and I did the only thing I could think to do.

The only thing that would keep my father's blood off the hands of the man I loved.

I opened my mouth and said,

"I challenge Sylvie for the role of Alpha Female of All."

There was no guarantee it would work. Since I was the current Alpha of All, it would be easy for her to turn down the fight. But I had the feeling she wouldn't, because anyone with eyes could see that Roman was a better fighter than I was. Sylvie's best chance at staying alive was killing me, something she'd always wanted to do.

Roman and Hansen stopped where they were, at the bottom of the stairs.

They looked at me with the rest of the crowd, but my eyes met those of the woman who had caused me years and years of pain.

And though I didn't *want* to kill her, to end my father's life with hers, I would.

Because if I didn't, she would do to others what she'd done to me. And that was something I couldn't accept.

Sylvie smirked at me, the crowd parting for her as she stalked across the floor.

I stepped down the stairs, avoiding Roman's gaze because I knew exactly what I'd see in his eyes.

Fury.

Alpha Females always fought before Alpha Males in a double challenge. And this time, there would only be one fight.

Instead of meeting Roman's, my gaze moved to my father's as my bare feet landed on the chilled tile. My father bared his neck toward me. A sign of respect from a father I'd never gotten to know. One whose actions I wouldn't have the chance to understand.

"To secret daughters." He murmured, lifting his head.

Though he didn't say it, I knew what he was trying to say. He had challenged Roman for me, and he wanted me to beat Sylvie for him. He'd accepted his death, and would go out in pride.

"To second chances." I lifted my chin, making eye contact with him one last time before I stepped toward Sylvie.

And then I stopped.

I couldn't do this without saying goodbye.

Spinning on my heels, I stepped toward the dad I would never get the chance to really know and threw my arms around him the way I imagined I would've wanted to, had I grown up knowing him. Though I wasn't a hugger when it came to anyone but Roman and my girls, I squeezed him tight and hoped I'd never forget the feeling.

"I'm sorry." My fierce whisper brushed his ear.

"I'm not." Hansen's fingers brushed my cheeks. They came up wet, and I realized I was crying.

For once, I didn't care.

But I did spin to Roman. He caught me when my entire weight smashed into him, dropping a kiss on my head before setting me back on my feet and moving back.

"I'll give you a better kiss when you make it out of this alive." He said, trying to sound like he was teasing me.

I could feel his anger, though, and his fear beneath that.

"Tell me if I miss something in this fight? It's been a long time since those MMA classes." I whispered into his mind.

"Of course." The softness of his words would've surprised most people who knew him, but not me. I knew how gentle he was behind the giant muscles and buzzed head.

"Done saying your goodbyes?" Sylvie mocked as I moved toward her. She was completely naked, having no friends to force her into clothes the way mine had.

I ignored the taunt. There was no honor in making fun of someone before fighting them to the death.

As was typical, the fight started the moment Sylvie shifted and lunged for me.

I dodged her attack, my muscles sore and tired after a few days spent in chains.

"You'll have to end this fast. She's got more energy than you." Roman's words were soft, barely a brush so that he wouldn't distract me.

I didn't reply, but knew he'd feel my confirmation anyway as I opened my mind completely to him.

I'd need his help to win.

Sylvie lunged again, and I barely dodged.

The battle became a dance—a shitty one. She attacked, I dodged. Again and again, I ducked or ran while she continued on the offensive.

I grew more tired, but she remained steady as she chipped away at my defenses—and energy.

Her teeth caught on my flank and I barely get away, blood dripping down my leg as I skidded backward. The desire to run was fierce, but I couldn't give in to it. I'd figure out a way out of this—I had to.

My next dodge was clumsier, and I nearly lost my damn head because of it.

"You can't win this fight." Roman said, his fear and frustration louder than his words as I lunged away in the nick of time yet again. *"Dammit, Hen."*

With a lunge of his own, Roman buried himself into my mind completely. His control merged with my own, and Roman's reactions became my own.

Sylvie's teeth snapped at my neck and rather than dodging the way I would've done, Roman and I ducked beneath her bite. Another spun, a slam of our shoulder, and she was the one skidding backward.

"Let's end this." Roman said grimly. I waited for Sylvie's next attack, knowing she'd come at me with less precision than she had before now that she was pissed.

She swiped at my face, but I ducked the swing of her paw. The turning movement placed me within biting distance, and we wasted no more time. I closed my jaw around her neck.

She leaped backward, blood draining from her wound. It was so like Ezra's that I almost pitied her.

But she was still raging, and enough of her throat was intact for another attack. We didn't give her the chance. I surged forward, snapping my teeth around her throat once again. I shook my head, tearing her throat out. Knowing the fight was over, my mate withdrew from my mind.

Sylvie collapsed, life draining around her ruby fur in a pool of crimson. It was darker, more deadly, than the hair on both our heads.

I turned toward Hansen, watching his face grow pale as his mate passed on. My dad wobbled, and Roman caught the man by the shoulder. Roman draped Hansen's arm behind his neck so he could lower my father to the ground as I stumbled across the tile, dropping to my knees at his side and taking his hand.

I said nothing, not knowing what to say, but he looked me in the eyes while his life faded away.

"You look so much like your mother." He whispered.

I nodded, clenching his fingers so hard I worried I'd break them. Hansen's eyes moved to Roman's.

"Take care of her." He told my mate, as Roman lowered him the rest of the way to the floor.

Roman released Hansen, and his fingers curved around my arms to hold me upright as the life left my father's body.

I held the man's hand until I knew he was gone—hopefully to wherever my mother was. And then I stood on shaky legs. Ignoring the tears on my cheeks, my eyes scanned the crowd. Daring someone else to challenge me, to call me out.

"You've seen what my mate will do to protect what matters to her. Go home to your packs and make sure you're ready to answer to us when we come check on your packs." Roman's voice was low, but it reached every person in the room.

And then he swept me up off my feet, hauling me away from the death and the pain the room contained.

He carried me back to his house—our house—and locked our bedroom door behind us. Our friends and family would gather here, I knew, but I needed a few minutes alone.

He set me on the counter in the bathroom and turned the shower on, coming back to wrap his arms around me and haul me under the water. His body shielded mine from the cold water falling, and he turned me so the water met my hair and skin when it had warmed. Roman's fingers wiped blood off my face and shoulders, cleaning my hands for me too without setting me down.

"You're pissed at me." I croaked, eyes closing as he rubbed shampoo into my hair.

"You didn't have to fight." Roman growled, washing the bubbles from my strands.

"I did." I said, simply. Because it was simple.

Roman growled at me, but slathered my hair with conditioner and let it sit while he cleaned his own face and shoulders.

My face met his neck, and he adjusted his grip on me.

"You could've died, Henley."

"You wouldn't have let me." I said into his neck. He scoffed but didn't deny it. When it came down to it, he *hadn't* let me.

My eyes flooded with more damn tears, and I was glad we were in the shower so Roman wouldn't know.

"Don't you try to hide your tears from me, Henley fucking Ellis." He rumbled, his hand stroking circles on my bare back as he held me to him.

"That's a new nickname." I choked through the tears. "Is it because I'm fucking an Ellis?"

His chest rumbled again with his chuckle, and I wrapped my arm around his back, squeezing myself to him.

"Yup." He kissed my head, then my mouth.

"Thanks for helping me win the fight." I wiped at my tears again. "Dammit, I'm a leaky pipe."

Roman snorted.

"I hope you leak on *my* pipe."

I smacked him on the shoulder, but a laugh choked out of me.

"You're terrible."

"The worst." He agreed, kissing my lips again.

He rinsed the conditioner from my hair for me and we stayed beneath the water for a few more long minutes until I finally sighed.

"Our friends are probably worried about us." I said softly.

"They'll wait as long as you need them to." Roman said, his eyes steady on mine.

"I'm ready."

I wasn't, but Roman let me make that call.

He was good to me like that.

Shut the water off, he gently wrung my hair out for me. My eyes traced the tattoo on his collarbone, the one he'd gotten just to match mine.

"You changed my entire life." I said.

"I know." His lips curved gently.

"Cocky." I commented.

"Only for you." He kissed my cheek, then my forehead, then my nose. Which I wrinkled at him, just to see his soft grin.

"What do you see in me?" I asked. The question had come from nowhere, it seemed. Or maybe it had come from my insecurities, which I'd managed to bury for the most part. "You're so damn perfect, Romeo, and I'm nowhere near that. You wanted me the first time you smelled me, but why did you keep coming back?"

Roman was quiet for a long moment.

"Do you remember when we were in my truck, right after we met? I drove you to get your stuff, and asked you a bunch of questions about your fingers."

I nodded, and he lifted the now-straight fingers to his lips, kissing them.

"It probably seemed small to you, but the way you spoke to me... Women don't talk to me like that. Like I'm their equal, or their lesser." He said.

I lifted an eyebrow.

"You liked that I was defensive as hell and a complete bitch?"

He chuckled, kissing my fingers.

"I liked that you didn't offer me whatever I wanted just because you were attracted to me. Most women do. You didn't give a flying shit about the way my body made yours feel, and that was sexy." His lips lifted in another of his grins that I loved. "And you were so damn defensive, I knew if I could slip past your walls, you'd love me with the same fire you used to protect yourself. Obviously, I was right."

Roman dropped a kiss on my forehead as he carried me to the closet and set me on my feet, drying me off. I could have done it myself, but he wanted to.

I grabbed a sports bra provided by the girls whenever they had stocked my closet. It was sheer and unlined, because that's who they were. The thing was a lot more comfortable than it looked.

Roman slipped a black long-sleeved tee off a hanger, handing it to me. I glanced down at the front, my cheeks stretching in a soft grin when I read the front.

"Pizzaologist?"

It was a double pun, since I could technically be called a mixologist with my fancy bartending skills. But damn, it had been a long time since I'd been behind a bar.

"Arla thought this one was better." He held up another one on a hanger.

"Pizza slut?" I snorted. "She's right." I snagged the 'pizza slut' shirt off its hanger and tugged it over my head, pulling some spandex shorts on beneath it. It'd probably look like I wasn't wearing pants at all, but I had no fucks left to give.

Roman pulled his typical joggers and t-shirt on, and we left the room together.

Our friends and family were talking amongst themselves, quiet enough that we hadn't heard them before coming out of the room. When everyone turned to see us, there was a moment of intensely uncomfortable silence that made my skin crawl.

And then the girls rushed me, giving me the biggest hug. My arms slid around the three of them, and I held them tightly.

"We didn't know what you had planned, Hennie, but we sure as hell didn't expect *that*." Arla said, squeezing me tight. The girls stepped back, and my eyes landed on Jamie's belly.

"Holy shit, you're round Jame." I gawked down at her bump. She laughed, cheeks flushing. It had only been, what, a week since I saw her? Maybe two? She was definitely, visibly bigger. And werewolf pregnancy moved faster than human pregnancy, but that seemed a bit much.

"I know. I think it's twins."

"Damn, you little overachiever." I poked her belly and she laughed, stepping back. Multiples were more common for werewolves. There were an equal number of single babies as twins, and one in ten women would have triplets. One in thirty would have quads.

"You need to stop putting your sexy ass in situations that make me want to kill people for you, girl." London scowled at me. I lifted my hands.

"So, so sorry." I drawled.

The girls were quickly replaced by the others.

Marie, Joel, Amy, and Oliver hugged me too, leaving Kyler the last one to wrap his arms around me. Roman's warning growl had us releasing each other after barely half a second, and I saw Arla's grin when Roman wrapped a possessive arm around my waist.

"We've only got a few hours to get the eighth trial done." Amy waved a needle in the air. I grimaced at the thought of Roman in another trial, but he squeezed me and murmured,

"You're worth it."

Amy, Joel, and I followed Roman into our spare bedroom—neither of us wanted anyone else's scent in our room. There'd been too much shit going on for us to be that stable.

My grandparents closed the door, insistent that it could still only be ruby wolves in the room when the trial was going down.

Roman went under for the trial, and I paced the room for the entirety of the two hours before he came out.

Arla ordered pizza for everyone afterward—because I was a pizza slut, after all—and we were up most of the night talking about everything except what had happened at the gala.

After the pain earlier in the evening, it was exactly what I needed.

CHAPTER 24

THERE WERE dozens of packs to visit and a shit-ton of Alpha of All crap to do, but we decided to go get things sorted in New York and finish up the trials first.

Amy and Joel left us with a promise that they'd find a leader for the Ruby Pack—which we were renaming the North Idaho pack. The group was giant, so I didn't think it was a big deal to have two Idaho packs. Everyone else seemed to agree.

We met the rest of the New York Pack in the skyscraper, in the ballroom we'd used for our mating celebration. Everyone was gathered there, and they all watched us move to the stage area of the room—which had a band on it last time I'd been there.

This time it held Molly and Thomas, and a few others I recognized as their enforcers from the last time I'd seen them. They welcomed us with half-smiles but most other people were glaring or solemn, so I knew that things with the pack would lean in their favor.

Even though we hadn't known how to stop the murders, the deaths were still my fault. That wasn't something people forgot easily, and I didn't hold it against them.

We spent the day going through votes and tallying who would stay in the New York Pack and who would join our Alpha Pack. The Wolfsbane Pack.

Around 95% of the pack stayed with Molly and Thomas, so Roman signed the skyscraper over to them. We took the deeds for every house —every insanely expensive house—in the upstate neighborhood, along with our seventy-four people (including our family and friends) and went up to the top floor to pack our shit.

Roman, in all his gentlemanliness, sent me to Arla's place to help her and Jamie while he boxed up our stuff. Probably because Arla had enough shit for five people—and Jamie was the slowest packer in the universe, even when she wasn't pregnant.

I had experience packing with her, so I was allowed to say that.

I called London to join us, since I missed all my girls, and we turned music on to make a party out of it.

Arla ordered Chinese food a few hours in. Twenty minutes later, there was a knock at her door, and I opened it up to find Roman's assistant. The teenager was holding a massive bag of takeout in one arm—and a laundry basket full of alcohol in the others.

Since when was this a drinking party?

"Arla." I yelled, gesturing the guy inside. He looked unsure about coming in.

"I didn't join your pack." He said, like it was a warning.

"I'm still your Alpha Female." I grinned. His eyes widened, and I pointed to the countertop. He set the stuff down while I grabbed one of Arla's gazillion purses off the hook by the door—this one was yellow, to go with her "sunny bitch" jacket—and pulled her wallet out. She always had cash, in every purse, because she was shit at remembering to move stuff between bags.

He set the stuff down, stepping back toward the door. I blocked the entrance, holding a bunch of bills between us.

"Take the money and I'll let you go." I said.

We'd had this fight before, and I refused to lose.

"Roman pays me." He lifted his hands, "I'll still be working for him when you live upstate. Last time I took your money, he smelled you on it and nearly threw me out of the window."

I grinned again, wider.

"He's a asshole, right?" I stepped closer, wiggling the bills. "And I'm a bitch. So take the money, or you'll leave this apartment in a body bag."

He stared me down, willing me to change my mind. I pulled another bill from the wallet and added it to my pile.

"Henley!" Arla hollered from her bedroom. "Where's my damn orange chicken?"

"My Wolfsbane Pack is pretty scary. Don't want to keep my people waiting." I pulled out another bill, adding it to the pile.

The kid groaned.

"I don't need the money. My mom just wants me to learn work ethic." He snatched the bills from my fingers. "And girls dig anyone with insider details on Roman's life. You wouldn't believe how many kisses I got with that story about the hickeys on your…" He glanced down at my boobs for barely a second before his eyes shot to the roof and he coughed. "Don't tell the Alpha about this conversation. Please."

And just like that, he left.

"That little shit." I mused, staring at the closed door.

Roman had trained his assistant too damn well.

I grabbed the food and alcohol, hauling it into the bedroom and dropping it on the bed we'd stripped down to the mattress.

"Since when do you drink?" I looked pointedly at Arla. Or the direction I knew she was—somewhere in the closet. There were six bottles of champagne in the basket, and a bottle of sparkling cider for Jamie.

Another question,

"And who the hell could drink this much champagne?"

"Since forever." London called from the bathroom. "She just does it on the DL so her brother doesn't freak out—and only goes for wine or bubbly."

"Except that one time I drank your vodka. That shit was foul." Arla agreed, coming out of the closet. "Don't tell Roman. He's an alcohol virgin."

I shook my head.

"That bastard drank in Ruby City."

All three of the girls gasped together.

"He didn't." Arla's voice was low.

"He did." I grabbed a container of Chinese food, sitting on the bed and shrugging. "Twice. Guess the idea of living without me was too much for his fragile self. I'm the whole damn package."

London cackled, dropping beside me and plucking a piece of shrimp off my plate. I smacked her away, but she was too quick.

"Shit. Never thought I'd see the day he went anywhere near drinking." Arla pulled her own food out of the bag. "Not sure if I should celebrate or cry for him."

"Yeah. But I'm pretty sure I'd burn this place to the ground if I found out he was fated to be with some other bitch, so I can't say I blame him."

"I get that." London nodded, reaching for more of my shrimp. I stabbed one and handed her my fork, too lazy to bother trying to figure out chopsticks. "Gunner and I are living states away, and if I ever find out he's even looking at another woman, I will still legitimately drive across the state to stab her eyes out. And then his."

I grinned. Jamie's eyebrows shot upward, and Arla laughed.

"You do realize there are pictures and videos of you prancing around mostly naked for any guy to look at all over the planet, right?" Arla leaned toward our model, humor in her eyes.

"You calling me a hypocrite?" London checked, her humor mostly vanished.

"No. Just pointing out a fact. You don't want him looking at other women; do you think he's ever wanted other men looking at you?"

"Well, in her defense, that's completely different." Jamie pointed at our model with her chopsticks. "He'd be cheating on her—emotionally, at least. She's just making a living."

"Valid point, Jamie and Co." I pointed my fork at Jamie. She pointed her chopsticks back, and we wiggled the utensils at each other before dropping them back to our food.

"Is the 'co' her baby?" London checked. Not offended by our conversation, it seemed. I hadn't expected her to be what with how open she was, but I'd end the conversation if she was.

"Babies." I corrected.

If Jamie thought there were two, I'd go with it.

"London doesn't think it's twins." Arla explained.

"I think we need an ultrasound to confirm there are two babies before we throw around giant words like 'twins'. Two babies is a hell of a lot more than one." London clarified.

"It is." Arla nodded emphatically. "Kyler's mom had one baby first and then a set of twins, and she's convinced two babies are four times the work."

I grinned.

"I'm so glad you finally brought your secret love tryst into the light." I said, biting into another piece of shrimp. Jamie was eating for three, and I was eating for at least two of myself to gain back the weight I'd lost. I'd be working out for two when we got moved in upstate, too, because I'd lost a damn lot of muscle.

Arla laughed, glancing back at London.

"I think we were talking about you and Gunner."

London grimaced.

"I know my modeling makes him jealous, but we've spent so many years fighting that I'm terrified if I stop, I'll have nothing anymore. No family. No money. No place to call home." Her shoulders lifted. "I've expected to lose him for so many years that the modeling became my backup plan. At least now, I'll have something. The fame, the money…"

"Don't forget the free underwear." I pointed out. "That shit's expensive."

I said it partly to make a joke, but mostly because I felt like London wanted the focus off her. In some ways, I think she was just starting to open up, the way I was. From what I'd gathered, Arla and Jamie had been much closer to each other than they were to London when I moved into the skyscraper. That still seemed true.

"So much free underwear." She agreed.

"So why hasn't Jamie had an ultrasound yet?" I looked over to Jamie, and her cheeks went pink.

"Oliver asked to come to the first ultrasound. I was too nice to say no —because the baby's half his—but I don't want to see him."

"Jame." I groaned.

"I know." She covered her eyes with the hand that wasn't holding her chopsticks. "I shouldn't have promised him."

"You're a grown-ass woman. Just get the damn ultrasound and tell him you forgot to invite him." I said.

"I'd feel guilty for the rest of my life." She sighed. "I just need to get over it. Pick a day and tell him."

"Let's do it now." Arla said, leaning toward Jamie. "We can all stay here—so you're not alone with him. And then we get to see your cute baby."

"Hell yes!" I exclaimed.

Jamie didn't look convinced.

"It's your belly, Jamie. Your baby, and your mate. You do what's best for you." London told her.

"I'll think about it." Jamie's fingers landed on her belly. "Maybe when we're all settled upstate."

That was that. We were friends, pretty damn pushy ones, but we'd never push something like that. London was right; Jamie had to do what was best for her, just like the rest of us would do what was best for us.

"Well then, should we break out the bubbly?" London grabbed a bottle of champagne from the laundry basket. "Because I'm going to need a buzz if we're going to get through packing two more times."

It was taking forever, but in our defense, she had a *lot* of shit. And I wasn't in a hurry because I was fairly confident that at some point, the girls were going to say 'screw it' and pay someone to pack for them.

"Let's do it." Arla agreed, grabbing her own bottle.

I didn't grab a bottle of my own. The world didn't need Bitchy-Drunk Henley when I had all this Alpha power at my fingertips.

"Okay, let's do the ultrasound." Jamie blurted. "I need to know if it's twins. Can one of you text Oliver for me?" She held her phone out toward all of us.

"I'll do one better." I plucked it from her fingers and typed in her code, clicking her call button and hitting Oliver's contact—pointedly not acknowledging that he was the last person she'd talked to on the phone.

"What are you doing?" She whisper-shrieked as I lifted it to my ear and the phone rang once before Oliver picked up.

"Jamie." His voice was warmer and happier than I'd ever heard it.

"It's Henley." I didn't want to crash his high, but didn't want him to start panting on the other end of the phone either. "Hey, Ollie. Jamie's getting an ultrasound today in her and Arla's apartment, if you still want to be here when it happens."

He hesitated.

Arla stepped out, her own phone to her ear.

"I do." He finally said, his voice much more neutral than it had been when he thought he was talking to his mate. "What time?"

Arla stepped back in.

"Twenty minutes." She said.

I relayed the message, and he said he'd be there.

"Damn, he wished I was you." I handed her back the phone, a bit of accusation in the tone. The best kind of accusation, since I was still 150% team Jamie and Oliver.

She blushed, biting her lip.

"He's been… trying, sort of. It's weird." She said.

And by weird, I figured she meant 'nice'. Because having your mate put in an effort after so long had to be nice. Even if it still hurt that he'd been distant for so long. But what did I know? I'd never been mated to a douchebag, so I didn't know.

We spent the next twenty minutes eating and chatting—mostly placing bets on Jamie's babies. She was far enough along to tell what the gender was, in werewolf-pregnancy at least.

Jamie was betting it was boy and girl twins. I had my money on twin girls—I couldn't see Jamie parenting a boy—and London was betting one boy. Arla had her bets on three girls-probably for the same reasoning as me, as far as genders went.

When the midwife finally arrived, Arla pulled me to the side of the room.

"Hey, you should know that the pack's midwife is Ella's mom, Mia. She's staying with our pack, probably because of Roman. She knows you're mated, but she always thought Ella and Roman would end up together so…" Arla grimaced. "Shit. I shouldn't be telling you not to talk about your mate."

Ella was the girl Roman had killed the last Alpha to save, so she would always be a part of him. And I knew he'd spent time talking to her mother, Mia, comforting her after the loss of her daughter.

Who had died because of me.

"It's not a big deal, Arla. She loves Roman like a son, and I love him too. I won't rub it in her face that I'm the reason her daughter died, or that I'm banging him."

She snorted.

"Always tactful, sis."

We went back to the living room with Jamie and London. Oliver was inside, not the midwife. His hands were in his pockets, his expression uncertain.

I really hoped he didn't say anything shitty to my pregnant friend, because I didn't want to kill him.

He stepped up to Jamie's side, his eyes widening when he saw her belly. His hands moved toward her stomach, as if it was an automatic response. But she turned slightly away from him, and he lowered them.

A petite middle-aged woman with buttery curls rolled a medical cart inside without stopping to knock.

"Jamie!" She smiled, going to my friend and wrapping her arms around her in a soft hug. "I've been waiting for you to call."

"You and me both." She laughed awkwardly, her hands landing on her stomach when the midwife stepped away.

Mia quickly greeted everyone else, her eyes landing on me last.

I waited for her response to me before deciding how to act. Mostly because Roman had held this woman while she cried—and because I was the reason her daughter was dead.

She looked at me for a long moment.

In the corner of my eye, I saw Arla and London exchange worried glances.

But I maintained eye contact, staring the woman straight on.

"You must be Henley." She said, not reaching toward me for a hug like she'd done for everyone else.

I didn't reach for her either.

"Did you know my daughter would die because you joined our pack?" Mia asked.

If that was the rumor going around, then damn, I didn't blame over a thousand wolves for choosing to stay the hell away from me and Roman.

"No. I never would have joined *any* pack if I knew that would happen."

She studied me. Looking for evidence of a lie—or evidence of truth. And I could've lied to her, but I was done running, done lying, and done hiding.

"My daughter was supposed to spend the rest of her life with your mate." She said. Her voice quivered, and I didn't blame her for it. Didn't even think about judging.

But I was an Alpha of All. And while that meant I had to be kind, I also had to be a leader.

"His scent changed for me the first moment he saw me. I wish I could undo what happened to Ella, but even if that were possible, Roman Ellis would still be mine."

I stared her down—not angry, for once. But strong, confident, and sure.

Her head bobbed. We'd found a relative peace, and that would have to be good enough because she was one of the few werewolf midwives alive, so I might need her someday. Doctors and human hospitals weren't a great idea considering some of our babies came out in their furry forms.

Mia had Jamie lay down on the couch, propping my friend up with pillows so she could see the ultrasound's screen.

Oliver sat behind her head, the way a spouse would. Though I imagined, if I were in Jamie's place, Roman would be propping me up with his body instead of the pillows—and he'd be so damn jittery I'd probably cuss at him to stop fidgeting.

Mia had Jamie pull her shirt up, and she grabbing a bottle of gel off a little warming plate. She squeezed the gel on Jamie's belly. My friend's bump looked huge to me, but I imagined it would get even bigger as she progressed through whatever time she had left in her pregnancy.

Mia turned the screen on and put the device over the gel on Jamie's stomach, swirling it around and watching the screen as she paused the device on one area of Jamie's belly. A thrumming sounded around us, and my lips parted as I realized what it was.

A heartbeat.

Life.

Growing in Jamie's damn abdomen.

"Oh my gosh." Jamie's fingers found her lips, her eyes widening. Oliver leaned toward her, wonder in his eyes too.

"Fuck." Arla stared at the screen.

London's fingers found my bicep. I hadn't even realized she was next to me, but I put my hand on hers.

Mia moved her device around, and the heartbeat grew different—more rapid, out of synch.

"What's that?" Oliver demanded. His hand landed on Jamie's shoulder, and I saw her lift her fingers to his. "Is the baby alright?"

"The baby's healthy. I'm just checking things." I caught the undertones in her voice but wasn't sure if it was worry or something else.

We waited a long moment.

"Here's your baby." Mia said, her voice lifting. The heartbeat went steady again, and I saw the tiny baby—arms and head and legs and feet and all that shit, so tiny I nearly swooned. "Baby A."

"Baby A?" Jamie's voice wobbled.

Mia moved the ultrasound thingy.

"Here's Baby B." This one was wiggling like a damn fish, tiny body doing little flips.

"Damn." I murmured.

Jamie was right.

Twins.

Mia moved the thing again, and I saw Jamie go white.

"And here's Baby C."

"Three babies?" Oliver's voice was low, panicked.

"Yes." Mia smiled "You've been blessed with triplets."

"Oh shit." Jamie gaped.

She never cussed, so the one word to her was like me stringing curses and Roman bombing the damn planet with 'fuck's.

"Multiples are much more common for werewolves, as you likely knew." Her voice grew gentler. Maybe she knew Jamie and Oliver had issues in their relationship—or maybe she realized the triplet bomb was a giant one.

"This is normal, and your body will handle it just fine. We'll watch you closely, and take care of you and your babies."

"What are their genders?" Jamie whispered. Her face was still crazy pale, and I doubted it would regain color in the near future.

"Three boys."

Her pale cheeks went green, and then Oliver was lunging for the trash bin. He made it back just in time for her to puke her guts into the bin. For once, it wasn't because of her morning sickness.

"I need to do a few more scans, but I can come back later tonight or we can reschedule if that works better." Mia said. "It might be easier if you have time to accept it, and if we can get the pack move done first."

Jamie nodded.

"Let's reschedule. I'll text you." Oliver said, taking over for Jamie.

"I'll text you." Jamie's voice grew harder, her eyes flashing at her mate.

I had a feeling we were about to see our mama bear in action. Maybe papa bear, too.

Mia eased away from the couple. Arla helped the midwife wheel her cart away from whatever shit was about to go down.

"They're my babies too." Oliver looked ready to go to war over this, but Jamie sure as hell wasn't backing down.

"You didn't want them." She snarled. "They're mine."

"And you're mine." He growled. "My mate—pregnant because of me."

Jamie stood. His hands went out to catch her, and she smacked them away.

"You don't get to decide to care now, after everything. I waited for you to notice me for years, Oliver. Years! You can't just change your mind after you made it so clear for so long that you felt nothing for me!"

"I've never felt 'nothing' for you, Jamie. And I always noticed you —Always."

"Well, you never showed it. And now, it's too late." She pointed to the door. "Get out."

He didn't budge.

"Get out, Oliver."

He still didn't move.

His eyes were looking wilder, his breathing picking up.

"Don't make me ask Henley to use her power on you." Her voice lowered.

My eyebrows lifted.

Don't bring me into this.

I wasn't about to start using my Alpha power to end arguments between mates when said arguments were perfectly rational conversations that needed to happen—though the people weren't nearly as rational as what they needed to discuss.

I inched backward, closer to the door.

Oliver wouldn't hurt Jamie—he was a good guy.

And well, maybe it made me a shitty friend, but I thought they should talk about this. If she was having triplets and he wanted to be a part of the kids' lives, he should get that privilege until he proved he wasn't worthy of it.

"This is between us." Oliver warned.

At least one of them wasn't hormonal.

Or at least, not as hormonal.

I moved closer to the door.

London beat me outside, and Arla and Mia were already out.

"Hennie." Jamie looked to me, panic in her eyes.

I groaned inwardly, turning to face the couple.

"Jame, you know I can't use my power to force him out when he's being good to you." I said gently.

She blinked rapidly; I guess she hadn't realized he was being good to her, or that he was trying.

"What do you want me to do?" I asked her, softly.

"I just-" She looked back to Oliver. "I want time. I need time to figure this out."

"The clock's ticking on us, Jamie. On this." He gestured to her belly. "Them."

Her eyes squeezed shut.

"A month. Give me a month. Then, we figure out what we're doing." She said.

He let a long breath out slowly.

"Three days." He countered.

Her eyes opened, angry.

"That's your counter-offer? Three days?"

He met her steadily.

"Three days." He said.

"Three weeks." She countered.

I slipped out as he said,

"One week, and I'm not budging. So take it or leave it. If you leave it, I'm not moving from your side until our babies are five."

The door closed behind me and I silently urged her to take his one week. It was a far more generous offer than most men would give her. If I found out I was having even one kid, Roman would probably strap me to his damn back in one of those hiking backpacks little kids and dogs hung out in.

But if we had three babies? He'd probably glue me to the couch with his own massive body.

"Well, damn." London whistled.

"Now I want a baby." Arla sighed.

I was thinking the same thing, though I'd never say it to Arla. Who knew what she'd do with that information.

I caught Roman's scent in the hall as we moved closer to my old place.

"Done packing up in there?" His voice tugged me from my baby thoughts, and I lifted my eyes to his.

"Not exactly." I said, noticing the boxes already stacked outside our door. That was my mate; effective as always. "Jamie slowed us down."

And well, it was true in more than one way.

CHAPTER 25

We moved into the upstate neighborhood quickly. Kyler wouldn't take his house back from me, but it was next to Arla's, so I left that alone. The neighborhood was kind of a ghost town, but I hoped it would fill up a bit more when time went on and people from other packs realized we weren't so bad.

Roman and I cuddled on the new mattress he'd insisted on buying, just to be sure the place didn't smell like Kyler, the night before his final trial.

"Oliver's pissy. Are he and Jamie fighting?" He murmured.

"Yup." I said.

"That's all I get?" He poked me in the stomach and I growled playfully at him.

"You didn't tell me about Arla's love affair." I countered. "I found out after they were already mated."

"That's hardly the same thing. She's my twin sister—and you and I are co-leaders of Jamie and Oliver's fan club. You can't keep secrets from your co-leader."

"You can't keep secrets from your mate, either. We're a team. If someone doesn't want me to know something, they shouldn't tell you."

"Fine." He nuzzled his nose further against my neck, inhaling my scent.

"Fine?"

"You're right. We're in each other's heads, we shouldn't have secrets. I like to know everything, and you love that about me."

"It's one of your hottest qualities." I drawled.

"I know. So tell me about Jamie and Oliver before I make *you* hot again." His fingers slid down to my core, but stopped without touching me.

"Asshole. I'm always hot."

"I know." His teeth scraped my neck. "Hot for me."

I smiled, my eyes closing.

This was it.

One of those moments you hope for, as a lonely teenager.

Laying in bed wrapped in your soulmate's arms, talking. Laughing. Loving.

And knowing with a certainty that loneliness was your past, not your future.

"Jamie's having triplets." I said. "Oliver wants to talk to her about something—co-parenting, probably. But she doesn't want to talk; they were arguing when I left."

"He doesn't want to talk about co-parenting." Roman murmured into my neck. "He wants her back."

"Back, as in what? They were never romantic."

"Back in his bed, I'd imagine. In his arms. In their home, where he can protect her."

"Well, he's going to have to do better than that if you're right." I said.

"Better than protecting her?"

"Yup. She won't move back in with him unless he wins her over first. She doesn't want protection—she wants romance and love."

He growled playfully.

"He shows his love by protecting her." Roman nibbled my ear, and I shrieked, wiggling away from him. A full-belly laugh shook my male, and his arms were iron around my waist when he nibbled my ear again. "Much like I do."

"Stop!" I smacked his arms, wiggling and screeching. "Bastard!"

"Do you surrender?" He laughed, holding me down.

"Hell no." I bucked against him, trying to get free. "You surrender."

"Why would I surrender when I have your sexy ass rubbing against me?" He grabbed my hips, rubbing me on his dick. I gave up fighting, flopping back to the bed and smacking Roman's shoulder with my head.

"How are you already hard again?"

It had been like ten minutes, tops.

"You smell good." He sniffed my neck, then kissed it. "And you feel good." He squeezed my hips and then my boobs and ass. "Plus, you're mine. What more could I want or need?"

"Good point." I agreed, relaxing into my male as his fingers stroked up and down my side. My mind went back to the ultrasound—the heartbeats. My own heart picked up, just thinking about it.

Roman's hand slid up to rest over my chest, feeling my quick heartbeat.

"You're nervous?" He murmured. "Since when does me touching you make you nervous?"

"Not nervous. Well, sort of nervous—but not because you're touching me." I grabbed his hand, holding it to my heart. "I was there when Jamie had her ultrasound."

Roman's voice went quiet.

"You met Mia."

"Yes, but—"

"Was she cruel? If she can't be kind to you, she's not welcome in our pack. I don't care who or what—"

"Romeo, she was fine." I interrupted him. His body relaxed. I hesitated to say more, and Roman growled.

"Who do I need to kill, woman?"

"I think I want to have a kid." I said.

Roman tensed—in a completely different way.

"Not now." I rushed to say. "We've got shit to figure out with all the packs. I don't want to bring a kid into an unstable world. But after we get things working well, and there's peace in all the packs… maybe we could try."

He said nothing.

I waited a long few minutes… and slowly grimaced.

"You don't want to. There's no rush, I mean, I'm fine with waiting longer, I just-"

Roman pounced.

He rolled me to my back, his body pressing into mine as he captured my lips. His tongue clashed against mine, his fingers exploring my body as he ravaged my mouth.

I dragged my lips from his when his fingers slipped inside my sleep shorts.

"Was that a yes?" I checked.

He kissed me again, hard, and rolled me over the top of him so he could grab my ass to tug my legs around either side of him.

"That was a *hell yes*, Henley fucking Ellis."

Roman kissed me again, his tongue delving inside my mouth until he pulled away, leaving me breathing hard and arching into him.

"Tell me what changed your mind." He said.

"What changed my mind about having kids? I told you before it was a maybe."

"What changed your mind *today.*" He clarified.

"It's hard to explain." I said.

"Try."

"I heard the babies' heartbeats. Life growing inside Jamie. Their tiny arms and heads and legs… It had to be the most amazing thing I've ever seen. I've seen a hell of a lot of death, but I've never seen someone create life. And maybe it's selfish, but I want that. With you."

He kissed me again, and when he pulled away, there was a fierce love thrumming between us, coming from him.

"I didn't think there was a perfect woman before I met you. Clearly, I was wrong." He murmured, pressing another hot kiss to my mouth. "Fuck waiting—let's have a baby now." He had my shorts and panties across the room in an instant and was climbing down me, moving his tongue across my stomach, toward my core. He had my thighs parted and my body hot before he even licked me up the center.

I pushed his face away before his tongue met my sweet spot.

"Romeo." I interrupted, sitting up. "I have an IUD, remember?"

He blinked at me.

"And our world's still a shitshow. Plus, I just barely changed my mind —what if it changes back?"

"If you're hoping that will convince me otherwise, you're wrong." He growled. "And there's probably a way to get that thing out of you. That's what YouTube's for."

"Roman." I scowled.

"I'll call Mia. She can do it. We—"

I slid across the bed, grabbing his face between my hands.

"Roman." I raised my voice. He finally stopped, his hands cupping mine on his face. We were both on our knees, looking each other dead in the eyes.

"I want kids, Hen. I've wanted kids since I was a damn eighteen-year-old Alpha teaching little people how to control their big feelings so they didn't shift in front of humans. And when I met you, when I fell for you, I knew you'd be the best mother on the damn planet. Because you're rough, and raw, and honest, and so damn real it still shocks me sometimes.

"It takes forever for someone to earn your trust, but when they do, you become their biggest fan and number one supporter. So when we have kids, I know I won't have to worry about them because they'll have you fighting for them, teaching them, and protecting them. And you'll be the best damn mother they could ever ask for."

He stared at me. Waiting for a response, I guess. But I didn't have one.

"What the hell am I supposed to say to that?" I tried to let go of him, but he held my hands to his cheeks. "You never told me any of that!"

"You weren't ready to hear it." He gave me a devastating smile, but I ached to smack him upside the head.

"How many kids do you actually want?" I demanded.

He shrugged.

"As many as you'll give me."

I tugged my hands away again and this time, he let me go.

"I'm going for a walk." I called out to him, easing into the closet to tug on some clothing. "Alone." I added when I heard him get off the bed.

"Don't run from me, Hen." He warned. Though I could hear the excitement beneath the warning, the dare. The bastard wanted to chase me.

"I'm not running. I'm walking." I called back.

He strode to the doorway, watching me dress in his clothing.

"I don't want you going out alone." He said, serious.

"Well, sometimes I need time to process things. Especially the gigantic bomb that is, 'surprise, I want you to birth a dozen babies, starting right after I watch a video about how to remove an IUD'." I drawled. "So yeah, I'm going out alone. And you're going to deal with it."

He chuckled.

"Not a dozen."

"How many?" I whirled back to him. "You told me, when we were first together, that you didn't care if we had kids or where we lived. You said if I wanted them, we'd have them. And that if I didn't, you would be perfectly happy just with me."

He didn't deny it.

And my accusation became a heated glare.

"I would get over it, Hen. I haven't brought it up because it doesn't *really* matter—you're what matters." He stepped closer to me, lifting his hands up like he was surrendering. "But we tell each other the truth now, and that's my truth. I've never said I didn't want kids—and I never asked you to have them. But you just said you wanted them, and I do too. I'm sorry if I overwhelmed you."

"I'm going for a walk." I repeated.

His eyebrows furrowed.

"We're going to talk about this, but first I need time to think. So I'm going to get in your truck and drive to the nearest town, and go for a walk where there are lights and people so you know I'm safe. I'll have a drink if I need to—and you're not going to panic if I come home tipsy. Because this," I gestured between the two of us, "is freaking me out the way people drinking sometimes freaks you out. Okay?"

The asshole actually looked amused.

"Okay." He nodded once. "But you carry your phone so I can track you. And I'm allowed to check in mentally every half an hour." He tapped his temple with his forefinger.

"That's fair." I nodded. Then paused. "Did you say you track my phone?"

His amusement grew so much I could smell it in the air, and I loved that damn smell.

"You're my woman. Of course I track you. After what we've been through, I'm not sure why you're surprised by that."

I blinked a few times and then shook my head.

"I'll add that to the list of reasons I'm drinking tonight." I told him.

He chuckled, not moving as I turned to slide past him. Our chests brushed, and something in me tingled at the excitement of the thought of trying to get pregnant with this man.

"Don't be out too late. I want to sleep a full night with you before the last trial tomorrow." His fingers brushed my cheek, and I grabbed his hand to pull it to my lips.

"There are always two ruby wolves." I said lightly. "You'll crush the trial."

I didn't want to consider the alternative, that this could be our last night, but I definitely understood his desire not to spend the night alone.

"I'll be back before ten."

It was eight, so that was more than enough time to deal with my feelings and come back. The grownup version of running from my problems, I guess.

"Perfect." He pulled his fingers from my lips, tucking a strand of my hair behind my ear and then leaning in close. His lips brushed the earlobe he'd nibbled earlier. "If another man touches you, I will tear him limb from limb." He murmured.

I laughed.

"You doubt me?" He lifted an eyebrow, pulling back.

"We're mated, Romeo, and there's no mating season for us. You're more reasonable than that."

He chuckled, the sound rich and low.

"It's cute that you think I'm reasonable. Try me, Hen. I've fought for you, and now you're mine. If someone touches what's mine, I'll kill them without asking questions."

I rolled my eyes, wiggling my fingers at him and grabbing my bag as I headed for the door.

"See ya." I called. When I glanced over my shoulder, he was shooting me with a finger gun. I threw my head back and cackled. "You're the hottest."

"I know." His words reached me as I shut the door.

My phone buzzed as I left, and I glanced down at the screen.

ROMAN: Come back horny for me

I snorted and texted back,

ME: One pair of wet panties coming right up

ROMAN: Can't wait to taste them

With another grin, I slid into the truck and turned the key.

I wasn't sure if I wanted to drink or not, but since I was heading for a bar, I decided I didn't want to go alone and dialed London's number. She answered immediately.

"Feel like hitting the town with me?" I checked.

Part of me felt bad for not inviting Arla and Jamie, but the last time London and I had talked just the two of us, things had been different. London had dropped the mask she usually wore, and I'd felt like I found a kindred spirit.

"Duh." She didn't hesitate.

"Sweet. I'm in front of your house." I said, hitting the brakes and parking in front of her place.

"I'm not dressed up." She warned, as her door opened and she came walking out in sneakers, an old sweatshirt, and faded cotton shorts. I hung up and unrolled the window.

"As long as you have pants on, you're dressed up enough for me." I called out the window.

She grinned, sliding into the truck.

"How's it going?" I checked, pulling away from her house.

"Eh." Her shoulders lifted. "I'm horny and lonely. Gunner hasn't texted, and even though I sent him away and told him not to, I still stupidly wish he would. My house is too empty—and now I'm sad I'll never feel a baby kick me from inside my damn uterus. How pathetic is that?"

"Pathetic." I agreed. "If you think creating life and having someone to share it with is pathetic, at least."

She sighed.

"You're not supposed to make me wish for more, Hennie."

"You could swallow your pride and just go find him." I said. "You know where he is—California, right? So hop on a plane, tell him you miss his face or dick or whatever, and figure out a way to make things work."

"Or I could seduce him into impregnating me." She mused.

"Or that." I shrugged. "It's your life. But personally, I think you'd be a hell of a lot happier if you just got over that sexy-ass pride of yours and tell him you're sorry, and ask if the two of you can start over."

We drove down the highway toward the bar I'd planned on going to. I'd been in town a few times as we'd moved in, grabbing random things from the store, so I knew where it was.

"I can't do that." London said, her attention out the window.

"Why not?"

"Because it feels wrong. He's the guy; he should be fighting for me."

"Relationships work both ways. It's give and take." I said, pulling Roman's big-ass truck into a parking space far from the door so I didn't hit any other vehicles. "I need to buy a car."

"You should get something cute." London changed the subject. Or at least, she tried. The air was heavy. "A red corvette, maybe?"

"That's exactly what I need. More red in my life."

London laughed, and I laughed with her.

And though we were in the bar's parking lot, neither of us moved to get out of the truck. I didn't even shut the engine off.

"Do you want to go in?" London asked.

"I thought I did, when I left the house." My eyes landed on the bar in my rear-view mirror. "But alcohol feels like the easy way out."

"What do you have against easy ways out?"

"Nothing. Easy is great. But there's always a reckoning after one takes the easy way out, and I hate reckonings. So I'm thinking I go with the hard way off the bat."

"What's the hard way today?" London tipped her head toward me, studying me. "I can't imagine you and Roman have problems. He didn't even flinch when you told him you weren't his mate."

I shot her a quick smile.

"That's different. It was a matter of dedication and promises. This is something entirely new."

She waited for me to spill. When I didn't, she waited longer.

And damn, it worked.

"I think I want to have a baby after we get things settled with the pack. I told Roman, and he flipped." London's eyebrows shot into her forehead. "Not like the bad kind of flipped—he was ecstatic. I guess he's always wanted kids—he just didn't tell me."

"Ugh, men suck." She muttered, tilting her mass of curly hair into the window.

"Roman's the best person I know." I said, bluntly.

I wasn't angry or irritated, but I had to stand up for my man. Especially the night before he was going to fight for us in the trials one last time.

"I know. That's why he sucks; he's too damn perfect. Gunner's like that too." She wore a grimace, and I lifted an eyebrow at her.

"I thought you hated him."

And I definitely remembered him nearly killing someone for dancing with London.

"I do, but I love him more. He's better than he probably seems—and definitely better than I make him sound. I kind of expected my feelings for him to fade when we separated for good this time, but it's like everything I feel is just building up into this big ball of misery and longing, and it's driving me insane." She shut her eyes.

"Sounds shitty." I said.

"It is."

We were silent for a minute.

"Do you want to go get a drink?" I asked her.

"No." She opened her eyes. "What's the hard way out, in my situation?" She looked at me like I had the answers. But I was the furthest thing from a professional when it came to relationships, so I just shrugged.

"What's the last thing you want to do?"

"Apologize and quit modeling as some big-ass grand gesture." She made a face. I smiled.

"Then that's probably the hard thing."

She groaned.

"I need a middle thing."

"Maybe try to accept the past?" I suggested, trying to let my words come out kindly. "I know what he did to you years ago was shitty. He should've made sure you wanted to be with him permanently before he slept with you. But you were young… have you ever asked him if he even realized that you might not know it was permanent?"

She looked away.

Honestly, I wouldn't have been surprised either way. Gunner did seem like a dick, but I really hadn't interacted with him much.

"What's the hard thing for you to do?" She changed the subject quickly. I didn't blame her—or protest the subject change.

"Go home and talk to Roman." I said. "He's ready to have a kid now, but I'm not. That's too big of a decision to make on the fly, even for me."

London nodded.

"Maybe you should go home and talk to him, then."

"Maybe you quit modeling and fly to California." I countered.

"Yeah, yeah." She waved her hand through the air. "I'm sure I'll get sad enough to do that eventually, but not tonight. Take me back to my lonely house, Hennie. Its time I learned how to write in a journal. I'll do some self-therapy. That can be my middle thing tonight."

I snorted, but went.

CHAPTER 26

ROMAN and I were up late talking that night. He apologized for pushing me, and I apologized for leaving, and that was that.

We didn't even have sex, just talked and cuddled. Kids didn't come up again; that wasn't something to worry about on the night before Roman's last trial.

Things moved fast during the day as we focused on unpacking and helping others move boxes into their homes. When Mia came by our place to talk to Roman, I nodded her way and made myself scarce, heading out toward Jamie's place.

She'd claimed the house she and Oliver had owned before—telling him to find another place to stay. I had smelled him in one of the spare bedrooms in her house though, so I had a suspicion they were trying to make things work already.

I found Jamie in her kitchen—mixing alcohol, of all things. There were dozens of bottles on her counters, and she had a laptop off to the side of the intricate setup on her kitchen's island. Cups of all kinds lined the countertops, and notecards with Jamie's perfect handwriting on them sat in front of each of the glasses and mugs.

"Jame?" I glanced between the bottle of rum in her hand and the shot glasses on the table. "What are you doing?"

"Hey! I was just about to text you!" She exclaimed, beckoning me forward.

"Alcohol isn't good for your baby." I said. "Tell me you know that."

She laughed.

"Of course I know that; I'm testing recipes. I bought the bar in town and I'm going to jazz it up a bit. Change the lighting, redo the walls." She shrugged. "It'll be cute."

"You could just ask me for the recipes." I reminded her, stepping up to the counter and leaning over the granite island. For a moment, it brought back memories of leaning over the bar top back in Kyler's club.

My club.

I was the opposite of sentimental, but I kind of missed that place. Which reminded me...

"I haven't talked to Bodhi in forever."

Jamie smiled. He was my blue-haired manager, and he was totally afraid of me even though we were friends.

"I text him every day. He's great, and the club's booming. I sort of started rebranding it for you." She bit her lip, watching me for a reaction.

"I don't have a clue what that means in your fancy business lingo." I said honestly.

"I renamed it and started redecorating" She admitted. "No one ever called it by its name, Hennie. Do you even know what it was called?"

"Of course I know the name. It's just stupid, so I prefer to call it 'the club'. I don't know what made Kyler decide to call his club 'Abstract'. It's so vague; like, are we talking paintings? Or a chunk of words summarizing a science article? Some tourists legitimately asked me if it was a museum one time."

Jamie laughed.

"I don't know what Kyler's thinking most of the time. Granted, I don't know what anyone's thinking most of the time."

"Make that two of us." We traded grins.

Mine, wide and devious. Hers, happy and calm.

"What did you name it?" I checked. Her cheeks reddened.

"I'd rather show you than tell you."

I shrugged.

"We can drive into the city tomorrow. Roman and I have a flight booked to go kick the Minnesota Alpha's ass the next day, though."

"That works." Jamie smiled again. "Would you ever consider selling me the club? I know Kyler gave it to you, and it probably means a lot to you, so I completely understand if you don't want to sell. But I'd love to run it, if you're willing to consider it."

She waited almost cautiously.

"You don't have to be nervous around me." I teased her. "You'd be doing me a favor if you took it off my hands. If you hadn't been taking care of it, who knows what Bodhi and his neon blue hair would've done to the place over the past month. Just bring over the papers and I'll sign it over to you. I've got more money than I need; you can have it."

She scoffed.

"I'll be paying you for it, but I will bring the papers over." Her scowl vanished, swapped for a hint of a smile. "And Bodhi's hair is green now."

I gasped.

"He didn't."

She laughed and nodded.

"That bastard told me he'd die before he put green in his hair. He swore that blues, purples, and pinks were the only colors in his future."

"Guess he changed his mind." Jamie said.

We laughed together, and she pulled his social media pages up to show me his hair. It was very, very green. But somehow, he still rocked it.

"So, you want me to look at your recipes?" I checked.

Her expression went sheepish.

"I want you to taste them."

I lifted an eyebrow.

"Roman's last trial is tonight, Jame. I don't want to be a drunken bitch when my mate is fighting for both of our lives."

"I know that." She scowled, like she was mad I'd even considered that. "I don't want you to drink them, just stick your finger in and taste it or something. I want to make sure the drinks are good before I add them to my menu."

"It's a good thing you're cute." I sighed, grabbing my phone and pulling up my contacts. "We're going to need some help with this. I can't taste all of these and stay sober."

We called London and Arla, and they were there twenty minutes later. London, wearing a massive grin and Arla, a wrinkled-forehead and a frown.

"You okay?" I checked with Arla. She groaned and dropped onto one of the barstools attached to Jamie's island.

"I'm finally getting back into my dissertation after so many months of drama, and it's like wading through shit. It's like another language to me, and I'm the one who wrote the damn thing." She grabbed the nearest cup and sniffed it, withdrawing quickly and peering at the card.

"Negroni?" She frowned.

"You'll like it." I told her.

She sipped it and looked pleasantly surprised.

"That's actually kind of good."

"Now put it down, there are a hundred more." Jamie swept it from Arla's fingers, handing it to me. "Make sure it smells right and dump it in the sink if it does."

I accepted the drink, sniffing it and nodding my approval. It was a simple, three-ingredient cocktail.

"You stirred it, right?" I checked. Jamie had worked with me enough times to know I was clarifying that she hadn't shaken the thing.

"Right." She turned to her computer, typing for a second. "What are you waiting for? Sip the drinks, and Hennie will check them."

London headed to the counter beside the fridge, leaning over the notecards to find one she wanted.

"Sazerac? What the hell is that?"

She looked to me, and I made a face.

"Has absinthe in it."

I'd never worked at a bar that had absinthe until I worked for Kyler, and I'd never dared taste any drinks with it inside it, with my tendency toward over-drinking. Drunk puking was one thing, but I wasn't about to risk hallucinations or death. I hadn't survived so long to die because of a damn glass of alcohol.

"Is it good?" She checked.

"Don't know." I said, lifting the nearest drink to my nose and sniffing. Whiskey sour—I nodded to Jamie without tasting it, because I knew the smell so well. "You must've made a thousand of these." I told her, carrying the glass to the sink but hesitating before I dumped it in.

"Maybe we should throw a party or something. Feels wrong to dump this much money down the drain."

"It's just money, Hennie." Arla said.

"But still." I set it by the sink. "We could call Kyler. He'd probably have some friends to bring over." I glanced pointedly at Arla, who grinned.

"Let's do it." She agreed as she grabbed another glass and sipped it. She immediately gagged. "You must've done something wrong." She gestured to the cup.

Jamie leaned over the counter, frowning and looking at the card before she laughed.

"Four Horsemen of the Apocalypse. It's actually pretty popular at the club." She said, exchanging grins with me.

"That's got to be poison." She held it out for me. I sniffed it, my eyes tearing at the combination of the smells assaulting me so close to my sensitive nose.

"Nope. Just a really strong drink."

I set that one on the counter beside the other one. London brought over her Sazerac.

"This one's good, Jamie." She called out, handing it to me. I sniffed it and put it with the others. I was confident Jamie's recipes were all good—I'd taught her, after all. And she was kind of a perfectionist on top of that.

I only tasted a few drinks—not enough alcohol to get me buzzed, but I still had fun with it. Jamie continued to mix the drinks, adding my tossed-out instructions to her document when I offered advice or info she didn't already know. Arla and London were both tipsy, laughing at nearly everything and still sipping drinks.

We had filled one section of the counter with mugs and glasses when the door swung open without a knock.

"Hen?" Roman called out.

"In here." I yelled back.

I smelled him and Oliver before they made it to the room. Both men scanned the kitchen, eyebrows lifting as they tried to understand what was going on.

"They're tasting drinks for my new bar." Jamie explained quickly. Roman's gaze landed on me, and I knew what he was wondering without him saying the words.

"I'm not working there, and I'm not really drinking right now. When you permanently become a ruby wolf, I want to remember it." I murmured mentally.

The grin he shot me was better than any response.

"You're not drinking." Oliver looked to Jamie, his voice half warning and half in disbelief. She met his gaze with a hard glare.

"Of course I'm not drinking."

They didn't look away from each other, and a tingle went up my spine.

Damn, they'd be good together.

"Which one would I like?" Roman asked me, crossing the kitchen to lean casually past me and look at all the glasses we'd abandoned. I smacked his hand away.

"You've got a trial to win tonight." I warned.

He grabbed a glass, lifting it to his nose and sniffing it. He withdrew quickly.

"Vodka." He complained, not tasting it.

I sniffed it.

"That would be a vodka martini. Delicious, actually." I said, eyeing him. "You tried vodka when you drank?"

He nodded confirmation.

"Don't know how you drink that shit." He said, grabbing another. Jamie threw a lime wedge at him. It smacked the back of his neck and fell to the ground.

"No drinking." She ordered.

Arla and London laughed like hyenas, clutching their stomachs—and the drinks they'd decided to keep, when they stopped tasting.

"You're too wimpy for vodka?" I lifted an eyebrow, lips twitching. "Jame, I think he needs to celebrate after the trial with a strawberry daiquiri."

She laughed. The other girls cackled again, and Oliver took up residence in one of the barstools the girls had vacated ages ago.

"Maybe a mimosa." She teased.

Roman grinned, shaking his head at me and picking up another drink. Our thighs rested against each other as Roman tipped the mug toward my nose. I sniffed and tilted my head to the side.

"Even you should recognize this one." I said.

He lifted it to his own nose and grinned at the scent.

"Pina colada?"

I nodded, and he took a swig.

"Not bad." He nodded his approval, offering it to me.

"I'm not into girly drinks, unlike some people." I smirked.

His low chuckle made me grin, and he took another sip.

"I think we're both plenty secure in my masculinity for me to drink whatever the hell I want." He tugged me closer, turning me and leaning against the counter as he pulled me into his chest so my ass could press into his boner.

Horny bastard.

"Yes, I am." He agreed, nipping at my neck and taking another sip. I snagged the mug from him, dropping it back on the counter.

"No alcohol for you." I scowled.

I saw his gaze change, just a bit.

"Not because of your dad, Romeo. Because of the trial. You could be the happiest drunk on the damn planet and I still wouldn't want you to drink before tonight." I told him, where no one else could hear. It was nice, being able to talk in private even when we were around other people.

"It's creepy when you have silent conversations." Arla complained, her words slurring a bit. She'd told me she was nervous about the trial, and I knew she was drinking to cope with her nerves and her worries about her dissertation. Which was fine, but drinking problems ran in their family. So I'd watch her like a damn hawk over the next few weeks to make sure it didn't become an issue.

"I think it's cute." Jamie said.

"I'm so fucking glad Gunner isn't in my head." London threw her head back and laughed until there were tears streaming down her cheeks—real, sad tears. Arla hugged her tight, but Oliver looked taken aback by the drama of the moment.

Jamie and I exchanged grins.

Roman's mind touched mine with an image of him sliding his hand into the front of my pants, his fingers finding my core. My stomach clenched, and I fought to keep myself from getting turned on so everyone in the room wouldn't smell it.

Jamie passed out the next round of drinks—skipping Arla and London. So really, she just slid two toward me and Roman and then slapped one down in front of Oliver. The look in her eyes was a challenge.

Damn, you go girl.

His eyes met hers as he lifted the glass and took a swig.

Their gazes remained locked even as he lowered the glass.

I didn't want to break the tension but knew Jamie would want me to, so I cleared my throat and lifted both glasses. Roman reached for one, but I only let him sniff it.

"What are these?" I asked, though I already knew the answer.

She confirmed it, and I set one down. Roman caught my free hand as I lifted the drink to my lips. I sipped it, letting him take my hand and fold my fingers so only my pointer was up. And then I let him dip my finger in the drink—and watched him lift the finger to his mouth and close his lips around me.

Our eyes locked, and he sucked.

Jamie groaned and Arla made a puking noise.

"Find a room, sex-crazed nasties." Drunk Arla slurred the command.

Roman released my finger and took the glass from me, placing it on the counter.

"We can help again tomorrow." He called over his shoulder, leading me out Jamie's back door and tugging me toward our house. We walked through the trees together, and I loved that even though the pack was loaded, none of our members had manicured backyards. The back of every house faced the forest, giving us open access to the trees.

We slid inside our place and Roman sucked a hell of a lot more than just my finger.

CHAPTER 27

OUR SPARE ROOM was full of people we cared about.

Arla, Jamie, and London. Joel and Amy and Marie. Kyler and Oliver.

Even Mia was there—though she'd stepped to the corner of the room, not wanting to bother anyone. I think she just wanted to keep her distance from me so she didn't let her negative feelings toward me affect Roman's trial, and I appreciated that.

It had taken some real convincing by Arla, but my grandparents had finally agreed that normal werewolves could be in the room with us during the trial as long as they stayed far away from Roman's unconscious body while he was out.

Amy gestured toward the bed, telling us it was time. I wrapped my arms around Roman's neck, squeezing my body to his.

His lips met mine and the kiss was gentle but strong. A promise that he would survive the trial and we would get the life together that we'd fought for.

I stepped back to the side of the room. Amy didn't want me too close to the bed since we were already so connected and I still wasn't allowed to intervene. It was probably a good idea to keep me away—the closer we were, the stronger our connection tended to be.

No one stood between me and Roman as he sat down on the edge of the bed, offering Amy his arm. I looked away when she injected the wolfsbane into his blood, turning back as Roman lowered himself to the bed.

His eyes closed and his mind was swept away almost immediately.

I saw through his eyes, seeing what Roman was seeing the moment he was out.

He was here, in our house, in the neighborhood. We were talking in our kitchen. It was simple—too simple—and made me damn suspicious.

Only seconds into the vision, someone shook my shoulders and the kitchen vanished, the guest room and our friends reappearing as I blinked back into reality.

"You can't intervene." Amy's voice was firm, her eyes hard. "It would cost you both your lives."

I nodded.

I knew that, but the trial and our connection didn't seem to agree.

"What did you see?" Arla demanded.

She and London had sobered up for the most part, but both were a little pissy. I didn't blame them; I was pissy too, and I wasn't even drunk. Just worried about my male.

"My kitchen." I said, looking to my grandmother.

"The final test is one of mental endurance." She explained. "It will be longer than the others, as it's the final determiner of whether he can handle the ruby mantle.

I nodded, hoping she was wrong about how long it would be.

We waited.

Ten minutes passed in silence, and then someone decided to carry chairs in. I didn't sit.

An hour went by, and then another.

I felt Roman's mind reaching for mine every few minutes and had to force myself to retain the distance between us. During his last trial, keeping my mind out of his had nearly snapped him out of it. This time, his body and mind hadn't responded to my pushing him away so I hoped to make it through unscathed.

Jamie was wiggling uncomfortably in the kitchen chair she occupied, so Oliver dragged a couch in. When Arla fell asleep on her chair, Kyler dragged another couch in.

I stayed on my feet, though.

Four hours had gone by when Jamie finally talked me into sitting down beside her. The fight to keep my mind out of Roman's was getting worse by the minute, my head aching and pounding.

The moment I sat on the couch, taking my attention off remaining upright, Roman's mind caught mine again.

This time, he was in a fight.

Werewolves surrounded him. Some I didn't recognize, some our own friends and family. Mine and Roman's scents were on the wolves, marking them as our pack the same way my scent had marked the bodies of those who'd been killed by wolves overtaken by my ruby power, forced by some freakish law of nature to protect me from perceived threats.

Roman was part-shifted, his arms and hands furry while the rest of him was human. He hauled a bleeding wolf on his shoulders while he made his way through the battle, kicking and clawing the other pack's wolves while he fought desperately for whoever was on his shoulders.

This trial felt different than the others. Usually, I only saw images or brief moments. Usually, it didn't feel real. This one felt so damn real it scared me.

I stepped toward Roman, assuming I was some sort of ghostly-spectator in this trial. Instead of going through things, I tripped over the body of a dying werewolf, and crashed to my hands and knees beside him. He was wheezing and struggling to breath, and I froze when I realized I recognized from the New York Pack. He was one of my old guards, the enforcers who had followed me around to protect me.

His lips formed the words,

"Help me."

The man's abdomen was wide open, hardly bleeding anymore because most of his blood was pooled in the dirt beneath him. There was little chance I could help him, and according to Amy, I wasn't allowed to interact with the trial.

A sharp slap on my cheek tugged me back to my own mind.

"You can't intervene." Amy's voice was sharper, angrier.

"I'm not doing it on purpose." I growled, looking around the room to try to regain my bearings. "It's like his mind is a magnet on mine. Stopping myself from going in isn't as easy as you'd think."

She looked a bit surprised for a moment, but quickly shook her head.

"You're going to have to fight it. He has to survive this alone."

"I know." I reminded her, leaning carefully into Jamie when she wrapped her arms around me.

"I'll grab you some coffee." Arla said, sliding off her couch. Kyler followed her into the kitchen, but I didn't remove my eyes from my mate. I rarely drank coffee because it usually gave me jitters and panic attacks, but to keep myself out of Roman's trial, I'd drink the shit.

"You should walk around the house a bit. Get your mind off it." Joel suggested.

The only things I had to say weren't things I wanted to say to my only living grandfather, so I replied by shaking my head.

Marie came around the couch to sit beside me, squishing me into Jamie's side. Both women wrapped an arm around me, and I was cradled between my friend and grandmother. It was a strange feeling, particularly because I had hardly seen Marie since finding out Roman was taking part in the trials, but my eyes remained on my mate.

The mental struggle was relentless. Roman's mind tugged, shoved, and stroked mine, trying to find entrance. I was on the defensive, but holding my ground against the guy I loved wasn't something I'd really practiced, and I was shitty at it.

When Arla and Kyler came back with the coffee, they handed out the mugs. I sipped my creamy, sugar-filled drink as Arla came around my couch. There was so much creamer and sugar in it that it may as well have been some kind of fancy dessert milk.

Marie scooted to the side for my sister, and the four of us squished together.

We all drank in silence.

"Did he look okay when you saw him?" Arla whispered.

I nodded, and she mirrored the movement, leaning into the couch and squeezing her eyes shut.

"I'm really glad he's got you—and that I have you—but my life would be a lot less stressful if you hadn't walked in." She said.

A tiny smile pushed at my lips.

"I don't remember walking in. Roman pretty much dragged me into the skyscraper."

She snorted.

"Oh, please. Even when you were afraid of Alphas, I saw the way you looked at him. It's the same way you look at a ham and bacon pizza."

A laugh-choke broke from me.

"Even then, I had eyes."

"When he left you in his office that first day, do you know what he said to me?" She asked.

I shook my head.

Her lips curved upward.

"He walked in like he'd lost his fucking mind and told me you were his." She brushed her hair behind her ear. "You didn't know him before, but he was different. More subdued and much less happy. I didn't even blame him for signing up for these damn trials because when you meet someone who brings you to life like that, you sure as hell shouldn't let go."

I looked back at Roman's relaxed body and pushed his mind away again, leaning into the couch cushions. Arla's eyes had gone to Kyler.

His mind slammed into me hard.

I barely blocked myself, but all it took was another hit and his mind swallowed mine whole.

I watched him kneeling on the dirt, bleeding from many wounds. He pulled a blanket over Arla's body, anguish in his eyes as he looked out at the group of female werewolves around him. There were many of them, all wearing skin and little else.

"This isn't over." His voice wobbled like I'd never heard it wobble. It was even worse than after the torture trial. "We can still defeat her wolves. My sister would want us to keep fighting."

Her wolves?

Who was the 'her' they were fighting?

Sylvie was the best bet, I thought.

I took a step closer to the group, and my foot landed on a small, broken branch.

It snapped, and when the wolves saw me, they didn't just turn.

They attacked.

Fur and skin and fangs flew at me.

Roman flew at me with them. His expression was feral, furious.

Like I was the reason his sister was dead.

Shit. I was the 'her' they needed to defeat.

I flung myself to the side, rolling away from the attack. Branches stabbed my skin, rocks slicing into me, but I didn't know the rules here so I had to keep myself alive in case dying in the trial would kill me in the real world.

The other wolves recouped faster than me, rolling over the top of me in a massive pile.

Shit.

"Roman, it's me. This isn't real." I shouted, as someone's claws sliced through my hip. Considering I was barefoot, wearing leggings and a tank top, I didn't have much to protect myself with.

"Kill her." He snarled. "It's the only way to free her wolves."

Double shit.

I ripped my mind away from his, trying to separate us, to get out of his trial. Nothing happened.

I felt water dripping down my cheeks and back, though I didn't see any wetness. The water had to be back on my body, but the trial still didn't disappear. Nothing changed at all.

A woman lunged toward me, claws out and fangs lengthening as her body flew toward mine. I was still on the ground, and prepared myself for collision as I tried again to separate myself from Roman.

As the woman smashed into me, my vision changed and I was ripped back to reality. I gasped, clutching my hip as I slammed back into my own mind.

"What the hell is going on?" Arla snarled at Amy. "She was talking, she couldn't have reached out for him.

I lifted my hand from my hip, and my eyes widened when I saw no blood on my fingers.

It really was just happening in his mind.

Already, I could feel Roman reaching for me again. I withdrew quickly, pulling my mind as far from his as I could possibly get with the mental connection we shared.

"Get her more coffee. The caffeine may help her stay aware enough to avoid his mind." Joel urged someone I couldn't see.

It would help, but I didn't know for how long. And Roman didn't look close to defeating me in the trial—if that was how he'd win.

"We could sedate her. Maybe she couldn't reach him, and she'd be protected." Marie suggested, crouching beside us. Her fingers found my pulse, as they had hundreds of times during my month in Ruby City.

"No." I wasn't considering that option. Not while Roman could still lose the trial.

"It may work, or it may make her too weak to fight when his mind seeks her out." Amy said, shaking her head quickly. "We won't risk it."

Marie looked like she wanted to argue, but nodded once.

"Then what's the plan?" She asked Amy.

"Distract her, caffeinate her, and get her talking." Amy said.

Roman's mind tugged again, harder, and my hand left my wound to clutch my head.

"Shit." I groaned, grinding my palm against my temple. He was getting stronger and more desperate. I had to wonder if he was trying to use our connection to call that version of me to him, so he could kill fake Henley and win.

"Tell us something exciting." Marie urged. "Something you feel strongly about."

My eyes squeezed shut, but the more I thought about it, the more I floundered and came up with nothing.

"I don't know." I said, fighting Roman's pull again.

"Why should I give up modeling and go talk to Gunner?" London demanded.

I shot her an incredulous look.

"You want me to talk about your relationship while Roman's trying to drag me into his trial and kill me?"

"I want you to distract yourself. So talk."

"He's not terrible. You said he'd never hurt you physically." I stumbled over my words as Roman reached for me. "He's jealous, and you're holding onto the past. Let it go."

My temple throbbed as Roman's mind ground up against mine—and grinding could be sexy, but this wasn't that.

"Fuck." I snarled.

"Do Jamie and Oliver." Arla said.

Jamie's eyes widened.

"Tell me what happened between you." I told Arla, instead. My eyes swept to Kyler, just off to her side, holding her upright while she held me.

Arla shook her head.

For someone so nosy, she was damn private when it came to her own life.

"I knew I wanted to mate with her the first time I saw her, in middle school. She knew answers to math problems the smartest guy in class couldn't figure out, but her eyes were sad. I wanted to make them happy." Kyler spilled words.

Arla grimaced.

"When we were sixteen, I finally got up the guts to ask her out. She told me it had to be a secret—Roman was dealing with a lot, and she was overwhelmed with being the Alpha Female. The last thing I wanted was to keep it hidden, but I was so in love with her I didn't argue. We were together for a year—talking, and kissing, and falling for each other—until her dad hit her."

"Stop." Arla told him.

He closed his mouth, and I wouldn't push for more. Not when it came to that topic.

Roman's mind rammed into mine, making the damn world spin. I cried out, and Arla's fingers gripped mine hard.

"We were making out, and he saw the bruise on my collarbone. It was the first time in years that dad had hurt me, and I didn't tell Roman because he couldn't control his Alpha power well and I was afraid he'd kill dad. I didn't want him dead, even though he deserved that and more."

Mixed emotions crossed her face. I imagined with her dad dying so recently, it was still a bit raw.

"Kyler went on a rampage—broke my lamp and a picture of me and Roman, even a couch. It scared the hell out of me. When he left to go kill my dad for touching me, I told him we were done. Said he was no better than my father. And I told him that if he ever touched me again, I'd tell Roman he was the one who hurt me."

Arla didn't look at him, but her eyes burned with emotions. The scent of shame was sharp in the air.

"You were sixteen, and scared." Kyler said, softly.

"I was the one as bad as my father." She sighed.

It seemed like they'd had this conversation before, but wounds like that could stay open a long time.

He kissed her forehead, then her lips, to shush her.

Crippling pain smashed into my head and felt like it was shattering my damn brain.

"Shit, shit, shit." I swore, both hands gripping my head as I folded in half.

Roman slammed his mind into mine with every ounce of strength he had, and damn, that man was strong.

My control wobbled and his mind crashed into mine with so much force that he dragged me into the trial like it was a walk in the park.

CHAPTER 28

I CAME to with Roman standing over me… Fangs bared in his human mouth and nails shifted to claws. My hands were tied in front of me with some thick-ass rope, my feet the same.

"Back off, Romeo." I snarled, hating the way he was trying to intimidate me. Even though he thought I was a different version of myself, it still freaked me out a bit.

The whole room inhaled, and my mate's eyes widened just slightly. I was probably the only one who would've known him well enough to see the change in expression.

Glancing around the room, I sized up the threat.

Yeah, it was a big threat.

What I'd assumed was a room was actually a gigantic tent, the kind you'd see in a fantasy war movie, and all four sides of the thing were rolled up so people could see in from everywhere if they were tall enough. And the thing was chock-full of werewolves, as far as I could see.

Roman was still at war.

And apparently, now the real version of me was too.

Somehow, I had to find a way out of this without intervening in the trial at all.

"Henley?" His voice was low enough that only those closest to us could hear, but their murmured disbelief told me that wasn't how he was supposed to react.

"Yup." I blew a puff of air toward my nose, trying to clear hair away from my face.

"Tell me what your next plan is." Roman seemed to switch back to the offensive, his eyes going hard.

Not good.

In our time together, he'd sure as hell never looked at me like *that.*

"Then what are you doing here? It's been two years since you deigned to be in my presence." He glared at me.

"Years? You've been in this trial for hours, Roman. Not years."

He blinked confusion, then shock, and then understanding.

"You're talking about the ruby trials. I finished them five years ago." He said. "What happened to you?"

"We need to talk in private." I said.

His scoff and the angry shouts in the crowd told me that was the wrong thing to say.

"So you can attempt to seduce me, like the last time we were together?"

I laughed—a huge, loud, booming laugh.

"The last time I attempted to seduce you, Kyler was in the skyscraper's prison cell and I tanked it. I don't possess whatever attributes a person has to have to successfully seduce someone."

A woman stepped up beside Roman. It took a minute for me to register who she was, but then it clicked.

Jamie.

An older, angrier version of Jamie.

What the hell?

"What happened to you?" My eyes swept her from head to toe.

"You happened to me, *bitch*." Jamie snarled back.

My eyebrows lifted.

Since when did she swear?

"You said you finished the trials five years ago?" I looked at Roman again.

"Enough questions." Jamie whipped a gun from her belt and stepped closer, pressing the metal to my head. "You lost the right to ask anything when you turned our men against us."

When I what?

My eyes went back to the crowd around us…

All women.

And everything clicked.

This was a trial of mental endurance, as Amy said. The fake me had gone insane and captured all male werewolves with my Alpha power, so Roman and the other women went to war with me. He had to prove himself strong enough to retain his sanity even if I lost mine.

My eyes went to the woman at his side.

Jamie. Currently pregnant with three boys.

Five years later, I took all male wolves…

Shit, she was going to kill me.

"I-"

Jamie didn't let me finish speaking. The side of her gun slapped my cheek so hard the damn room spun.

Ouch.

But if I'd actually stolen away Oliver and their boys, I deserved it.

Somehow, I had to make sure Roman won the trial without interfering, because apparently that would kill both of us. As far as I could guess, just being there was interfering. So basically, I needed to get the hell out of there.

And death was the only way out, as far as I could see.

"Kill me." I commanded Roman, my eyes colliding with his.

I wouldn't actually die, since my cut had healed before I left the trial last time.

Jamie's gun slapped me again, nearly hard enough to break my nose.

Damn, that hurt.

"Lock her up. A night in prison will get her talking." Roman snarled, turning and stalking away.

I stared at his ass while he walked away, feeling the blood run down my lip and chin.

No version of Roman could possibly believe a night in any kind of prison would change my mind about anything.

Even after five years of this, the trial's version of me couldn't have grown weaker-willed. She was controlling a damn army of male werewolves.

So he either believed me, or wanted to torture me himself.

Jamie looked suspicious too, but jerked her chin in a nod, grabbing my arm and lifting me like a damn bodybuilder.

Shit, she was strong.

She hauled me through the flood of women—who parted for her the way they'd parted for Roman.

Throwing me into a makeshift prison cell, she locked a door made of metal bars before leaving me alone. It was a bathroom with barred windows and reinforced walls. A quick search of the cupboards proved them empty, and the mirror that should've been over the sink had been removed.

The water still ran in the sink, but not the shower/tub combo.

I sat on the toilet seat, mentally trying to pull myself out of Roman's trial like I'd done the last time. This time, I couldn't budge. I was trapped in the damn vision created by the wolfsbane running through his system.

Hopefully, not for five years.

It was quiet for a long time, but I waited.

I'd had worse than rope bindings in a bathroom.

I wasn't sure how much time had passed when I finally heard voices. A door slammed somewhere, and Jamie's angry voice met my ears.

"This is a trick, Ellis." She snarled.

"I don't know that it is." He said, his voice much calmer than he'd seemed in the tent. "Did you see the way she looked at us?"

"She was pissed."

"No, she was *normal*. The way she was before." Roman urged. "You were busy with your boys, but I spent almost every minute with her. I watched her lose her mind, Jame. I watched her descend into madness. But the Henley we just saw is a completely different person than the one I lost."

"She's tricked us before." Jamie wasn't even phased by Roman's arguments.

"I don't think she could fake this. I don't think anyone could fake this." He said. "Come with me if you want. Make sure she isn't using me. But we've got to talk to her."

I heard Jamie's groan, and then their footsteps. Crossing the bathroom, I leaned up against the bars and wrapped my fingers around them.

Roman stepped into view, his body position more tense and angry than I'd ever seen it.

I met his glare head-on. Not with my own glare, but with neutrality. Calmness.

If the other Henley had gone crazy, I needed to be the opposite.

"Why did you ask me to kill you?" He demanded.

There was an awareness in his eyes, like maybe he was starting to figure out what was going on.

"Just do as she asked and get it over with." Jamie snarled.

"Go strengthen our boundaries. Double the guard, in case this is a trick." Roman told Jamie, not taking his eyes off mine. "After we've broken her connection to the male wolves, the people will decide her fate."

Jamie jerked her head in a nod, throwing a scowl my way as she left.

"They don't know I'll die if they kill you." Roman said, when she was gone.

I tried not to let my surprise show. I hadn't been ready to play dumb and shut my mouth when I first landed back in the trial, but now I had to. There was no way to know if we'd really die because I interfered, but Amy was worried which told me I should be careful.

"They should know. Jamie was there when Hansen died with Sylvie. It shouldn't be a question. And here you are, looking exactly the way you did when you appeared near my pack months ago. Wearing the same thing you wore when I went into the ninth-"

I stepped up to the bars, grabbing his face and kissing him hard.

There was no way to know if the win would count if Roman won because of me, so I needed to get him to shut up.

"Shh." I said. "Stop."

"The way I see it," He lowered his voice as the backs of his fingers slid over my cheek. His chest brushed the bars, his t-shirt thin enough that he would've been able to feel the chill on his skin. "There's only one option here."

I didn't step closer, unsure what he meant.

He tugged a key from his pocket and inserted it in the lock, turning it and opening the door. When he stepped inside, he locked the door from behind and tossed the key out of the bars, into the hall.

Shit.

"I'm sure we can come up with more options." I said, eyeing the key.

Too far to reach.

Would I mentally survive being tortured by my own mate? I wasn't sure.

"If I'm right, and this is a-" Roman began again, but I cut him off before he could say what was going on. I didn't know if that mattered, saying it out loud, but I didn't want to risk out damn lives over it.

So I grabbed his face again, kissing him harder.

"Roman, *shut up*." I urged.

Amy hadn't said what had triggered the end of the trials, but I was fairly confident the damn thing wouldn't count if he went and figured out it wasn't real.

"If I'm right, I get out of this hellish life and back to the real world. If I'm wrong, the war would end. Mates would be reunited. Jamie would raise her boys, and there would be peace." He said, trailing his fingers over my arm. "If this is really a trial, I guess it's asking whether I value my own life over the lives of everyone else. And the answer is no."

His knuckle brushed the underside of my chin, and he dipped his lips toward mine so his breath tickled my nose.

"You've always been the love of my life." He murmured, leaning closer.

His palm met my chest, and I didn't move away from him.

I'd asked him to kill me; now he would.

But he didn't cut into *my* chest.

I looked down in horror as his claws pierced his own heart. Blood blossomed from the wounds, and he fell to his knees. I fell with him, grabbing his neck and chest and shoulders.

Life began to fade from his eyes, and I was ripped back out of the trial. Thrown back into my own body.

I gasped for air, sitting up quickly and reaching out with my arms. They caught someone, but the someone was too hard to be Roman. My vision cleared and I found Arla leaning over me, her fingers at my neck.

"Thank—"

I pushed her away, shooting to my feet and lunging for my mate. Our bodies collided as his eyes opened, scanning the room. A breath of relief escaped him before he crushed me to him. His fingers slid into my hair, pulling my body tight against his as he held me—clutching me and not letting go.

"None of it was real." I told him, lifting my head so my hazels could meet his blues, a fierce surety in my eyes.

He just crushed me back to his chest, holding me tighter.

"I know." He said. "I knew the whole time. But I didn't know how to get out until you showed up."

My mind reached for his on purpose this time, and he opened for me in an instant. I saw what he felt—like the whole thing had been one big nightmare. The longest damn nightmare of anyone's life.

"Rome." Arla threw her arms around us both and Roman squeezed her into our hug.

"Oof." I complained, both of them squishing the air from me as I was between the twins.

"The trial sucked." Roman said gruffly, like that was all the explanation she needed.

And well, it might be all the explanation she got. I doubted he'd want to tell anyone he'd seen me go power-crazy and turn every male werewolf against them.

"Well, at least it's over." Arla said.

"Massive understatement." I wheezed, breath not coming easy in the Ellis sandwich.

Roman chuckled.

"You have no idea."

His lips met my forehead, then my cheek, then my ear.

He kissed my whole damn face while Arla removed herself from our hug so I could breathe again.

"We need to order some pizzas." Roman said. "And a movie—a damn chick-flick. The funniest one you know. I need something happy. And if anyone suggests I let go of Henley, I will remove your head. You've been warned."

Arla snorted, but I grinned.

"I need therapy." He muttered, his fingers tangling in my red hair. My fingers brushed over the stubble on his chin—bright, ruby red. The exact same color as mine.

"At least no one told you we look like siblings in there." I teased, voice soft. His lips curled upward.

"I forgot about that. Damn idiots."

"Morons." I agreed, kissing him.

His lips opened my mouth, his tongue sliding gently inside. It wasn't a hot, or passionate kiss. Just a soft, warm connection that reminded us both we were still there, together.

"I love you so fucking much." He whispered into my mind. *"Don't even think about going crazy."*

I laughed into his mouth, pulling away so I didn't choke on spit.

He grinned up at me, my favorite damn image in the world.

"Hey lovebirds, get off the bed before I vomit." Arla called out. "Go make out in your car while you grab us some pizzas. I'll get the movie—and some snacks."

I laughed again, and Roman's chuckle rumbled our chests.

My favorite damn feeling.

"We can grab the pizza." Amy and Joel said, their smiles nearly as large as mine and Roman's.

"Don't worry about it." I slid off the bed—and then was pulled back on top of Roman, by the man himself. He slipped off then, his arms around me as he lifted me with him. "We want to make out in the car." I grinned at Amy, who shook her head at me.

"Oh, to be young again." She said.

"I'll kiss you in a car any time you want." Joel said, kissing her on the head. She smiled, and I was warm from the inside out.

I hadn't expected any of this.

Not the family, not the love story—and definitely not the happiness. But somehow, by some miracle, I found it anyway.

And now there wasn't a chance in hell I would let it go.

CHAPTER 29

"WHY AM I WEARING A BLINDFOLD, JAMIE?" I complained. "I don't even own this place anymore."

After a long night of movies, good food, and far too much laughter, we'd waited until ten before heading into the city. I assumed the rest of our people slept in, but we hadn't gotten any sleep.

Partially, because of sex.

Mostly, because of the trial.

Even though Roman had known it wasn't real, parts of him still felt like five years had gone by. Coming out of that was rough. He had a hard time sleeping—and a hard time looking away from me, out of fear he'd look back and I'd be gone, or crazy.

We'd talked about it, and he let me into the shit that was five years in the bleakest damn trial. Roman had watched me lose my mind—something he assured me he wouldn't ever let happen in the real world now that he knew what to watch for.

Through the whole night, we just hung out and talked and listened to music together like a normal couple, and I loved every minute of it.

Even though we were talking about the alternate reality in his trial, and our shitty pasts.

Jamie still wanted to show me the changes she'd made to the club—which was officially hers, since I'd signed the papers. And for some reason, she'd insisted everyone needed to be there.

"Stop asking and let me surprise you." She chided.

I rolled my eyes behind the blindfold, but couldn't hide my smile.

Roman ran a finger along the curve of my lip, and I felt his appreciation as he led me from the car.

"Okay, turn her and set her up right there." Jamie instructed him. "More left… More left… Come on, Roman. It's not that hard." She complained.

I laughed, and Roman scolded me with a squeeze on the ass as he stopped me.

"Is this left enough?" He growled playfully.

"Well, now you're slightly too right. But close enough." She sighed dramatically. "Alright, pull it off."

Roman started to untie the blindfold, but I pushed it over my head.

My eyes landed on the gigantic, glowing white lights of the bold-lettered name above the club's front doors. It was the middle of the day, but there was still a bit of a line out the front.

"What do you think?" Jamie demanded.

I studied it.

The lettering was large but simple. All caps. It looked awesome.

The club's new name… less simple.

"Crap. You haven't kept your tattoo covered in months, so I assumed it was fine. And a bunch of the reviews mentioned the mysterious bartender with the tattoo, so I just assumed, and—"

"It's perfect, Jame." I said, being completely honest.

Because she'd renamed the club "WOLFSBANE".

It was just a word. A myth, a legend, sure. But ultimately just a word.

One I'd been called out of cruelty.

One I'd suffered for.

One I'd hated.

And one I'd come to accept, if not love.

I had always been Wolfsbane, and I always would be her. My scars were still healing on the inside, though my mate had healed them on the outside.

I was still her, but now, I was loved. My past had settled in the past, and my future was so much brighter.

The club was the place everything changed, and it deserved to be marked as such.

"Thank goodness. I was so worried." She breathed, throwing her arms around me and hugging me tightly.

Roman let go of me reluctantly, his hand still on the small of my back as Jamie and her baby bump pressed into me.

"Want to see the inside?" She pulled away, eyes bright with excitement.

"Definitely." I grinned and she caught my hand, tugging me inside. Roman grabbed my other hand, and the three of us breezed past the bouncers at the doors.

I'd expected it to be a madhouse considering the line out the door, but it was only half-full despite the people outside. Arla and London waited by the door, and we stopped in front of them.

"So, we still owe you a bunch of bet money." London said. "Or rather, we did."

Arla grinned.

I couldn't decide if she was grinning because it was a lie and they'd already spent it all, or because of the memories of what she'd done with that bet money.

"We decided that with the rest of it, we wanted to throw you a real mating celebration. Somewhere you wanted to be, with people you wanted to celebrate with. And a dress you didn't hate." My sister explained.

I looked around again and realized I recognized the majority of the people inside the club. My old co-workers were there, along with friends I'd made in the pack before all the drama hit. Even Lilac and Sky were there, grinding on some assholes I recognized from speed-dating. The people I didn't recognize, I was sure Roman knew.

"This had to cost more than the money you owed me." I said, looking between the girls.

"I covered the rest." Roman's lips met my neck. I tilted my head, turning to look at him. And loved the grin he wore.

"You knew about this?"

"It was his idea." Jamie admitted. "The last mating celebration didn't go great, and you technically weren't even mated. This time, we planned it just for you two."

I let go of Roman's hand long enough to hug all of the girls tightly. Next, I threw my arms around Roman, squeezing him tight enough that he probably couldn't breathe. He just held me tighter.

"Your dress is in the storage room." Jamie smiled. "I set up a mirror, too. We figured you'd rather have Roman help you get ready this time."

It was true—and luckily, they didn't seem offended.

"Go, get ready." London shooed us toward the back room.

I grabbed Roman's hand and tugged him in that direction, waving over my shoulder at the girls.

As we walked, I waved greetings at the people who called my name. I'd chat with some of them when the party started—hell, maybe I'd even chat with *all* of them. This was my party, after all.

We slipped into the storage room, and Roman shut the door behind us. It didn't lock, but Jamie had put a sign on the door that warned people away.

Someone had dragged in a metal clothing rack with only one dress bag hanging from it, along with a soft-looking gray couch and a vanity mirror with lots of lights attached.

Walking to the clothing rack, I grabbed the dress bag. It was a silky black thing, and I hoped that didn't reflect the dress within. I could do without another Alpha fight at this mating celebration redo.

Tugging the zipper down, my eyes widened at the dress within.

Soft white fabric.

A high neckline.

Long sleeves.

My fingers trailed down the garment almost religiously, and I gently spun the hanger so I could see the back.

Wide open.

It was my favorite style—a mix of comfortable and sexy.

"Do I need to send my sister back to the store?" Roman's words warmed me as he approached, his fingers finding my waist as he stepped up so his back rested up against mine. His eyes swept over the dress, and I felt his approval through our bond.

"Not this time." I said, slipping out of my jeans and tossing them and my top onto the couch. Roman's hands slid over my bare shoulders and arms, down my waist, and landed on my hips.

"I'll never get tired of touching you." He murmured, his lips landing on my shoulder. "Feeling you against me." They met my neck. "Your skin on mine." He kissed my cheek.

"That makes two of us."

I tugged his arms tighter around me, pulling us closer together so his nose met my throat. His chest rumbled as he inhaled my scent.

"Remember the first time you kissed me?"

My lips curved upward.

"Of course. Right here, in this room." I gestured to the storage room around us. Roman chuckled.

"I had no idea what you were doing, but when your lips met mine, and I felt your fingers on my skin…" He growled, low in his throat. "Damn, I wanted you."

I kissed him, and his lips trailed up and down my throat again. I felt the tickle of air on my collarbone before he switched to the other side of my neck, and I realized he was marking me with his scent.

"Does it bother you?" He murmured.

Though he didn't clarify what he was asking about, I knew.

"That you're being clingy?" I lifted an eyebrow, and our gazes met in the mirror before he lowered his nose back to my throat.

"You like to be free." He said.

"Yeah, and you make me free." I shrugged. "You're only clingy because you survived a nightmare to keep us both alive. So no, it doesn't bother me. I kind of like that you need me extra right now. Usually, I'm the one who needs you more."

Roman scoffed against my throat.

"You can't seriously believe that."

"I'm constantly in danger, Romeo. It comes with the territory." I lifted a strand of my hair.

"Well, now we're both in the same territory." He dragged my fingers up to his chin and I skimmed them over the scratchy red stubble I loved.

My heart was so ridiculously warm and happy.

He kissed my fingertips, then finally let go of me.

I shot him with my finger guns, and he shot me back as he settled on the couch. He was content to watch me—with great humor—as I put the sticky-bra on and wiggled into the dress. It was mermaid-style, so my thighs barely fit in the thing even though I was still skinnier than usual. But it was surprisingly comfortable when I managed to get it on.

There were a few buttons from my ass to lower back, so Roman came over and did them up for me while I leaned toward the mirror, getting up close so I could see better while I swiped on some eyeliner and mascara. I'd never be a pro when it came to makeup, but I didn't really care.

Rubbing the foundation in with my fingers, I stepped back and checked it in the mirror.

Good enough.

"Not *good enough*." Roman growled, his fingers latching to my hips again as he licked up the side of my neck, making me shiver. "So damn perfect you shouldn't even exist, let alone have chosen me."

"Well, it's a little too late for me to change my mind." I smirked.

Roman's eyes narrowed playfully.

"Take that back."

"Or what?" I taunted, stepping out of his grasp and putting my hands on my hips. I'm sure it looked funny in my white dress, but I didn't give a shit. Playing with my mate was too much fun.

"Or I'll make you." He grabbed a bag of hamburger buns off the shelf and tore the package open, lifting it in the air. "What'll it be, Mrs. Ellis? Surrender, or die?"

His grin was wicked in the best way as his fingers clenched around the burger, squeezing it into a bread-ball.

"I'd rather die." I called back, bending my knees so I was ready to dive out of the way.

Roman launched a bun, and I jumped to the side. Another followed quickly, and I hopped back to where I'd been.

This was harder in a wedding dress.

Scooping the bread-ball up off the ground, I chucked it back toward him. Roman ducked to the side while I attempted to fold myself in half to avoid the one hurtling toward my face.

"Is that all you've got?" He taunted, tossing a few more my way. I grabbed my own bag of buns off the shelf, tearing into it and throwing out buns like frisbees. Two of mine hit Roman, and he laughed when two of his hit me.

"You can do better than that." I called, shooting the buns as fast as I could. Roman dodged, rolling toward me even as my buns hit him.

Roman jumped to his feet, sweeping me into his arms—and then smashing a bun into my face.

"I win." He grinned.

I slammed two buns over his ears, rubbing them all over his head.

"Now I win."

My favorite of his deep, rumbling laughs shook us both.

"You're the fucking best, Hen." He grabbed my face, dropping his buns and kissing me on the mouth.

I dropped mine, kissing him back with just as much passion.

"Get your tux on." I flicked his nose, and he bit my finger. "We've got a party to attend.

"Yes, ma'am." He caught my mouth in his one more time. "And in case I forgot to say it earlier, don't touch any other men."

I snorted, shoving him away when he laughed.

"Bastard." I grinned.

"You forgot cocky." He said, maintaining a serious expression.

"I definitely didn't." I glanced down at his lower half and he pulled me in for another kiss.

"So damn glad you're mine." He muttered, kissing my head again.

And I was just as glad he was mine.

EPILOGUE

ROMAN- AROUND 2 YEARS LATER

I GLANCED down at my phone, mostly out of boredom. We'd been meeting with the same packs month after month. A big part of being Alphas of All was settling disputes, and some of the packs had long-standing grudges against each other.

Henley had been up late the night before, puking her damn guts out. We'd been trying for a baby for nearly a year, but I guess it's harder for some people than others. She managed to blame herself for that—as if it was her own fault that her body wasn't growing a baby. And every time I tried to tell her that was bullshit, she'd just shake her head and tell me I couldn't understand because I didn't have a damn uterus.

I wanted to punch the wall every time she said that.

To be honest, I had a few times.

Hen put a punching bag up in our room to cover the hole; she was good to me like that.

We hoped it was a baby every time she got sick, but when it came down to it, we met with a lot of people from all over the world, and she just got sick a lot. This time was no different.

"Are you paying attention?" The Nevada Alpha demanded, after I checked my phone for the dozenth time.

These meetings usually ran themselves—or I guess, Henley ran them. I just knocked heads around when necessary.

"Heard every word." I lied. "I'm just checking up on my mate. This is between you two."

I flipped my phone over, so I wasn't tempted to keep hitting the button to light the screen up.

The Alphas argued a bit more. Things got heated, and I hoped they'd fight so I could punch one of them and be done with it. They didn't, though.

The guys were moving toward an agreement when my phone vibrated. I ignored it, not wanting to irritate them. It vibrated again, and again, and I couldn't help myself

I flipped it over.

Henley had sent a picture, so I typed in my code and pulled up our messages.

There, on the screen, was a picture of a pregnancy test.

I had to read the explanation on the stick.

One line=not pregnant, two lines=pregnant.

Glancing back at the line area, I stilled.

Two lines.

I sat up quickly, glancing at the rest of her texts.

HEN: OH SHIT

HEN: THIS CAN'T BE HAPPENING

HEN: FUCK

HEN: FUCK

HEN: FUCK

HEN: COME HOME

HEN: ACTUALLY DON'T, OR NEVADA AND UTAH WILL BE SUSPICIOUS

HEN: BUT SHIT

HEN: WHAT IF IT'S A FALSE POSITIVE?

HEN: I'M GOING TO THE STORE

The bubbles disappeared, telling me she was done texting. I stood, not considering how it would look to the men. My heart was pounding out of my fucking chest.

Pregnant.

We were having a fucking baby.

I reached my mind toward Henley's. She liked to text so she wouldn't bother me when I was in meetings and shit, but I preferred the mind-speak. We were damn lucky to have it; why not use it?

"Wait for me. I'll pick you up." I told her.

She didn't answer, but I felt her agreement.

"I've got a family emergency. Work things out yourselves or come back next month. One of my enforcers will see you out." I said, hurrying out the door.

I yelled to one of my newer guys as I passed him—our pack had started growing insanely fast, after we met with all the packs and people realized we weren't shitty. The fact that they wouldn't have to shift every night with the moon in our pack was also a mega bonus. So, I had a lot of enforcers at that point.

"Is something wrong?" Kyler jogged at my side.

I'd held a grudge against him for a while, but had to give up on it when he mated with my sister. The rest of our family was too shitty for me to have issues with my brother-in-law.

Though my mom had come out of rehab more stable than she'd ever been, she was still my mom. And for me, that meant I couldn't really trust her. She'd never babysit our kid, but she would still be in his or her life.

Shit, I was going to have a kid.

"Hurry." Henley exclaimed into my mind.

"Roman?" Kyler waved a hand at me, jogging backward now.

"Shit. Sorry. Distracted." I ran a hand over my head—then realized I was wearing a hat. "Something came up."

Henley and I were on the same page as far as telling people went—we wanted our close friends and family to know about early pregnancies, so that we didn't have to keep it a secret from them if the worst happened. We were grown-ass people, but even grown-ass people needed support.

"You freaked out those Alphas, man." Kyler nodded toward the Alpha of All building. It really needed a new name.

"Hen got a positive pregnancy test." I said.

Was that even the right way to say it?

Hell if I knew. Or cared.

Kyler's eyes went huge.

"No way. Congrats, man."

Arla didn't want a baby for years and years—if at all, she said. So I'm sure Kyler knew even less about that shit than I did.

"She's worried it's not real, so I've got to buy her every kind of test they have so she can pee on a dozen more sticks." I explained, like that was a normal thing to say.

"Damn. Are you telling people, or what?" He asked.

"Just you and Arla, Jamie and Oliver, and London."

"The usual." Kyler bobbed his head.

"Tell anyone else and there's a legit chance Hen will castrate you." I warned. "I'll help her."

He grinned.

Kyler was a good guy. Not good enough for Arla, but still good. He made her happy, so I couldn't complain.

At least to anyone other than Henley.

"No worries, I'll keep my trap shut until Arla brings it up to me." Kyler said.

I nodded, and he headed back to the Alpha of All building.

Me and my truck were back at my house in five minutes—half the time it took if a person obeyed the speeding laws.

Which I rarely did.

Hen had our front door open before I even put the truck in park. I hauled ass out of my vehicle just in time to catch her when she threw herself at me.

"I can't believe it." She said, spewing words. "A baby, Roman. A fucking baby. We can't raise a baby—we suck at folding laundry. And we're horrible cooks! I don't think we're ready, maybe-"

I shut her up with a kiss to that perfect, gorgeous mouth of hers. And damn, I loved the feel of her lips on mine.

"We'll figure it out, Hen. We always do." I ran my hand down her hair, and she nodded rapidly.

"Let's go."

We hit the road, Henley sitting so close she was practically in my lap, bouncing nervously. She probably didn't even realize she was doing it.

"Our baby will be a ruby, right? I mean, the odds are high. Really high. But you weren't born one, so—shit." She threw the door open as I parked.

We were just in time for her to puke all over the asphalt… and the little car next to us.

"Shit." She muttered again, as I handed her a bottle of water. She swished and spat that on the ground too.

The car's owner walked up, gawking at the mess. I strode over to the chick, handing her a bunch of cash.

"Sorry. My wife's pregnant." I said, walking around to her side of the door and hauling her out.

"I'm fucking pregnant." She whispered, gawking up at me.

"I know. It's insane." A grin tugged at my lips. "We need to celebrate. I'll order pizza and soda on the way home."

We were quick in the store, leaving with a basket of at least twenty pregnancy tests of different brands and colors. I didn't give a shit—if it made her feel better, she could buy every damn test the store had.

We ate pizza, but Henley only made it through half of a slice before she ran back to the bathroom to puke again. And I felt fucking terrible, but also thrilled.

She was growing us a damn baby.

And holy fuck, I couldn't wait to be a dad.

THE END.

PLEASE REVIEW

Here it is. The awkward page at the end of the book where the author begs you to leave a review.

Believe me, I hate it more than you do.

But, this is me swallowing my pride and asking.

Whether you loved or hated this story, you made it this far, so please review! Your reviews play a MASSIVE role in determining whether others read my books, and ultimately, writing is a job for me—even if it's the best job ever—so I write what people are reading.

Regardless of whether you do or not, thank you so much for reading <3

-Lola

AFTERTHOUGHTS

This trilogy started with a quote by F Scott Fitzgerald.

"I'm not used to being loved. I wouldn't know what to do."

When I read that quote, I'd been trying to figure out who Henley was and I felt strongly that it had to be her theme. Henley came to life, then. An abrasive, defensive chick who'd walked through hell and survived. Too abrasive, in some ways, but it was the only way I could tell her story.

Henley wasn't someone who knew what it felt like to be loved, and that shaped her entire life. All of her decisions, and all of her experiences. She looked for excuses to push people away—especially Roman, because he fought especially hard.

And Roman… if you've read my note at the end of book one, you know that in the first version of that book, he was a controlling jerk. I didn't intend for him to come off like that when I was writing, but it's a hard line to walk, the line of an Alpha Male who's strong and tough but still gentle. A line he crossed a bit in this book as he dealt with his own stuff, but one Henley was ready for at this point.

Even before I rewrote Roman, his and Henley's relationship was inspired by Tarryn Fisher's words:

"When you find someone who breaks you open and makes you feel things, you fight for them."

And I guess that's what this trilogy came down to when everything was said and done in this final book. People finding things that made them feel, and fighting for them.

For Sylvie, that was Ezra and the children she wanted so desperately. For Roman, it was Henley. And for Henley, it was just about everything. New York and Georgia. The women whose situations mirrored her own. The Alphas who hurt her. Her girls. Definitely Roman. The entirety of the family she built, moment by abrasive, bitchy moment.

Anyway, this afterword turned into a bit of a rant, but I've loved every minute of telling you Henley and Roman's story. Their world will stay with me forever, and I hope some part of it stays with you too.

Thank you so much for reading!

-Lola

ALSO BY LOLA GLASS

Burning Kingdom Trilogy

Moon of the Monsters Trilogy

Sacrificed to the Fae King Trilogy

Shifter Queen Trilogy

Rejected Mate Refuge Trilogy

Outcast Pack Standalones

Mate Hunt Standalones

Wolfsbane Series

Shifter City Trilogy

Supernatural Underworld Duology

SAY HI!

Check out my reader group, Lola's Book Lovers
for giveaways, book recommendations, and more!

Or find me on:
TIKTOK
INSTAGRAM
PINTEREST
GOODREADS

ABOUT THE AUTHOR

Teller of stories. Wrangler of children. Buyer of Chinese food. Creator of art. Lover of life.

If that's too vague for you, Lola is a twenty-something with a *slight* werewolf obsession and a passion for love—real love. Not the flowers-and-chocolates kind of love, but the kind where two people build a relationship strong enough to last. That's the kind of relationship she loves to read about, and the kind she tries to portray in her books.

Even if they're about shifters :)

Made in the USA
Columbia, SC
02 July 2025